T0355000

WHISPERING
VOICE
FROM THE DARKNESS

TINA LAWLER

ARCHWAY
PUBLISHING

Archway Publishing books may be ordered through booksellers or by contacting:

Archway Publishing
1663 Liberty Drive
Bloomington, IN 47403
www.archwaypublishing.com
844-669-3957

ISBN: 978-1-6657-0291-1 (sc)
ISBN: 978-1-6657-0292-8 (e)

Library of Congress Control Number: 2021902880

Print information available on the last page.

Archway Publishing rev. date: 02/18/2021

CHAPTER ONE

CHOSEN ONES

"We need to do something with that group of people who refuse to bow to our demands."

"What do you have in mind sir?"

"Those people, they call themselves the Chosen Ones. They're few in number now, but our intelligence has informed us that they're recruiting more people into their group."

"I have heard of them; some people can hear him but our investigators who infiltrate their meetings aren't able to hear him. We've had some of the investigators who have converted over, claiming they did hear the Voice. We are searching for them to arrest them."

"Sir, they're non-cooperatives. They could end us."

"What's the plan?"

"Sir we take them out. We eliminate them; cut them off from any and all means of survival. For many years, we have been imprisoning many of them and killing them systematically. They treat each other well and aren't criminals, they just interfere with the rest of us by claiming that certain lifestyles are wrong. We don't need someone telling us what we can or cannot do. Most of the world agrees with us and are trying to do their part to comply."

"Has your plan been fully developed?"

"No, sir. Our people are still working on it. We should have everything in place soon. Our scientists had developed microchips many years ago that was used to track animals. Our secret technology agency has been working around the clock getting these chips developed and are close to having them ready, they are inexpensive and can be mass produced without having any delays. We provide them generously with a lifestyle to keep them in line with our thinking; they live in a town that is only for these scientists and we are bringing in any supplies they need so they won't have to leave and risk everything we have been working to accomplish. So, I am thinking that we could use this technology to put this under the skin of every person who wishes to have a job, to buy or sell, get medical treatment, or any kind of goods or services. This chip will allow us to scan them and if any person doesn't have one, then we will be able to take their property and possession. They want people to join. We don't need a bunch of loonies running around, brainwashing people into hearing the Voice. It could be disastrous."

"I agree. Make it happen and as quickly as possible."

"I am on it, sir. I'll let our people know the urgency."

"You need to be absolutely sure about this or it could come back on us."

"Yes, sir."

"Once this plan is up and running, we could use this as some entertainment. We can have hunting games to get people to help bring these undesirables in for us, quite amusing, if I do say so myself. Those people will be running around trying to find food, clothes, shelter, and other essentials they'll need, and it should be easy. It is the sport above all sports. w\We can charge for it as other sports charge fees."

"Sir, that's great, but the legalities…"

"It's nothing to be concerned about. There are ways around the legal system. Remember, I have the power to make things happen."

"Yes, sir, you do."

"It's time that the world knows who I am. Now go, talk to our people, and I'll finish my work here."

"Yes, sir, and I might add, I think you alone can make our world a perfect place."

"We'll meet in a few days to finalize everything. I need to make some phone calls." The people he intended to call in were on the government payroll. They did legitimate scientific work and developed products that were needed to serve the government's purposes only. But when President Gerrin wanted results to be consistent with his agenda, he would have them make statements that he himself would write up for them to sign. Of course, they were compensated very well. These scientists lived in mansions and had every luxury the president would give them, without having them live a life that would usurp him. He refused to be upstaged by those who worked for him, and he planned to take it all back when he was finished with them. He thought of himself superior in every way in comparison to the "common" people, which just so happened to be every person alive.

Gary was the senior researcher on the team, as he had several degrees and was considered to be an expert on several projects in the world, including the microchips he had been working on. He knew the danger of these chips for a person of interest to the government. They could easily track one of them and monitor their movements. These were very small devices which he was originally told would only be used on terrorists and criminals. He had believed it at the time, but now he knew he had been lied to. Most of the people in his lab had very specific work they were working on, and he alone knew the whole operation. The Attorney General for the President came to him for advice. If they needed propaganda, they would invite other scientists to go before the Council to testify. They were pawns who were only trying to do their jobs and be left alone to work. They did what they had to do and comply with what they were asked to do.

Gary was secretly working on an instrument to prevent this intrusive device from invading his life. He worked at his house, and had been working with Barry, another scientist who had left. They had some impressive inventions that neither one was willing to share with the world, so they shared secrets and kept them close. The two of them had gone to college together and had maintained a close friendship ever since.

The phone rang in the lab, "Lab, this is Gary."

"Gary, do you have a time when we can meet?" Marshal asked.

"How about meeting with me about three o'clock this afternoon?"

"Can you get your top guys from each department to come?"

"Yes, I will meet you in the conference room on the second floor at three."

"Thank you and be prepared to give an update on what you have ready."

"Good day to you," said Gary as he hung up the phone. He punched in a number and relayed the message to the lab supervisor, who agreed to have them meet at three. Marshal was a cruel man but he was careful around the scientists, so as not to dirty his own hands using public humiliation. Gerrin was afraid of the intellectuals, but he would never admit it. If not for those around him, he would not have been able to keep his power and he knew it. He was tempestuous and intimidating. Marshal would never be able to lead a massive amount of people; he had the cruelty to give him the edge Gerrin needed. He had them investigated and watched closely; there were hidden cameras and listening devices in place so as to listen and watch everything that was going on in and around the labs, even going so far as to place the devices closer to home around the scientists outside the lab. And he was aware of the minutia of their lives. On several occasions, he heard some of them talking about him negatively and they would mysteriously die shortly afterwards. It became known not to talk about him anywhere indoors, and even outside was questionable.

Gary decided to take his lunch break early. He had some things to finish up first and it took a few minutes. He went into his office after clearing his lab table and putting the things in their proper places. In his office, he straightened his desk and checked his emails, answering the ones that needed a response and that left him a stopping place. One of the other researchers asked him to finish up on a project. "I have the QA department testing now, and so far they have been performing the way they should. We have come a long way with the chips. At one time, they were limited to what they could do, but now we can do so much more with them. I have been hearing good things. After the afternoon meeting I will check with them. How are you doing with your project?"

"It is working out very well."

"I am going home for lunch. Go get something to eat so I don't have you wasting away."

"I will be going in a few minutes."

Gary hung up his lab coat on the hook in his office and headed out to his car. He got in and was thinking about what he was going to do at the meeting. He was uncomfortable with it. "I think it is time for me to retire or maybe start patenting some of my inventions," he said aloud. Closing the door and starting his car, he headed home. Retiring sounded great. He had plenty of money saved up, as did his wife, Carol. They had been married forty years. She was the president of the bank where she worked and lately had been talking about doing some traveling. The house they lived in was in an upscale neighborhood and was a mile from his work and a half mile from hers. When he pulled into the driveway, he saw her car. The garage door was just going down so he knew she had just arrived. He got out of his car and walked to the front door, unlocking and going in. She met him with a kiss on his cheek.

"You had a good morning, didn't you?" he asked.

"I am always happy to see you, even after all these delightful years."

"I am one lucky man. While we eat lunch, I would like to talk to you about something."

"Ok, let me microwave some leftovers and we can talk." She pulled out food from the refrigerator and had it heated up within a few minutes. "There, let's dig in," she said. Between bites, Gary told her about his plans to retire. "I am tired of the way things are going. The work we are doing is going to do harm and I don't want to be a part of it any more. I am thinking about marketing the inventions I have. What do you think?"

"I love that it is an idea I have been waiting for you to get around to. Let's do it! I will retire and help you with the marketing. I have a lot of connections around the world. All those business trips will finally have a purpose! This is what I have been wanting! Let's put in our notices today."

"Carol, you are an amazing woman!" Gary was so relieved. He was looking forward to spending more time with her and she had been hinting about it often in the last couple of years. Timing was good.

"Honey, I will put my notice in at the three o'clock meeting this afternoon."

"I am putting mine in as soon as I get back to my office. I have a meeting with my department heads. I am so excited!"

They finished their lunch at a leisurely pace and cleaned up the kitchen before saying good bye and leaving together.

When Gary got to the lab he went in and put his lab coat on. He sat down at his desk to answer some messages, emails, and read some letters that he planned to take care of the next day. Time to check with his associates to the see the progress of their projects. These were some highly intelligent people working here. He admired them and would miss them when he left. After going back to his work space, he was not concentrating on his work, so he thought he would get some things put away and finish up some filing. It was almost time to meet with the general, so he replaced his lab coat on the hook and headed to the conference room, stopping to speak to his secretary as he started out. He walked slowly to the conference room, not looking forward to seeing the general, who was already there when he got there, as were the other scientists. "Come in Gary and have a seat," the general said in a blustery voice. "These guys have been filling me in on what they have been doing. What is your take on how the work is going?"

"I believe we will have these ready for production within six months. They are being tested right now and the tests are looking positive, so far we haven't seen any real problems." The researchers further filled him in on the progress and the general was pleased.

"Gary, you have done an outstanding job with this project. You will have a tax-free deposit made into your bank account."

"General, I appreciate that I have that. I have some news; I am putting in my notice to retire. Carol has been wanting for us to have more time together so we both want to retire. Don't worry about a thing; I have a replacement in mind that will do an excellent job for you. I will check with him and if he agrees, I will give you his name."

"I hate to see you go but I understand. Give me a letter and the recommendation as soon as you can. Thank you for your service." He stood up and came around the table to shake his hand. The others could not believe he was about to leave. "I will get back with you soon to check on your progress. Thank you gentlemen, have a good day," the general said. He left the room with a rushed air about him. He could hardly contain his excitement. He called Gerrin and reported to him.

Gary didn't like what he knew was about to happen. Finishing his day without accomplishing much of anything, he put his lab coat away. He straightened the lab and his office, turned out his office light, locked the door, and left for home.

He was home before Carol got there, which was unusual because he was the one who normally worked late. Going into the kitchen, he started dinner. He liked to cook, and found some steaks and went out to get the grill going. Steaks were sizzling when Carol walked out and gave him a hug and kiss. "How did it go?" he asked.

"I did it and I am glad I did," he said.

"It was good for me too. Those steaks sure do smell good."

"Carol, these microchips I have helped develop are going to be injected into people and it is not honest. I think it is to force people to turn from the Voice and I don't plan to get one. What about you?"

"Same here, you and Ben had created some shelters for the purpose of having a place to hide. There had been stories on the news. We might want to start making plans. I am not going to reject the Voice. I am with you. We need to talk to our pastor about it."

"Not only are you beautiful, but you are one smart cookie."

Retirement came as Gary and Carol started making plans as they were led. Their pastor had the church involved, as those within the church rejected the idea and were causing trouble for those who knew the truth.

The spirits are gathered around the Voice. There is anticipation as the Voice is ready to instruct them for their upcoming duties. With a voice of great authority, one that would strike down the enemy with just one word, spoke "You must go all throughout the world to collect the ones chosen to perish by the hands of the Council. You are to stand by them; the Chosen Ones will be forced into turmoil so you must be there to guide them."

"What shall we do when we go to our assigned Chosen One?"

"Give them comfort and keep reminding them that we will be with them until the end of time, even the worst of times, and they can endure because they have been given great strength. Remember, our enemies will labor hard to separate them from us."

"We're going to lose a large number of the humans. These are trying times for all of humanity. We will work as hard as we can to defend them. They must learn more and more to be completely dependent on me. The choice is theirs and we don't want to interfere with their free will; that is the only thing that is theirs. They have to choose to listen to me and know that the truth will set them free. I am saddened that so many of them won't listen to me and to know how much I love them. The ones who choose with wisdom and an open heart will be appointed as my Special People; in turn they will be rewarded with riches far beyond human value."

"We will go and do as you command us."

In the unseen world of eternal fire and painful misery, the Serpent was holding a summit with the dark spirits. Not only was it a place of pain and misery, but the smell was of sulfur. It was the most grotesque of places with the ugliest of being living there. The place was ridiculed as mythical to scare young people; no living person who was unbelieving thought this place actually existed, until they were put here. The Dark Spirits were the soldiers who fought the Serpent's battles, and had for as long as time existed. He called them together to update them on the progress of their successful campaign. They were fighting to regain possession of human territory they'd lost on earth.

"The humans have indulged in self-gratifying behavior. They destroy themselves by their own actions. I don't always have to take the blame for some of the things they do; they want to do that on their own. I like to let the Voice know about it. I have seen the Voice and have some important information that he's sending his Spirits to strengthen the Chosen Ones. He is allowing us to work on humans, as He always has done in the past the difference is that humans are listening to us more. Humans are easier to deceive as we have progressively shown them how old fashioned the Voices ideas are. The Voice says any pain we inflict will only make his Chosen Ones stronger. I'm going to crush them and pulverize them into the nothing that they are. We will take back our power and reign over earth!"

"We need to open the human's eyes, that if they do not submit to us we will have to punish them accordingly, we will bring suffering to them like the humans have never known. We have staged everything to prepare the most physical and spiritual pain and suffering. The humans with children will watch as their young ones die in the worst ways we can inflict. If we can convince them that they need to survive, we can convince them that their Voice has no intention of protecting them. They need to feel alone, helpless, and without the Voice they so desperately cling to. Maybe feeling instant relief from their hunger and pain, they will succumb to us. They need to be persuaded to turn to our side, away from their Voice. We will make our voices far too loud for them to hear any other voice. We'll exploit the human's every weakness to pain and turning them away from their deity. They will think our truth is the only truth that makes sense. We all know how the humans will always take the easy path."

"They love effortless handouts and we will give them what they want."

"What if this plan is unsuccessful?"

"Whatever may happen, remain persistent without stopping to doubt yourselves. The results we want all falls on the successful work you perform on the humans. They should watch as those around them are being killed. They should watch as their loved ones, their friends, everyone, takes their last pitiful breath. They should watch their faces as death, my beautiful friend, envelops their human flesh. If nothing else, threats to their children are powerful enough to dissuade them. Humans are programmed to protect their young ones; most will do anything to protect them from harm. If the young are ill, they will do what they must do to make them well. Put most of your focus on the young. They'll give up their convictions for the children. Taking the minds of the children is how we capture the next generation. Oh, and remember, cause divisions among friends, and family member. With control over the children, we can control them all."

"We have worked for many years to take the hearts and minds of the children. We have thought of various methods to condition them into acceptance of what we want them to accept, and it has been rather successful. We incorporated our ways into their education, the system taught them our ways as being normal and harmless. We took over their hearts and minds, parents were not watchful enough or they would have been able to stop us. Their children's shows are wrapped up with our lies. Even the youngest are exposed to us; no one knew. Their parents use TV's as entertainment for the young ones. No one was or is safe from us. We are everywhere and parents were deceived. We used a few to create dissension and intimidation; no one is or was immune. Oh, how I hate the Chosen Ones, they have become too strong, we must fight or we will lose."

CHAPTER TWO
WORLD COUNCIL

The World Council had assembled and President Gerrin was preparing to speak. The members were standing around drinking coffee and eating food. They were discussing further the meeting and what it meant. There had been phone calls between them as to the reason the meeting had been ordered. It wasn't a surprise since special meetings were frequently called, but something about this one wasn't normal. They were speculating, based off of rumors that this meeting was pertaining to the newest technology that had been developed. The claims were that it would make the world a better place.

The meeting started. "May I have your attention, please? If everyone will take their places, we will get this meeting started." The council members scuffled to their seats as quickly as they could. Everyone had questions and had been anxiously waiting to find out what it was about. "I appreciate your patience. I know you all have been waiting patiently to know why we called you in today. We preferred to wait until we knew with certainty what we wanted to do before we gave a proposal of our ides to the Council. Many of you have heard about the new technology that has been developed that will control the world's population and help control the issue of global problems we had been facing. You should have the notes in front of you, summarizing the proposal." There was a shuffling of papers.

"Now, what is needed is to have a Constitutional amendment to make this proposal legal. Many of you have submitted your thoughts to me pertaining to, specifically, a group of people we call the Undesirables. They call themselves The Chosen Ones and that is why this meeting has been called. For those who do not know, they are claiming to hear what they refer to as The Voice. This group of people feel exempt from obeying the laws that our government has set forth and are choosing the laws of their God. This not obeying the laws of the land; therefore, it is in the best interest of our world's society that they are no longer allowed to roam so freely within the general population, spreading their propaganda against us. We can imprison and eliminate these people, who are now deemed terrorist threats. We will hunt them, torture, and kill, or simply imprison these people, at our discretion. The Voice they claim to hear tells them that it is their provider and that we are the enemy. They think it protects them and this voice takes care of them. Several members of the Council know just how preposterous this is, so we want to show them just how wrong they are. This is the best thing for all of humanity and our implemented ideas of perfection. What we are proposing to do pertains to this new technology. We are asking to put a microchip inside the forearm of all people who have chosen our way of thinking, who are on our side. This chip will be scanned when the person wants to buy or sell products. Without this microchip, the person will be unable to receive medical care. We want to know who is on our side and to eliminate those against us, because, Council, anyone who is not on our side is the enemy. This microchip will cover all forms of services anyone can or may receive and this will, in turn, force the undesirables to be with us, or be eliminated, that is the choice they are being given. It will solve the problems we are facing in our world. We will then be able to rule them and to have true and absolute peace on the planet, at last. With them obeying laws that are different from ours they are causing dissension everywhere. We also believe that there are going to be many who will refuse to cooperate. Furthermore, the plan we have come up with is to get those off the streets into contained areas. We want to give an incentive for people to bring the undesirables into the holding areas where we can put them to good use that will be more cost effective than hiring our own people to do this work. For this, we propose a hefty financial boost. The ones we imprison can be spared to use in entertainment in the stadiums, or they can be put to the same good use as the ones in the camps. Some can be used for personal pleasure whether for shooting or for slaves. Please, your thoughts."

"What makes you so sure this will work?"

"It will allow us to weed out our enemies. We cannot live without food, correct? Well, they must agree with the state verbally, with witnesses, and renounce any and all connection with the Voice and the undesirables. Once they have done this, they will have the chip inserted into their arms. We simply cannot allow our enemies to enjoy freedoms if they do not cooperate with us."

"I think that's a great idea. I for one do not like the idea of undesirable people walking amongst us." There were rumors that there was going to be a change that was going to bring relief to those who were suffering from the total world economic disaster. Some stories were favorable but there were some that didn't bring much assurance to the people. There was more uncertainty than not, and people wanted to be relieved of their poverty.

The Voice was addressing the Assembled Spirits. "The beginning of the end is here in the world. It is dire that we work to prepare our Chosen Ones. They must know that they will be given the strength that they need during these times of peril. I want care to be given to those certain Chosen Ones, it is time for them to get ready."

The Spirits assigned to the Chosen Ones stepped forward to address the Voice, "We sent prophets who serve you to the Chosen Ones and there are those who have listened to your voice. We are now preparing them for the task that you ask of them, it will be done."

In the dark world, all the hosts were having a meeting, discussing the developments that were taking place on earth.

"Now is the time that we shall act. We will take over control of the humans that do not serve the Voice, they are weak and vulnerable and easily manipulated. They will give into what we want from them. They're more concerned with their own selves that anyone else. The time to act is now."

"What have you done to prepare?"

"We persuaded the World Council to single out the Chosen Ones for elimination. There are many of us acting as World Council members. They have no idea it's us, so we're safe from being exposed. They believed everything we told them. Lies, so easily accepted as for the good. We give them money and power and our actions are without question. Money is a powerful tool to blind the eyes of the greedy and power seeker; bribery has done its service in blinding the infidels. If any of them decide to back out or question the motives behind this, we can just manipulate them through the threat of having their money and influence taken away. They allowed themselves to be used like puppets. If only the Chosen Ones were this easy. Their Voice protects them well because He tells them He will and they believe it. We will increase our persuasion to pelt them from their protection."

Every news station had made a major announcement about the newest developments in the economy. Any person who wished to make any business transaction or work had to get a microchip that would be scanned upon purchases, trading items, being hired for new employment or keeping their jobs. Even if they worked, they wouldn't be paid. The microchip also served as the new way to receive medical treatment, all type of services rendered were only allowed for those with the microchip.

To obtain the microchip, an allegiance had to be made to the World Council. The World Council promised to World Sport. The World Council felt that all possessions and money would best serve to be in their control. In the beginning, there was resistance to the new control. The Council was able to convince people that with their cooperation they would be protected, the alternative option was less than desirable. People had begun to think that the whole idea made a lot of sense. Resistance decreased as hatred of the Chosen Ones increased. Chosen Ones were trying to lead people astray from lives of prosperity so the world wanted the undesirables dead.

CHAPTER THREE
GEORGE HEARS THE VOICE

As he was sleeping with his mouth open, a line of drool seeped out of the corner of his mouth. He lay on his back, and in the midst of his dreams, he was walking through a dark forest; everything within the forest was burned. There were no sounds, just the deafening silence. No birds calling, no wind, nothing but the silence. The strangest thing about the dreams was how he felt, so overwhelmingly hopeless and alone. All he did was roam about the burned forest trying to find another person, anyone could help him. But he found no one, he was so utterly alone. The nightmare was so vivid that he woke up in a cold sweat.

Even when he did sleep, it never felt like he was resting. He was constantly tired, and he was exhausted mentally and physically. His nightmares were becoming more frequent. It seemed more than not were filled with the most terrifying nightmares he could ever remember having before in his life. It was even to the point where he dreaded the thought of sleeping; he would wake up, every night, with a dry mouth and be on the same thin, sweat-stained mattress that reeked of too many odors to identify. But on that night, he was abruptly awoken by a voice he had not heard but sounded vaguely familiar from a time he seemed to have forgotten. The voice was calling his name. The voice was soft, gentle, and soothing. He had become accustomed to voices all day, all night but none were like the one calling his name. The voice called his name once more, and this time he knew it wasn't his imagination or a dream. It was real.

"George."

"Who are you? What do you want?"

"Listen to me, George. You are soon to be free from imprisonment. I have plans for you."

"What?" He was half awake.

"George, I am the God above all the gods of the earth. I am the Lord above all rulers. I am the Alpha and the Omega, the beginning, and the end. I am the Lamb and the Lion. No other god of the earth has the power that I possess. I am the One and Only. I have secured your freedom. I want you to listen to me."

"Who are you?"

"I am a voice that guides you, the Voice, I am God."

"You're not real."

"You will soon see how wrong you are. I am real; you cannot see me, but I am more real and have been here forever longer than you can even imagine. I have talked to you for a long time and you used to hear me, the times has come for you to listen to me and you are now listening to me again. I am with you and I always will be here with you."

"What do you want with me?"

"You shall find that out in due time, just trust me."

"Trust you? I don't even know you! I don't trust anyone."

"George, the time will come when you will know to trust me again. I shall free you. I am here for you."

"Do you even know where I am? There's no freedom for people like me. Just leave me alone."

"I do know, George. I will take you out of here, and renew your life. I can do anything I want to do. For now, sleep and get your rest."

George went to sleep and it was the best sleep he could remember in a very long time. When he awoke the next morning to the noises of prison life, he shook the night's event off as another dream.

George had been on death row for ten years. He had been convicted of homicide during an attempted robbery and had confessed to other murders he had committed in angry rages during those robberies. He had thought that day of the crime he would make out with cash and be gone, and all of his plans had gone awry. And now, George was rotting away in his prison cell on death row for what he'd done, when he'd killed innocent people he never felt any remorse for. He never felt the guilt of taking lives. Because of lack of remorse, his heart had hardened and he was full of bitterness. He didn't care about anyone; he was only concerned about getting his sentence appealed and getting out of prison. His selfishness was what drove him. There seemed to be no hope for him, or at least that's how he regarded himself. His death sentence was soon to be consummated. The end of his life was in the near future. What was done was done; he didn't care. He'd committed crimes his whole adult life, and there was no going back; it was the end of the road for George and there was nothing left.

He lay there, thinking about one event in particular. It was before he'd been put on death row; he thought about it more than he cared to. He had found a couple who were stopped alongside a highway. They were looking at a map with the overhead light on in their car. It was late at night and they appeared to be lost. When the couple had stopped, he approached their car, and they jumped when George rapped on the window. The man lowered his window. That was when George put the gun in the man's face, demanding their money. The couple handed it to him. They knew they were about to die and were praying for him and forgiving him for what he was about to do right before he shot and killed them. He kept thinking about them. He could have gotten away with that crime since there was no evidence that he had done it. The gun he had used was one that he had stolen. He confessed to it only because the police had made him believe they had a witness. They didn't know it was him, only that they knew that he had been in the nearby town about the time of the couple's deaths.

George had been so angry about his misfortune of the day that he decided to shoot them out of frustration. He had hitchhiked to try to get back to his home town. He had gone with some friends in hopes of having a place to live and it hadn't worked out so he was trying to get back home. The ones he thought were his friends had abandoned him and left him to his own devices and he was angry and homicidal. They were some ratty looking guys who were headed in his direction and they were going to take him as far as they could. His ride back home had turned off and gone in another direction, leaving him to get most of the way home on his own. He was trying to get another ride when he saw the stopped car. He didn't steal the car because of an approaching car that had emergency lights flashing, which he knew was a law enforcement vehicle. He ran off into the nearby field and kept going. He didn't bother hitchhiking back into town; he made his way back by going through the fields and brush away from the highway. By late morning he had found his way back to town, hungry and thirsty as well as being filthy.

George leaned against a fence that wrapped around the track, where he had begun running around the previous year. His body was in much better condition as a result of weight lifting and running. When he looked in the mirror that morning, he was amazed at how different from the first day he had walked into the confines of the prison. Since the first time he had heard the voice he realized that he was important to someone. His life had purpose and meaning and he cared about others. Every day he spoke to the Voice and he had learned that he could feel good about himself; at times, he found that he was smiling for no reason. The other inmates mocked him, but it didn't faze him. He felt like a new and different man.

Thinking aloud, "I need to finish my run. It looks like a storm is coming." Pushing off the fence, he sprinted back to the gate so he could go back to his cell. Not many in this place worked out like he did. Many thought being locked up had made him crazy. He smiled knowing they were afraid of him, for a very different reason. Hanging out in the yard, some of the other men were curious about his strange attitude. "Hey, George! What's up with you? You act like you're above us." The inmate nudged the inmate next to him, and pointed at George with a smirk. "You used to fist anyone who just looked at you and you used to shaft our stuff man. Hey man, what happened to you?"

"I have been talking to someone who told me I was going to be free." That set them to mocking him and laughing at him in derision.

"George, your head ain't on right. You're crazy! You need to stop before they put you in isolation; they put the crazies in there."

George only smiled. Nothing could get him down; he had met guys who talked like him. The difference was he knew he was going to be ok and he knew he didn't have to worry about what anyone said. He went about his daily life and let the other inmates wonder about him. He didn't comprehend the impact he was having on them; he only saw what they covered with their derision. Some of them would be changed because of what they saw in George. One of the guards, Ken would come by his cell and talk to him. Ken was a kind man and he never mocked George and he made him feel like he was a human.

George was a five foot nine man with dark brown hair and dark brown eyes; he weighed one hundred eighty pounds. His build was thick and muscular after he had neglected himself so he had gotten flabby and then he decided to get back into shape. His prison clothes were tight around him and made him appear to be larger in size than he actually was. Women were always looking at him and flirting. During his junior year in high school he had a girlfriend he really cared about, and then she moved away when her dad was transferred with his job to another city. They had a hard time staying in touch so eventually they broke up.

CHAPTER FOUR

ESCAPE

At 2:34 am, George awoke with the feeling that he was not alone. He thought at first it was a dream but the voice was persistent. "George, wake up." He'd been in a deep sleep and was slow in becoming aware of what was going on.

"George! Get up!"

"Who's there?"

"George, get dressed, it's time to go."

George stumbled as he put his prison-issue clothes on. The light was that of the dim fluorescent lights, high above his head, outside of his cell in the long walkway. He could see from a distance that the guards had flashlights. They were conducting their nightly rounds to ensure that every inmate was in their cell, asleep. He hit his head on the cold stainless steel sink as he reached for his shoes. In his hurry to put his shoes on, he attempted to stand up too fast. "What am I doing?" he asked the Voice.

"The time has come. I have work for you to do, trust me. You are to meet with the Chosen Ones when you leave here. They are waiting for you now, I sent them."

George had managed to clumsily get dressed. He wasn't sure if his clothes were clean, but at that moment it didn't matter and he wasn't going to wash them at that time. He felt exhilarated; he was well-prepared for what was to come. He had been reading and learning about the way he was to live and was influencing the others around him without knowing he was doing so. He grabbed the Book as he was looking around at what little he had in the cell with him. He didn't see anything that was of any importance to him. He had known for a while that this exact moment would happen, but it seemed almost surreal. George asked himself if he needed to take anything.

"No. There is nothing here that you need." The Voice knew exactly what he was thinking. Strange having his thoughts answered.

"Follow my instructions, George, and trust me."

There was a click and his cell door opened. Surprisingly, it didn't make its normal loud squeak as it slid open. He walked out of his cell, his home for the last decade. He looked to his left, then to his right. No one was in sight.

"Hmmmm." He thought. The guards were normally here doing their rounds by now.

"Keep moving, George."

He took a deep breath as he moved silently along the walkway. He could hear his fellow cellmates snoring. They were all condemned to death, his cellmates, and what friends he had, only because they all were in the same predicament. There wasn't a single one of them who even cared. They had all filed for appeals, thinking that their sentences would be appealed. George thought for a second how tomorrow he was going to be yet another nameless inmate put to death for his crime he shook it off and kept moving.

Walking along the walkway, George realized that he was passing security cameras. They were watching his every move, yet no alarms had been set off. It seemed that only seconds ago, when there were guards coming down to his end of death row. There were always guards posted and he thought he was about to be caught, he passed one who didn't look up as he walked by him. He stifled a nervous laugh.

George had already put some distance between his ell and where he was headed. Every time he got to a security gate, one that either had to have a code punched in on a keypad or a security key scanned in front of a sensor, the gate opened by itself with a soft click. "George, I'm right here with you. Don't worry. I am guiding you through all obstacles you face."

"This feels like a dream," he thought.

"No, George. This is not a dream. I am with you."

He was approaching the office area where the guards conjured when they were finished doing their rounds and were talking. He heard their voices, as these guards were about to conduct their rounds at a different cell block than the ones who he had seen earlier. He quickened his steps. If he got caught it wasn't going to go well at all.

"You won't be caught, George. I am with you; you are almost free."

It had only been about fifteen minutes since George had left the confines of his cell as he was going slowly, but it had seemed like ages. He approached the very last gate of the prison section of the prison unit. It, too, clicked open. Then, George noticed he was in the front of the prison where the administrative offices were located in the foyer. It was vacant at this hour of the day, since they were only there during regular business hours. The camera lights were flashing their steady red, silent flashes, indicating they were operational. All the windows had bars on them for the protection of the ones sitting in the offices. The chairs here were soft and lined up along the walls. The room was blue and soft in comparison to the rest of the prison. The night lights and the red exit sign let him know that he was heading for the front door. As he approached the double glass doors, he pushed against one of them and it opened freely. The outside lights were bright.

His heart was beating a little less by now. He knew he almost free. There was a door separating him from his freedom. They unlocked as he got near. "These are supposed to be locked," he thought. "Ah, I get it," he chuckled quietly. The Voice had upheld his promises as he had said he would. He was outside, and took another deep breath, but this time of the night the air outside was cool with a slight breeze blowing softly and rumpling his hair. There was one last gate; it was the armed guard controlled main gate. In the watch towers looking over the large area where George was, the guards could see everything and had full authority to shoot at will. The armed guards were not paying attention to what was going on and George crept along quietly.

"George, keep going. They can't see you."

"Ok." Deep breath.

George was on autopilot. His feet moved without him thinking about it, and before he knew it, he was out of prison. The guards in the watch towers had no idea that he had simply walked out but he now had a mile to walk until he was still off prison property. He tried not to bring attention to himself as he took off.

"Now George, walk to the end of the paved road. There will be a car waiting for you there." The Voice told him.

He was breathing in the air and not smelling the rancid odors of dirty bodies, dirty yellowed teeth, halitosis, and the other persistent odors that were in the prison. Some of the wild flowers were in bloom and he thought nothing had ever smelled so good. Running on the track, he could smell them but being free made them smell even better. Off in the trees, he heard an owl hooting and night animals scurrying about. Looking up in the sky, he saw the stars twinkling as if they were cheering him on. He started jogging down the road. He had been in prison for so long that this made him feel like a wild stallion, free of restraints. He felt free and glorious! The running made him feel like at last, he could stretch his legs out. Suddenly, he heard the alarm, and they now knew he was gone. The blaring sirens were a stark contrast to the quiet of the night. The guards must have gone on their rounds right after he had left; that was the reason the Voice had told him to hurry. He very quickly got off the road and ran alongside it and into the brush to escape any possible detection. The short ground vegetation growing low to the ground was making a grab for his legs but he was scarcely noticing the stinging. He had to get out of there.

On the night George was to escape, Jeremy and Kendra drove to the place they were to meet him, and for a while they were wondering if they were in the right place when he appeared, right on time. When he got into the car they introduced themselves, but they weren't prepared for what they saw. They were expecting a mean looking man who looked ready to kill at any provocation. They saw a man with gentle eyes and that was both polite and respectful; he gave them a small smile as he greeted them. He was quiet and watchful. Joann had known him for a long time and she explained to them about his history. When she had seen him the last time, George was a mean looking man and she had told them what to expect when they picked him up. The Voice had not misguided them. Joann, a church member and good friend, had been feeling like a death row inmate was being selected to leave prison and lead people in a venture not yet known to them. She'd been so persistent that others were joining her in praying about it, and as it turned out, she was right. At the time, she was unaware that the prisoner was to be George. It turned out to be a nice surprise for her.

Back at the prison, there was chaos with the warden on his way in. Guards were checking the videos in hopes they had missed something but they couldn't find anything on the tapes. George had seemingly vanished from the maximum-security prison. His cell was upheaved in hopes of finding any clue. He couldn't have gone out any way except out the front gate. The videos showed him entering the cell after dinner and guards walking by from time to time. The guards had no idea how he had gotten out, as the prison was on lockdown, and by that time, other inmates had awoken with all the bustling about. They were questioned relentlessly for hours without finding any helpful information. The inmates were envious of his escape. Guards were all over the prison checking every inch of it, without results. No one had seen nor heard anything. He was simply gone. One guard noticed his Book was missing and the clothes he had on.

When George had jumped into the car with people he'd never met before, he was overwhelmed by them taking the time to come pick him up. Jeremy and Kendra had brought food, drinks, and new clothes. They introduced themselves to George, while thinking that they were never prepared for what they saw in him. Police vehicles passed by the very car driven by Jeremy and Kendra, with George in the back. Little did they know that the one person they were looking for had gone right by them going in the opposite direction. Jeremy was driving at a normal speed and everything had happened so quickly that road blocks hadn't yet been set up. George didn't turn around to watch the vehicles pass by as he knew he was not going to get caught.

It was dark outside and he had no idea where they were taking him; he just knew he was safe. George was tired, so he leaned back against the seat and soon was asleep. Jeremy and Kendra looked back at him from time to time. Neither one of them could imagine the stress he must have felt, slipping out of a maximum security prison, and death row at that.

The warden arrived and was informed of the progress they had made, that the videos had been checked, but that there wasn't a single piece of evidence that led to the facts of his escape. Guards and inmates had been questioned, police were called in and an APB was put out on him. The warden ordered the videos sent to a forensic lab to have them analyzed. What the warden found out about George was the changes in him were very real; the other inmates had come to see and respect the transformation in him, even as they ridiculed him. He had changed so much they had a hard time believing he was the same man they had first met when he came to the prison. He didn't have any violent tendencies. He cared about others, and if he had to die, he was willing to accept his fate. Life in prison had changed him, and he had learned to listen to the Voice. At first, it shook him up, but later the company he had with him comforted him. The other inmates told him about George talking to someone and they had thought he was talking to himself as if he was having a conversation with another person. The warden sent word to the forensic lab describing what the inmates had reported to him. The fact the warden had to face was that George was in his right mind and maybe, just maybe, he was talking to another person, unseen, or he was finding comfort in his own way.

George woke up as Jeremy pulled off onto a gravel road when the shaking of the car jarred him awake. Kendra turned around as he was stretching and yawning. "We're on the farm," she told him. George could see it was early morning, with the sun making its appearance behind the trees. In his early years, he had worked on a farm, and he was thinking how well kept it was. He tingled with excitement at the thought that he would be able to work here like old times. The car windows were down and he was inhaling the earthy odors of the place. He heard roosters crowing, cows mooing, and dogs barking. He looked off to the pasture beside the road and saw horses grazing. "Like back in the day," he murmured to himself.

Jeremy and Kendra were talking to each other about things they needed to do. Both appeared to be in their mid to late forties. Kendra was slim and pretty with a quick smile and a way about her that seemed calm and confident. She had shoulder length light brown hair and hazel eyes that lit up her face when she smiled, and that seemed to be often.

Jeremy must have been working on a farm for a while with his strong frame. He was sitting tall behind the steering wheel despite of the fact that he had driven all night. He had dark brown, neatly cut hair. His eyes were light brown and George thought he most likely was a take charge kind of guy who knew how to take care of the people who worked for him. This was going to be interesting and he was feeling excited about his place here. Jeremy wanted to get some mowing done while Kendra would help Mariann bake some bread, he had heard Kendra tell him. George was curious. "What can I do to help?"

"There's always work to do around here. You can start by helping harvest our crops and we need help with the up keep. Have you ever done this type of work before?"

"I have, and I really like working outside. I don't mind working in all types of weather. I'm really ready to be able to help out here. Thank you for all that you are doing for me and taking the time out of your schedule to come get me."

"It's our pleasure having you. You'll be meeting a lot of people who work here. Everyone is excited about you being here."

"George, are you hungry?" He hadn't eaten any of the food they had packed for him. The sleep had left him feeling a bit energized, and he was wondering how Jeremy and Kendra seemed to be unaffected by the lack of a good night sleep. "Must have taken a nap before leaving," he thought.

"I am starving."

"Good, the food here is no prison food, I'll tell you that. We have the world's best cook."

"Great!"

Jeremy pulled into a space under a metal roofed carport. George noticed that everything back here was clean, neat, and tidy. Everywhere he looked the place seemed well maintained and in the right place. He didn't see any piles of discarded junk, which was surprising, because the farms he had seen may have been clean, but here and there would be a pile of junk sitting somewhere, usually rusting equipment and useless, rusting parts from old outdated farm implements. He couldn't imagine being useful, but maybe that was the reason for the efficiency of the place. Jeremy turned the car off and opened his door, got out, and stretched his cramped legs as he started walking toward the back door to the house, with Kendra walking behind him and George behind her. The smell of breakfast made them realize how hungry they really were, and they walked faster as the aroma begged them to get moving. Two dogs jumped up on them, greeting them with licks and nuzzling. They picked up their pace to get into the house with the dogs and other animals scurrying about. One of the dogs was checking him out as the other one was excited about seeing their human masters.

Jeremy opened up the door and allowed Kendra and George to walk in before him. They were hit by the delicious aromas of food; breakfast was about ready. "Mariann, would you come here, please?" Kendra called out to her. Mariann put down a towel she held in her hand and walked over to them. "George, meet Mariann, our cook and housekeeper. Mariann, this is George." George shook her hand. "I am pleased to meet you, Mariann."

"It is my pleasure, George." She went about cheerfully greeting the others who were getting the others ready to eat, and she ushered them through the dining room to get them cleaned up before she would allow them to eat.

Mariann was cheerfully greeting the diners and she hustled them through the dining room. "No breakfast unless you glisten," she bristled with pretend firmness and a glowing smile. George could tell that she loved this family and they loved her. He couldn't help but feel a bit envious. His stomach was urging him to hurry to get himself cleaned up to suit her. The smell of the food alone made his stomach growl with hunger. He followed the other three men as they made their way to the bathroom where he was waiting his turn to get cleaned up. As he waited, he listened to them chatter about the work that was waiting for them after breakfast, giving him a bit of background on the general work they did. They weren't ignoring him, they were turning to him to include him and let him know what they were doing. George was ready to do some meaningful work and was eager to get started.

"Sit down everyone," Mariann ordered them as they entered the dining room. The whole group sat down at the large dining table, waiting for the breakfast. The food was blessed While eating, there was laughing and bantering back and forth. Even though he had just arrived, George felt so much as if he had always belonged. The other people on the farm knew who he was and what he had done, and they all had things in their own lives they were ashamed of and knew how they had been changed, so it was easy for them to accept George and make him feel at home. The food tasted gourmet to him even though he was just eating eggs, bacon, pancakes with orange juice and coffee. It had been so long since he had eaten food this good.

"This is the best food I've eaten for a long time," he told Mariann, she laughed, "Honey; you've been locked up for way too long. I make this food every day. I'll get you fattened up, for sure. You're going to like it here, I know." She gave him a sly wink as she was trying to make him feel welcome. George wasn't expecting it, so they were getting a good laugh at his expense. He was starting to understand that they were... happy. There was camaraderie here and it was comforting. The effort to include him didn't feel forced and he was pleased how natural it felt to be with them.

Jeremy replied, "Mariann, you, my dear, are the best cook in the world!" Mariann's face turned red with embarrassment.

"Why, thank you!"

Mariann was in her sixties with shoulder length, shiny gray hair that had been cut into a fashionable, attractive style with her blue sparkling eyes, and a quick smile. Everything about her gave off an aura of a grandmother, loving, and always taking care of those around her. She stood five feet two inches, on which she carried a few extra pounds. Her husband had died ten years before she had come to live on the farm. She was not only the cook, but a mediator around the house, making sure everyone behaved, as she considered herself the only one who could keep them in line. No one argued with her on that account. They all loved her and she was a full member of their family. Her dry sense of humor was throwing George off a bit and the joy in her was undeniable.

She hadn't always been a cheerful person; before her husband, Jack, had died of cancer she had been a very unhappy person. She had to be on prescription drugs just to get up in the mornings, in which she dragged herself through the day. Before Jack had died, they were both miserable. When he died she was at the end of her rope. At Jack's funeral Kendra invited her to go to church with her and picked her up on their way, where she found the Voice. She grew in the knowledge of Him and learned that she could be happy. Mariann was working at a job she didn't like and was having a hard time being in a situation she wasn't feeling good about. Kendra was watching the new person emerge and wanted her to feel and be useful, so she asked her to come live with them as their cook and housekeeper. The arrangement worked out to everyone's benefit, one that no one regretted.

After breakfast Mariann shooed them out so she could clean up and start lunch preparations. She could always be heard humming, which was part of her daily clean up. Everyone in the house loved hearing her little tunes, but none of them would interrupt her. No one knew the tunes but it didn't matter. She was an important part of their lives.

CHAPTER FIVE

THE BUNKER

"Let me take you on a tour of the farm," Jeremy suggested. "Kendra, do you want to come along?"

"No, I really need to get some work done in the office," she replied.

"We will be back by lunch time, darling."

"Behave yourself, honey. And George, get ready to be shocked." She winked and went into the office for work.

Jeremy led George to a shop that was at the back of the barn where a golf cart was parked under an awning at the side of the barn. "Hop on," he invited George. He started the quiet motor and drove off in the direction toward the back of the property. "There is a special place I want to show you, it has been camouflaged as a hidden place that has been a work for years. It will surprise you, as it's different from anything you've ever seen. When my dad bought it years ago, he got a really good deal on it. Originally it was owned by the state, and since he was a scientist, he was allowed to buy a waste dump as it was within his area of expertise. You see, it is a nuclear waste disposal site, and he was working on some experiments, so the state made a deal on it and now it is mine. My dad found a way to make a safe underground living area. The Voice provided everything we needed for it. He had heard things about future trouble for Chosen Ones, so he planned ahead. His friends from his church thought they would be alive during this time so they worked hard to have it ready, but they're now all gone and their families have moved away."

Driving along both men were chatting like old friends when Jeremy drove the cart over a small rise on a path barely discernible since it wasn't used very often and the cart was usually driven along the fence lines. The look on George's face was funny to Jeremy, even with the warning about how different it was from the farm. It was a big pile of junk and the size of it was astounding to George, and in no way did he expect this. "This is it?"

"This looks bad and it has actually been planned this way. It looks like a landfill and smells like one on the surface. When you go inside it's something entirely different as you will see. Come on." Moving along, slowly navigating all the discarded trash, George was in disbelief. "This has all kinds of junk here, old cars, appliances, clothes, and every sort of unidentifiable trash. Where did it all come from?" he asked.

"We have had people who volunteered to haul off other people's trash as a public service. They were members of our church who had equipment as a part of their businesses and they hauled all this over a long period of time to keep outsiders from being suspicious; some of the trash was hauled to public landfills so anyone who might have been watching us didn't give us much thought. It was a long process, sometimes very difficult, so we wouldn't have anyone asking questions. We had all kinds of events out here and people would come and go as regular visitors."

"Come on, let's go inside," he said to George, sidestepping through the trash that was scattered everywhere. The trash was not only on the pile but was scattered all around haphazardly. Jeremy knew exactly where to go. George was not so sure and fumbled through the piles. Stumbling through the debris, George noticed that they were in a darkened tunnel and it was hard to see, but Jeremy was following it as if it were normal to walk through the trash heap. The tunnel had been cleverly hidden. "Don't worry, you won't get hurt. It is actually safe to walk through here; if there is a threat of this entrance being seen, we would put more trash around the door and the path we came in to discourage anyone snooping around. I forgot to bring a flashlight, so just follow the sound of my voice." They were walking at an angle that was sloping down as it was going under the large tank that was looming overhead. George was listening to Jeremy talk about it and he was telling him about the braces holding the tank up as supports. Much of the waste had been removed as his dad had used a great deal of it in his inventions; the same technology had been patented and was being put to use for the same reason as it was being used inside the bunker, which George was about to see in a minute. Looking back, Jeremy could see him and was guiding him through the tunnel and he stopped to wait for George to catch up to him. The path was smooth and easy to traverse. He opened a door that was hardly discernible in the darkness. He pulled out a key to unlock the door that was tilted at an angle and looking like a broken door from a storm shelter, "Why the lock?"

"To make it seem stuck, just in case someone we don't want here tries to get in and it can be locked from the inside when it is necessary. Notice that to unlock it you have to find the bolt, it has been purposely hidden." George took him at his word. After his eyes adjusted to the dark interior, he could see some light ahead of them. He walked towards it and saw a large open room with some light. The light was radiating from the ceiling with enough illumination to help him to see that it was an acceptable residence. Going into the bunker was an experience; the floor sloped down and around as it descended to the bottom where the living area where it leveled off. It was the size of the tank that loomed above it with the glowing of the faded glow of ceiling tiles, and George saw what he had been talking about. Jeremy had walked ahead of him, so George was standing and looking around to see what he could in the dim light. Jeremy switched on the light and George was taken aback by the size and the fair comfort of the place. It could easily hold a number of people. It wouldn't be as spacious when necessities were brought in for survival, but it was impressive. Thought had been put into this place.

"My dad found a way to use this toxic waste safely. It glows, so he made special glass containers for it. It isn't enough light to live by on a daily basis but it is enough to prevent total darkness. My uncles were also scientists so they worked together on it. We have trusted the Voice to keep us safe with the poison around us, but my dad secured it so well I doubt we'll ever have to worry about it. Give me a minute and I will turn some other lights on." He found the light switch, and the whole room was illuminated.

"It has electricity?"

"This place is made for long term living." George looked around; it was a huge. The walls were lined with something George couldn't identify and it was painted a soft white. The floors were flat rocks that had been carefully placed to keep from having tripping hazards and to be easier to clean. It was made for surprising comfort.

"It looks like you have been getting ready for a nuclear war, this is the sort of thing cults do. Is this what this is about?"

"In a way, that is what this is, except we are the Chosen Ones who the Voice has been telling that the time is coming when the world will be hunting us down to kill us because of what we believe. We don't advocate overthrowing the government; we don't arm ourselves with weapons of mass destruction, or other weapons to go about killing people, because they don't believe the way we do. That isn't what we're about. There will be weapons we will use for hunting food. We know something is about to happen and the Chosen Ones are preparing according to what the Voice tells us so that we may live."

"He has called me to help with this?"

"Yes."

Jeremy took George into the depths of the bunker, and he was impressed by the setup of the facility. It was well stocked with all the necessities needed for survival. "Is there a water supply here?"

"There is, the water comes from an aquifer located a couple of miles away, so the water is perfectly safe to drink. Heat detection devices can't be used to find anyone in here. This is a state of the art facility, with everything we need."

After George had time to look around and see everything the bunker had. Jeremy glanced at his watch and told George, "We need to get back or Mariann will have our heads for letting our lunch get cold."

"Lunch time already?"

"We've been gone for a while."

They left by going back through the tunnel, the way they'd gone in. Jeremy secured the entrance and they took off for the house. George asked more questions from the fascination of what he saw, and all the work that had been put into completing the bunker.

CHAPTER SIX

MR. CONLEY

He worked construction, which had been his favorite job, out of all that he worked besides working on the farm when he was younger. He had worked several different jobs since keeping employment was difficult. But he liked the job, his co-workers, and the fact that he didn't have to work inside behind a desk in a stuffy office. His co-workers often went to bars after working hours. He was always invited, but politely declined, until one day, after a particularly stressful day, he joined them. That was where he found alcohol and drugs. The drugs, more than anything, were a release. He felt uninhibited, free, no stress. It was freedom from his reality. He was lying in bed, sleeping off the previous night of partying, when his phone rang.

"Yes," he said after sitting up and picking the phone off the charger dock. His instincts told him this wasn't good.

"May I speak to George Conley?"

"This is George."

"This is Dr. Kiser from United Care Hospital. We found your name and phone number in his wallet. I have some bad news for you, your father was admitted here about an hour ago with symptoms of a heart attack. We did everything we could to save him but there was nothing we could do. I am so sorry to have to tell you that he has passed away. You will need to let us know what to do with his body."

"I'll get there as soon as I can." He was in shock. His dad seemed so healthy. Lately, he was stressed about money. He'd planned to go see him soon, but there was never enough time. Between work and partying, he just hadn't enough hours in the day. George crawled out of bed feeling like the night was heavy weight on his chest. He was sore and his head throbbed from the hangover. He went into the bathroom to brush his teeth and take a shower; he looked in the mirror and groaned at what he saw his eyes were blood shot with his hair standing on end. His stomach felt like it wanted to empty itself. Stumbling and his head feeling like and atomic explosion in progress, he got cleaned up, dressed, and out the door. He made it to his car, turned the key in the ignition to start it. The drive to the hospital took only fifteen minutes but seemed to take an hour. Finding a parking space, he sat for a minute to take a deep breath as he had to go inside, stumbling slightly he made it to the emergency room doors. Slowly walking through the doors, he approached the information desk. The receptionist called a nurse, who greeted him with a solemn smile. He was led to an office and told to be seated, and that the doctor would with him in a few minutes. He was sitting and rubbing his temples when the doctor came in.

"I'm Dr. Kiser," he introduced himself, shaking George's hand. "We did everything we could. Do you have plans for what you want to do?"

"Would you call the funeral home?" He gave them the name of the funeral home that had taken care of his mother's funeral.

"We can do that, my condolences to you, sir." The doctor sat with him for a couple of minutes before George got up to leave.

"Thank you, doctor," Dr. Kiser led him out. He left to go home, walking slowly to his car. He felt the need to go get a case of beer to numb his encroaching pain that was starting to poke at him, but he resisted. There wasn't anyone else.

Eight years ago his mother had died of stomach cancer at the age of fifty one. George had wondered if his mother's death had caused his dad to do the dishonorable things he had done; he cheated on his mother and lied about his indiscretions. His mother's death had hurt his dad, even if he didn't show it His dad was only sixty-one. George was feeling even lonelier and was already having regrets. Mr. Conley had deeply regretted what he had done to her and had remained alone ever since.

As George left the hospital, Dr. Kiser watched him go and was concerned about him. He had smelled alcohol on his breath and he was hoping he would be all right. He looked worn down, with his blood shot eyes; he didn't appear intoxicated, but he was certainly hung-over. Picking up the phone, he called the nurses' station and on the second ring a nurse picked it up, "Nurses' station, this is Jan."

"This is Dr. Kiser. Have you called the funeral home about Mr. Conley's body?"

"Yes, doctor, they should be here later today."

"Thank you, Jan."

Walking to where he had parked and stumbling until he finally spotted it, George got into his car to drive home, and he was feeling sluggish and nauseous. All he could think about was to get back into his bed, go to sleep, and wake up to everything being as it was before. He still missed his mother and now his dad was gone. Already he felt guilty about not taking better care of him. When his mother had died he had the same guilt and now he thought about how he had messed up by not being there for his father. He should have been there. He needed a drink but it wasn't the time. He had things to take care of.

Later, he thought, I'll go out for a drink later. Driving slowly along the streets to the one he lived on, he got to his driveway and parked. As he got out of his car to go inside, he had a change of heart and got back in. He decided to go to his dad's house. The hospital had given him his dad's possessions; his house keys were included with everything, including his wallet with a few dollars in it, some loose change, drivers' license, two credit cards and a pack of gum. He got back in his car and laid everything on the front passenger seat. Sitting there staring at the items, he felt tears burning his eyes and when he looked up he saw a couple of teen-aged boys watching him intently, so he started the car and drove the short distance to his dad's house.

The house already seemed empty when he pulled into the driveway. With his mother's death, the emptiness lingered. He sat in his car staring out into the emptiness he was feeling, after a few minutes of sitting, he decided to open the car door, and as he did he reached for the pile on the seat and headed for the front door. He rattled the keys that were on the ring to find the one that fit the door lock, when he found the right one with trembling hands. After he managed to get the door unlocked and had gone into the house, he kicked the door shut behind him. He stopped to take a good look around. There wasn't much left, as it appeared his dad was moving out. George stopped to think about when the last time he had been there and he realized that it had been months since the last time he had visited. There was a sharp stab of pain in his chest; he knew it was guilt. Tears were running down his cheeks as he quietly let his emotions take over. He walked over to a chair and sat down so he could calm himself. Time was going by and after what seemed to be hours, he looked up and saw that the sun was overhead and the clock showed it to be close to noon. He sighed and slowly stood up. He made a tour of the house and found the rest to look about the same as the living room. He went into his dad's office to find a will and see the state of his affairs. He was an only child, so everything would be his if the will didn't list anyone else. In the filing cabinet, he found the will and he confirmed that he was the sole heir. Letters and bills were lying scattered on the desk, and he picked them up to organize them in a pile. George found delinquent bills and credit card debt. He was surprised to see the massive debt his dad had accumulated, with an eviction notice from the bank. A bankruptcy folder was buried under the papers. His dad was deep in debt. "This is why he was stressed about money," he thought. His dad's car was parked in the garage; he had thought about it after he had been in the house for a while. The car wasn't terribly old and it had been paid off so it wouldn't be repossessed. It could be sold.

George started going through the house, cleaning it and taking out the trash. He was wondering where the rest of the property was, when he looked out the window and saw the next-door neighbor opening his mail box and pulling out its contents. He lingered at the mail box, looking at each piece of mail. George went out to speak to him, "Hi, Mr. Harvey, how are you? I haven't seen you in a long time." Mr. Harvey clearly noticed how bad George looked.

"Hello, George. I'm doing well. How's your dad? I haven't seen him this week." George felt tears burning his eyes.

"He died this morning from a heart attack." Mr. Harvey's smile left his face and sympathy replaced the smile. George had always liked him. He'd been a good friend to his dad, and they would always stop to chat for a few minutes when George came by to visit.

"George, I am so sorry. I knew he wasn't feeling very well lately; he said he had gone to the doctor and was told there wasn't anything to be concerned about. He didn't look good to me. Is there anything I can do?"

"Thank you, Mr. Harvey. Right now, I need to make funeral arrangements. Do you know what happened to his stuff? The house is pretty much empty."

"He was being evicted as you may know by now. He had sold off most of his things to try to pay his debts. We were going to let him stay with us for a while, and next week I was going to let him work for me. He was a hard worker. As for the rest of his things, he had a charity come by to get what was left. He asked me not to call you; he didn't want to worry you and when he got back on his feet, he planned to call you to let you know what was going on. I'll be sure to ask my wife which realtor he was going to list the house with. She was helping him get organized. I'll give you a call after she gets home from work."

"Thanks, I appreciate it," George sniffed. Mr. Harvey went inside. While he was out, he checked the mail box and found more delinquency notices. Thinking about what needed to be done, he decided to box up a few things and go home. He would have to call in to work and get started on the funeral arrangement and accomplish everything here. Seeing the mess still scattered, he checked around and locked the front door behind him. In the car, he sat for a minute looking at the empty house, started the car, and headed home.

Arriving home, he didn't bother to turn the lights on. Instead, he sat in his dark duplex apartment, grief pouring out. The phone rang but he didn't feel like talking to anyone; probably his friend wanting to go out. Why didn't his dad call him? His mother had died much too young and if she hadn't died, things could have turned out differently. He wasn't so sure and perhaps dad knew it too. George bent over with his hands covering his face, sobbing uncontrollably. How had things become so bad? He had to do something, but just the same, he admired her. They both loved her, George knew she was always busy with something but just the same, he admired her. He saw how much he resembled her. He looked like her and had his father's mannerisms. As his mother was dying, he could hardly recognize her as the attractive lady she had once been. Her death was horrible and painful. His losses were too heavy for him. Hurting and overwhelmed, he threw himself on the couch and fell asleep, restlessness and waking up every hour or so he made it through the night.

Before the sun was up, so was George. Taking a shower, he got dressed. He glanced at his reflection in the mirror, only to be shocked at who was looking back at him. He couldn't believe he looked even worse that he had the day before; it was a stranger looking back at him. The face was puffy with red rimmed eyes and dark circles under them; he groaned as he got himself ready to go out. There was more cleaning to accomplish at his dad's house.

He checked his answering machine and saw the flashing red light on it. Mr. Harvey had called to tell him the name of the realtor. George wrote it down on a sheet of paper that he stuffed into his pocket; he would call after the office opened. On the way over to his dad's house, he stopped at a convenience store for a much-needed coffee. The caffeine helped clear his head, and by the time he entered the house, he was feeling a little more prepared to tackle the job he had to do. As he pulled into the driveway, Mr. Harvey was out in his yard and he came over to offer George some help. They got busy and it didn't take long to clean and pack. Mr. Harvey told stories about Mr. Conley that made George smile in remembrance of his own life with him.

With the house neat and tidy, he began making the calls he dreaded, but he managed to push through the tasks he needed to get done.

An appointment was made for after lunch to pick out the casket and the day for the funeral. The next Wednesday, Mr. Conley was buried beside George's mother, and after the service George stayed around as the mourners tried to give him comfort. People had liked Mr. Conley, despite what he had done. It was a nice funeral, as far as funerals go. Most of what happened was hardly noticed by George. He tried to eat the food that had been brought to the church by the church members, but he wasn't feeling up to eating. He mumbled his thanks to the people as he left to go home to the silence of his apartment.

The realtor had called and left messages about prospective buyers for the house; the house was going to make a family a fine home. The Conleys hadn't owned it long before Mrs. Conley had died, and they had lived in the comfort that money provided them. It no longer felt like a real home.

George was already sinking lower. He went to a bar where he drowned his sorrows with liquor. In the morning when he woke up, he sat up in his bed wondering how he had gotten there; he had absolutely no memory of getting back to his apartment. His head was splitting and his stomach was revolting, but he needed to go to the bathroom. Getting on his feet was strenuous, swaying and stumbling, he made it. The days he had taken off for the funeral had turned into weeks and his money ran out, so he had to make some money quick. He had to give up his apartment, pawn his sellable belongings, and sell what he could for the rest of what was left. His so-called friends no longer let him stay with them anymore, and he was making no effort to help himself. He had met Joann and she wanted to help him; he wasn't ready but she wasn't about to give up on him. George was headed for trouble and she tried and tried. Joann would find him and offer him food and help, and she knew where to find him so she would bring food to him. He rejected her time after time, and she still refused to give up on him. She had known his parents and had attended the funeral; the look of him told her he was in serious trouble, and her heart went out to him. He was stealing all the while avoiding her as much as he could. She prayed for him; he had grown bitter and he was not able to see any hope for himself. The once strong and daring person he'd been turned cold as his anger and resentment grew.

Joann would see him on occasion as he went to places to get away from her. She would find him and try to get him to come see her at the shelter, but he refused. Seeing her made his guilt more acute, and he knew she was a kind person who truly had a good heart and a loving spirit. She reminded him of his mother and that made him feel worse.

He indulged more into his drug of choice. His past haunted him every day of his life, and all he wanted was to get away from it. The one person who could help him, he rejected.

Even though George had been in prison, in his younger days no one would have guessed that he had ever be where he was now. His family was upper middle class, his father was a successful businessman who had always been able to provide his family with everything they needed and wanted. George's older sister, Carolynn, was the ambitious type; a good quality to have to make a difference in what she did, and she was on the road to great success until she ended up in a physically abusive marriage. After years of brutal abuse, she committed suicide. George never moved on from her death, as they had both been close as kids.

George knew his parents loved him and his sister; they just never had much time for the kids. They were professionals and worked long hours. He was sent to his grandparents to spend time with them instead of having his parents around. They were life savers for the two of them. In high school, they died two years apart and it was hard on them. The family went on vacations together and they went to many interesting places and it was times George felt loved, and his parents let him do the things he wanted to do, but they were always on the phone taking care of business. The feeling of being alone started during those tumultuous times for him. He had loved his grandparents; they just weren't his parents and he was hurting. He longed for a normal home life like sitting at the breakfast or dinner table telling stories about their day or having fun in the back yard. His family appeared from the outside to be the perfect family; the kind of family others envied. Their community admired the family. They kept up the façade. George's father spent more time at work and with his mistress than he did with his wife and kids. George's mother would drink when she wasn't working, rather than taking the time with her children. The family was shattered from the inside. All George ever wanted was for his family to spend time with his mom and dad. It was hard for him to understand why they were living their own lives instead of living happily together. He was given everything he asked for. The allowance he was given was generous and he was taught how to look the part of a preppy boy, and he did it well.

Teachers, his parents, everyone, had always foreseen George as the one to follow in his father's footsteps. They knew he would grow up to be successful, with money and all the luxuries most people only dream of having. But at age of twenty-three, George couldn't stand his life anymore. He began a downward spiral into a life that opposed the one he'd grown up with. Bitterness was a thief that turned his heart to ice. It had a grip on George, eating away at him. He had planned on going to college using a football scholarship that he had earned during high school. He was a smart guy; he was grieved by what his father had gone through. He never learned to deal with the anger and resentment. He postponed going to college for a year, and the year became two, then three, then four, five. After all the years of putting it off, George just never went to school to fulfill his dream. He eventually thought of higher education as impossible, something he could not and would not do. He bounced from job to job, feeling dissatisfied and unhappy. He knew he needed to make some changes.

CHAPTER SEVEN

JEREMY

Years before, the bunker had been created, just for what would soon come.

"I've done some experimenting, and I think I figured out some uses for toxic waste," Barry said.

"I read the notes you wrote. Genius findings," Jake told him.

"The Voice told me that I need a plan for a future day when during Jeremy's time, possibly ours, he will need a place to hide along with the Chosen Ones. He told me to help Jeremy. Adam and Chance are needed too."

"Then we need to get started and get it done. I know of a toxic waste dump. The state will sell it to me for a bargain. No one else will go near it and I can make it safe enough for living conditions. No toxic waste is being put into it anymore," Barry said.

"We need to keep our findings to ourselves or it may be making the future for him dangerous. The Voice has been giving me some help. There's a group of wealthy people who go to another church and understand the future events as they are unfolding. We can approach them and maybe we can set up similar places around the world for such a time," Jake said.

"That is a good plan. This weekend maybe the four of us can go out to this place and look around."

"I'll give them a call," Jake said.

The weekend came, and all of them drove out to the place Barry had found. Barry had his Geiger counter with him. As they were riding around the place, they noticed the farm house that looked as if it had been sitting empty for a while. A short distance behind the house was a house-sized barn, which also needed repairs. Riding along further, they saw signs warning about biohazard waste. With the Geiger counter in hand, they weren't concerned and continued along their way. Barry knew how far down the tanks went and what was in there.

"This stuff glows. If it leaks there will be problems, so we need to find a way to make it safe. It's good for dark places and if we can build under these tanks, we will have a safe place. I've been working on some special glass the Voice showed me how to make. I'm planning on using it as lighting. Do you think you could help? We need to make air vents that will have to have filters to prevent the outside from being able to detect odors such as cooking."

"You know we like a challenge. This will be a good project." Jake said and the other two brothers agreed. Barry was a forty-year-old with a brilliant mind. He was a lean muscular built man. All four brothers had to wear glasses. Both parents had blonde hair so each of them inherited the hair color and blue eyes. They all were similar in their features with different personalities. The others were all above average in intelligence. Barry was the youngest. He was the most ambitious out of the brothers, and the brothers were motivated by him. Barry worked with toxic waste from which he had made breakthrough discoveries.

Jake was forty-three and the one who was quiet. He was a deep thinker and usually the voice of reason as the brothers were growing up. He had kept them out of trouble most of the time during childhood. The other three of them were rowdy, always chasing girls. Their parents would have him with them when they were out doing their fun activities and he kept them out of trouble with his reasoning. He helped with stabilizing chemicals that were developed and problems that were discovered later.

Adam was forty-six and was the one with the dominant personality. He was the one the girls first noticed out of the four of them. Slightly taller than the others, he called the other his little brothers. He was a gentle man who smiled frequently and his smile dazzled women. He worked with chemical storage and the development of chemical safety procedures. He had ideas he wanted to follow through with, on his own, to make money.

Chance was the prankster, he was forty-seven. He kept his brothers from being so serious, and he was one who told jokes and told stories with a serious expression. None of the others ever knew what to expect from him, what and when he would pull a prank on them. He once went to the chemical facility in a fluorescent safety suit to the horror of people outside the facility where they worked. In the years they had worked, there one accident had occurred and people of the town hadn't forgotten. The brothers grabbed their throats and made choking sounds and throwing themselves to the ground as if in pain and having trouble breathing, which made the people around town scatter. The brothers were reprimanded for it, even though they still laughed about it. Chance was the Chemical Transportation Specialist.

All of them had outside interests in working with chemicals for personal financial benefits. They had a purpose for what they were working on. Having a purpose to do what was part of the heavenly calling, and having been given gifts, the brothers were confident in their work. They worked in secrecy. Together they had developed technology in their garages that was helpful for the plans they were implementing.

Barry purchased the land. He knew of people in several commercial industries who also had the calling to fulfill a future purpose; they wanted to help out with this project. Barry decided to make the place look like a land fill so the men started hauling off trash around town. Construction would start when they had made the waste safe to get up close to it. Using the Geiger counter, they started digging beneath the huge tank. So far they hadn't found any leaks. It took about a year to complete the digging. They put in concrete and steel girders to secure the area as they were digging so it was braced as if free standing. To lighten the tank, they made use of the waste inside, which they could sell to government secret agencies. They conducted testing to ensure stability.

All tests gave them the results they were hoping for and there were no signs of leaking.

Chance had an idea. "Why don't we get one of those old windmills? They can be fixed to be fully functional to produce plenty of the electricity needed. Barry, you know more about how to do that than we do."

"It can work. I know where one is and I think I can get it cheap," Barry said. Jake suggested, "There's an underground aquifer at the far side of the property. We could have running water in the place. If we put in a filtration system, it should be safe, it will be tested. Also, we can have the drainage into the stream not far away with a purifying system from the bunker to the stream. Within a couple of years it would be about all it would take to finish it."

"We should be able to put several bedrooms in it if we make them small." Within a month everything had been arranged. The bunker would have complete modern touches to it. Even though the people living there would have to give up their normal lives, they decided giving the project a touch of luxury would help with the transition.

Barry and the brothers worked out all the kinks with the tiles. It had been challenging but the end result was successful. The tiles were slabs of glass filled with toxins between layers, similar to energy efficient windows with the use of high tech processes. Chance got busy getting them ready to install in the bunker.

Barry was determined to make sheets of the special glass and use them as ceiling tiles. This would require a structure to hold them in place. He used the steel that was used to support the tank. They had a welder help build bridges and multi-story buildings. He was serious about doing the job right. It took about a year to complete the digging. They put in concrete and steel braces to secure the area as they were digging, so it was braced as if free standing. To lighten the tank, they made use of the waste inside, which they sold to government agencies they used in the underground facilities. Most of the toxic waste was used up and other waste sites were being emptied of their content in the same way. They conducted testing to ensure stability. All tests gave positive results.

Mr. Jordan, the welder, owned his own business and trained young men in his trade. He was also a member of the church the brothers attended. This church was active in reaching out to the community; they trained people to live independent lives instead of turning to government for handouts. The church congregation was interested in being involved in showing how much they loved them, and how serving was more rewarding than a life of debauchery. The church was an important part of the community as it was active in changing lives. This church was an exception to what the churches had become; no power.

His colleagues thought he was crazy to attempt what he did. It was in the tiles and the tiles had gone through rigorous testing. The ceiling above the tiles had been heavily coated with a specially made coating to keep the tanks from leaking. The outer walls were being lined with concrete and steel reinforcements to prevent water from leaking in and from the possibility of cracking. The heavy coating on the walls was an extra protection and an air system was installed to circulate and keep the air fresh and clean.

Others in the church who weren't working on this particular project were busy with their lives doing the work of serving the community and tending to their families. There was a sense of urgency, and their work was progressing as needed to have it ready and waiting for the assigned time. Work around the world was also progressing as believers were preparing for what was believed to be coming, and others were living as if they could live forever without any worries. Pipes were in the process of being laid. It was slow and tedious digging the trenches, laying the pipes, gluing them, covering the trenches, and starting again but at last they saw the bunker insight. The plumbing was completed and the hookup inside the bunker was finished. Some of them went ahead to get the pump installed and the pipes set for the final hookup. The final preparations for a complete bunker were put into action. Chance, Jake, and Adam were following the calling of the Voice and left with their wives to help with shelters in other countries to build shelters. Their children were grown, with some of them in college or married with children. They had hoped to come back to retire but they ended up staying too long and weren't able to leave, so they were in hiding with Chosen Ones where they were. Adam was caught and killed. Chance was helping move people around as needed, and Jake had been injured, so he had to be confined to a shelter, staying busy as an advisor. Their wives were helping tend to the shelters.

When Jeremy was in college, he had met Kendra. He knew she was the love of his life. Both were freshmen at the same time so they graduated the same year. The families were close friends. After graduation they got married and move to Jeremy's home town. Jeremy worked in agriculture and worked for the state. He loved his job.

Kendra was a business major so she worked for a corporation to help develop new products and improve the way businesses were run. They were busy with their jobs and helping Jeremy's parents with the farm. It was fun going out to the farm; they had barbecues and had fun celebrating. Life was precious to the family. They invited their church out for functions and they had a nice barn to use. The place was kept in perfect working order.

The years were flying by and Jeremy's mom and dad were getting older and becoming frail. One day his mom called Jeremy in a panic; Barry had had a heart attack and had been rushed to the hospital where he died later that night. It was difficult for the family but not unexpected. Two years later, Kendra tried to help take care of his mom but she had been having a hard time after Barry had died, so Jeremy and Kendra had moved in with her to help take better care of her. She died in her sleep and was at rest.

Jeremy and Kendra took over the farm. They still had their jobs so they decided to find someone to help with the house. A woman at church had lost her husband and she was having a hard time. They asked her to come live with them and become their cook and house keeper, she accepted. Her name was Mariann, she did her job and they loved her. It was like they had a new mother. They also hired men to work outside with the work. Jeremy knew how to hire good people; their farm was running like a well oiled machine. This was one big happy family.

CHAPTER EIGHT

CINDY AND LUCY

"You are being hunted down as if you are animals; I want you to put your full trust in me. He will find you and Lucy. He will take you and I will rescue you. I am here always. Worry not, my child. I will shield you from death and the trials that I put you through." She thought she was dreaming.

Cindy woke up at one in the afternoon. And after getting herself up, she sat at her table in her small kitchen, feeling tired and old. At just twenty-five years old, she was numbed by life. Only drugs and caffeine kept her moving, powering her through endless days and nights. She knew she wasn't eating enough, which left her feeling the weariness even more. Mostly her fatigue was the emptiness she felt from the job she worked. Changes needed to happen, and soon. Her hopes were high; she knew she was smart enough, just that she needed to find a way out. Ghost was her handler and he would not just let her walk away. For now, she was going to eat and think of a plan. Lucy was smart, so together they might be able to think of something, for now she would do what she had to do, like it or not.

The phone rang. Cindy sighed and slowly rose from the table to answer it. In a tired voice, she answered, "Hello."

"Cindy! Hey! What have you been doing?"

"I just got up. Why are you so happy today?"

"I have money! We are going to have a fun afternoon. Let's go!"

"No thank you, it's ok. I'm a little tired."

"No excuses, you're coming with me."

"No, really, it's ok. There was just something that happened last night."

"What happened?"

"Come over and I'll tell you."

"Be there in fifteen minutes."

Cindy hung up the phone and yawned; she stretched out her tired body before sitting back down to eat her toast and coffee she'd fixed herself before the phone rang. Cindy nibbled slowly at her toast and started thinking about what had happened last night.

She thought, "I need a shower." So, before her friend arrived, she got up and took a hot shower. When she got out, she took a quick look around and realized that her small little living space was too messy for her taste; she picked up everything that had been tossed around. Cindy was compulsive, maybe a little too compulsive, about her living quarters being tidy. She had grown up keeping her living home neat and clean, which her friends thought was funny. Even though her mother knew it wasn't normal, she didn't mind. Her friends had liked to come over to her house, mostly because they liked her mother. She treated them like they were her children. They were close and Nancy liked having her friends over. There was an endless supply of snacks to be devoured, and her mother was 'the really cool' type. Nancy would help them work out problems they were going through. Cindy cherished her mother so much. But then there was a tragedy. Cindy's family was taken away from her because of an act of violence.

Nancy and Cindy's dad, Jacob, had a relationship with each other that they could write a best selling book about. They had been married for twenty-eight years and had settled into a happy life of comfortable middle-class living. Cindy was the joy of their lives and they did everything together as a family. As she grew up she had moments where she gave her parents problems and times where she had trouble coping, but she always knew they loved her. Cindy wasn't able to get away with much since both parents were in agreement with what she was allowed to do; she was given discipline when she needed it. They were a strong and loving family who had times of hardship and trials but they stuck together. Cindy was a good student in school and was encouraged to go out for sports and have interests of her own. Times were happy for her. Nancy was a substitute teacher who taught in the public schools, and she was good with kids of all ages. She taught elementary through high school; she took the opportunities, as they presented themselves, to teach life lessons and good living to the students as she had a sincere care and love for them. Making a difference was a source of pride for her and she stayed busy as she was a very popular teacher who was asked to fill in often.

Jacob worked for a well-known company where he was an account executive. He loved his work, but they were defrauding the government. He was keeping copies of records of illegal transactions and was keeping the records in their home safe. Knowing what was going on made him unhappy and he was in distress. He was planning to turn the records over to an examiner after he moved on to another job. Several of his resumes had generated responses from potential employers. Nancy had their church pray with them about it. The family knew they might have to move and Nancy and Jacob were concerned for Cindy's sake. Cindy was excited about a new adventure. She was in junior high school, and Jacob still worried for her, but the stress of being involved in illegal work was getting to him. There were some possible interviews coming up, so he was planning to take some time off to make it to them. He was emailing information to the potential companies as they were requesting it.

One morning, Jacob was feeling especially down, and Nancy called him to invite him to lunch to give him some quiet time so they could talk. Cindy was in school, so Nancy had time and she wasn't working that day, which was unusual for her. Her plan was to go pick him up early from his office so they could avoid the noon lunch rush hour and have a quiet lunch. After straightening up the house, she got herself ready.

Parking her car down the block from the front door to Jacob's office building, she walked to the front doors and entered the building, where it was cool and fairly quiet, so she thought Jacob may not be so busy. He wasn't expecting her so early. Greeting the receptionist who was busy at the front desk, they exchanged friendly smiles as Nancy kept going toward the elevator. The elevator took a moment and a couple of men got off, and she got on as she pushed the third-floor button where Jacob's office was down the hall. The door to his office was closed, so she knocked and heard him say, "Come in." Opening the door, she watched as his face lit up when he saw her. She rarely came to his office as he was very busy. "Sweetheart! What are you doing here so early? I thought you were coming in a little later." She went to put her arms around him and gave him a kiss.

"I have decided to snatch you away from here and take you to lunch with me a bit early, even if it is against your will. You are officially being kidnapped for an hour or so," they laughed.

"Definitely not against my will, let me tell the others that I will be back after a while," he picked up the phone and told the person answering it to take messages for him. He hung up and they headed for the elevators. Already he was feeling much better.

Nancy took him to her car, and after they had gotten in and buckled into their seat belts, she maneuvered in and out of the traffic of the small city where they lived. The restaurant where she was going was the one he had taken her to the first date they had together. It was always a special date place for them throughout their married life, and it only took a few minutes to get there, and as they were getting the car parked, they noticed a man out in the parking lot who appeared nervous as he was pacing back and forth. He seemed to be overdressed for this particular time of year. He was wearing loose faded jeans, an army coat that was several sizes too big for him. His hair was down to the middle of his back and it was thin, stringy, and dark brown. Under the coat, he had a dirty white t-shirt, with a brown checked button down shirt that was not buttoned. On his feet, he had tattered tennis shoes that were in desperate need of replacement. He was thin and looked as if he hadn't eaten in a while. Nancy had a bad feeling about him as she looked him over. She was wary of him but quickly forgot about him as they were having an animated conversation about some things going on a Jacob's office that morning. Jacob held the door open for Nancy as she walked in, and were greeted by the hostess. She knew both of them as regulars and she knew the waiter or waitress would get a good tip from them, so she was planning to seat them where a friend of hers was waiting tables. She was always glad to see them as they were very kind people, and she had them seated right away as the place was slow but picking up at that hour.

The waiter, a longtime employee, greeted them and took their drink order: water for Nancy and iced tea with lemon for Jacob. The waiter left to give them time to decide and as they made up their mind as to what they wanted, the front door opened and in walked the man from the parking lot. They recognized his clothes, but his face was covered with a mask. He had pulled out an assault rifle and was pointing it at the hostess, who screamed. The manager was nearby, and he came running over. "What can I do for you? "He asked the intruder.

"You took my job and now I am going to kill you," he hissed. And without another word, he started shooting before anyone had a chance to move; it happened very quickly. The manager was the first one he shot, and the the bullet hit him in the chest. The hostess was the next one to go down, the other people in the restaurant were shot as witnesses. The staff who were in the kitchen had come out to see what was going on, and they too were killed. Jacob and Nancy were among those murdered. The man left and disappeared without being identified, and anyone who heard the conversation were murdered. The place was a gruesome mess, and when a customer came in, he called the police, who arrived within minutes to find the murder scene. The cameras were of no help in finding him.

When Cindy wasn't picked up from school, the principal started calling Nancy and Jacob. He found it strange Nancy hadn't picked her up. He knew Nancy very well and knew she would never leave Cindy without calling. He called the police, and they came to get Cindy, where they met with a social worker who told her what had happened to her parents. Cindy was devastated. Her life in foster care began. Since there were no other family members who could have taken guardianship of her, she became a ward of the state, part of the system. Like kids in the same situation, she was moved from one home to another. During that time, she suffered unmentionable abuse. No one was there to save her from it, and she just had to go through it completely alone. Every time Cindy thought about her past life, she would just try as hard as she could to forget her family had loved her. The memories she had kept with her lasted a long time. Eventually they were lost, so she had nothing left as visual reminder of her parents. In her heart, she would always have them.

She went to school and graduated. Cindy was, and even now, was a beautiful girl, which did get her attention that made her uncomfortable. She was five foot seven, weighing one hundred twenty pounds, and she had long dark brown hair, and big crystal blue eyes lined with long black lashes. She had the potential to be a model; it wasn't something she wanted to do. Her personality meshed well with everyone, she was 'that girl'; the one the boys liked and the girls wanted to be like.

"Cindy, Cindy, I have plans for you. I will free you from your entrapment. I will guide you through all the turmoil, as I have already. I have plans for you, listen to me, now. The lady you spoke to, listen to her. She was sent by me to show you what you need to do. Follow my voice and you shall be free."

Cindy felt much more awake now. The shower had done a lot of good. She didn't feel as tired now so she got dressed in loose fitting jeans and a plain pink t-shirt with two buttons at the top of the round neck line, a silver shell jacket with matching pink buttons. Her clothes hung off her thin body. The finishing touches were when she put on some makeup. She did notice some wrinkles around her eyes. Oh, I have lots of gray hair, I need to color it. Wrapping her hair up into a ponytail, she gave herself one last glance in the mirror, and walked out of her bathroom

As she walked towards her kitchen the doorbell rang. She gave a quick look through the peephole in the door and saw her friend Lucy. She opened the door and they gave each other a hug. Lucy wore tight jeans, an animal print t-shirt with a black ruffle on the bottom that hung to just above her knees and a short cropped black leather jacket. She had ankle high boots that had a gold belt around them attached to gold buckles on the sides. To top it off, her wrists jingled with gold bracelets and gemstone rings on every finger with gem stones. Her hair, light brown in color, fell down to her shoulders in natural curls. Cindy envied her for the natural beauty and that she could pull off wearing anything effortlessly and managed to make clothes look good. She was the more fashionable of the two, put together and coordinated. Cindy figured it wasn't her clothes that were noticed, but Lucy herself captured the attention.

"Hey!"

"Hey! You look great!"

"Just took a shower."

"I really hope you changed your mind and you'll go shopping. Just give me a couple of hours. I want to get away from all of this. Please?"

"Ok. But I need to get back early for work. OK?"

"Ok, ok. Now let's go." Lucy laughed.

Lucy was all Cindy had, and Cindy was all Lucy had. They looked after one another, as much as time and life allowed them. "Tell me what happened last night," Lucy inquired.

Sigh. Cindy wasn't up to talking about it, but she began, "It was kind of early, and there was this nice lady who was walking by. She started telling me about this Voice she hears. She said this voice wanted to talk to me, and she invited me to her house for lunch. I had a dream last night and I heard a voice talking to me, telling me to trust it."

"That's like, weird. Most people treat us like trash and try to steer clear of us. Dreams are dreams. So what are you going to do?"

"I don't know, it's not like I'm going to see her again."

"Give her some credit, she's not mean or anything, was she?"

"Yeah, she was nice, let's go."

Lucy was just an all-around happy person. Cindy wondered why she was so happy, considering Lucy was also an orphan. But she liked Lucy, everything about her made Cindy happy, even though Lucy's drug of choice was alcohol, with occasional indulgences in drugs. Lucy had a magnetic kind of personality.

Out the door they went for what Cindy hoped would be a fun, relaxing afternoon.

They were looking for clothes at their favorite store, when they ran into Jenny. Jenny was one of the girls who worked at night like they did. They invited her to join them, to which she agreed. The three made some purchases, and decided to stop for lunch since none of them had eaten much that morning and they were hungry. Being with her friends had cheered Cindy and she was surprised she was so ravishing hungry as she was.

"I don't know what I am going to do. Ghost has been hitting me a lot lately and I don't know why. He says I'm being punished and don't know what I am being punished for." Jenny told them while they munched on onion rings that they had been dipping in ketchup.

"He doesn't say what you did?" Lucy asked. Cindy nibbled at her food, keeping her head down. She had been there. Ghost had punished her, not explaining why. They finished eating and sat at the table, continuing their conversation.

"He has been hurting a lot of the other girls too. Some of them have been hurt severely and I'm worried about them. One of them got beat so bad she was scarcely recognizable. I don't think she was alive, and the other girl was beaten so bad she had lots of broken bones. They took her out so I don't know if she was alive at that time, I think it will probably happen to us. Ghost doesn't care what he does to us as long as we keep working. He'll do it to anybody. I want to find something else to do with my life. I am tired of feeling so used," Cindy piped in. It was true, she hated what she did, what men did to her. She wanted something more.

"This isn't life; it's just sailing through our time alive." Lucy agreed. Jenny sighed, she was ready for something different but getting away from Ghost was not going to be easy. Getting away had only one path, being found and killed, disappearing without anyone knowing what had happened. The police weren't able to do much about it; Cindy and Lucy didn't have family to look for them.

CHAPTER NINE

LEAVING

Cindy had an idea. "Hey, why don't we go see where that nice lady works, the one who came by to see me. She told me where it is. I really like her and hope I see her again, and maybe she can help us get out of this. The least we can do it try."

The place wasn't far away from where they were, so they walked to the address and found it easily. There was nothing remarkable able about the building. There were bricks that had come loose and were lying on the cracked sidewalk. It was obvious someone was trying to perform the upkeep on it. There were weeds around it that had been mowed down recently. Cindy liked Joann and the way she was caring, taking time out of her life to find her, and her kindness. Homeless people were going in and out of the building so they decided not to go in. The three decided they would go back later, when it wasn't as busy. They started back to their apartments when the afternoon began to fade into evening. It was time for work. Each one said good-bye, promising to go out again for some fun. They all worked in the same district so they saw each other often, but there was usually no time to talk. If they were caught talking, it meant Ghost was going to hurt them. Getting themselves ready to go out, they walked over to where they were to wait. It was a slow night and

Ghost was going to be in a rage. It didn't matter to him if it was slow and not the fault of the girls; he just didn't care.

The nice lady was out looking for Cindy and she found her leaning against the door of a closed café. It was a cool evening.

"Hi, Cindy," she greeted her. "How are you?"

"Ok, I guess. I'm ready to go home," she replied. "Oh, I told my best friend about you. I want her to met you."

"I would love to meet her!"

"Do you have time right now?"

"I sure do." Lucy was down the next block so they walked down the street where she was staring off into space. As Joann and Cindy walked up to her, she gave them a big smile.

"Lucy, this is the lady I was telling you about," Cindy told her.

"Lucy, I am Joann. It's so nice to meet you." Joann gave her a warm friendly smile.

"Would you go with me for a cup of coffee?"

"That sounds good. My feet hurt. We need to be careful to watch for Ghost," Cindy answered and Lucy agreed with a nod.

"I know of a nice coffee shop a short way from here. My car is a couple of blocks away; we can ride." Walking to Joann's car was making the girls nervous, and they kept looking around to see if Ghost was lurking somewhere. They got to her car and Cindy got into the front passenger seat while Lucy got in the back behind her. Joann was talking about things the Voice had told her about them, and both of them looked at each other. They arrived at the coffee shop where they went inside and found a booth with Joann sitting on one side and Cindy and Lucy on the other. Joann had a way about her that had the girls relaxed and comfortable; they were surprised by what Joann knew about them. "I really didn't know about you until the Voice told me to get you out of here. He wants better things for both of you." The girls were quiet.

"Lucy and I have been talking about leaving this life behind. We want to get out of it but Ghost doesn't just turn loose any of us who choose to leave. He would rather kill us than for that to happen," Cindy told her.

"The Voice is much more powerful than the Ghost, so nothing will happen to you that He won't let happen. He has a plan for both of you. I know what work you are in, but I don't think that was your plan. Something hadn't worked out for either of you. The Voice sent me here and I think you are supposed to go with me. I need some help at the homeless shelter I run. I want to get you away from this, and come with me. Would you be interested? You can stay with me in my home. I could use some company in that big old house." Cindy and Lucy looked at each other with amazement.

"Obviously, the Voice has been telling you this because you know things about us that we haven't told anyone here,"

Lucy said, "Thank you, are you sure? I mean, it's not like people really care about us."

"The Voice is never wrong he wants you to give Him your hearts. I would be thrilled to have you join me. I care about you and want for a better life for you, if you will allow me to help you." Both of them were happy and ready to change their lives. In their hearts, they knew this was the right thing to do.

"Would you like for me to go with you to get your things?"

"You want us to go now?"

"I really do. Are you ready now for change?"

"Yes," they said simultaneously.

"No time like the present." Cindy saw Ghost driving down the street.

"Oh no!" she said. "Ghost won't let us go. He'll kill us if we leave."

"Does he drive up and down the street often?" Joann asked.

"He patrols, but he may not be back for a while."

"How long will it take for you to get your things?"

"We don't have much, so not very long."

"If you get only what you don't want to leave and leave the rest, I will provide you with anything else you will need."

"That will only take a minute or two."

"Here is what we will do then, Cindy, I will drop you off and take

Lucy to her place and leave her and then I will come get you, and then go back to get Lucy. If you need more time, I will keep watch."

"I think that will work," Cindy said. They got into Joann's car, and she took off headed towards Cindy's apartment with Cindy directing the way for her. At her apartment, she jumped out and raced up the steps, unlocked the door, ran in, and closed it behind her. She clicked the lock in place. 'It's finally happening,' she thought.

Joann drove off with Lucy directing her to her apartment a few blocks away. Lucy did the same thing at her apartment. Joann went to get Cindy and as she drove up, she dashed out of her door without even locking it, and jumped in Joann's car with her small bag of her possessions she had brought with her. In her excitement to go, she hit her head on the door frame of the car, but she hardly paid any attention to the pain even as a knot formed on her head. Joann noticed, "Honey, are you ok?"

"Oh, yes, I am fine!" Joann wanted to stop to make sure but Cindy urged her on with a laugh and wave of her hand. Joann took off. Joann kept looking at her with concern as she noticed the knot was well formed, but Cindy seemed not to pay any attention to it in her excitement to be out of the dreadful life she was leaving. Lucy was also ready when they drove up, except she closed and locked the door. Lucy was ready to go; she got in carefully so Joann didn't need to worry.

"Girls, I am so happy to have you with me!"

"We have to get out of this work. It wasn't the direction we wanted our lives to go; we are so thankful to you."

"Be thankful to the Voice for making sure I was listening." Cindy and Lucy were apprehensive about Ghost, but Joann reassured them that the Voice would take care of them. Soon they were talking and chatting happily with their new-found happiness, and Joann was sure about taking them into her home. Pulling into the garage, they grabbed their small bags and got out of the car as the garage door was closing. Joann opened the garage door that led into the kitchen, where there was an aroma of recent cooking. Joann opened the refrigerator to find something for them to eat.

The night was deep, and Joann was tired and ready for bed as the girls were finishing up. Yawning, she announced that she was going to sleep. But first, she showed them to their rooms and where to find whatever they might need. Tomorrow she was taking them shopping before taking them to the shelter. She planned for it to be a short work day for them. Cindy and Lucy took a shower before crawling into the comfortable beds. They each had their own room; the rooms were bright and cheerful with the obvious touch of Joann's personality. Each girl was happily nestling down under the lightly flower scented sheets and blanket, inhaling the sweet aromas of their new lives. They were sound asleep in no time as fatigue overtook them, sending each into peaceful dreams.

All of them slept in late, and when they got up they ate a leisurely breakfast before getting ready to go out. The girls were admiring Joann's beautiful home. Joann smiled as she watched them checking out their new home and seeing the hope that lit up their faces. To her, it was only possessions; to them they were seeing treasure. Not having to look forward to the life they left had them bouncing with energy and hope. Joann was smiling at their youthful exuberance. Joann made omelets for breakfast with homemade rolls and juices of their choice. Cleaning up the kitchen and getting dressed for the day, they were ready to go out and start the day. The weather was nice and shopping was fun. They went to lunch at a small café that served specialty sandwiches that had them talking about a return visit. After they finished their lunch and shopping, Joann took them to her house to put their things away and to change into some work clothes. They went to the shelter so they could help her prepare the evening meal. Already the girls loved their new jobs. They were seeing themselves in this permanent change of their lives.

Joann had dreamed of being a wife and mother ever since she was very young. As a child, she dreamed of having a home to keep, a husband to care for, and a big family. When she met the man, Eric, who worked for her dad, he had introduced them when her mother took her with her to go see her dad at work. Somehow, she had known she would marry him. She thought about him often and as she found out later, he was thinking about her too. They met again sometime later and they started talking, he started calling her, and they started going places together. In time, they decided to get married, and the wedding was everything she had ever wanted. Having been married for a year, she found out they were going to be parents, and both of them were so excited and waiting for the arrival of their new baby girl. Seeing their new baby for the first time was beyond anything she thought was possible and they were a happy family. Eric had joined the Special Forces in the military, so he was away for long periods of time. But Joann had hidden secrets from everyone. Only she knew how she had survived unspeakable things from her childhood. Just when she thought that her life was finally as she wanted it, as a wife and mother, everything that she knew would be turned upside down.

Joann grew up with her cousin living in her family home. Her cousin moved in with them because his mother died from a drug overdose. She liked her cousin and was happy that he had joined her family, and it was like having a brother. Shortly after he moved in, the monster that he was came to light. It happened at first only once every few months, and then it began occurring every week. He was touching her inappropriately at first, and then he started molesting her. She knew it was wrong what her cousin was doing to her, but his threats made her too afraid to say anything. Her cousin did dreadful things to her, making her feel dirty. Over time, she didn't fight back anymore; there was no use. He would threaten her, telling her that if she said anything he would kill her entire family during the night while they were all sleeping. He was sent to prison a few years after coming to live with them, and was charged with the rape of a younger child. The police had questioned her, but she was still too afraid even though they knew what he had done to her. There was nothing they could do without her testimony.

After Joann was married, she was left with her self-esteem at a low point, but marriage was what she wanted. She cast those feelings aside so that she could fulfill her life goal of being a good wife and mother. She had never told Eric about what had happened; one day she was going to tell him about it.

Eric was an officer in the Special Forces with a unit that was needed in extremely dangerous situations, and he was trained to neutralize certain elements where he was sent. He was able to live out his life's goal by serving and being the good soldier that he was. When he was told that he had to leave to fight battles elsewhere, he was thrilled, but Joann was devastated. Battle was dangerous but duty called for him to go. When he left, she felt so alone. He wanted to be in the thick of the action with the men he commanded.

Being a strong woman, she did what she could to survive. She received benefits from Eric's death, but that wasn't a replacement for him. She had been a homemaker since being married, so she had to find a job. She did, but the money just barely covered her expenses. Her daughter Cass was growing up quickly, but there was the stress of taking care of herself and Cass. Cass helped take her mind off other things. There were nights where Joann broke down in tears. It was so hard to grieve and still live her life. Life still had a ball to throw at her. Cass loved the outdoors. She played in the yard on nice days and she loved it. She was playing with her ball in the front yard one afternoon while Joann was washing the dishes as she watched her play in the yard. The neighbors greeted the little girl, asking her to come by when she was done playing. Cass thought the neighbor had asked her to come by at that moment.

At that instant, a driver who was texting on his mobile phone, without his eyes on the road and going well over the posted speed limit, drove by just as Cass ran across the street to play with the neighbor's daughter who was playing in her front yard. The little girl's body was so badly broken and Joann had witnessed the whole thing. She was thrown into shock that she was barely able to move, and when she did she was unaware of her movements. Joann couldn't make it in time to stop her from running into the street. She would feel like it was her fault for a long time that she had lost the family she had loved so much. Cass was only eight years old. Joann was inconsolable for quite a long time.

Cindy and Lucy were no longer women of the night. Joann had done not only the greatest thing for the girls, but done what the Voice had instructed her to do. She had taken in the girls into her home. The girls were finally at ease with their lives, with the exception of one thing: Ghost. Their handler wasn't happy they had left. He had been sending threats, and hiring very rough people to find the girls. Cindy and Lucy had brought him the most money out of all of his girls, and he wasn't about to let them leave so easily. Ghost was determined to bring them back.

Joann listened to what the girls told her as she wanted to know everything about them. After she had met Lucy, they had all become close friends and as time had passed, the girls began trusting her and Joann ad no regrets about bringing them into her home. They were beautiful, smart, and she knew they had had good parents. She was pleased with them and knowing they were safe from what they had lived every night. Both of them were happy to be helping her around her home and at the shelter, never complaining. Joann had given them jobs at the homeless shelter. They cooked, cleaned, ran errands for the shelter, and did general upkeep of the place. They stayed so busy they didn't have time to think about the life they had given up, they loved what they were doing.

Joann was extremely satisfied with how much the girls had turned their lives around and was happy and fulfilled. They loved their jobs and seemed to find contentment helping those who had far less than they did. Never did she ever imagine that the two girls, who had once worked on the streets, would be her best workers. Life seemed so good and the routine was good for them.

CHAPTER TEN
BEWARE OF THE GHOST

"They left, none of my girls leave, they're not allowed to. I told them when they started working for me that the only way out was being six feet under. What did they do? They had to sneak out and now they're hiding. I don't think that's going to work, not for me. They turned over a lot of dollars for me, and their clients ask for them specifically. I'm going to make sure they pay for this. First, I'm going to find them. Then, they'll be punished. I don't know who they think they are, leaving me out like this. I did everything for them. They had nothing before they came to work for me. They were both damaged before working for me. Cindy had nobody, Lucy left her family. How could they do this?" Ghost was agitated and he was taking it out on his crew who worked for him. "What do you mean you can't find them?" he demanded. "I told you where I have already looked. If you don't get them in here now, I'll make you pay and it will not go easy for you, so get out of here. Get out there and bring them to me. I'm losing a lot of money because of them. Go! Don't come back unless you have them!"

The thugs quickly disappeared. They knew he'd do as he said. Ghost was notorious, and his reputation had preceded him where ever he went. People knew he wasn't one to mess with. Finding the girls was the top priority, and he wouldn't stop until he did. He wouldn't stop with killing the girls. He was planning on taking care of anyone associated with them, even that lady who he saw with them. Ghost was a man who did whatever it took to get what he wanted, there were many dead people to prove it and it didn't faze him at all. He found pride in his work, and even more so, the fear he'd instilled in this town. Fear of him was intense, and anyone who even thought about turning him in, were killed. The law hadn't been able to pin anything on him, which made him confident he could do what he wanted. This was a man who believed he could get by with anything, and it seemed that way. Those who did what Ghost asked them were paid for their silence, even though they were afraid of him, they had a warped respect for him. His loyal workers lived well, as long as they did want Ghost told them to.

"We need to find the two girls they're going to regret they left."

One of the thugs shifted uncomfortably in his chair. He knew it wasn't going to turn out well for those two girls. They were both beautiful, and the thought of what was going to happen made him uneasy. Ghost never did the work by himself; instead he had a couple of guys who took intense pleasure in inflecting pain. When inflicting harm on his victims, faces were never touched but body parts that were covered were fair game. The torture was degrading and the abuse would cause such pain and suffering the victim would beg for death, and there were those who got their wish. Ghost considered his victims insignificant; to him, no one would care they were dead. Many of them believed them to be with other family members and not knowing they were missing which made disposing of them much easier.

"Get some more of our guys out patrolling the streets so we can end this quickly."

"Yes, boss."

Ghost sat back in his chair at his desk drinking beer, on a high from his latest fix. He was livid but pleased at the same time because his two prized possessions were about to find out what happens when they leave. If only he could find those two useless girls. He should have known they would be trouble they had seemed to always be having trouble listening to him. He slammed down his fist on the desk, causing all the piled-up work to shuffle, and he picked up the phone. "Get my car!" He was going to go for a ride. He had so much built up tension, he needed to unwind. The phone rang. "Hey boss. I think I know where they are. Word on the street is they've been working at this homeless shelter, in Old Downtown on Front Street."

On the street, across from the shelter, there were old abandoned crumbling building were some of the homeless had taken up residence. The odors inside were deplorable. Windows had been broken with glass inside and outside, along with all the other trash that the wind had blown up against it. Where the doorways were recessed, there were piles that seemed to be climbing up the wall and the doors. Occasionally paper currency would be blown in from the direction of a shopping center with people being careless about loose bills, and the wind would blow it up against the old buildings as if making a deposit.

"Go to that shelter," the driver drove to it. "Stop, let me out here and you drive down the street and wait for me, be where I came to see you." Ghost got out and he watched as his driver turned around and parked a block away with the front of the car facing him. He walked over to a pole and stood smoking a cigarette. When homeless people went in and out of the building, he looked inside, and he was sure he saw Cindy and Lucy standing at a serving table filling plates and smiling at them. "Dumb chicks," he said out loud. He raised his hand for the driver to come over, and he drove up and Ghost got in. "I want you to find out what time this place closes."

The driver took ghost to his apartment where he came up with his plan. He thought it was a good idea, and he was feeling deliriously happy. Going to the refrigerator, getting a beer, and sitting down in his plush easy chair, he was going to sleep very well tonight. Chugging down the last of the beer, he went to bed and fell asleep.

Right before twelve o'clock, he woke up and stretched before climbing out of his comfortable bed. He reached for his phone to call his girlfriend, another short term one who put up with him in hopes of getting as much out of him as she could. Buying stuff was the only way he could keep one, and then they only put up with him for so long and then they moved on. "Hello," she said answering her phone.

"Hey, babe. I am coming over tonight, will you be home?"

"I work until eight and then I will be."

"Until then," he hung up. He got up to get ready to go to work. He had made his rounds, checking on the girls before coming home early this morning. Maybe he would get a nap in his office when it was slow. In the freezer, he found a pastry that he put in the microwave and got himself a beer to wash it down. Taking his breakfast out on the patio to eat it, he finished it off by sitting back, putting his feet up on one of the patio chairs as he smoked some weed. Yawning, he went inside with the trash, he went to take a shower, and he burped noisily and scratched himself.

Dressed and approving of himself in the mirror, he was pleased with what he saw. He went to call for his driver who was there in fifteen minutes.

As Ghost was growing up, he had lived with both of his parents until he turned ten when his father had walked out on them. He drank a lot and when he was home, he beat him and his mother in his drunken rage. Ghost was afraid; his mother was powerless to protect him. This life went on until one night his father was arrested for having killed a man in a bar fight when he and another man got into a knife fight and his father killed the other man. The police had been called, when they got there, they witnessed the killing. He was tried, convicted, and was serving a life sentence in prison. His mother had worked two full time jobs to survive, leaving Ghost to fend for himself. At first, he tried to do as his mother asked of him, but with her gone all the time he got bored, quit school, and joined a neighborhood gang. The gang required loyalty for acceptance and Ghost needed acceptance. He was soon making a name for himself and was standing out, even taking over the gang. He became revered and he loved the power.

One day as his mother was coming home from one of her jobs, a rival gang drove by her house and shot her as she was unlocking the door. She fell to the ground, instantly dead. She was shot in the back

and as the bullet went through her chest, it ruptured her heart. A rival
gang had known where his mother lived and retaliated. A neighbor saw
what had happened, and called the police who arrived within minutes
along with an ambulance. It didn't take long to identify the killers as
the neighbor knew the killer. Ghost heard the sirens as he was walking
down the street where he lived. It was true, but he didn't want to believe
it. Ghost knew what time she got off work and the time when the bus
would drop her off at the corner close to their house. He ran to his house
where he was stopped by the police. Her body was gone and he saw the
spilled blood from the devastating death. This was a turning point that
changed everything for him. "That is my house!" he told the officer as
he was sobbing and struggling to get to the door.

"You can't go in; this is a crime scene," he was told.

"My mom," he cried.

"Boy, I'm so sorry. Is there anyone I can call for you?"

"No," he said turning around and walking away. He was walking
aimlessly, not knowing or caring where he went. He looked up when one
on his homies walked up to him. "I just heard what happened to your
mom. Let's go get the one who did this." He didn't care what happened
to Ghost's mom, he was looking to kill off the rivals.

"Yes, let's go get a car." The gangster left, and Ghost stood where he
was, seething with anger and hatred, ready to kill someone.... anyone.
A car pulled up beside him after a few minutes. "Come on, get in." It
was no secret where the rivals were, so the driver went to find them.
Ghost saw that every member who was in the car had a gun. All of them
were primed and ready. Getting close to the rival's hangout, the tinted
windows went down and the guns came up, ready for action. They saw
the car and the gangsters were able to see who they were, sudden fear
showed on their faces as they started to duck down, but too late. Ghost's
gang started shooting, killing every one of them standing by the car. The
shootout was over within seconds. The driver hit the gas pedal and shot
out of there with the tires pealing and leaving marks on the road. In the
distance, they heard the sound of sirens; they were well out of there by
the time the emergency vehicles arrived.

The news that day was full of details about all the deaths. It was all very gruesome. A total of seven people had been killed. Ghost was the suspected killer but the police weren't able to make a positive connection, because there were no witnesses alive. His mother had been killed was all they had. Ghost never got over his mother's death. He became angrier, bitter, and his hatred intensified as time went by. He became more abusive and he was only eighteen.

Later in the morning Ghost wanted to make sure it was the girls he actually saw. "Take me back to the shelter. I have some questions I want to ask that crazy old lady who runs that place." In another fifteen minutes they were in front of the building. The driver got out and walked up to the door. Lunch was about over, and he didn't see the girls, but he could see that Joann was cleaning and pulling pans off the serving line. "Do you have Cindy and Lucy working here? I am a good friend of theirs." Joann didn't trust him, so she wouldn't give out any information, and he left. He knew they were there; he had been looking around while talking to her, and knew they were here somewhere, so he left.

Back at the office, he was fuming and ranting while trying to get some work done.

He called his driver from his office to have him waiting so he could go to the shelter on Front Street. As it was getting dark, he got out of the car and walked across the street from the shelter. Ghost stood at the intersection where he had a clear view of the shelter. He was going to get the girls and make an example out of them; teach his other girls what happens when they try to leave. He couldn't believe they would leave him like that after all that he had done for them, and he was determined to show what happens to those who disrespect him. He was still ranting and raving in his crazed mind.

He had heard from his people who worked for him on the streets that Cindy and Lucy were working at the homeless shelter since the afternoon when he had informed of their possible whereabouts. So, he decided to wait out front for them to leave. He wasn't going to let his investments leave this time. "Get ready to pay for what you did." He turned and left.

CHAPTER ELEVEN

KIDNAPPED

"We're getting a little low on bread," Cindy informed Joann.

"Is there enough for now?"

"I think so."

"We'll get some more after lunch."

Lucy was in the back, finishing the cleaning in the kitchen to be prepared for the evening rush crowd. She sang to herself while she worked. "I love this, go figure," she thought, and then laughed.

"Are dirty dishes really that funny?" Joann asked. She had walked into the kitchen right at that moment.

"Oh! Joann, I didn't know you were in here."

"I just came in to check on how you were doing."

"I was just thinking about how much I actually love doing this. You know what? This kind of work is fun. It's funny to me that one time I totally thought it would be lame, not anymore. I love it."

"It is satisfying working here, isn't it? I've been here for a long time and it feels good to help others in need. The people who come here have been through horrible things, but for the most part, they're pleasant to be around."

"Yeah."

"Oh, I just remembered something I needed to tell you. Earlier today, some man came in here and was asking around about where you and Cindy are. He was an unsavory looking guy and I didn't tell him anything. Do you know anything about that?"

Lucy's normally rosy cheeks turned pale. "Yes," she said in a weak voice. "He thinks he owns us. Ghost would kill us if he found us. We were fortunate to get away before he knew we were leaving. He won't stop until he finds us, if he does..." her voice trailed away.

"Don't worry, sweetie. You have protection."

"Joann, you don't understand. He'll kill us! And you, if he knew we lived with you."

"Lucy, The Voice has brought our paths from two into one. We do this together. He got you out of your old life and brought you here. He gave you strength to get clean and sober. There is nothing for you to worry about. He will guide you in the direction you need to go."

Cindy walked into the kitchen. "Hey! Luce, what's the matter?" Joann told Cindy about the visitor during the day. Cindy sat down on a stool, without saying much. "The Voice told me that Ghost would come looking for us. He said we don't have to worry about him. Ghost will be punished." Lucy stared at her for a minute. "I feel like this was going to happen. We never could have expected him to just let us go."

During the evening dinner rush, no one had time to think about what may happen after Ghost found them, but during the cleanup they talked about it. It was unsettling to have Ghost getting so close to them. After they closed the shelter, they left out the back door, remaining vigilant and looking for anything that would indicate someone was around. They walked down the alley and onto the main street. They knew that Ghost could be anywhere, and that even just walking to Joann's car could mean their lives. The street lights were dimmed from years of neglect. The lack of lighting only added to the fright of the situation. They all got into Joann's car and she drove them to her house. The buildings left around the area were dark and added to the discomfort of the situation they were facing. Because the street crime had gotten so bad, the buildings fell into disrepair from the harsh living and social conditions, and it was as if the dilapidated buildings were taunting them. The shelter had become a haven of hope for those who had fallen on hard times. Those who needed a hot meal and a place to rest went to the shelter, knowing they could get replenished from their hard lives living on the street. The shelter was one of only a few places here that still stood up under the management of the church; it was like a mountain amidst a desert. The church provided the upkeep on the building, so it stood out in the midst of the other buildings on the street, ones that were still being used. Several of the churches had been considering coming in and taking over the street to use it for providing homes and places for training and employment for the down and out community they were trying to reach out to.

"You will come get me at six thirty tomorrow night." Ghost told his driver as they left the shelter."Ok." Ghost gave him a one-hundred-dollar bill. The driver knew it was to keep him quiet. He drove Ghost to the bar. The day was a quiet one, so he did get his nap. He spent time planning to get some of his employees in compliance; they had no business trying to think on their own since he was the smart business man. He was worried about them figuring out his weaknesses and exploiting him, taking over; they were all jealous.

He was excited about going to get his girls back; the thought of those pretty ladies paying for their crimes against him had him antsy. Focusing on his days' work was not working, and he went out to sit at the bar to chat with the patrons, which helped. About five thirty he went back to his office, and it took an hour to finish up. He left his address book out instead of locking it up; he was going to adjust some entries in it. The phone buzzed, "Yeah."

"Your driver is here." He hung up, walked out the door, locking it behind him. Passing through the bar. He glanced around; more people were coming in. He waved to the bartender as he walked by. The driver was standing beside the front door, and when he got near it, he opened it for Ghost, letting him go ahead of him. Closing the door, he walked to where Ghost was waiting, and the driver opened the car door for him. Ghost silently got in and the driver closed the door, going around to the driver's sid. They started off for the shelter, and on the way, they picked up two other guys.

"Park in the alley so make sure you are right in front of the back door. Be ready to leave quickly." Ghost walked around to the front of the building where a line had formed to get inside for dinner, Ghost and the three other men followed the line inside, Joann was standing and greeting each person and giving them a smile, when she saw Ghost and the three men with him and she knew something was wrong, she started back to the kitchen, but the men rushed past her pushing her to the side and rushed to where he saw Cindy and Lucy working. They snatched the two women and pushed them out the back door to the alley and the waiting car, Joann tried to fight them off but wasn't able to. They girls were screaming as they were roughly pushed out the door and Ghost wasn't concerned about them and the screaming.

The men had them in the waiting car within seconds and the driver had them out of the alley before the stunned onlookers could react, except for Joann. "Well, now. Hello, ladies. It is so nice to see you again." He was smirking at the fear he saw on their faces. "I am not happy with you two," he said. The girls were down on the floor board so they weren't able to see where they were going, they could feel the car as it went around corners and they could see they were still on the same side of town. In a couple of minutes they came to a stop, the thugs got out and one of them came around to open the door for Ghost, he got out with them dragging the girls with them. The girls were aware of the building and the stories that were told about a person who entered never came out alive. A door on the building was unlocked, they all went inside and the door was locked behind them. The only light on were the low security lights. The thugs had Cindy and Lucy in their strong grip, they were dragging them down the hall to a lighted sign that read "exit." The door was opened and they stepped out on a landing for the stairs. Cindy was pushed toward the steps with Lucy right behind her. One thug was leading the way and the other three were close behind. They must not have been moving fast enough to suit the men because they were being pushed to move faster, both of them had to grab the hand rail to keep from falling. The stair well was dimly lit as was the lower floor.

In the hallway, there were doors on either side and they passed by until they were led to a heavy door made to keep intruders out. Ghost pulled out a key from his pocket and had the door opened with the girls being pushed inside, Cindy screamed as the door was relocked behind them. They were shoved to the floor where they were kicked.

"You have been very bad girls, you have been disrespectful, ungrateful, and I don't appreciate that in my employees. I have taken care of you, I have loved you, and I only ask that you do your work to repay me. Is that too much to ask?" Both of them were crying.

Ghost was walking around them as they lay terrified on the floor huddled together trying to comfort each other. They watched in fear as he was coming closer and closer to them. Both of them knew what was to come and neither of them were expecting to come out alive. As they were trying not to panic, they could hear the Voice speaking to them. Ghost and the other men were cursing at them in hopes of adding to their terror. Both girls started to settle down and bracing themselves for what they knew was about to happen. Each one of them were grabbed and the horrendous agony began. The pain was extraordinary. Their screaming was in vain as there was no one around to hear them. They were feeling the presence of the Voice but they also could feel every blow to their bodies.

They cried out to the Voice, which infuriated the men who were abusing them and fueled their anger. Ghost was laughing at them and ridiculing what he saw as their stupidity. Deep down he wasn't laughing as he was wondering how they could endure this and still be thinking about the Voice. This was something that he had never seen before. He wanted them dead. He hated that they were not submitting to him, as usual. The satisfaction that he usually deprived for what he was doing to them wasn't there and they were not giving in to him. "Let's get out of here to give them time to think about this and we will come back later to finish them off." With that, they left.

The girls were left unconscious and unrecognizable. At the shelter,

Joann cried out. The car was out of sight, those two wonderful girls were gone; one of the men standing nearby, Sam, gently touched her arm and wrapped his arms around her. "Let's call the police, I got the license number." Joann was spurred to action as she and Sam went to make the call to the police. After the call was made, Joann turned to Sam, "Thank you Sam. You kept your head and I didn't."

"I was in Special Forces, I can find them."

"You think they'll be all right?"

"Of course, Joann, they will be. The police should be here any minute now. I'll give them the description of those guys. I know them enough to know what they look like. They work for Ghost. I didn't want to get involved with him but they took Lucy and Cindy. I know what they're going to do to them. Ghost didn't take it lightly that they left. You know what's weird, Ms. Joann? I wasn't going to come in today. I felt like for some reason, I needed to be her today."

"Sam, the Voice was talking to you." Sam stood still for a moment pondering this. "I think you're right," he smiled. "I think he has been talking to me a lot lately. It must be him since I talk to myself and this voice kept telling me things that I don't tell myself." Sam laughed to himself.

"I need to get lunch served before I have a riot out there. There are a lot of witnesses for the police to interrogate."

"Let me help you with the serving. Where do I clean up? I can get a couple of others to help. Why don't you sit down and leave this to me, you are in no condition to be doing this. I will take care of everything."

"Thank you so much."

"It's the least I can do."

The police arrived and after speaking briefly with Joann they went around the large common room, here there were a number of tables for their friends to sit, and eat, speaking to anyone who was willing to give them statements. They were able to get enough of them to talk, that they had enough evidence to make an arrest. Word had gotten around that the kidnappers were Ghost's men. All of them were afraid, because living on the streets like they did, they knew Ghost, or at least his reputation.

"We have been trying to charge this guy; he's killed people and his crimes are enough to lock him up for life. If you all can help us, we can put these criminals away for a long time. Once we catch them, we can pressure them into confessions. We can have them make confessions against each other. We'll get these guys off the streets."

With that assurance, there was an air of relief in the shelter. Before the police left, Joann and Sam gave them the details of what happened. Joann told them what she had done to get Cindy and Lucy off the streets and what they had told her and how they had been afraid of this happening. Wrapping up the statements from all who would talk to them, they left to make their report and to put out a bulletin on Ghost. Finally, Sam and Joann sat down at a table in the dining room. There was food on the floor that had been walked on and spilled beverages with paper napkins sticking to the sticky substances. Paper plates had managed to miss the trash cans. A few of the shelter's clients were hanging around since they really had nowhere else to go, and they were talking to each other in hushed voices. Sam's friends were cleaning the kitchen, the rattling of pots and pans echoing throughout the kitchen. One of the helpers was working to clean up the dining room. Everyone was talking about the kidnapping. Some of them were discussing what they would do to them if they found the Ghost's men first. But in reality, no one was brave enough to stand up; to him. Joann was shaken up, but she knew that her girls would be ok. The Voice was there to protect them from Ghost. "Guys," Joann pleaded with them as they sat at a table in the shelter. "Please find them. I can't stand the thought of those two being with…him." Her voice was quivering; George and Sam knew she was heartbroken. Based on Ghost's reputation, they also knew the longer he had them, the probability of finding the girls alive was dramatically lowered. The time was for them to get out and do some looking on their own.

"Joann, we're going to find them. Not only that, but alive. I promise. Don't worry, the Voice is with them." Sam did his best to comfort her, but it was difficult because he too was worried. He was on a mission to find and return them to Joann, who loved them more than they had been loved in a long time.

"Please find them," she repeated. Tears streamed down her face as she wiped them with a towel from the kitchen. "I'm so sorry to cry, I just..." Her voice trailed off.

"No, Joann. There's nothing to apologize for. Why don't you go in the kitchen and get yourself a cup of coffee? It'll give you a chance to sit down and calm your mind we can come up with a plan."

"Joann, I have a friend who got out of prison with some help. I think he can help us find them."

"Not the one who just made the news?"

"That's the one."

"George?"

"Yes."

"I've known George for a very long time. He was a convicted murderer on death row. He's always scared me a little, but I've seen what a good guy he is."

"I had been writing to him when he was in prison. He was telling me that he could hear the Voice. At first, I thought prison had made him loony, but I don't think that any more. I know now he was telling the truth. Wouldn't you know the day after he got out of prison was the day he was going to die? I had planned on being there, you know, when they injected him."

"He has some great tracking abilities. It was sad his life went in the direction that it did, he had potential. I'm happy to see he turned over a new leaf, like he did. He called me a few days ago, and told me what he's been doing. He did say he wants to meet. I'm concerned about being followed so I'm not sure."

"The Voice will tell you what to do."

Sam had served with Special Forces and was highly trained. He had served his time. War had been hard on him and he had nightmares which left him exhausted. A soldier's life in combat left marks on his mind, upon return from war, Sam had thought he would be living it up, but life didn't turn the way he'd planned. He had money to live on to give him a comfortable life except, inside left him feeling unfulfilled, useless, war had wounded him. He had seen so much death and destruction. Without the environment of combat, Sam was lost. Shelters were his choice when the weather turned cold. At the age of thirty-six, Sam wanted some changes in his life. Joann had been working with him since he had returned to the civilian life. He was a six foot two, two hundred twenty-two-pound man with a muscular body. He had black hair in a buzz cut and brown eyes made him a very handsome man even with his stressful life leaving worry lines on his square jawed face. He still retained a little bit of his youthfulness. He dressed casually and he wore worn looking clothes that made him appear youthful and somehow interesting. Laughing wasn't something he did very often, but when he did, his smile made him seem youthful, even ten years younger. Being in a war zone had left him hardened. Dealing with those who had less than he did was his passion and had immensely helped him cope with his PTSD, as well. Joann had been working with him to show him his potential and he had gotten to a place in his life where he was well-adjusted to being civilian, even though there were times when he longed for war again. Joann was his best friend and he helped her cope with the things in her past. She had confided with him about the early days in her life when she had been molested, it made Sam angry but he was there for her as she was for him, they were a team and they understood the others deep pain. There was comfort between them.

He had played football in high school and had been quite popular back in those days. Mostly, he played sports and chased the head cheer leader. She thought he was obnoxious and found him annoying, persistently rejecting his offers to date her. That didn't stop him throughout his high school years. He never did get a date with her, that didn't stop him throughout his high school years. After graduating, he joined the military, in Special Forces. Just like football, he excelled at it due to his well-known determination.

Being the parents of Sam wasn't easy. They knew his prospective and tried their best to get him to study more in school. Sam was a great kid, but he was a daredevil. Drugs and alcohol were never a problem as he was a leader type and embraced it, he was the type to come to the aid of the underdog to protect and defend the ones who were bullied. The cheerleader he had tirelessly pursued had forgotten about him, as he did her. She had felt that he was too cocky for her taste. Upon graduation had passed they moved on with their lives; high school was only a memory.

In the war Sam had met a young woman who captured his heart. He saw her as much as he could. War took him everywhere so their time together was few and far between. One day he went to see her for a few days, but her home was empty. No one was there so he searched for her but to no avail. Coming home he continued his search for her without success. He had heard that she had moved to another country to pursue a career in her work with the development of medical devices where she was making more money than she would have at home.

Once he had served his time in the military he tried to readjust to his new life. He wanted to apply his skills as a former soldier into employment, but the problems from post-traumatic syndrome disorder had taken a toll on him and he wasn't able to keep a job for long periods of time. A trust fund had been set up by his grandparents, so he had money to live. His inability to have a stable life left him with feelings of inadequacy; he was too ashamed to go home to his parent's house, they had begged him to come home to stay with them but he had declined.

"Thanks to you, I've heard the Voice of God."

"I love you. You're just like a son to me. I will be here for you when you need me. Now, we need to find George."

"There's a farm Jeremy's dad had purchased years ago, I work for them from time to time. So, you want to go with me to try to find him?"

"Yes. Let's go now, maybe he's there. If not, at least we can rest an eat some of Mariann's good old country cooking." The police had asked them to stay around for a while in case they found some information to capture Ghost and his cohorts so they did and waited until the next afternoon before heading out to the farm.

George and Jeremy were working on repairing some fences that had become loose, the work was refreshing for George as he was finding his mind was refreshed and he was feeling like he did in his younger days, except for the reassurance he was a new person. His new family was so good to him and having a newness of life with the work he was doing for others had him sleeping and resting better.

"We have gotten so much done, you really know your stuff around here," Jeremy was saying. This work is making me feel useful and I am feeling much better. I have done a lot of this type of work before."

"We are so happy you are with us, how about going in for dinner?"

After collecting the tools and trash, they loaded it on the golf cart and they had just ridden along to the loose fence rails in the fence line where they had finished the repairs. It took a while to get the tools and supplies put back into their proper places, pausing to catch their breath and get a drink of water they headed for the house and their waiting dinner. It was time for eating and watching a game on TV, relaxing in their chairs for some much-needed rest. Riding along they saw a vehicle coming up the road with a dust train behind it as they were approaching the house. "I wonder who that might be at this time of day." Jeremy was wondering, "We'll know in a minute," George answered.

As they got closer Jeremy noted, "That looks like Sam's truck." Getting closer, he said, "It is Sam's truck and that is Joann with him. Ummmm."

"Hi, Jeremy," Sam called out, "George is that you?"

"Hello Sam! It's me and it is great to see you!" Joann approached, "George, I haven't seen you in such a long time, you are looking good!"

"Thank you, I am feeling great these days. I have been thinking about you. Sam has been writing to me in prison and he has been telling me about what you have been doing. I am happy to see you, especially after all that you had tried to do for me."

"Why don't you stay for dinner so you can tell us why you are here, you look like you are upset about something."

Kendra walked out and looked at Sam and Joann and immediately took them inside. Jeremy told her they would be staying for dinner. Entering the house, they could smell the food. After getting cleaned up they sat down to eat. Joann picked at her food. "We need some help." Joann told them as tears came to her eyes.

Sam took up the story as he related the kidnapping and the possibility of what most likely would happen to Cindy and Lucy. "We have some of the homeless people on the streets to help find where they are and we need to get back to find out if there is any news about them. The police asked us to stay around in case something came up but they haven't gotten back with us so we have decided to try to find them ourselves. George, would you come with us to help find them?"

"I will go with you."

"I want to go too," Jeremy said.

Jeremy got together some things he thought might be useful in their search along with some food, water, first aid equipment. George and Sam got back into Sam's truck and headed for town towards the shelter before they were going to the building allegedly where the girls were being held that was located in the more deserted and desolate part of town with empty dilapidated buildings. At the shelter one of the homeless men said he thought he had seen Ghost in one of the buildings along Front Street "Sam, what do you know about these buildings?"

"Most of them have basements and this one they are supposed to be in had a secure room where sensitive records were stored, a good place to take someone and keep the screams from being heard from the outside. At the time it was built, the room was considered to be burglar proof but that has been proven wrong." They were driving around the building where they spotted a couple of expensive cars parked out in front that seemed out of place for this neighborhood. "I am guessing this may very well be the place where we will find the girls," George surmised. "We need to be very careful as these guys mean business."

"We need to check out the building to see if we can find a way in and be on the lookout for anyone who may be watching us, maybe some of your street friends can help. We need to hide our trucks where we can get them in a hurry if we have to move fast." They found a food spot; the evening shadows were starting to envelope the world and the shadows covered them. They alley was a good place. All of them were wearing dark clothes and they were walking quietly towards the building. The parked cars they had seen earlier were gone. They walked around in hopes of finding an entryway in, where they found a window at ground level that caught George's attention, he stooped down to examine it, at first, he thought the bars on it were in solid until he started prying some of the bricks loose. Sam was looking around and saw a piece of scrap metal laying down the street a little way, he retrieved it and handed it to George and he started taking out the remaining bricks. It took several minutes and with Sam's help the window was removed. Soon the bars came loose and they had their way into the basement Entering the basement through the opening with some effort, the three of them stopped to listen. They put the window back to disguise their entry, no sounds were heard within the darkened building and being as quiet as possible, they made their way out of the room they were in and were making their way down the hallway that divided the basement in half. Looking in all directions they made their way along listening and stopping to check in rooms along the way. It was so quiet they thought the girls weren't in here; the only light was from exit signs and dim lights used for security; after having covered most of the rooms they thought they heard something, they froze. "Look for a heavy door and check for any signs of activity," Sam suggested.

The place was coated with dirt from having set for a long time and former occupants having left trash. They kept moving through empty beer bottles and some wrappers from fast food that looked recent that was around a door where it was more solid than the other ones they had passed.

"This may be what we are looking for," George said. Sam thought so too. They tried the door and found that it was locked. They heard voices coming towards them so they retreated into an empty room and waited. They heard three voices and as they peeked out the door and saw the men enter the room. A few seconds later they heard screams, George, Jeremy, and Sam froze. They recognized Ghost as he had gone in and closed the door.

"This is a very simple lock," George said in a whisper. I can get us in using the screw driver you brought in Sam. I have gotten into harder places than this."

Ten minutes went by before the door opened and the men came out and the men's voices faded as they left. "Go and let's get this done fast," George said. They went into action and he had the door unlocked and they were inside within two minutes. It was quiet, to quiet. It was dark so Jeremy searched along the wall for the light switch and after finding it turned on the overhead lights. The girls were lying in awkward positions on the floor and they didn't look like they were even alive. The room was dark and when the light was turned on to allow a small amount of light from the light fixture that was in need of having the bulbs replace, they checked the girls, they had been severely beaten and they found that they were still alive, barely. "Let's go call the police and get an ambulance." They hurried out leaving the door to the room open as they made their way out. George needed to get out of there before the police arrived so he took Sam with him as they cautiously went to the truck and they got in after procuring the keys from Jeremy and headed to the shelter where Joann and Kendra were waiting with the shelter still open as they were waiting for some good news. Rushing inside they told Joann in a hurried voice, "We need to call the police," Sam ran to the phone, he dialed and they listened to him tell the police dispatcher about the location of Ghost and they heard him end the call by telling them he would meet them there. Jeremy stayed with the girls in the basement of the building as he attempted to give them first aid.

"Are they ok?" Joann asked anxiously.

"They are, barely," George said. "This building has seen a lot of horrible things Ghost has done."

Sam had left to meet the police at the building where they met the police and the ambulance as they explained what had happened and what they had done to find the girls. An officer broke down the front door and the others followed him inside as they made their way to the basement and the room where the paramedics found them. Sam asked them if they were still alive and was told they were but needed to get to the hospital ASAP. They both were given IV's before being put on stretchers, they looked lifeless and Sam felt a pang of pain for them. The paramedics had them heading out with them where they were loaded in the ambulance and taken to the hospital. Both girls were strangely aware of someone gently lifting their bodies and setting them on something a bit softer than the floor and the movement from dim light to bright lights flashing and the fresh air. Someone had found them. They saw people moving around through their swollen eyes and heard sirens; they felt the movement of the stretchers as they were loaded into an ambulance that was the last thing they were aware of until they woke up in the hospital. Sam and Jeremy stayed to give their statements explaining how they found out where they were, and how they got in. The paramedics felt sure they would have died soon and the police believed Ghost would have come to finish them off. "You have been a good help in being a witness for us, now we think we may have enough to put them away. If you find out where he is, give us a call, we will pick him up. We will put out an APB on them. Do not try to apprehend them yourselves.

"Thanks guys," the officer said to them and he left to turn in his report. When he got into his vehicle he sent a report about the two females being found and an APB was sent out.

"We need to go get Joann and take her to the hospital to wait for the results on the girls, it will keep her busy while we go after Ghost," Sam told Jeremy.

"I want that man put away after what I just saw. The girls were in really bad shape, let's go," Jeremy said leading the way to the truck.

Other police officers were in the building going through it, there was plenty of evidence that many crimes had been committed in there and it was going to take a while to get things sorted out, forensic experts and detectives had already been called in, to protect evidence they secured the building, they knew they were onto something that was bigger than anything they had dealt with before. They were going to crack some cold cases, they felt sure. A police officer was outside on the sidewalk talking to the news media.

They went to get Joann from the shelter and Jeremy took her to the hospital. "How are they?" she asked.

"They look bad, really bad but we have to trust the Voice to get them through it. I am going to take you to the hospital and will return a little later, George and Sam are going with me to find Ghost so we can notify the police as to his whereabouts."

"Please be careful, I don't want to lose any of you."

"We are only locating him, don't you worry, just be there for those girls."

CHAPTER TWELVE

GHOST HUNTING

"What do you think we're going to do?"

"Man," Sam scratched his head. "First thing, we need to do an initial sweep, find the exact location, and stake out to watch for anything that might clue us in. We'll do a recon to give us time to figure out the rest of this scenario."

"Not a bad idea. Let's go. If we don't find the place within a few hours, then the clients here who offered to help maybe can do their own tracking. No one will even pay them any mind if they go snooping."

Sam was thinking about the further possibility of finding the kidnappers. Everyone knew they hung out at Ghost's office, which was slightly hidden inside of a bar that was not ten minutes from the shelter. "George, do you want to go find those guys?"

"You don't even need to ask, buddy."

"Let's move. We can see if they're there, and if they are we can notify the police. We've got to get them off the streets."

They headed towards the bar and when they arrived, they noticed there were a lot of people in there, most of them looking like the type of people you don't cross. This was definitely dangerous, but they had to find Ghost and his thugs.

Ghost wasn't going to stop at getting the girls, even if they were in the hospital. This had to end. Ghost's reign of terror was coming to an end. They sat in Sam's truck for a while, assessing the exterior of the bar. "Tell you what, man. I'll go in and look around. Do some recon on the place. Is that cool with you?" George asked Sam. Sam gave it a quick thought and said, "Yeah, but be careful."

"I'll be back in a few minutes. If I'm not out in fifteen minutes, come in."

"Sure thing, I'll stay out here and watch."

George got out of the truck, knowing that by entering the bar, his life was in grave danger just by being there. But the adrenaline, much like his escape from prison, was driving him forward, to enter the bar where Ghost himself could very well be.

He walked in, and the smell of stale alcohol, urine, and rot hit his nose, he automatically felt a splitting headache and nausea, but he kept moving. In front of him was the open bar area. There was the bar itself at the back of the room, where every bar stool was occupied. The room was full of tables and chairs, with probably about twenty-five or thirty people occupying the place. Beer bottles and trash littered the dirty, sticky floors. Loud music from a juke box in the corner made it impossible to hear anything. There were game machines and a pool table along the right side of the room, where there was a game of bar pool going on. Signs advertising the different brands of alcohol lined the walls. To the left, there was a VIP area, where a party was apparently being held. It seemed like everyone in the room was so severely intoxicated that no one was going to pay any attention to him. Immediately to his left, there was a hallway where the restrooms were located. He walked down the hallway, past the restrooms and at the end of the hall was a door. Definitely a private room, George thought. 'Let's see what's in there.'

He opened the door, and was greeted by Cindy and Lucy's kidnappers sitting around the room in chairs. Right at that moment, Sam barged in. "Come on, buddy. You've had too many beers. Let's go and I'll get you home." He turned to the kidnappers. "Sorry guys. He's been drinking and he just up and walked into your bar, and somehow found your office. If you'll excuse us, I'll just get him out of here."

"I don't think so. You'll stay right there." One of them told Sam. Sam saw what he thought looked like an address book sitting on the edge of Ghost's desk, he grabbed it before anyone had time to think and he headed for the door, one of the men pulled out a gun and aimed it at them, pulling the trigger, but the only sound was that of a click. It was a beautiful sound, since it had jammed when he tried to shoot them. The kidnapper stared at his pistol in disbelief. That had never happened before. The other kidnappers in the office, somehow, were frozen in place. Even as George and Sam ran out of the office, out of the bar, and into the truck, none of them moved. "I will be your Shield, your Rock, your Protection," The Voice told Sam and George.

As they left the bar, the bar tender was on the phone. They didn't know who he was talking to, but weren't planning to stick around to find out. They rushed out and jumped into the truck and as they were headed back to the shelter, it was then that they stopped and took a breath as they had almost been shot. George felt his torso in disbelief for bullet wounds and found none. "Wow." Sam countered, "I know. Did you notice when we ran out of there that none of them moved? They were frozen. The Voice told me that He's out Protector. Did you hear it?"

George stared at the floor. "I did. I should've been shot but He prevented it." They found a phone and called the police to report where some of the kidnappers were at the moment. They were headed straight for the shelter, but as they made the short drive, several police cars with their sirens on were going in the direction of the bar. "That bar tender must have called them." George remarked. They didn't say much the rest of the way. They were both shocked by the fact that a weapon had been fired at them, and yet they hadn't been shot.

As soon as they got to the shelter, Jeremy walked in right behind them. The people were shocked by the sight. "Where have you all been?"

"Don't worry. We care of something." George didn't want them knowing where they had been or hat the crew almost did to them.

Jeremy had important news to share. He had walked in as they did. "Ghost has not gone to the building but we think he will be going back to check on the girls. I hope we can find him before he finds out that they are in the hospital and goes to kill them." One of the homeless people was standing within ear's reach and offered, "I know where Ghost stays; he is at his girlfriend's apartment all the time. He doesn't let her out very often, to work is about the only place he allows her to go without him and we've seen them together. One of our friends says that he saw his car at her place."

"Do you know where the apartment is, sir?"

"Yes, sir, I do."

"Would you be willing to take us there?"

"Yes."

"George, Sam, come with me." The homeless man and the three guys piled into Jeremy's truck. Before they took off, a couple of their friends stopped. "We're going too."

"Ok, we're going by to see if Ghost's car is there. If it is, we're calling the police." As they drove to the apartment, George yawned wide, closed his eyes, and whispered, "I could sleep for a week." It would soon be dawn and there had been so much accomplished this night they would all be ready for a long sleep.

"We'll rest soon. Don't worry. We'll go back to the farm, eat, and then get some much-needed sleep." After winding street by street, directed by the homeless man's directions, he yelled out, "THERE!" Jeremy slammed on the brakes. "Here?"

"Yes, here. That one right up there, with the hanging plants on the balcony. That's his girlfriend's apartment." He pointed at the third-floor apartment with a balcony that was covered in hanging plants. It was obvious it was a woman's apartment.

"Do you know where a pay phone is around here?"

"Yes, sir. Right down there at that store." The homeless man took Jeremy to a store that was less than a block away. He made the phone call to the police to inform them of where Ghost was, and that his car was there. Just a couple of minutes later, the police showed up with their lights flashing without sirens. Ghost was finished, he was going away for a long time. Sam gave them the address book he had snatched from Ghost's office. They drove down the street and stopped to see what was going to happen. They watched as the police came out a few minutes later with Ghost between them in handcuffs. He was thrashing about and by the way his mouth was moving, he was probably swearing at them and claiming his innocence. He may not have known about what had transpired in the last few hours after leaving the girls for dead.

CHAPTER THIRTEEN

DR. PERRY

Dr. Robert Perry was a sixty-year-old man with once brown hair that had mostly grayed with age. He stood at five foot eight inches in height, weighing one hundred and ninety pounds. A former smoker who gave it up when his wife, Jacie, made him quit out of concern for his health. She was justified as she usually was. They were competitive with each other in ways that made them better partners in life; he playfully retaliated by making her lose forty pounds. It became a long-standing joke between the two of them about the price of their vices. They had been married for twenty-three years, and they had grown close and loved each other more deeply than the day they had first been married. They had met when he hired her in his private practice clinic as his charge nurse.

Jacie weighed one hundred twenty pounds and stood at five feet, six inches, with blonde hair and strawberry blonde highlights. She laughed and the smile lines on her face showed it, his favorite thing about her was the laugh lines around her eyes and how much her laughter meant to him. He had much on his mind as a doctor, but she lightened him up with her cheery laughter. She was good for him. When Cindy and Lucy were wheeled into the emergency room they were met by nurses who immediately took their vital signs and checked them for any permanent or potentially fatal injuries. It was hard to tell they were even alive and if wasn't for vital signs, they wouldn't have believed it. Dr. Perry had been paged and he headed to the trauma room as he had just finished up with a patient. Dr. Perry headed to the nurses' station to get information about the incoming emergency patients.

"What do we have here?"

"Two women, both in their twenties, they appear to have been assaulted; they were found in a basement in an abandoned building. The paramedics thought they were dead at first. Their vital signs were at the time of their arrival were fairly normal, they are a little high and that must be an occurrence stress." They told them of their suspicions and the police were present and were taking their statements.

"Which room?"

"They are in rooms two and three."

Walking into room two, he saw the nurse working on Cindy. At first glance, he could only tell she was female by her long hair and the clothes she was wearing. He moved closer to the bed and saw that she was petite. The size of her head made her look like a circus character. He looked at her chart as he turned to the nurse.

"How are her vitals?" He washed his hands and put on gloves from a dispenser hanging on the wall next to the sink.

"Elevated, but not fatal. Patient is stabilized for now."

"Get her to x-ray first and send the x-rays to me and get a full body scan after the head x-rays are done first, I want them when they are ready." She called the technician who told her she was on her way. Looking at Cindy, she was thinking about her own daughters. This could have been one of them. Dr. Perry took off the gloves and tossed them into the trash can that was by the door and he left the room. He went into exam room three where a nurse was tending to Lucy.

"Did they come in together?"

"Yes."

"The situation is the same with this one?"

"That's what the paramedics said, doctor." He examined Lucy and found very similar injuries on her; both girls were unconscious, which, in their condition kept them from feeling the pain and he hated to think how bad it was going to be when they woke up. They would need to be put on pain medication. He told the nurse to get the same x-rays for Lucy as he had ordered for Cindy. "Page me when the x-rays are ready." He tossed his gloves into the trash can.

Dr. Perry went off to check on another patient while waiting for the technicians to get the job done. He went into see a twelve-year-old boy who had a nasty gash on his head. "Jared, how did you do this?"

"My brother and I were jumping up and down on my bed. I guess we kind of forgot about the ceiling fan," he said. His mother was standing by the exam table rolling her eyes. "I'm surprised these two haven't gotten permanent brain damage the way they act." The mom was clearly exasperated, distressed and worried.

"Let me check it out buddy. I don't think you will need stitches. I will give you a shot of antibiotics. Mom, you can get a prescription filled for a pain reliever. Just watch him overnight and if he acts in any way that worries you, you'll need to take him to his doctor for a follow up. He should be ok. Keep him home from school tomorrow just in case and watch for any unusual behavior. Check him every couple of hours throughout the night, ceiling fans can hit hard and I don't see any problems at this time, but just keep an eye on him."

"Thank you, doctor."

"The nurse should be in shortly and you should be able to leave. Young man, be careful when you're playing. We don't want you back in here." Jared ducked his head in embarrassment. The hospital was fairly quiet at the moment but that could change any time as the ER was unpredictable. He had made his rounds so he thought this would be a good time to take a break. He was hungry so he went to the cafeteria where there was a room reserved for doctors. A buffet was laid out. He decided to have salad, some delicious smelling salmon with a whole wheat roll and iced tea. He got a plate and filled it and made his way to a table, a couple of his medical colleagues joined him and they sat down with him as they ate they discussed some cases they were working on as they ate. As they finished up and were getting ready to leave Dr. Perry was paged; he put his dishes in the container sitting by the trash can and left to catch the elevators.

On the first floor, he went to the room for viewing the x-rays, he found the envelope with them in it and the names on them. First, he pulled out Cindy's and put them on the viewing box and turned on the light. 'Impossible,' he thought to himself. He picked up the phone and dialed.

"This is Dr. Perry. Are you sure you sent the correct x-rays?" Yes."

"You didn't mix them up with someone else's by any chance?"

"No, they were the only two patients we have had in here in a while and there was enough time we had them here and the next patient that we couldn't have mixed them up."

"Just checking, thank you." First, he went in to see Cindy; she was lying quietly with her eyes barely open. He wasn't sure she could see him.

"I'm Dr. Perry, I'm the physician in charge of your care. I must say, young lady, you are fortunate. How are you feeling?"

"I feel like I am dead, or should be."

"It is amazing that you are alive. I know you're not feeling too good right now, but I have some good news for you. You have no broken bones, no concussion, at least your head is ok, I'm surprised because of the swelling on your face and head is so severe. The other x-rays show no signs of permanent injury. I haven't found any internal bleeding, so you should heal up nicely. You have plenty of bruises but otherwise you should do fine after a couple of weeks of rest."

"The Voice will help me heal."

"I hardly ever hear of anyone who hears the Voice any more. He has been talking to me too. I am going to give you something to help you to sleep, and I'll check back with you later." He left her as he wrote a note in her chart and handed it back to the nurse. She went to fill the med order.

He went in to see Lucy. "I am Dr. Perry I'm your physician today. How do you feel?"

"I'm hurting."

"You should be feeling better in a short while. You'll be given pain medication. The x-rays show no permanent damage. Why do you think that is?" He wondered how she would answer.

"The Voice told Cindy and me that we would be ok; we know we must go through bad things sometimes. This isn't anything we would want to go through again, but we know the Voice is watching over us." He was thinking about their answers, he knew something unusual had happened.

"The nurse will give you something to help you rest and will make you sleep. I'll check on you later." He made notes in her chart, instructing his nurse to give her the meds, and she left to call the pharmacy and have them filled.

"Thanks," he told her as she smiled at him; he returned her smile and went to his office with the lab results on Cindy and Lucy. Sitting down he looked over what he had. For two small women who came in looking like they did, they had no serious injuries and the lab results confirmed it. They should have been entirely broken, even dead. There was nothing wrong, except for bruising and severe swelling.

"I'm going to talk to her friends and family. Where are they?"

"They are sitting in the waiting room, they haven't gone anywhere." He left to find them. There was a group clustered together in a corner where they were gathered to pray. "Cindy and Lucy's family?" he asked. They all turned towards him as they stood up. "We're their friends. They don't have family."

"How are they?" Joann asked.

"They're in pretty good condition, with consideration on how badly they looked when they were brought in. They are severely bruised. They have no internal damage. I will keep them overnight for observation and if they are up to it, they will be discharged in the morning. There's no internal damage and no broken bones, they will be hurting for some time but otherwise, they will be ok. When they leave here, they will need a lot of support to get through the trauma, they should be waking up in a while, you can see them for a few minutes if you would like. Both will need to get plenty of rest. I will give you a prescription for pain relievers for them that you can have filled at the pharmacy, otherwise they should fully recover."

Dr. Perry went to his office to finish up some paper work, he left word at the nurses' station to call him when the girls woke up and he finished the paper work. As he put everything into the filing cabinet and finished making his rounds, a nurse called him to let him know the girls had awoken and he went to the room where that they shared. "Are you feeling any better?"

"I'm hurting and my brain doesn't feel as fuzzy." Cindy said and Lucy agreed that she felt much the same way.

"You may feel this way for a while but you will gradually start getting better. Are you up to talking to me for a minute before your friends come to see you? I wanted to ask you about the Voice."

"Sure!" Cindy said.

"He had been talking to me very quietly; he speaks so softly I have to really listen. Am I hearing the same Voice you are?"

"Yes, sir," Cindy answered him.

"He told me to stay in touch with the two of you and I thought it was strange until I saw the tests results we did on the two of you. I called to confirm that there wasn't a mix up in the results and there wasn't. Both of you should have died from the trauma to your bodies. I realized that I was witnessing a miracle only the Voice could have done. Before you were telling me about the Voice I thought I was imagining it. My wife, Jacie, had been hearing him also. I thought she just had a vivid imagination until I heard what you said."

"This hasn't been a fun way to meet you but I am very glad to have met you," Lucy said.

"I agree, Jacie is a nurse here. Would it be ok with you if I sent her in to talk to you before you check out?"

"We'd be honored to."

"Thank you, ladies. I'm discharging you two in the morning. I'll send your friends in to see you." With hat, he left. Their friends came in to see them, much to their relief. Upon entering the room Joann was taken aback by the look of them and she was quiet for a while at the shock of seeing how badly bruised they were. All of their exposed skin was black and their faces were swollen. They saw the girls' slight smiles and the relief on their faces and they had a sparkle in their eyes. Joann gave them a light kiss on the cheeks of both girls. They encouraged them with kind words until the nurse went in to inform them that visiting hours were over. They left promising to come back first thing in the morning. Joann decided to take over their recovery. Before visiting hours, Dr. Perry had come in to check on them and he was satisfied that they were going to be recovering well after they left and left instructions to put them in a private room. He had questions but for now he was going to do his job and hoping to talk with them after Jacie had gotten their phone number.

The next morning Dr. Perry and Jacie came in to see the girls. "I'm Jacie, Dr. Perry told me about what you told him about the Voice. I have been hearing Him for quite a while. He thought I was imagining Him. I asked the Voice to talk to him for a long time, and I am grateful to you for your witness to him. You two validated what I've been saying. You are two very remarkable young ladies. May I come visit you when you get out of here?"

"Yes, of course. Our friends will welcome you."

"Honey, let me go see about getting your discharge papers so you can go home. I would like to get your phone numbers, if you don't mind. And I'll get you wheel chairs."

"Here, let me write down our phone number for you," Cindy said.

Joann and the whole bunch were waiting for them as they were wheeled out to Joann's car where she had parked. No one was more excited than Joann to see her girls. All she could think about was to hold their hands and reassure them that everything would be ok, and to give them the comfort that they were there to watch out for them and would be there for them. It was, at last, over.

Joann turned to lead them out, but Lucy grabbed her arm and whispered, "Joann, thank you."

"Sweetie, you are more than welcome. I'm so happy you're alive and safe."

"Me too, Joann, but I mean for everything you have done."

"There's nothing to thank me for, Lucy. Now, let's go home."

It was a relief for them that it was all over. No more worry that Ghost would be a cloud hanging over them. They had obliterated fear.

"Ok girls, it's time to go home." A nurse brought the wheel chairs and they were wheeled out to Joann's car. Jeremy, George, and Sam assisted them, to get them safely in the truck. Though packed tightly they were comfortable as they drove to the farm with the two men riding with them in the car to assure their safety and comfort.

Mariann had a hot lunch ready upon their arrival at the farm. The farmhouse smelled of fried chicken, all the trimmings and iced tea. Everyone gathered at the large dining table and filled their empty stomachs of Mariann's marvelous food. When they were finished, Mariann shooed them out, and they all took a nap. The afternoon was spent quietly with Cindy and Lucy being pampered.

The next morning, they sat around the TV while Mariann made them breakfast. The night before was of great comfort to all of them. They were watching the morning news. The arrest of Ghost and all the men rounded up who had been on his payroll was played out in front of them on the news. The story was even grizzlier than they had first believed as more had been found in the basement that was sickening to them.

CHAPTER FOURTEEN

FOR SALE

After a long rest at the farm, Joann took the girls back to her house. They had done nothing except lay around and Joann made sure they wanted for nothing.

"How are my two girls doing?"

"Hurting a little, no, a lot but I'm so happy to be here, Joann." Cindy piped up, even though it hurt her ribs to talk. It would be a while yet until they were fully recovered.

"Good. Definitely better today," Lucy said.

"Good, good. Ok, dears. Are you two hungry?"

"Yes."

"Oh yes."

"I'll make you breakfast, then."

Joann had started on their breakfast when she heard Cindy ask, "Joann, what happened to Ghost?"

"He was caught. The guys found him and called the police, who went and arrested him. Sam and Jeremy gave them his address book that had names and addresses of many of his people and they're on the hunt for the others who work for him. They've already nabbed a couple of them. You don't have to worry about Ghost or his gang ever again."

Cindy and Lucy shot a look in each other's direction. That was the best news they could have gotten. It was finished.

"And, the police seized all of Ghost's assets. He undoubtedly won't make bail. But I just want you girls to understand how much protection you had. The Voice was there with you, keeping you alive. The police investigated the basement where he kept you two. He'd been using it for a long time for similar crimes, and worse than what he did to you. If it wasn't for the protection of the Voice, you girls would have been dead."

"We are so grateful to the Voice. He gave us a second chance."

"Your breakfast is almost ready."

"Don't you need to get to the shelter?"

"No. I'm not leaving either one of you until you can both get up and around without pain."

"What about the shelter? They need you there."

"The shelter will be fine. There are other workers there, the homeless understand. But when you ladies are ready, they do want to see you. Until that time, you will not move a muscle. You two are going to get rest, and I'm going to take care of everything you both need, I am here to take care of you." She set their breakfast plates on the coffee table in front of them. Cindy and Lucy slowly rose from their laying position on the two couches in Joann's living room, wincing in pain, and ate their food. They already felt more energized. Joann was taking good care of them. The Exalted Dark One sat down sulking. This is unacceptable, he wanted every soul. Failure was not an option; it wasn't going to be easy. Through the centuries there were so many who couldn't be cracked, they stumbled and fell and yet The Voice picked them up, dusted them off and they kept going. The more he thought about it, the angrier he became. He brewed in his increasing anger. Since the world had turned against the Chosen Ones, he was sure he could get to those few. Public opinion was a valuable device, and peer pressure had proven to be quite effective. Many had turned from their convictions when they were ridiculed long enough. He hated the ones who couldn't be swayed. Oh, how he hated them.

Politicians were in the spot light and were afraid of looking as though they were unconcerned for the minorities, the population who had to work for a living, making it easy for the Dark Ones. He used pressure and accusations of hate and discrimination to sway those weak people. Forget what was right by the Voice. Squeeze people into believing that ideas about right and wrong weren't updated to the times for now. It was working beyond the Dark Forces expectations. Accomplishments in their realm were going great, but would get better, much better. There was no room for failure.

The World Council were back in meeting to discuss the business of the microchips. "Mr. President, we have the microchips ready for immediate execution so people can get them before the set time limit."

"You have done very well. I thank you for all your hard work, a bonus is well-deserved. I thank you for putting your time into this. It is of utmost importance, as you all very well understand."

"The next order of business is to ratify the Amendment to the Constitution to make sure there are no impediments to the amendment process. We'll need to make an official announcement to be sure there are no difficulties. The Council as a whole is more than eager to vote on it. There have been no objections."

"Then, I suppose we could just vote without waiting. Are there any objections, Council? No? If you are in favor of this amendment please raise your hands in agreement." All hands went up to vote the amendment in. "Well, is there any new business that we should discuss?" No one had anything more to discuss.

"Let this session be adjourned."

This session being of importance and highly anticipated, the media was in a wild frenzy to report the latest development of the microchips. The work on them was to make it easier to track people who had them. It would be a long time before they were perfected to track but tracking with them had become a much easier task with all the work that had been done.

The next morning, they sat around the TV while Joann made them breakfast. The night before was of great comfort to all of them. They were watching the morning news.

"As of last night, the World Council has finally made the decision that all of the population will now be required to have a microchip inserted into their forearms. The chip will allow every person to receive medical treatment, to buy, to sell, or to trade. It will make it possible for a person to be found if they are lost. Each person will have protection if they are in trouble. All persons have six months from today to get the microchips inserted into their arms. Anyone not taking the chips will be imprisoned, put to death, or possibly put into labor camps, this is mandatory. This is Samantha Ortiz, and this has been your morning news." A feeling of dread came over the house. Life as they knew it had taken a nasty turn for the worse.

George and the rest of the group were meeting at the farmhouse. They sat in the large living room discussing their plans. "We'll need to start selling all of our furnishings and anything else that's not completely essential, so we can get money to finish up the bunker. Mariann, do you know anything about preserving fresh meat?"

"Oh, you bet I do. My grandparents taught me."

"Good. You'll need to put your skills to work. Kendra, you work alongside Mariann, as well as keep the bunker in order and keep our supplies stocked."

"Will do."

"Good, Sam, you'll be our guard and lookout, and Jeremy and I will find fresh meat for us. Everyone will help the others, even if it's not your assigned duties. We're a team, let's work together. Cindy and Lucy, you two are young and smart, with more energy than the rest of us, you'll help me. It's time to move. As of now, we will no longer maintain the farm, it needs to look abandoned. Our main focus is now only the bunker." Jeremy said.

Cindy asked, "When are we officially moving into the bunker?"

"We know the day when it is mandatory for the world to be having the chips implanted so we will be inside before that time. It will be getting more dangerous as the time gets closer; I have been hearing stories about soldiers who are already looking for possible victims to round up, rewards are being distributed to those who round up people without the chips. People have already gotten the chips, so we need to hurry and get the supplies we need now. We won't be able to get anything in the near future. We need to hurry, time is of the essence. What we need to do is split up once we get money. We'll go to a larger city, so we can blend in without drawing attention to ourselves. Once we get what we need, we'll come back here. And most importantly, listen to the Voice."

"The news said there are military troops patrolling the street," Kendra said.

"That's why we're going to blend in. Please, everyone, please be careful. There's no safety anymore."

"We need to make sure that we buy enough to last for a while. The law enforcement militia will randomly stop anybody, and a lot of people have been arrested just for carrying large amounts of cash on their person." Cindy said.

"Anyone with cash needs to bring it so we can get started and go about their daily routines and going on shopping trips like any family would appear to be doing," Sam informed the group. "The government has spy drones everywhere. They can and do watch activities. So, everyone really needs to remain cautious, but go and get what we need. The Voice is with us."

"Also, if you own any items with computer chips in them, get rid of them immediately. That's another way the government is tracking people. We can no longer be people of technology." Cindy shared her thought.

"You're such a smart young lady, Cindy dear," Kendra told her. She admired the girls. While they were young, they were very intelligent and had practical understanding in knowing technology.

"For now, Joann, continue going to the shelter. Girls, you too. We don't want to raise any alarms. There will be a time, soon, that you will need to stop going but for now, keep doing what you've been doing. When the time comes, you can come up with a legitimate reason to stop going, like poor health. Cindy and Lucy, you might want to start working fewer hours. Think of a plausible reason." George told them.

"It's time to get started on selling our possessions. Sam, might I suggest that you leave your truck broken down somewhere. It'll give an alibi for your disappearance. Let's get busy selling our belongings then we can go get our supplies. Be safe, everyone."

They all left the farmhouse to plan the disposal of their assets. Time was not on their side anymore. Jeremy had several pieces of equipment to sell, so he chose to put out a newspaper advertisement so he could reach out to a mass buying audience. The faster and sooner his items sold the better. Joann and the girls went back to her house. Their bodies had recovered and they were ready to get to work. Joann decided to have a garage sale, and she was planning to sell her house. If anyone asked why, she would tell him or her that the house was just too big for her and she wanted an apartment that was more efficient. She and the girls went through everything and boxed up items for the sale. They worked during the evening to get everything ready, because they were having the garage sale that as soon as they could get everything ready. As Joann got her things in order, she looked around and saw how much she had, but also how fortunate she had been. The things she had were all beautiful, and some of them were expensive, but the knowledge that the money from these items would sustain her and the group of Chosen Ones gave her great satisfaction she was able to do as much as she could. She didn't want the stuff anyway and it was only materialistic items that made her home beautiful. Her appliances were of good quality so she was planning on taking them to the shelter. They needed those things more than she did. They would use the appliances, and she knew it was a blessing to be able to give them to those who needed them.

Sam had rented a storage room where the few of his belongings were. He went through the storage, and threw out most of his stuff, but there were a few items that he wanted to donate to the shelter. They needed the stuff more than he did. He wanted to bless the homeless, his friends, and giving them things they could never get for themselves. Lately, he hadn't had flashbacks, and he knew it was because of Joann and her care for him, she had him talking and getting him to talk about the trauma he had gone through had helped him. He couldn't even begin to show his appreciation for the comfort that she had provided him; she had kept him so preoccupied that he was being haunted as often by the memories of his service as a soldier.

Cindy and Lucy had very few belongings, but what they did have they put in Joann's garage sale. They didn't care about the things they had, so putting them in the sale wasn't a problem, they kept some of their clothes and personal items and the rest they put into the sale. They were guided by the fact that they wouldn't need most of the stuff and the space was at a minimum. Joann put an ad in the newspaper for the garage sale after they had organized and it was set to go. Joann was busy getting her sale in order when the phone rang. "Hello?" she answered it.

"Hello, Joann! This is Sam. Is there anything I can do to help you ladies?"

"Actually, yes, if you don't mind, would you take some things to the shelter for me?"

"I was about to take some things over there myself. I'll be by and pick up your stuff."

"Oh, Sam! Thank you!"

CHAPTER FIFTEEN

GARAGE SALE

The weekend had finally arrived and the ladies were tired from all the labor of preparation but were excited about the sale. They had worked for days to get their things ready. It was a slow start to the morning, because all of them were so tired.

"Ladies, we're about to have a busy day. Wake up! It's time to sell!"

"Oooook." Cindy moaned, not really wanting to get up out of bed. The last couple of days had been exhausting.

The doorbell rang, and the voices of George, Sam, Jeremy, and Kendra could be heard coming from the living room. "Let's get dressed, Cindy," Lucy told Cindy. "Yeah, it's going to be a long day." They quickly got dressed and joined the rest of their sales group.

"Good morning, everybody," Cindy mumbled. She wasn't much of a morning person.

"Mariann will be coming by later to bring us some breakfast." Kendra told the girls. Cindy sleepily asked Joann, "Could you give us coffee in an IV? We could use it." Joann laughed and shook her head in amusement. "Coffee will be ready in a minute."

The girls went in to put on their makeup to get ready for the day ahead of them. "Um, Lucy, why the makeup? It's only a garage sale."

"Yes, I know and we need to look good to sell. Need to charm the customers." Cindy laughed. Only Lucy would get overly made up for something as simple as a garage sale, but she made herself up to look nice, she would have done it anyway. The rest of the group could hear them giggling from the bathroom. An hour later, the garage doors were opened to find there were customers already waiting for the sale to start. Once the doors were open, people began browsing the selection. In Joann's normal fashion, she greeted everyone with a smile and spoke to the people coming in, she knew many of them.

"Oh, Joann! Do you mind if I put some things in the sale?" Kendra asked.

"Sure, we can make some money today! Go right ahead."

Sam, Jeremy, and George set up some more tables they had brought. The guys handled the heavier things, while Cindy and Lucy set up the smaller items. They all laughed and had a great time, and the customers loved it. Their laughing was making it hard to keep people's minds on the browsing; they bought and were pleased by the bargains. The sale was tiring but they enjoyed every moment of it. Kendra noticed the items that Joann was selling. "You have tons of antiques, Joann."

"Yes, I'm pricing them low, so maybe some antique dealers will want them. Or maybe just collectors." Mariann arrived outside, with food to feed everyone. She was in and out making sure they all had full stomachs. She brought her homemade lemonade that was astoundingly delicious. Nothing went better with her food than her lemonade.

"Mariann, we're all going to have to shut down this sale to take a nap. I'm so full." Jeremy remarked.

"Fantastic! At least you've had enough to eat." Mariann retorted. "My family never goes hungry, haven't you figured that out by now, dear?" She laughed, they all did.

All throughout the afternoon, there was a steady flow of customers; most of the items were gone. Then, a man in jeans, button up shirt, and a Stetson hat, pulled up and got out of his van. "Sold out?" he asked.

"Just about."

"Tell you what, ma'am. You make me a deal, and I'll take what's left."

"I will do what I can, sir!"

The man left with the rest of the furniture and household items, having gotten a bargain on them. It marked the end of the sale, to everyone's relief. They were all tired from the work it took to get the garage sale ready, plus they were ready for a nap after the feast that Mariann had provided.

"Oh, what a day!" Kendra said.

Joann counted the money from the sale, and when she was done, "You won't believe this! Five thousand dollars!" They all cheered. That was more than they thought they would make to get them what they needed for the bunker. "Once I sell this house, we'll have more than enough." Everyone went home for a much-needed nap. Jeremy checked to see if he had any potential buyers for his equipment and there were interested parties. He soon had his equipment sold.

By the end of the month, Joann's house had sold and she decided they would move in with Jeremy and Kendra. Joann had turned the shelter over to new management and the place was running smoothly. Mariann and Kendra were busy getting the bunker set up.

CHAPTER SIXTEEN

MEDICAL STAFF

Dr. Robert Perry and Jacie had heard the news about the microchips at the time the world had gotten it, and as followers of the Voice, they knew they had to do something. "Do you still have the phone number for Cindy and Lucy?" the doctor asked Jacie.

"I sure do, I have been staying in contact with them. They are getting a hiding place ready for the Chosen Ones along with all the others who were with them when they were in the hospital."

"Would you call them to see if you could use us to serve the others as medical staff, please?"

"I already did, they have a place for us."

"You are so gorgeous and loaded with brains. We have the clinic, which is fully stocked, that we need to sell. I will buy more drugs and things we might need under less than modern circumstances. Would you see about ordering things such as bandages and whatever else we need to supply a clinic?"

"I can and will. The bunker has electricity and running water, it even has modern appliances that have no computer chips in them. I understand that they are as state of the art as they could manage. We might be able to have a refrigerator for the drugs we will use."

"Good, I have some of the best equipment around here so I think selling off the equipment in this clinic will be fairly easy, especially at a discounted price."

Jacie had phone numbers of the other friends of Cindy and Lucy, so she was busy calling to make arrangements to get supplies out to the bunker. Sam had his truck and either Jeremy or George would come with him to get a load from the clinic. George was having to be aware at all times of the possibility of getting caught so he was not out and around as much, mostly he stayed on the farm. The doctor and Jacie had told people who asked about the closing of the clinic they wanted to retire and spend their retirement taking life easier. Jacie called patients to set them up with other doctors and they understood, at least they thought they did. There was so much to do she asked to see if Cindy or Lucy could help her with getting records taken to the doctors who had taken their patients. Cindy was more than happy to help; they borrowed Sam's truck when he wasn't using it. She was efficient and finished the work in a few days; she took supplies out to the bunker which helped Dr. Perry get through with getting the equipment sold, he finally had all the large items gone, including the desks, waiting room furniture, shelves, and free standing cabinets. They used plastic boxes to store most of their other supplies.

A doctor stopped by one afternoon to make an offer on the building, Dr. Perry owned it and he gave the other doctor a good deal on it, they shook hands. A week later he had a check in his hand, "Since we won't be able to buy or sell, we can withdraw our money from the bank and find out how to best use it. Our cars have some prospective buyers so we should be able to make a fairly sizable contribution towards the care of our new family. The house will be in the new owners hand in a few days."

"I have noticed that we are being watched by the patrols coming by here more often. The time is getting close for the deadline to take the chips, we need to be careful about what they see," Jacie said. She heard about the ones who hadn't taken the chip were being stalked.

They started trying to look more casual as they did what they had to do; everything was sold and now they were about to be without a home or transportation, it was time for them to go to the bunker to get it set up. The friends had used the money and put it to good use, the bunker was well stocked, thanks to all who were working together as a team. Sam came by and they told him what was going on, "Do you have your things together that you will be taking with you?"

'We can be ready in an hour."

"Let me drop you off and I will go down the alley, when you are ready, come out and we will be off. The clinic there needs some organizing." There were no patrols in sight so Sam left the Perry's at their house with suitcases in their hands and waiting by the back gate. Sam drove slowly down the alley as he watched for any sign of patrols and he stopped by the back gate where Robert threw the suitcases in the back, got in the front with Jacie and Sam took off. They were warmly greeted when they got out to the farm; they were the first ones to be actually living in the bunker at the time. Time was running out and others were moving in as they set their affairs in order for the final preparation of their shelter until the time came for George to get everyone inside.

CHAPTER SEVENTEEN
THE TIME HAS COME

The day had arrived, when the microchips were to be inserted into the forearms of those receiving them. It was proclaimed the World Chip Day. But unofficially, it was also the day that began the start of the hunting down of the non-cooperatives. Lists had been made of people who had refused to take the chips, and everyone who had the chips inserted was given the list. There was not a person the world who didn't know someone one the list. All of the Chosen Ones were chosen by the Voice, some were to live the rest of their lives in prison, some to be shot and killed, some to be beheaded, and some to die painfully and slowly. Many of the Chosen Ones had been tracked down prior to the start of the hunt, just so the hunters could claim their rewards sooner. The hunt showed the true rawness of true human nature; what was in the heart was nothing more than the black filth of sin. The human condition was raw and was showing its true color, blackest of black. Without a voice of conscience to guide and keep in check the deep evil that lurks within every person, humans were without the restraints to care about what they did to each other. There was no longer morality; no distinguishing of right or wrong. The world was unlike anything ever experienced throughout history. The Chosen Ones were being killed, imprisoned or in hiding. The world was celebrating the evil in all its forms. The Dark

Spirits were celebrating as they never had before; because after thousands of years, they were at last able to make evil the right thing right in the minds of humanity.

They knew they had to eliminate any trace of the Chosen Ones. If nothing else, they had to keep those ones from making any appearances. It was time to force the ones who chose good to disappear. The Forces of the Dark World knew their end was close, so their work in the humans was going to count for something. They weren't planning on going easy after all they'd worked too hard to go down without a fight. Anyone else who opposed them, small number that they were, were going to have the ultimate of all punishments. The Dark Forces were going to rain down on them more than ever before. The Ones who were left were strong, but they were human, after all.

The Dark World knew how well humans could be deceived. The number of humans willing to set aside their moral code for refuge from their suffering was ever increasing. The Dark Spirits reveled in their success of shielding the truth from humans, making so many souls turn from the Voice, without regard to life after death. Humans only thought of the moment, their souls gone now for the taking of the Exalted Dark Spirit. Humans were not interested in the Voice who reasoned with them. It was hard to listen when the possibility of starving and dying was right in front of them. Faith was good only when life was easy.

For a while, humans were in frantic chaos while trying to obtain the microchip. There was no longer any regard for others, Spiritual wellness broke down.

A few months after the news announcement had been made about the microchips, things settled down. People got the microchips, and they found themselves relieved from their hunger and uncertainty of the future. Those with the chips had money in their pockets and food on their tables, at last. Freedom from what they knew was to come. But, there were some that hadn't listened to the Voice and found themselves greatly struggling. They knew that their procrastination for preparations had led them to having nothing. The Voice had been warning his People, some were to prepare places and some had other tasks assigned. They had to find the other Chosen Ones, which proved to be extremely difficult. Chosen Ones were assigned to find the Ones who needed help. Homes had been confiscated, no way to buy food, and a very real possibility of getting caught. In human folly, the Voice takes care of His people for those who fully put their trust in the Lord of Lords, they kept their hope and were never disappointed.

The Voice was not willing for any to perish; He didn't give up until the appointed time that was to come.

CHAPTER EIGHTEEN
DARK FORCES

There was a buzz of excitement with the Dark Forces. They had worked hard and keeping up with their deceptions had been paying off. They were almost certain that the Voice was soon to meet his defeat in the raging war. The Voice spoke so quietly that it made the work of the Dark Forces much easier. Centuries of their hard work were finally seeing results.

The humans now had every reason to ignore the Voice. The humans were willing to do anything to prevent them from hurting so that all they focused on was saving their own skins. Now that so many humans were complying with the Dark One, it was time to focus on those who listened to the Voice. The dark spirits had decided it was time to silence them before they had the humans out of compliance with the darkness. It was time to make better use of entertainment and the news media to numb their minds from knowing the truth. Humans needed to have their consciences soothed and believing what they ere doing was the right thing to do.

The Exalted Dark One was quiet as the dark spirits were partaking in a great jubilee, in celebration of their victories. He watched for a while, but finally held up his dark, clawed hands to quiet down his warriors of darkness. "Dark Spirits, you are happy that you have seen success through your work, but do not think this is over yet. There are still those who will give their lives to the Voice rather than give in to me. This is not finished yet." A hush of silence fell over the large numbers of dark spirits.

"They are having new recruits to be Chosen Ones; they will be set loose soon. They have nothing to lose. The Voice has been underestimated, as more humans are listening to it now. We have accomplished a great deal of our work with the new system established. But, not enough time has been spent with those who were imprisoned. The new recruits could cost us a great deal. The Voice thinks that even the weak humans are worth his attention. My opinion and his differ greatly. There was brooding among the dark spirits. This was the war of all wars that they would not lose. No one was exempt."

CHAPTER NINETEEN

THE RESCUE

The bunker was a place of celebration. New friends had been welcomed into the group. They had been on rescue missions to get Chosen Ones the Voice had sent them to rescue. After a time, the outside world had settled down. The patrols had lessened. They listened to the radio they had with them. Chosen Ones were caught and sent to prison and from time to time there were announcements of events where the Chosen Ones were being used for hunting games, like animals. Some of the Chosen Ones were used for target practice; they were restrained in order for hunters to practice their shooting. The shelter prayed for them, asking the Voice to make their suffering not in vain. The Voice wanted several of the friends to go to an arena to rescue some the Chosen Ones. George spoke, "Sam, I need you to stay here to guard the place. Cindy, Lucy, Jeremy, and Kendra, I would like you to help me."

"I still see the drones flying over. The farm looks so run down. Great job everyone! No one's paying any attention to it, especially with this toxic waste dump out here. The soldiers don't want to come out here."

"After tonight they may be coming around. We cannot be complacent." George replied.

"When do we need to leave?" Lucy asked. "With all the work we do here everyone if is in great shape. We've been able to get into town in three hours. The arena will take another thirty minutes once we get into the city limits. We should get there so early so we can have an extra twenty minutes for observation time."

"We need to leave in an hour, then," Kendra said. "Make sure our back packs have enough for us and our rescued friends."

Mariann came in lugging backpacks. "I think this should get you going," she said.

"Off we go," George said.

"I have a bad feeling. Something doesn't feel right," Cindy said.

"I do too," Kendra replied.

They had to go, bad feeling or not, the Voice sent them on a mission, and they did as He told them, regardless of the outcome, the Voice would be there, watching over them.

"The Voice told us to do this, so we will do it," Jeremy said. They each grabbed a back pack and started their walk into town, they were ready.

They tried not to use the same path every time they left so as not to leave a trail that would lead back to them. A drone could spot a trail very quickly, with having high optic lenses that could see in the daytime and nighttime.

They had learned how to walk without leaving evidence of the presence. Their movements were calculated and efficient, with many hours of practice on the farm. No one was allowed to talk and only when absolutely necessary and even then, in quiet whispers. They moved quickly and silently. Three hours later they reached the outskirts of the town. Along the way, they would come upon people who were out doing activities, hiking, dirt bikes, working, and other outdoor events. They had places where they could hide as they made their way to the arena. Soldiers were all around, patrolling the area. Hearts were beating hard. They were moving quickly as they knew they didn't have much time before the sports in the arena started. The work they had to do was dangerous; a blatant act of defiance towards the very government that had once made laws that protected them from acts of violence. What they were doing was enough for them to be shot and killed on the spot.

They were in town and had to watch closely so as not to be caught. Where they were walking was mostly abandoned but nonetheless, patrols drove through the area on their way to bases that were scattered around in cases of emergencies. They stayed in alleys most of the time to have easy hiding places. Nearing the arena, they were in an alley behind an abandoned building with weeds grown up and all about them, snakes could be a problem. So far there wasn't anything of great concern; they saw nothing to be alarmed about. Jeremy was in the lead. Then he stopped suddenly. "There it is," he whispered. "Let's hide our back packs where we can grab them on the way out."

"Hey, this looks like a good spot," George said. There was a dumpster in a dark alleyway. They put their packs behind the dumpster, where their things were completely hidden from view from the street. Stashing their back packs, they headed in the direction of the arena. They could hear the buzz of a couple of thousand people cheering. The group knew they were cheering for the deaths of Chosen Ones. Evil was having a field day; it was in taking pleasure in the control of those who refused the Voice. The arena was close to the spot where they were so they took extra caution and were creeping and staying as low as possible.

Once they got to the arena, which was football stadium without the green field, they found a side door that had been left unlocked. Carefully, looking in, they looked and didn't see anyone so they slipped inside. The air was cool. They noticed some unpleasant odors; some they guessed were from a pile of trash that had not been picked up by the sanitation department as it was not done regularly on this side of town. Up; ahead in the hallway, they saw a doorway they slipped through. Still they didn't see anyone. Everyone was around the arena where the action was about to start. Moving along they could hear the crowd getting louder. Moving slowly, they saw the open arena where they saw people being lead, hands and ankles bound with chains. "Those must be the Chosen Ones we're here to rescue," Cindy said. Looking around at the crowds they noticed the audience had rocks the size of softballs, some bigger, in their hands. They noticed there were not only guards but also members of the crowds standing inside the arena. They paid large sums of money to be allowed inside, in order to reach the victims. They milled about, overwhelmed with anticipation. They wanted the massacre to begin so that they could take the lives of the Chosen Ones. Their eyes were hungry, like ravenous wolves. They loved killing Chosen Ones; in fact, it had become a lifestyle to do so, for those fortunate enough to have the money. Chosen Ones as they had been told were not human so it was deemed to be a favor to mankind to eliminate them.

"We were told to do this, so let's go. Have no fear, for He is with us." George said. The guards were dressed in military style uniforms, were unlocking the chains on the prisoner's hands, but not their feet. They wanted the prisoners to stay in one place as much as possible. It made it much more fun for the crowds. The Chosen Ones were standing at attention, in the same place where their hands had been released. There was no fear on their faces, by looking at their facial features were as if they knew it was over and they had accepted their fate. The group of friends was in awe of them, and how they were in complete peace of what they knew would happen, only moments away. The guards made their way out of the arena and the crowds were worked into frenzied chanting that had begun from the seated spectators. Kill them! Kill Them! Kill Them! Kill them! A guard riding on a horse was guiding it with the reins around the outside ring of the arena. The signal to begin throwing the rocks was when he left the arena. The crowd chanted for him to leave. They didn't want to wait any longer. The air was filled with evil excitement. The guard rode around for a few minutes longer, and then galloped the horse out. Stones were thrown, coming only inches from the guard's head. He dodged his head to prevent getting hit himself. The very exact moment that the guard rode out of the arena, the friends ran out. The crowd was silent, but only for a moment. The rocks were thrown. The rocks were not hitting anyone so they started throwing the rocks harder and faster. The rocks were missing their targets completely; it had never had before, the crowd was stunned. It was like there was a wall of protection that surrounded the prisoners; the rocks hit and came close and short of the prisoners without causing harm to them. The friends walked over to the prisoners and led them through the doorway they had exited just a moment before. The only one who threw rocks was the ones in the front rows in order to prevent the spectators in the upper seats from hitting the ones who were down on the lower seats. The rest of them were only paying for watching the show. The ones with the rocks had to pay a much higher price for their seats.

Kendra had come to comfort the females who were led out. Jeremy and Kendra were the last ones to leave. Just as they were about to be out of the arena into safety, a rock hit Kendra on the back of her head. The only sound to be heard by Jeremy was when the rock hit Kendra on the back of her head. Kendra fell down leaving the back of her head cut open and she started to fall and Jeremy wasn't aware of what had happened but had felt the thud and heard the thump. It took a few seconds for the realization to hit him as he had to catch her and he saw her eyes close. The crowds went wild. Jeremy picked her limp body up and they left back the way they had entered by the side door. He held back his emotions, knowing it wasn't the time. But he was feeling the pain but wanted to get out with all of them and into a safe place. At that moment there was not time to check on her condition, they had to leave, and fast. No one could see was the Spirits of Light were everywhere, surrounding the Chosen Ones. They held the crowds back, they guided the rocks that were being thrown, and the guards were immobilized. Helping Jeremy get Kendra out, they reached for their back packs in the alley where they had left them with the rescued prisoners following them. It was dark out so they were under the cover of darkness. They had to find a place to take Kendra. Jeremy was holding back sobs, but carrying her limp body was the hardest thing he had ever done. He knew where her spirit was, but her body…the face, lovely, beautiful face…he could see the life fading from it. A short while later they found a hiding place. Jeremy laid Kendra down.

She was still breathing. Standing over her he tried to get her to wake her up. They were both a mess but Kendra wasn't feeling the pain which would have come later. She opened her eyes and looked at Jeremy. "See you soon, my love." With that, she took her last breath.

Quietly, George said, "We need to go. I am so sorry." Jeremy knew he was right. Picking her up he numbly carried her, he barely noticed her weight as his sorrow was so intense. He stumbled along and George stepped in to help. The sorrow for all of them was overwhelming. They knew they had to be quiet. It would be a long, emotional walk home. They had to stop along the way, using the rest time to offer comfort to Jeremy. The rescued ones felt his heart breaking; they had their losses and understood what he was going through.

In the World of Light, the Voice welcomed Kendra. "Welcome home, my daughter! You have served me well, and you shall then be rewarded. For now, and eternity, you shall have no more sorrow, no more tears, no more grief, and no more pain. Come now, my child. For you will live in my land of paradise, in spirit, with my love encompassing you."

The friends made their way back to the bunker. They burst into tears when they were in the safety of the bunker's walls. The ones who knew her were shattered with grief.

Mariann had prepared hot food for the group, which had grown considerable. The sat at the large table in the bunker and reminisced over Kendra. The freed prisoners were trying to comfort the grieving group. One of them commented, "All of us understand what you are going through. We were forced to watch as they killed our families. The worst was when they burned our kids alive. Trust that you will see her again, he has that dear lady in his hands. And He will be with all of us. The Voice welcomed Kendra into His arms. Be sad, but remember that she is with Him now. All of us were in prison because we refused to worship what the World Council said to worship. We knew we would never see our families again on the earth because of that choice. We weren't afraid of the idea of dying, because the Voice has been with use every step of the way. The army of the Voice is greater than the sorrows we have today. We are here for you and we will share your grief. You are not alone, friends."

Jeremy and the group were put at ease as they realized what they were saying. "When we bury my lovely Kendra, let's have a party and celebrate what she meant to us. She will be greatly missed but we will see her again."

"Jeremy, Sam and I will dig a grave under one of the trees early in the morning, so her body may rest in the way she deserved." George wanted to do something for a lady that the Voice had sent to help him. She deserved something better than that, but they couldn't risk being spotted by the drones, so they had to bury her body quickly. But to bury her under one of the big oaks trees would honor her.

"Thank you, my friends."

CHAPTER TWENTY

THE BURIAL

At the arena, crowd was left stunned. The only one they hit was the pretty one someone hit as she left. Something strange had happened, those prisoners should have died. They paid good money to see this show. Why didn't the guards catch the prisoners and the people who just walked in and walked out with them? Rocks were strewn all over the arena floor; those prisoners should have been hit. There were soldiers and guards everywhere. What they had just witnessed was beyond comprehension. It instilled fear in the spectators. There was no way that had just happened.

The rescuers had stood up against a huge crowd and held them off. It was decided that a scientific explanation was needed. They refused to call it a miracle. If it was called a miracle there would be a need to acknowledge the Voice. It needed to be referred to as a mysterious phenomenon. Yes, that is what it will be called. There are still Chosen Ones around so they need to be found. No one will be allowed to make a fool out of the believers of The Supreme One. No, it was unacceptable. The Supreme One couldn't have such disrespect like that. He had said this would happen. After all he had done to save them; he was the great protector and provider.

Cindy and Lucy helped prepare for the funeral. Mariann was given a sedative by Dr. Perry and Jacie sat with her to comfort her doing the best they could do. The men went out to dig the grave. In the morning they would bury Kendra. The entire group helped in one way or the other. It was a difficult time for them as Kendra was so much a part of them and she had a heart for all the people she encountered. Her presence was already greatly missed and their grief was profound. Jeremy was so devastated that he wouldn't eat and sleeping had left. George and Sam weren't to be easily comforted. The rescued ones from the arena stepped in and gave them comfort, all night they spent the time talking and referring to the times and how they would meet her again. She was where she would be happy and the time would come for them all to be together again. Early in the morning Sam went out to take up his watch. The funeral was simple but somehow the most beautiful one anyone had ever attended. There was renewed hope and a sense of close companionship amongst them. They went back into the bunker after covering up the grave with leaves and tree branches to disguise it as a part of the landscape. Their tears of sorrow became tears of joy as they started celebrating the person Kendra was as opposed to the shell of a body she had left behind. Jeremy's grief was losing its grip on him. He would see his love again, whenever his time came.

The rescued prisoners spent time in helping with the work that needed to be done so they would not suffer from hunger and would be well supplied. The bunker was coming together to realize that they had to pull themselves through this so they could function and be useful with what they were called to do for others. They read the Book and found the comfort they were in dire need to have and at last they were ready to move on. Their visitors were called to move on and they gave some words of wisdom before they left. The bunker settled into life without Kendra, the sorrow lessened and they grieved together and found the Holy One was in their midst.

The Dark Spirits were furious. They were ranting and raving, cursing the Voice. They savaged earth, creating disaster, wreckage, and death throughout the world. It wasn't over yet, and they were sure that it wouldn't end like this. The Voice was not going to take from them what rightfully belonged to them and the Voice knew they were undeserving to have His mercy, it was freely given. The world, and the pathetic humans in it, was theirs. All theirs and they were going to claim what belonged to them. The Dark World was not happy. The Dark One was ranting. "What have you done? You let those creatures get away! You let the death of Kendra strengthen that group. You failed me!"

One Spirit responded, "The Voice is helping them, He guides them and protects them. We've been relentlessly attacking and harassing them. Greater is he who is with them than he who is in the world. The Voice keeps deflecting our arrows. They overcome everything we throw at them. They become stronger by the day. Our power over them is getting weaker. They ignore us because they only want to listen to Him. He thwarts our every move. They are standing together like a triple corded rope. We're losing our power over them." The Dark One brooded. He had souls to conquer, and it wasn't going the way he thought it should.

CHAPTER TWENTY-ONE
LABOR CAMP

In the days after the death of Kendra the group renewed their strength, courage, and resolve but they were aware of their limited food supply. The leaders of the group came together to talk to the Voice about what they needed to do. "We are in need of more food and we don't know what we need to do. We only know that our needs will be provided as we trust." The Voice, in His gentle, loving manner, replied, "I will send you food. Every morning, go out early to find flakes on the ground. Gather them up to make bread. This bread will be filling and keep you healthy. Once a week, I will send you an animal, which you are to let Mariann cure it so you have meat to sustain your bodies. There will be birds I will send, use them. At certain times, I will show you where to go to get fruits and vegetables. I will cause the earth to supply your food; I will cause plants to grow for you use."

"Thank you for all that you are doing for us and making it possible for us to survive," George was getting a sense of how faith was working. The love he had gotten from the Voice, the care. There were no words. "I am sending more of my people to you. There is a labor camp with some of my people I want you to go rescue. The armed guards are expert marksmen. I don't want you to be afraid of them. They are guarding the pastors and witnesses who have been standing up for me. They are in this labor camp where they are being brutally abused."

"When do we go?"

"Tonight, I will lead you," the Voice said.

"Who else needs to go?"

"I want Sam, Jeremy, and Dr. Perry to go. Cindy, Lucy, and Jacie need to stay to get ready. Sam should go out to shoot down some drones that will be flying over. When you get these Chosen Ones back here, I want you to help to get their bodies healed. Care for them as I have cared for you. I have a place ready for them to go. There is a search going on to find you so stay where I guide you."

The labor was ten miles away. Not knowing how they were going to get there and back they knew they had to trust. There was a lot of work they needed to do. Dr. Perry worked on getting supplies ready. "Jacie, would you get some cots set up? Be ready for anything."

"Yes, dear I already have a triage set up."

Mariann was busy putting together a stock of food for them. She was working so hard Dr. Perry was getting concerned about her. "Mariann, you need to rest more. You have plenty of help, you don't have to do it all yourself."

"Please, will the rest of you help her more? She doesn't look like she is feeling well."

"Lucy and I are going to put her out of the kitchen at least for cleanup," Cindy said.

"Good." Mariann wasn't happy about leaving the kitchen, but she didn't feel well, so at that moment she knew rest was more important. She had so much to do that she hadn't done in the past and they wouldn't be able to just go out to eat so they were dependent on her to prepare their food. The ladies could handle the kitchen while she recharged her tired body. She stayed close by to talk and keep them company.

George went out with Sam, hoping to be able to help him with the work that needed to be done. As they stood outside looking around they saw some horse a short distance away grazing. "I think we just found our transportation," Sam told George. The horses allowed them to approach.

"They must belong to someone living around here. A fence must've broken down. Let's go ahead and use them for our trip."

"No saddles but they have bridles," George smiled. He had seen many amazing things that had happened since he had first listened to the Voice, even if he went back to prison; he knew he was changed for the better.

"The women and other friends should be ok with the food supply we have. I'll go out and find the food that we were promised so everyone can stay inside while we are gone. "Sam said.

Jeremy was warning everyone to stay inside until they returned. George and Sam walked in, "We found some horses we can use to get to the camp." George announced. "They have bridles but no saddles. We'll have to improvise a way to hold our equipment on them."

"No problem," Jeremy said, "You're on a farm, buddy. I have some things that we can use." Jeremy went right to work and sure enough, he had some used canvas bags and rigged them up. "Jeremy, you are a genius!" George said.

George assembled everyone together. "Ok, we are about to leave. This is a dangerous job we're about to do. We are going to trust that we will be back safely. This is what it feels like to be led out of prison. I never would have believed I would be breaking into prison. If I get caught, it'll be death after I am tortured. I am going because this is what I have been told to do. "George was willing to do what he was he needed to do. This wasn't his first time to obey and he was ready and willing to go. They were assembled in the living area solemnly comprehending the situation. "Whatever happens and one of us does not come back, remember we will all be together one day," George was saying.

"Guys! Stop, you are going to be coming back, we will be waiting for you. You will get the job done and we are going to be here to help finish what you have started," Cindy announced.

"We are out of here. Cindy, you are right. And thank you, we need to go." The bunker emptied out as everyone went out to see the men off. They helped them get the horses loaded with their supplies, finally, they mounted their horses and they were off. The horses were young enough that they were energetic and ready for a run. "This sure beats walking," Sam said.

"I would have thought you would be used to it by now," George teased him.

"I don't mind but it's a nice change, for sure. We'll probably walk bow legged for a while after we get back."

"Remember to maintain an awareness of our surroundings. Listen for anything or anyone who may be near." Sam reminded them. "It should get easier as it gets later into the night." Each man was thinking their own thoughts as they were riding. Sam stayed on high alert. He decided to take the lead A few miles down the road he steered them away from some lights he saw. He spotted flashing lights in the sky and they were getting closer, they stayed under the trees. George got out a rifle and shot the drone to disable it. It fell to the ground with a crash and the men hurriedly got away from the area. Most of the terrain was barren and they were closely watching for more of the drones they knew would be coming their way. Overall, the ride was going smoothly and the men were having quiet conversation. They had come to see each other as brothers. They worked so closely together and were like a well-oiled machine, there was someone who would mediate arguments as they had learned how to work out their differences, there were some arguments from time to time, it became a family affair when it happened and they settled it and moved on with no hard feelings, their lives depended of it.

After a couple of hours, they were nearing the labor camp. "Let's tie up the horses close to the camp. Somewhere that will be easily accessible to us when we get back out," George said. They found a spot and tied the horses on a long tether so they could graze on the grass.

"There are a lot of lights. This place is as bright as day. We need a distraction. Let's wait here and see what we can come up with," Sam said. For a while there was only the occasional guard walking about inside the fence, nothing was happening. As they were waiting, they noticed three cars drive up to the gate. Out of the cars teenaged kids were getting out and they appeared to be intoxicated. "Our distraction has arrived," George said. "We only had to wait." Within a little while they were seeing that the teens were causing trouble. They quickly headed for the fence on the backside of the camp. They could hear one of the teens screaming, "I want to see my dad! Don't you know who I am?" Guards were running over to the gate. The gate was opened and the guards were working on settling them down and to get the boys to get them back in their cars and out of there. The guards were trying to reason with them. One of the boy's fathers was a guard at the camp.

"Go home to your mother young man," the guard, apparently, his father, ordered him.

"Dad, Jonathan wants to see his dad."

"It's not allowed. All of you go home or you'll be spending the night in there," the guard said. "Who isn't drinking?" All of them were. "I need to call someone to come get you." The teens had calmed down and the other guards were finding the situation amusing. A call was made to arrange transportation for the boys to get home and to arrange for them to come get their cars later the next day.

Sam and George, out in the back, were busy cutting the wire on the fence. There was razor wire all around the top. They had to work carefully, because one small wrong move would result in their hands or arms sliced open. The fence was carefully opened for them to get in safely and to close it enough when they got out so as not to be so noticeable. Sam stood guard as George worked on the cutting. The guards weren't paying any attention to them. The grass hadn't been mowed down in quite some time, so, the men were easily hidden in the dark of night. They carefully slipped through the cut fence and not sure where they were going, headed for one of the barracks they saw up ahead. Sam was closely watching. They found a door that was out of sight of the guards. Since there were no locks they opened it slowly and went inside, closing it behind them.

They heard some soft moaning. The light was dim and after a couple of minutes their eyes adjusted to the buildings darkened interior. Most of the men were sleeping. They went to the bunks and found four men who were awake moaning and in pain. "We are here to get you out," George informed them. "We have been waiting for you to come, we knew we would be leaving," one of them said.

"We need to hurry," George said. "Do you think you can walk?"

"All of us are hurting but I think we can."

"We'll help you. You can lean on us." As gently as possible, the friends helped the prisoners to their feet. None of the other inmates stirred. They headed to the door and Sam opened it, peeked out, and motioned for them to follow. They were all grimly aware of the proximity of the guards. Getting out was going to be harder to do than getting in.

"Do you still think you can walk?" Sam asked. They moaned, but answered back that they could or at least they would try.

"First, let's focus on getting you out of here. We have a safe place, and a doctor is waiting for you. He will give you some immediate treatment and food and water for now until we get you to our shelter."

"Thank you! We need a doctor." Sam was checking to see where the guards were located. The teens must have had beer in one of the cars because the guards were drinking them. They were all sitting around laughing so the friends picked up their steps and as quick as they could get the prisoners to the fence and helped them get through it.

"Try to stay as low as you can," George told them."

"The horses are up ahead." Sam looked behind them and saw that the guards were unconcerned about their duties. They were having their own party, so the beer they were drinking was distracting them from what they were doing. Staying low, the group made their way over to the horses. The men were put on the ground to try to get some food and water into them before they could travel. The freed prisoners were in so much pain and malnourished and it was obvious that they had been beaten frequently with all the old and new bruises that were visible on them. They managed to get to the area where the others were waiting for them and as gently as they could, they were set up by a tree to prepare them for the journey to the shelter. It was difficult for them to feed themselves, and Sam and George helped them to eat the food they had brought with them before they could travel. With food in them they were feeling better but they needed to be treated by Dr. Perry. He tried to tend them with what he had brought with him; it would have to be enough for now. Dr. Perry saw the multiple bruises and abrasions but wasn't able to check their injuries at that time since it was imperative that they get moving out of that vicinity. The prisoners tried to help themselves up on the horses but they were weak. With teamwork and effort from the rest of them, the men were finally on the horses.

"Getting some good food has really helped. We are hurting but I believe we will be all right," the others agreed. The horses had eaten and had water so they were ready to go. The trip back to the bunker took longer with the men being in pain and the pace had to be slowed down. As they were nearing the downed drone Sam saw another one that was hovering over it and it was turning in different directions. Sam took out the rifle and when the drone was scanning the far side of the field across from them, he took aim and disabled it, causing it to crash close to the first one. This time they couldn't take any chances, someone was going to show up and find out who had crashed the prized spies. Running the horses to get away caused immense pain for the freed men but it couldn't be helped. They clamped their mouths closed to keep from screaming. The trip seemed long and the weakened men were struggling to stay conscious. When they returned to the bunker they were in so much pain that Dr. Perry immediately gave them shots to relieve the suffering before he examined them.

"They are severely malnourished," Dr. Perry told Jacie. "They have had some food so after I check them out we need to let them rest. When was the last time you ate?" He asked them.

One of them piped up, "It's been a while. I'm not sure exactly. They are starving people, only giving us enough food and water to keep us alive and able to work. We are beaten but only enough to allow us to work. It's like the Holocaust all over again."

"Well, it looks like you all have some broken bones, plenty of bruises, and cuts. It looks like we got to you in time, barely. You will all be lying around for a couple of weeks to heal up. Don't worry about a thing now. We have a lot of people who will help you and let you rest. It's time to heal and a time to find out where you will need to go after your recovery."

The men now freed and safe, went to sleep. They slept peacefully knowing that they could sleep at last and get the much-needed rest.

Sam noticed some white flakes on the ground the next morning. He had Jeremy bring some buckets outside to collect them. This must be the food we have been expecting, time to get busy. George went outside with them to help. He put some in his mouth, "Mmmmmm, this tastes good! Mariann can put her magic touch on this," Jeremy said.

"After we get some sleep I'll find the meat we were promised," Sam said.

"That means I will go out to see what I can find, the fruit and vegetables," George added.

"We are being given substance but we have to work for it," Jeremy said with a laugh.

CHAPTER TWENTY-TWO
PASTOR LARS GOES HOME

In the bunker where the Pastors Lars, who had been rescued from the labor camp was recuperating from his injuries and was healing well. He was gaining weight and his health was rapidly improving with Mariann's good cooking and Jacie's close monitoring. The Voice wanted to send him out to his shelter to be with his family and help his Chosen Ones to learn and grow under his leadership. The Voice had made some incredible hiding places and many of them were nice, no one was going hungry, all their needs were being met.

A messenger was sent to Lars's shelter to inform his family that he was coming home to be with them. They waited to find out where they were to meet and the messenger arrived to tell them to meet at a river that they all knew about. It took a while to get ready. The plan was to take food for the overnight trip and food for getting back to the bunker for them and Lars would have his care taken over when the escorts were at the meeting place.

George, Jeremy, and Lars were on their way on a fine clear day with the sky filled big with clouds that were providing comfortable shade from the sun, a good day to leave. All of them were rested and ready. Lars was fully recovered and excited about seeing his family. The route they were traveling had become familiar with time. In an emergency, they could find quick hiding places from the natural terrain or from planned uses of logs or rocks they placed in natural looking formations. There were some lush underbrush and trees that were full and green. It was safer to go from one of these places to the next. Stopping from time to time to rest they would eat and drink the water they had with them. The hiding places were handy for their stops with shade and a chance to look around to check for any problems they might encounter. Crossing roads was challenging at times and on occasion they would see people out and about so they had to use caution as they travelled. Late in the afternoon they came to the dry river bed and as they started to cross they noticed a drone that was flying close to them and it had spotted them. George got out the rifle he had brought with him and shot down the drone, there were sparks flying as it plummeted to the ground with a loud crash. The drones were not large in size and could be difficult to spot as they had been built to be smaller and more efficient so it took good eyes to see them. They had been spotted so they didn't know how long it would be before someone would show up and they would be caught. With a sense of urgency, they took off and as they were in the middle of the river bed when Jeremy looked behind him and was alarmed, "There are soldiers behind us!" They froze. George took action, "Get going!"

Making their way across the dry river bed they made it to the other side and turning around they knew that they couldn't get away so they stopped. "They have been tracking us for a while and we will not be able to get away," Jeremy said. With the men in sight the soldiers were running to catch up with them. There was nothing to do but wait. As the soldiers had gotten in the middle of the river there came a loud roar. Looking up towards the upper part of the river they saw a tsunami size wave headed straight for them. They tried to get away but they were not able to run fast enough as the wave was bearing down upon them and they were helpless to get out of its path. The wave hit them was the fury of violence.

As the men watched in disbelief, they saw the soldiers disappear in a blink of an eye. It appeared that anything close to the banks of the river had been torn loose and was being forced down stream. Standing where they were they saw trees, cars, roofs of some houses and other types of buildings and everything the water was carrying in the rush as it was being pushed along to be deposited somewhere along the way. Most likely there would be bodies of humans and animals that had been swept away with the sudden rush of the giant wave. Behind them they heard someone greet them, "Hello, we saw what had happened. That was some kind of salvation, wasn't it?"

"Yes," George answered.

"We were sitting around waiting for you to show up when we heard the gun shot."

"We had been spotted by a drone that I shot down. We are in danger so it would be a good idea for us to move to safer quarters for the night."

"I have our people packing up and getting ready to leave right now."

"There will be other soldiers coming and they will be sending more drones, which should be arriving shortly."

As they were talking they were moving toward the camp and the other campers were about finished with having their supplies ready to go.

"I am Quincy, I was sent to get Lars."

"I am George. Meet Jeremy and Lars. We are very happy to meet you and I can't tell you how happy to see you."

"If you will come with me we will get all of us out of here to a safe place." With that they started off with the other three men they had met. The first thing they did was to head in the direction of a thicket of trees where they could stay under cover. Quincy had some camouflage netting he had brought with him and it was proving to be useful. As they were traveling under the trees they soon heard the whirring of the drones and they could see that the area was covered with them as there was a manhunt to find them. When a drone was overhead they would stop and hunker down so as not to have their movements spotted. Quincy took a route that wouldn't get them directly to his shelter so as not to lead possible pursuers to the other members in the shelter. They found a place where they could spend the rest of the night that was hidden with a small stream of water close by. They were able to build a small fire to cook and get their stomachs filled. They didn't stay up talking for very long as they needed to get moving quickly after some sleep. It seemed to them they had just dozed off when Quincy woke them up. "It will be light soon so we need to eat and get this place cleaned up." Somberly they quickly ate some breakfast and had they campsite cleaned up within twenty minutes. They had to move fast.

They were fortunate to have all the trees that were around them and where they were traveling it didn't look as if many people came this was. It was filled with all sorts of prickly brush and critters of the unsavory kind, which was good for them. George noticed that there weren't as many drones and the he wondered if the commanders thought they had taken another route and avoided this forsaken place. Jeremy knew where they were going as he had grown up around here and Quincy had wandered around here in search of provisions. For whatever reason it was, they were able to make good time and they were soon only seeing an occasional drone.

By midday they came to the shelter that Quincy was from and where Lars was going to be for a short time before going on to be with his family. It was set back in the undesirable area that had been cleaned up and had a covering of the briars that surrounded it. They were greeted with enthusiasm and welcomed with relief as Quincy's family was there with him as were the other men's. Sitting down to talk about how to get back to the bunker, they came up with a plan that seemed to be travelled with time on their side.

George and Jeremy left and headed in the direction they had talked about when they came to an open field they had to cross to get to where they needed to go they came upon an apple orchard. Jeremy found some apples that he picked off the tree hoping no worms had made their home in them when he saw George stop and was listening, he stopped also. There was some moaning coming from somewhere close by. Both of them slowly crept over to where they could hear it and that is when they saw a man leaning up against a tree, he had been hurt and was looking as if he hadn't eaten in a while. They walked over to him to try to help him. He weakly looked up at them before closing his eyes from the exertion.

"I am George and this is Jeremy. We are going to help you. Take a drink of water." Looking around them they didn't see any food or water. From the bottles of water, they had with them, they held him up and patiently helped him to drink. When he signaled that he had had enough they worked to get some food in him and it took some time, when he had eaten he tried to sit up with Jeremy's help.

"I am Micah and I have been out here for several days. I am one of the Chosen Ones. I had been staying out here and finding food to keep me alive during the summer months and staying in the barn of a family who leave to go to another place where they spend the winter. I have managed to find food until I caught something that made me sick and I fell. I don't think I broke any bones but I haven't been able to get up and around since the illness got me down. I thought I was going to die." He was already feeling better and had gained some of his strength. Jeremy touched him and he didn't seem to have much of a fever.

"We will help you and get you well again."

"What is your name and where are you from?"

"I am Micah. My wife left me for my best friend who is an attorney. I had a hardware business that was profitable and we were living well. She thought I wasn't keeping her in the lifestyle she wanted so she left with the attorney. It just so happened that my friend's wife had found out about him and my wife she had plans of her own. She had been his secretary and had set up an account where she was taking his money. One of his friends was pretty smart about divorce proceedings so he helped her and she cleaned him out before he knew what was happening. When my wife found out that he had nothing, she left him. I don't know where she is but she didn't want anything to do with the Voice so she refused to take the chip. Her plan was to turn me in for the reward but I heard her discussing it with one of her friends and I left and have been out here hiding for a long time." He was talking about it, not with bitterness but with sadness.

Micah was thin from being out here and not being able to sit around but having to find food. The clothes he was wearing were hanging off his thin frame. He was about five feet, six inches from the looks of him. His hair was a sandy blonde and thinning in places. He might have been about forty years old. The color of his eyes was a hazel color when he had them open and they could see them. The jeans he wore were faded and the red plaid button up shirt was torn in places.

It was getting late so they thought it would be a good idea to spend the night under the trees. The smell of the apples was pleasant and appealing. Looking up at the stars and the light breeze blowing they talked and came up with a plan to get Micah back to the shelter where Quincy was living. They didn't have to go after all, by early morning Quincy himself showed. He had been told to come to this place where he was to meet someone. All of them were surprised to see each other again so soon. George and Jeremy helped to get Micah on his feet after they picked up some of the apples for them to take back to his shelter. Quincy was struggling to keep Micah on his feet so they went with him to get them safely back. It meant another day of travel but they didn't want to leave them in case of trouble along the way. They soon found out that they were right in doing so. Micah was still too weak to travel. George made a liter so they could carry him. They made frequent stops to nourish and hydrate him. Huffing and puffing they managed to get him to the shelter where he was immediately given the care he needed. He fell asleep soon after getting there after he was cleaned up and given more food and water.

George and Jeremy wanted to get back so they took their leave once again going the same route. When they got to the apple orchard they picked up some apples and once again spent the night there so they could get a fresh start in the morning. As of that time there hadn't been any drones spotted. It was humid and there was the possibility of some rain as the clouds were getting heavy and they felt a few drops of rain. They would have to cross the river that had flooded and it was close to them within five miles by the description Quincy had given them. On the way, they heard some shooting and they found a hiding place so they could find out what was going on. Moving closer to where the shooting was going on they saw a unit of the military who were having some target practice. It was then that they figured they were still being hunted down and they hoped the shelter hadn't been suspected. "Let's move back,"

George told Jeremy, "we will have to go around them away from where they first spotted us." Moving back far enough away they made their way further downstream to where they could cross over and make their way home. Slowly they found protection as were making their way when they came across a patrol of soldiers who were looking over what appeared to be a map of the area with a commander pointing out particular spots on the map and discussing them. They were not close enough to hear what they were saying but it was apparent they were looking for something and they suspected it was them.

"From what we have seen so far, I think they are closing in on what they believe to be us," Jeremy was telling George.

As they were moving back around them, the commander suddenly looked up and pointed in their direction, the men froze. They hunkered down and moved silently and as fast as they could. When they were in the trees and out of sight of the platoon, they looked back and saw that the soldiers were moving across the spot where they had just left. "That was a little too close," Jeremy whispered. They took off running and didn't slow down until they had put quite a bit of distance between them and the platoon. By this time, it was late afternoon and they had passed several houses indicating they were near a town. George was guessing that they were about fifteen miles away from the soldiers and hoped they were not coming back this way for a while. George saw a landfill that was below them as they stood at the edge of a manmade hole about the size of a lake in a city park. On the other side of the landfill they saw some old rusted out vehicles that had weeds growing up around them. George was wondering why they had been left and not used for recycling, not a worry. They walked around the landfill trying to stay hidden from prying eyes they were on the other side in a few minutes and looking for a place to spend the night. Some of the cars were stacked in a heap so they meandered through them and found a small travel trailer that didn't look as if it had been parked there for a very long time. Pulling the door open with some effort, they went inside. It was smelly and dirty but they figured they could put their sleeping bags down on the old couch and a mattress that was in there and have reasonable accommodations.

The landfill had fires burning so they weren't worried about building their own fire. George went out to find some fresh meat in the woods they had left and he didn't have to wait long before he had some quail for their dinner which they roasted over an open fire. Jeremy had found some paper to start a fire and some wood that was all around the edges of the landfill. It wasn't dark yet so they just rested and they planned their next days' journey. The small town was located along the river bank and as far as they could see, the wave hadn't affected them as it did town upstream, there was debris along the banks. When the time came for them to get some sleep they had to smash the windows in the trailer because of the horrible smell and the staleness of it. The smell of the trash was not easy to palpitate but at least they had a slight breeze to keep them cool and comfortable.

Just before the sun was coming up over the horizon they woke up to the sounds of heavy machinery getting closer. George jumped up right before Jeremy and he was panicked. "We need to get out of here and quick."

They grabbed their belongings and scrambled out the door of the trailer. "Wait!" Jeremy said. "We on't want them to get suspicious."

"You are right. We need to act like we are vagrants who are just spending the night." They walked around poking through the trash as if looking for anything that could be sold. One of the men on one of the huge machines stopped and yelled at them, "Get out of here, you bums!" as the men were walking away the waved their hands behind them in a dismissing gesture. The machine driver yelled back, "Aren't you that guy who was on death row who escaped?" George momentarily froze, long enough for the driver to know that he was right. "Get him!" the driver screamed at the others. Jeremy grabbed George by the arm and they took off at a run with the overweight men trying to follow behind them with them being left behind. Jeremy kept George at a run and not stopping, both knew they were going to be pursued.

They continued down the river bank until they came to a spot where it was shallow and they could go across on the rocks. Barely being able to stand on their feet as they crossed they got to the other side. They could hear sirens screaming behind them in the distance so they kept running. In a pasture, they saw from the tree line where off in the distance were some horses that were tied up on some fence posts so they made their way over to them. They could hear a couple of kids a short way away as they were involved in some activity that had them laughing and making noise. Jeremy walked over and got the horses and brought them back. Getting on them they walked them until they were out of earshot of the kids and then they were off at a full run. By the time they were in they were in the tree line they saw drones flying overhead. The trees were close enough together that they were allotted protection from the cameras.

By the time the sun was starting to go down they were fairly close to the bunker so they got off the horses. They took the saddles off the horses and swatted them to get them out of there. The horses went off and the men walked at a quick pace to get back to the bunker. It was already dark when they got back and they filled the friends in on their experiences they had since they had left.

CHAPTER TWENTY-THREE
THE WORLD NOT TURNING TO THE VOICE

The Dark Forces were all equally excited about the work they had accomplished so far. "Our work has paid off. Now we can finally silence those who oppose us. They've been in conflict with us for so long we can now rule; our reign will be as supreme as anticipated for the next millennia."

"There's still work to be done. Push forward, and do it with full force. The Voice won't be giving up so easily. He speaks to his followers quietly. Drown His voice out, no mercy. Humans are such weak creatures; they are powerless without their Voice and His protection. Distract them, as they are easily distracted."

"Is there anything new we need to do?"

"No, same as you've been doing. Wave money and power in front of their faces; show them what can happen if they have everything they want. When there's an opportunity, be there to jump in. Crack them wide open. As they weaken, exploit their weaknesses; give them the incentives to sway. Make them think they are entitled. Hit their weaknesses from all around. They need to forget about their Voice. They should think that we care, that we want the best for them. Be loud, but don't scream." "This has been successful for us so far."

"Continue what you've done, go. Take back what is ours. This world and the humans in it are ours."

The Chosen Ones were being close to extinction but they were still being kept under the umbrella of protection, some were dying but not enough of them.

Times had changed from when churches were the center of social activities, they were the voice of God speaking to humanity, and they were the rock of society. People prayed together, stayed together, people married, had children, and raised the children together. Fathers went to work and the children knew someone would be home for them. Divorce became easy, poverty stalked families, drugs and alcohol was more important than tending the children. Fathers were no longer around, mothers who tried to tend the family left to them had to work to provide and sometimes two or three jobs. No one stayed any longer at home to be with the children and to make sure they were being taught. Night life was the way people believed they could find happiness. Children were left to fend for themselves or left with friends and relatives. Discipline of biblical worth was condemned as damaging to the children. The government wanted to control children and parents believed the lies or were clueless about what was being taught and felt helpless to do anything about it. Schools taught lifestyles that the Book taught against and condemned as fatal. People didn't want to be seen as intolerant and so it went. The Church had no back bone to stand up and say wrong so all rights were given away. Deterioration of the once stable society was gone, replaced by the Dark Forces agenda. The strong grew stronger and the weak became weaker. The weak were the dominant ones in the societies of the world. Divorce was the solution for marriage in trouble.

Deviant behavior became normal as people were convinced the few and noisy were right and to be pitied as minorities needing special treatment. Dark Spirits were having their days as fear set in on those who wanted to do what was right and Chosen Ones were refusing to give in and losing everything. Little children were harmed by pedophiles as the world was inundated with it everywhere. Pornography was impossible to control and the ones who could make the difference were lax in doing so. Parents were too busy with their own interests to be around for protecting their offspring and not taking the time when they were around. The privileged few were given whatever their eyes desired, no consequences for their actions. Many children were learning that they were owed, they weren't given the important boundaries needed for life lessons, and these children became the little gods to the parents who were clueless to what the future was for them. The over-protected and neglected, either way, society was doomed. Gangs life, lying, cheating, and stealing to get through life, bullying and killing, there weren't enough law enforcement to keep up and no one wanted to.

The Ten Commandments and praying to the Devine and Holy One was offensive to the few, who were trouble makers of the world, God who created law and order was offensive, the One who made laws for harmony in the world was offensive. Laws were made to suit the politician who decided what was right and not what the Supreme God wanted for the protection of His creation.

Serving the One who is Truth and could provide was removed. Self-control was for someone else to practice, if a person saw something another person had, just take it, steal it, or kill them to get it. The cycle went around and around much to the delight of the Dark One, his plan was to drown out the voice of the prophets of the Holy One, it was easy as he prepared the world and it listened to these spirits as the spiraling of evil took over.

The murder of Chosen Ones started way back since the beginning, their lives were nothing in the world, and it was even celebrated. Free speech of the Chosen Ones didn't count as freedom, filth had infiltrated entertainment and was appalling, yet these producers of incomprehensible trash were proud of their accomplishments. Sexual content with every form of perversion was put out and even biblical behavior was portrayed as being out of step with the times. Celebrities promoted and bragged about their pervasive behavior as young people were idolizing them. The deceived were sinking lower and the Holy One was being drowned out by those whose hearts were yearning for the glitter of evil. Right become wrong and wrong became right. The Church was retreating in cowardice.

Those who engaged in Dark acts were accepted. The Exalted Dark One was pleased; he was taking souls as he pleased. He bragged to the Voice to let him know that he was keeping his Chosen Ones until the final day. He'd save the best for last. He was determined to take every one of them and was stepping up his tactics. These humans needed to feel they were deserving of whatever they wanted. Humans were so weak. The humans who listened to the Voice would be pressured through ridicule and bullying to convert to the Darkness. Death threats for noncompliance were being carried out and the murderers were treated as heroes.

The Holy One let people make their own choices, not one person in the end could say they weren't warned for in their hearts the Word was known to them. The prophets of Light were warning of the impending doom for those who refused to listen and change their ways, they would surely die.

CHAPTER TWENTY-FOUR

ABOUT JENNY

Jenny was a twenty-one-year-old girl, with strawberry blonde hair and freckles scattered on her cheeks. She had the air of one who had the most, which was a persona she lived up to. She stood five foot six inches, weighing one hundred thirty pounds. Growing up, she'd decided she was better off living on her own. She thought the rules her parents imposed weren't her style, and she loved her independence. At twenty-one, she had finally understood her parents' rules. She wanted to go back home, but was too ashamed to admit she was wrong for rebelling against them. Her life was hard and she had been afraid of Ghost. His presence, even lack of presence, was imposing, and she had seen what he would do to the other girls if his rules weren't adhered to.

This wasn't the kind of life she had envisioned for herself. She loved to draw, which she did and art school was the direction she wanted to go. Her dreams for her life had not been realized and she had so many regrets. She had held one of her roommate's hands as she watched her die after Ghost had gotten hold of her. When she took her last breath, some guys came in and grabbed the body. Jenny went into the bathroom and threw up. She couldn't understand why a life could be so devalued the way Ghost treated it; she cried and cried. In the middle of the night she heard a voice speak to her. "Jenny, my love for you is boundless.

Only through me, shall you be free from the chains that bind you into slavery. I shall wash you clean and make you as an infant; to grow like a flower in my peace."

"Who are you?" she asked.

"I am the Voice. Someone is trying to kill you so I am sending Cindy and Lucy, two of my Chosen Ones to get you. They are the ones who worked with you."

"What about Ghost?"

"He's been taken care of, so no need to worry about him."

Jenny was happy and was waiting for her rescue.

CHAPTER TWENTY-FIVE

RESCUE

Cindy had been helping Mariann when she realized the Voice was talking to her, one of the girls, Jenny, who she used to work with was in need of her help. "Lucy, we need to get Jenny, she is in danger and I feel like I am being asked to go get her."

"Of course, I will."

"It might be late before we get back but I think we need to get her before it gets late."

"Sam, will you go with us?"

"I will go with you, get together the things we many need and I will be ready."

"Thanks, Sam." Cindy and Lucy got busy with their packs and had them ready within a short time; Sam was ready as he had said he would be. George was out so Mariann said she would tell him they had left. With all the walking they did, they had been able to cut their time getting into town and they had found easier ways getting there. "Do you know where we need to go?" Sam asked them.

"If we can get there before dark, I think I can find her easy enough."

"We should hurry so we will find her before she goes to work." There was one way of getting into town that allowed them to stay clear of the highway, the problem was they had to keep clear of houses and be watchful of people walking around or being found randomly. Because of their need to go as fast as they could, they didn't talk. They came across people but weren't spotted. Sam was ever the watchful one, there were some close calls but otherwise they were making good time. Close to one home they heard a couple arguing, the man started hitting her, she fell to the ground crying as he stood over her, kicking her, finally she lay very still. They weren't sure if she was dead or not, they had to hurry and couldn't take a chance getting caught as much as they wanted to help her. On their way back, Sam planned to stop to see if he could learn anything. This world was a miserable place; he was saddened by it all.

Cindy and Lucy were feeling it also, they knew how she felt. Cindy felt a sense of urgency to keep going. It looked like they would be where Jenny was in time, they kept up the steady pace. All of them were breathing hard. With a few cuts and scrapes, they were close to where Cindy hoped to find Jenny. The place was in the district where they used to work and close to where Jenny lived, hoping to be in time, Cindy told Sam where she thought they might come across her. Sam looked around and thought the alley around the corner from her apartment would be a good spot, he got them hidden and they had to wait. It was getting dark when they heard a girl crying, Sam peeked around the corner. "Cindy is this Jenny with that soldier?" he whispered.

"That's her," she replied apprehensively. The soldier was dragging her down the street and he was hurting her.

"Ok, ladies, grab some bricks that are lying over there," he pointed back into the alley by a dumpster where they had been hiding and they grabbed a brick for each of them. They walked back to where Sam was watching. Jenny was close so the three of them were waiting tensely but ready to move. As Jenny and the soldier got right in front, Sam leaped out and charged the soldier, Jenny saw him coming so she dropped down and Sam hit him on the head with a loud thump with the brick and the soldier fell to the ground unconscious. The girls dropped the bricks they had in their hands. Jenny was stunned until she saw Cindy and Lucy; they picked her up off the ground and hugged her.

"Girls, we need to move quickly," Sam told them as he was grabbing them and pushing them back into the alley. "Are you ok?" he asked her.

"I am ok. He was going to hurt me, I heard him bragging to one of the other soldiers about what he was planning to do to me, I don't think I would have survived."

"We are taking you with us, the Voice told us to come get you," Cindy told her.

"I was asking Him to rescue me."

"Is that soldier dead?" Lucy asked Sam.

"I am not staying around to find out." Sam had them out of the alley and on their way out of town as quickly as he could. Jenny seemed to have only had a scare and minor cuts and bruises, other than that, she was doing well. She was chattering as they walked with the nervous energy that had built up from the previous experience. She was given comfort. They went slower on her account; the walk was uneventful with the sun having gone down and darkness having descended. When they got to the house of the couple who had been fighting, Sam left the girls in a safe place and quietly moved to the house to see about her. He saw her sitting on a couch with her face bruised and swollen, at least she was alive, for now. The man was sitting at a table eating his food and watching a sports game on TV. Sam was relieved. He walked back to the girls and they headed for the bunker, they were there without any problems, people were at home or out partying.

When Sam brought the girls into the bunker, the friends greeted Jenny, giving her hugs. "Are you hungry?" Mariann asked her.

"No, I ate food Cindy and Lucy brought with them. I am good, thank you." She was introduced to the friends in the bunker. Sam listened to the radio and learned that the soldier had died as a result of a the massive blow to his head and it was currently under investigation.

A week later as they were listening to the radio and keeping up with current events, they were hearing stories, waiting to find out if they needed to go to the rescue of any of them. The soldiers were patrolling streets in search of the trophies that had a cash reward for being hunted down, the Chosen Ones. They knew they were still around and were determined to find them. There were those who were having trouble finding a hiding place, some had been found as they were roaming the streets and were trying to find a new shelter without a plan.

George and the friends were told about some Chosen Ones in dire need of help. They asked Jeremy to go with him. They had gone to the edge of town and were trying to come up with a plan while keeping out of sight of the patrols.

"The house we're headed to is close to here," George told Jeremy. "If we go through the trees just up ahead we should be there." The house was two miles from them on the opposite side of the road; Jeremy had known the couple who lived there. Getting close to the house, they stopped to look and listen. Twenty-five minutes later, they came to the trees George had mentioned. Looking around for any sign of movement, they proceeded to move forward cautiously. Jeremy saw the house first. "That's it," he said.

"Stop for a minute to be sure it's safe," George said. Pausing and watching, they noticed a vehicle driving up to the house. George and Jeremy crept slowly closer to observe the activity. Two soldiers got out and walked up to the door. They paused and one said something to the other one and the second one went around behind the house. The first soldier opened the door and stormed inside. After a couple of minutes both soldiers were coming out the front door dragging the couple out who were to be rescued by the men. Both of them were dreading what they were about to see.

The couple was doing as they were told in compliance, but that didn't matter to the soldiers. One of the soldiers took his rifle and hit the man behind the knees causing him to fall forward. The woman dropped down beside him. She was crying his name and holding on to him. The other soldier hit her on her back with his rifle. Both of the soldiers were laughing as they committed the horrendous deed, it was a sport to them to inflict suffering on another human being. Each grabbed one of the couple and stood them on their feet, while squeezing the back of their arms as hard as they could, both of the couple was in pain, and it was visible on their faces. The man was limping and the woman was having trouble breathing. She was crying and the soldier hit her with his rifle and she crumpled to the ground having her breath knocked out of her and in severe pain. Her husband attempted to come to her aid but was landed with a rifle across his stomach. He doubled over to his knees again and fell to the ground, holding his stomach. He doubled over to his knees again and fell to the ground. One of soldiers grabbed the man up by his hair with one hand and with his other hand pulled him by his arm and stood him on his feet, he was not able to stand so he fell down again. The two soldiers picked him up and one of them held him up while the other one took sadistic pleasure in working him over as the demonic spirits were working through him. The soldier was laughing as the demons within him knew he had another to take with him when it was finished with him, the man assed out, he started falling and the soldiers let him hit the ground hard with him lying face down and the ground and as the life drained from him, he looked up and saw a bright light, he smiled. The other soldier hit the woman again in the stomach so hard that she wasn't breathing. Both soldiers were yet to be finished with the man; fortunately, he was already unconscious, ending their criminal activity with finishing off the young man. The taller of the two looked over to the woman, and said with a sneer, "You're next, sweetheart."

George and Jeremy turned away in horror and vomited. It wasn't heard above the bloodcurdling screaming in front of them. The woman was picked up and set on her feet. She was a small-framed woman so she was easier to hold up than the man. The other soldier took out his heinous activity on her, she collapsed. A soldier finished them off as two shots were fired and they were mercifully out of pain. The laughter was loud, ringing throughout the abandoned country side. George and Jeremy were sick. Jeremy said, "I can't endure this, how can anyone be so brutal and heartless?"

The Voice greeted the couple into the heavenly realm. "My son, my daughter, you did not die not in vain, but for the work well done. I welcome you into the eternity of paradise. You shall not die again, but live forever, with me."

George and Jeremy stood watching the soldiers. "Let's stop them," Jeremy said.

"The road curves back around behind us. If we hurry, we can catch them."

They turned around and started back. They could hear the jubilant celebration of the soldiers. They didn't act like they had just killed two innocent people, but more like they had just won the lottery, they went on about the nice reward they were about to get for this couple. The bodies were tossed into the back of the truck. "Oh, man! It's going to be some food money we're getting on these two. How about taking the wives to a nice dinner after we get paid?"

George found a spot where he and Jeremy could hide from the approach of the soldiers. He was thinking back to the times he didn't think twice about killing. This time it was different, he wanted to save the lives of other people. He couldn't bear to witness this again. He knew they would be in good hands now, he had never liked the killing that he had done, but at the times he did it, it was what he thought of as self-defense and he now knew it wasn't. It wasn't something to glory in and have pleasure.

In a while they could hear the truck coming down the gravel road and they saw the dust that was picked up by the moving vehicle. Both of them picked up the largest rocks they could find and handle comfortably. Crouched down with their muscles twitching in anticipation, they were ready. "My God, forgive me, I don't want to kill again. I ask that if I must do this, it be for your name." The truck was almost by the tree on their right. They had decided this would be the best place to throw the rocks in front of the truck. They had picked up rocks that were large but manageable for throwing. Each of them was going to throw the rocks right before they arrived at the spot where they were hiding, on each side of the cab. The truck was speeding down the road. They were close enough to the men they could see their faces glow in the dash lights. "Go!" George shouted. They leaped up and at the same time the truck swerved as they were startled by the sudden appearance of the two men. The soldiers were momentarily stunned and didn't have time to react. The truck swerved off the road to avoid hitting the rocks in the road and they hit a tree and the truck crumpled as the soldiers were thrown forward. Neither one was wearing seat beats so they were thrown through the windshield. George and Jeremy ran over to them and to check on them They went on each side of the truck and opened the doors, dragging the soldiers out. Both of them were seriously hurt, with their faces broken with gashes that left their faces beyond recognition. "Should we leave them like this?" Jeremy asked.

"Those are really bad head injuries. If no one knows where to find them they won't survive very long without medical attention so let's get out of here. Let's go get the bodies of that couple and start on our way before it gets any later and our friends start to wonder about us."

The bodies the soldiers had tossed into the back of the truck where they were left lying in a crumpled heap. The men gently and reverently lifted them up and started back to the farm. They had to make frequent stops to rest. "If only we could have gotten here sooner," Jeremy said.

"They were meant to go home or we would have been able to save them," George answered. "They don't have to suffer anymore."

"The Devil gets the two who killed them. At least the streets are safer from them."

"It'd be great if we found those horses we used for the labor camp rescue."

A couple of miles down the highway and off in a pasture they found the horses. The horses were as docile as they had been before and as gently as they could, they put the bodies on the horses. They'd been walking for a while, when they were stopped suddenly by a rattling sound. The horses were nervous, walking the horses back slowly from the snake and waited, the snake finally slithered off without feeling the threat, it was gone. "Whew! That was close," George said letting out his breath he had been holding. "It must not have been to cool for it to have left as quickly as it did," Jeremy said.

"Too close,"

A few minutes later they knew why the snake had been in their path. Soldiers were walking down from the road, close the where they were going. The snake had kept them out of sight and diverted them from the eyes of the soldiers. "Why don't we back track and head across the road and go off into the brush on the other side. We are being watched over and given protection," George breathed. Keeping out of sight, they walked back and found a place where cars weren't visible on the road. They crossed over and walked into the grass and brush hoping the horses thudding hooves would keep the snakes away. They were making good time back to the bunker. As usual, Sam was out and about keeping the residents safe. He saw the two men and the horses. He went inside the bunker to let everyone know that George and Jeremy were back. As they waited for the men to get closer, they could see the bodies. "OH, no!" Joann gasped. "What happened?"

"We didn't get there in time and we watched as they were murdered for their stand for their beliefs. Their deaths were horrible. We had to watch as it..." George exclaimed, his voice trailing. He felt tears coming, so he stopped talking.

"I've been preparing graves for such a time that's all too common," Sam told them.

"Sam, you're doing great with all that you do!" Cindy told him.

"It feels good to be useful around here," Sam said.

The bodies were brought inside and the women were preparing them for burial and early the next morning as soon as breakfast was over the funeral was held with Dr. Perry giving the farewell speech.

The men of the bunker were working to keep everyone safe and food for them when one day George was helping butcher a cow they had killed when he heard a word being spoken about an upcoming event. "George, I am sending a severe drought to the land. I will give you extra food that you will need to store. Your water will be safe and I will keep your food from turning bad. I will be sending other Chosen Ones to you to preserve their lives."

George called everyone together to plan out how they could streamline the bunker and make use of their days. He talked to Cindy and she thought they should go to the farmhouse to get any extra shelves they could find around there and the barn. They could set up the shelves and move supplies into a section of the bunker where it was fairly cool and no one wanted to sleep and in there that it would be perfect for storage. With extra shelves, they could stack and move things higher and utilize the wall space more efficiently.

Lucy looked around and came up with a plan to move their clothes into one of the rooms that had empty wall space. Her plan was to use dividers so everyone had their own space. She saw that some of them could double up and they could have some extra rooms. It would make everything a bit tighter, but not uncomfortable.

Dr. Perry and Jacie rearranged their little clinic so they could sleep in there. It was decided to use a small room for incoming patients. The doctor was pleased when Jenny asked if she could help Jacie. "Jacie can teach you how to change a bandage and care for wounds. You were such a great help when we had those patients from the labor camp."

Sam went out with Jeremy to spend their days hunting. They found more of the wild growing herbs for Mariann. The men found some potatoes that no one even knew had been planted. It appeared they had been growing for quite a long time. Many more of the pleasant surprises were in store for them. Each day that went by they understood just how well protected and preserved they were being kept. He had told them he would take care of all they needed according to his riches in glory, even to the end of time and He had. They weren't able to survive without their full trust in Him.

Chosen Ones remained in hiding, but always going where they were sent, sometimes, some of them didn't return. They were kept busy with various missionary errands instilled in them. Many were scattered around the world, and small groups were growing as more non-believers converted. As they were led, they were saving some out of the Eternal Darkness. Chips were being taken out. Out in the world without the Chosen Ones, the nastiness of human evil and spiritual decay was spread. People were going to work each day, but getting sick and dying by afflictions that were caused by denying the Great Physician. Diseases without cures were creating havoc. Governments were blaming Chosen Ones for all the problems, that they were creating these diseases and spreading them to punish others for not joining their lifestyle. Non-believers refused to hold themselves accountable for their own behaviors and they were without hope.

CHAPER TWENTY-SIX

JEFF SHOWS UP AT THE BUNKER AND THEY BLOW UP AMMO FACILITY

"There will be a man who comes to you. He will be most unexpected, but welcome him."

They were busy keeping food and supplies ready. Jacie spent much of her time helping out with all chores to be done. Mariann and Joann were taking over much of the care of the residents in the bunker. The two of them had grown to be close friends. They had much of the same interests. Cindy called them chatter boxes, which they accepted with insincere glares, Cindy laughed.

Each morning the flakes were gathered outside. Mariann had become creative with turning them into various tasty dishes. Lucy was out and about and had found some herbs that had grown wild. She took them to Mariann who used them for the meals. There was a steady supply of meat that was sent to meet their needs. Sam had noticed animals taking over the property. He guessed the fences were down from neighboring farms. The broken fence was to their advantage to cover up their hiding place, as well. One morning Sam went out the door and he froze. He was looking at a soldier, in uniform, standing right in front of him by the door. His eyes, unlike other soldiers were soft and kind.

"I am sorry to startle you," he said.

"Welcome," Sam said.

"My name is Jeff and I'm now a believer. I'm ready to change. I was led to come here, that is how I found this place," he said.

"How can that be? You're a soldier."

"I didn't take the chip."

"How did you manage to have gone so long without a chip?"

"I have tried to do my job quietly; mostly I stayed away from my superiors as much as possible and have been over looked. I was a soldier long before the chips were required. My family was hiding me. They didn't know I didn't have one. I just kind of slipped through the system. They just found out that I didn't have one. I left to protect my family. By the way, this place is awesome!"

"Come on in and see how awesome it is inside."

When he walked in the residents there were standing and looking at him in disbelief. This was the guy? None of them were expecting a soldier to be the one sent to them.

"He's one of us. Don't worry." Sam informed them. Sam explained to them what had happened. "I tried to get as many of them killed as I could. They kill people all the time and I was trying to protect as many of the Chosen Ones as I could."

"Welcome!" He was greeted as if he was a long-lost friend.

"I have some things I need to get in here," he told them. "I took some guns from the other dead soldiers."

"We'll help," George said as Dr. Perry, Jeremy, and Sam headed for the door. They walked out and this soldier led them to his equipment. "May I ask you your names?" The others introduced themselves "Here we are," he said. "I know how to get into places average people could never get into. The security that's used isn't as complicated as you might think. No one with my unit even knows I'm missing. I left a trail so my family will think that I am dead. The trail won't lead anyone here."

"You may be very useful. We are very happy to have you here." Joann said. She proceeded to make him his own space.

"I'm ex-military. Nice to meet you," Sam said, as he shook Jeff's hand. "Jeff, tell us more about the information you have." He told them about some places where they stored equipment and how to get in to them, he could at least.

Joann told them about some Chosen Ones who she had been told needed their help. "A short distance from the shelter I ran I noticed some activity that I think may be some of our friends who have been creating a hiding place. They had been stopping by the shelter occasionally have been hearing on the news about additional patrols in that area. I am wondering if they are trying to find them." Joann said.

"We can blow up their ammo storage facility," Jeff said. "I know the exact time they'll be away from it. Since they don't see us as a threat, they don't guard it very well. We can distract them enough to get to that shelter to get them out of there."

"We need to have a plan to help us to succeed in this mission," Jeremy was saying. Jeff organized the plans for their way into town. He had so much inside information for making it happen. George knew stealth, Sam had keen eyes and Jeff had the ability and knew how the militia ran their operations. They were a great team. Getting explosives would be the tricky part but Jeff had a plan for that also. He had a key to get into the place where he had access to some explosives. If he kept his eyes covered, he could slip in and be out in no time. There were cameras monitoring the entire area but the guards were bored and didn't pay much attention. He also knew when the place would be vulnerable.

"I never thought much about security around here. Some places are on high alert but not here. Tomorrow you and Sam can go with me and we can check it out," George said. "Joann, tell us more about the location." The hiding place was in an unusual spot that wasn't very well hidden and she was surprised it hadn't been found already. Jeff was sure he knew exactly where it was and how to get the people out of there.

"Everyone needs to stay attentive to every detail for this to be pulled off smoothly," Sam informed them. They spent more time trying to

come up with possible scenarios they might encounter. After finalizing
the plans, they chose to eat and get to bed early for starting out before
the sun was up. As they were leaving the next morning Jenny gave Jeff
a kiss on his cheek that turned his face a bright red, and Jenny laughed.
They started off making good time into town. It was a way to get to the
place Jeff told them about. They had to duck the patrols. When they
got there, all of them became alert to possible trouble. They had to duck
down on a number of occasions before they came to an open field, and
crossed it. Since they were in the run-down side of town, mowing was
not done very often. Jeff told them to use caution but he was positive
that none of the guards were paying the slightest bit of attention. Still,
they were careful. Getting closer, Sam was keeping his eyes moving in
every direction. Creeping up to the gate, Jeff pulled his cap low over
his face; he went to the gate as if he had gotten orders to do so. George
and Sam stayed back to keep from arousing suspicions. Jeff went inside
leaving the gate unlocked but making it to appear as if he had locked it.
George and Sam watched him approach the building and he unlocked
it, disappearing inside.

Once Jeff got inside he saw a friend sitting at the desk. "Hi Jeff," he
said, "What are you doing?"

"I need to get some things for the commander," he replied.

"Sure thing, Jeff. Do you need any help?"

"No, just getting a couple of things."

He knew he had to hurry. He went to the back and grabbed the
explosives he needed. He threw some rope into a canvas bag to cover the
things he had that might lead to suspicions that he was taking. As he
went by his friend, he opened the bag to show him what he had.

"See you later, Joe." If he did, it wasn't going to be in a friendly way
that had just happened. George and Sam saw him casually walk out of
the building and towards the gate. He acted like he was unlocking it,
opened it, walked out, locked the gate, and headed towards them. It
helped that he was wearing his uniform. As he got close to them he said.
"Let's get out of here." Crouching low they took off as fast as they could
without visibility and noise, there were some military vehicles arriving

as they were leaving. Getting out of the range of the supply building they stopped to rest, "A friend of mine was at that desk, but he thinks I only grabbed rope." Opening the bag, he showed them. Thirty minutes later they were on the street where the shelter was located, Front Street. "There's the shelter, Joann said the place is right down the street. Look there are patrols, just as she said," Sam said. "I know where she was talking about."

"The ammo storage is right over there," Jeff said pointing to a seemingly abandoned building. "Let's go around and sneak to the back. All we have to do is get these explosives that will have a timer and throw it over the fence and we will have time to get out of here." Fifteen minutes later they were behind the building. "Go as fast as you can. These are already put together. I got the smaller bundles so we don't blow up everything around. Right now, there isn't as much ammo here since this is a distribution center and inventory is low. Collateral damage for them isn't a concern to me at all as it can't be avoided. Ready? Ok, quickly." They jumped up and ran to the fence. They had ten minutes to get out of there and they didn't waste a single second of it. Watching the time, they got down and covered their eyes and ears. The first explosion was loud but the next explosions they heard sounded like fireworks that needed to be seen and heard from miles away.

Lifting up their heads they could see the soldiers rushing over to see what was going on. The flames from the fire were shooting up into the sky. The three men took off for the place where the Chosen Ones were in hiding. They were trusting that the Voice would help them get to the right place. When they got there they were met by a man who looked at Jeff and thought things had gone wrong. Jeff knew what he was thinking, "We're here to help you. I'm one of the Chosen Ones. What do you need?"

"We got all of our stuff out of here but have not been able to leave. We're trying to get to another shelter. Can you help us?"

"Where is it?" Jeff asked.

"It is only a couple of miles from here and there are five of us. Will you help us?"

"Get them and we will go while the soldiers are busy with the explosions."

George went inside with him and rounded them up. There were two men and two women with a boy of about ten years old. "Can all of you walk?"

"Yes."

"We need to get moving or we'll risk detection." George said. Sam took off in the lead. George and Jeff surrounded the rescued to protect them the best they could. They had to go slow to avoid detection since they were moving away from the explosion as law enforcement departments were moving towards it and people were curious as to what had happened. News reporters who happened to be out driving around town started heading towards the explosion, which made them look suspicious if anyone were to see them. Sam was taking them away from well-travelled roads and streets to places less likely to have traffic headed towards the excitement and places that would offer better covering for their trip to safety.

Soon they met up with the contact person who was to take these Chosen Ones to safety, saying goodbye, they headed back to the bunker. Jeff gave them the run down on how he had managed to get the job done. They talked and were having a great time and they got back to the bunker in what seemed to be only a short time. It was late and the travelers were exhausted.

CHAPTER TWENTY-SEVEN

THE HUNTERS

Jeremy wandered over to the fence line and found several broken boards. That explained livestock wandering around near the bunker. He had seen deer in the area as well. They would be able to get a nice supply of meat. Just as he was turning around to head back, there was a cracking of a shot fired and he was hit, falling to the ground. He was conscious and writhing in pain. He saw two people walking towards him. They were dressed in hunters' attire.

"Are you all right?" one of them asked him.

"I don't know, I'm hurting," he managed to get out.

"I am so sorry, man; we thought you were a deer."

"We can take you to a hospital, if you want."

"No, my doctor friend will be here in a minute. He can take care of this. Thanks anyway."

"We can help to find him."

"He heard the shot, he'll be here soon."

"You sure?"

"Yeah, I'm sure," he moaned.

"Ok, we're out of here." Both of them were nervous and they took off in a hurry.

Sam was there before they were even out of sight. "You're bleeding; did one of them shoot you?"

"Yeah, it was an accident. They wanted to take me to a hospital. The colors of our clothes have a down side being out here."

"Here, let me help you up. Can you walk?"

"I think so." Sam helped him to his feet, Jeremy winced. He was bleeding from his left shoulder.

"Man, you're hurt. Let's get back in and have Dr. Perry look at you. This is not good."

Jeremy was going into shock so Sam was half dragging him along back to the bunker. As they got closer to the bunker Sam saw Jeff and yelled to him. Sam had heard the shot and was starting to go find out what it was. Jeff looked up and saw them. He came running over and put Jeremy's other arm around his shoulder and both of them got him inside.

"Dr. Perry, Jeremy was shot!" Sam shouted. "We need help!" Dr. Perry rushed over and guided them to put him on one of the exam tables. "Roll him on his side," he commanded, Jeremy winced with the pain. Dr. Perry started cutting away his shirt. The bullet had entered his shoulder but there wasn't an exit wound, it didn't look good. The bullet had pierced muscle and ligament.

Jacie came in and started cleaning the wound. "Jacie, give him a sedative and when that starts taking effect, I'll cut the bullet out of him. Jeremy, this is going to hurt, even with the sedatives. I need you to be as still as possible, you should start feeling better in a few minutes. I need to stop this bleeding."

"I understand, doctor. I'll do my best to stay still."

Jenny gathered the medical equipment they needed. She wasn't able to do any of the treatments, but she was giving the doctor and Jacie as much help as she could. Dr. Perry was getting ready to cut the bullet out when he was shocked to see the bullet was sliding out as if it were being pushed and all he had to do was take his medical tweezers and simply pull it up and out of Jeremy's shoulder. The wound needed stitches so Dr. Perry finished with cleaning the wound and stitched it up, Jeremy was not feeling the pain. "How bad is it?" Jenny asked him.

"He's going to be fine."

"I can't believe how easy that was to get out, it slipped out easily, and I have never seen anything like that before. It was as if it were being pushed out." Jacie, Dr. Perry, and Jenny looked at each other, and then turned to Jeremy with shocked faces. Without a question, Dr. Perry knew that Jeremy was going to recover without any serious side effects; he would have a scar he could brag about. An hour later, Jeremy was lying in bed. He moved with some pain but otherwise was doing well. Dr. Perry had given him a shot of antibiotics and pain meds, which had made him sleepy and he was sleeping quietly, he would be fine.

When the hunters returned to town, they were scared. They listened to police reports to see if that man had been reported dead. A week later, they didn't hear anything so they decided to go back to find out why. At the site where they had shot him, they didn't see any signs of his body. They crept up closer in the direction they thought he came from. Sam and Jeff were out doing some hunting. They saw the hunters approach and that they were going in the direction they had come from. They thought these were Chosen Ones so they were leaving to go into town to bring back the authorities to arrest the two they had found and possibly the others they believed to be out here somewhere. This time they felt they had hit the lottery. With the reward they would get, they were already making plans for spending their money. As they were rushing to their truck they were so busy spending the money that they were not paying attention to where they were going. In their hurry one of them stepped on a pile of loose rocks that was on the side of a large hole that had been dug for some unknown purpose. His ankle twisted and as he was falling he grabbed his friends's arm, causing both of them to tumble. They were falling and hitting rocks causing bruising with cuts and scrapes, possibly broken bones. When they finally landed at the bottom, to their horror, they found themselves in a pit of venomous snakes that were striking with fury for them intruding into their den. Within minutes, both men swelled up and quickly died. There were so many bites on them it was creepy with all the punctures. Jeff and Sam thought it was peculiar that they had not seen the snakes around, especially since they were constantly out hunting. They realized that they were being watched over.

Following behind, Jeff and Sam had been watching to see what the men were going to do; they watched as the men feel into the hole and the snakes striking them. Each one winced as they knew the fate of them. Going over to the hole, they threw some rocks in the hole to cover their bodies, the hole wasn't very deep but it was a dangerous one. They went to find the vehicle the men had come in and found it a little way away. "Let's use this truck to go where we are being sent," Jeff said. Sam checked to see if the keys were in it, and they were, he checked to see if the gas tank was full, it was. Earlier in he day they had been told to go somewhere to find one of the Chosen Ones who needed their help.

CHAPTER TWENTY-EIGHT

DON'S RESCUE

Sam and Jeff felt there was someone in dire need of being rescued. Neither one had any idea of where to go but went to see where they would be led. Going back to the bunker, Sam and Jeff gathered supplies. They packed food, water, and an extra set of men's clothes. "Hmmmm," Sam thought. Jeff was headed for the door and Sam followed, and they took off through the tall grass. As they walked by the hole where the two soldiers were buried, they looked and saw that flies were already buzzing about, and animals would arrive soon enough. Trekking to the truck, they checked to see if anyone was nearby. There wasn't so they walked to it. It was an older model truck that the owner took pride in keeping in good condition; it was dark blue and had been equipped for hunting. These guys must have been avid hunters; Sam wondered why they chose this area to hunt. They must not have been very smart to have gotten themselves killed the way they did.

Jeff got in to start the truck and he found that the truck owner had left the keys in the ignition dangling, both of them were relieved they didn't have to go to the bodies of the men to retrieve them from the pocket of the owner, neither one wanted that job. Jeff started it and it was purring. Sam got in and since they had to go over rough terrain they had to drive slowly and carefully looking for good places to travel so as not to tear up the truck. They headed in the direction of town going through the fields off the highway; they avoided houses and places that had the appearance of being occupied. Jeff drove to the dry river bed where he had to find a place to cross. Sam kept a watch while Jeff navigated the rocks and holes. Sam spotted a place that looked promising and Jeff stopped as they evaluated the place, it seemed safe so Jeff drove slowly and eased the truck over it trying to stay on the flat rocks and the truck held up nicely. The middle of the river had gravel and silt. Easing through it, they got to the other side without breaking down or getting stuck. Jeff gave a sigh of relief.

"I am not sure the shock absorbers on this truck are going to survive this tip," Sam said. Jeff was thinking the same thing.

Going was slow and methodical but they finally came to the edge of town. They had to navigate dirt roads and fences, it was problematic at times but they did it. Stopping, they were trying to figure where they needed to go, Jeff turned right, driving at a slow speed. In a rundown place, he made a left turn and drove along until he came to an alley that had a pile of large card board boxes that had been used for shipping major appliances, braking, driving at a crawl down the alley they saw one of the boxes move as they got out and approached it. The saw a man in the box and he was looking up at them as he was lying on his left side, he was emaciated and weak. "Need help, friend?"

"You want to help me? Everything I had was stolen and I have been left here to die."

"We have been sent here to help you, what is your name?"

"Don."

"I am Jeff and this is Sam. We are Chosen Ones."

"I am too. I didn't take the microchip; homeless people are ignored and I haven't been able to find food since I got sick. Other people have been taking whatever food I so get. I have been begging for help and have been feeling helpless."

"Lift up your eyes to the hills and know where your help comes from," Sam told him.

"That is what I heard a while ago, as I have been here waiting."

"We are here to take you with us. Are you ready to go?" Don nodded. Jeff got on one side of him and Sam got on the other as they lifted him up and helped him get into the truck, Sam drove this time as Jeff got out the food and water. Most of his clothes had been stolen off his body, he had no shoes on so they helped him with the things they had brought with them, the clothes were loose on his thin frame but the shoes were a perfect fit. As soon as they had him dressed, Sam started the truck to get them out of here, they hadn't seen anyone about and thought maybe something was going on around town that had people's attention, they hadn't been listening to the radio so neither one knew but they were thankful for the quiet. Sam eased out of the other end of the alley and saw no one so he started back, he took a different route home than the one they had come into town on and saw why they had gone the way they did.

The law enforcement officers had the road blocked and were searching everyone who came through. Sam turned in another direction to go back the way they had come, he was carefully watching to make sure they weren't being followed, which they weren't.

Jeff was giving Don some food to eat to fill his stomach and water to quench his thirst. Sam glanced at him and he figures he was about forty-five years old. "What kind of job did you have?" Sam asked him.

"I was a warehouse manager with a good company when the chips were required I had to quit my job. My wife had gone to her sisters and had been gone for such a long time. She called me and asked if I had gotten my chip yet. I told her no and she said I needed to get it before the time expired or I would be picked up and arrested. At that time, she had just gotten one so I knew I was in trouble. I had accepted the Voice but she thought He was ridiculous and refused to believe in Him. Before she left she had told me to change my ways or she wouldn't come home. I told her I wasn't going to change so I haven't seen her since. I have been by our house several times and have seen patrols watching it carefully so I am sure she is counting on the reward she would get for turning me in. I had read about what happens to people who don't take the chip. I look the part of a homeless person so it has been easier for me to keep from getting caught. My wife was the cause of my children's deaths. Her drinking and partying ways were the result of a crash was caused. One night she was driving home after having picked them up from the baby sitters after she stopped at a bar with some of her work friends for some drinks. She was so drunk that she didn't know the kids were dead until the next day and even then she didn't seem to care too much. In the crash, she came through it without a scratch." He had a sad look on his face and Sam and Jeff gave him a reassuring pat on the shoulder.

Up ahead Sam saw some soldiers walking around stopping vehicles so he chose an off road that was barely there and drove along it far enough away from the road they had been on to get off into the pastures behind farm houses. One thing he took into consideration was making traceable tracks. The ground was dry so it was easier. There were some rocky places that would hide tire tracks so he took that route. At an open area, up ahead was a herd of cattle that a man on horseback was herding so Sam drove in a wide circle around him, he was having to go a long way around and with the truck bouncing around, he was worried about how it was affecting Don, he seemed to be handling it well. With food in his stomach he had improved and was chatting with Jeff.

Severe drought conditions were a concern and Sam hoped the truck wouldn't cause a fire. It was Jeff who noticed some teenaged kids riding horses through the thick dense grassy fields, he also saw them smoking cigarettes, "Oh, oh," he said. The kids were laughing and showing off for each other when they watched as one of them threw his cigarette on the ground and they took off on their horses oblivious to the danger. And as if on cue, the wind picked up, smoke was curling around them as the fire started, it was between them and in the direction they were going. Sam stopped as they needed to figure out a way around it, they needed to go in a big hurry as the fire was spreading rapidly. He hit the accelerator, causing Jeff and Don to bump their heads hard enough to have to put their hands up to protect them. Sam tried to out run the fire by driving where there wasn't any smoke, the river was up within a quarter of a mile and he made a dash for it as he found a good place to get across. There wasn't much grass in the river so it was safer and he could slow down, looking over his shoulder he saw the fire was taking over everything behind them, houses weren't far away. Thankfully, the ride back was less eventful, barring the bumps they had to endure.

By the time they had gotten to the bunker, Don was doing much better. Jeff and Jeremy took him inside where he was made right at home. He would need more care to fully recover but he was in good hands. Sam went out to return the truck to where they had found it. He left the window down in the same way that it was originally when they had found it parked there. He checked to make sure he hadn't missed anything, satisfied all was as it should be, including wiping fingerprints off of it, he walked back to the bunker. He went by the hole where the bodies were, animals had already started tearing them apart. He didn't realize soldiers would be coming to look for them and would find them soon.

In the bunker, Don was being cleaned up and tended to as he was being animated and making everyone laugh; He was nothing like when they had first encountered him he was younger looking than he had first thought. George was talking about where to send him when it was time.

A couple of weeks later as Don were recovering as he should and he was ready to go out to a shelter. For someone who was close to death, he was energetic and enthusiastic. George found him interesting and spent time talking with him. Don was a very down to earth kind of man who had magnetism about him that George thought would be useful to the town of Maple Wood. He was a funny guy who made them all laugh, between him and Lucy; it was a constant comedy show. George was having second thoughts about sending him off; he didn't want to be self-serving so he reluctantly chose to send him for he greater good, sigh.

Plans were to find out what Don could do and find out if Maple Wood would be the right place for him. George worked with him and he discovered he was a multi-talented man. Sam and Jeremy took him out to get him trained in survival, he taught them a few things as well. Dr. Perry wanted to give him some basic training, just in case. Don was a good student, if not for any other reason, being around him was fun. Time slipped by and it was time to get him where he could be serving his purpose. Maple Wood was struggling and needed help, he knew where it was so he worked on getting ready to go, it was a nice little town, getting there would take a couple of days to get there. Uncertain about what lay between where they were and Maple Wood, he wasn't sure about, but that was where he was needed.

On the day he was to leave for Maple Wood all the friends got together for a farewell party for Don, he was such a good part of the family; he was going to be greatly missed. They all gathered around him to give him hugs. Each one remembered how he was when he first came to them, barely alive, and now he was fully recovered and displaying great energy and inner strength, he had humility with a beautiful sense of humor. There were times when some of them were sent out to the different shelters so some would see him again and some would only see him in the eternal life, either way it would be a pleasure. As he walked away, they stood watching him go, he turned to wave.

He was feeling good, he was singing to himself as he walked along, the friends had warned him about the dangers he would possibly encounter along the way, being cleaned up he would most likely be harmed if found as opposed to looking homeless. The walk for a while was uneventful until the evening started drawing near, he was staying away from open areas as much as he could, and he heard some loud talking near a grove of trees where there must have been a large group of men. Military, he moved towards some large boulders to watch, sure enough, he had come across a training camp. What he noticed was that they were drinking and he thought it was beer. Why would they be training and out here drinking? He was thinking they had some time off from whatever they were doing and one of them had gone out and got several cases to relax, not what their commander would have approved of, wherever he was. Don stayed where he was to watch.

After a while he was thinking about getting out of there to find a place to make camp when he noticed the men were laying down to sleep and no one was on guard. 'That's interesting,' he thought. 'Those soldiers are drunk.' He started moving closer to the camp; and as he did he noticed things he might find useful. As it started getting dark the soldiers were wiped out cold, still Don moved cautiously into the midst of them, and not a one of them stirred, he moved around boldly, keeping his eyes on them. He found some knives that might come in handy, a cot that hadn't been unpacked, some extra clothes, boots, and some food, all of which he carried out with him. A way away from their camp he stopped and looked back, no movement. Now he had to decide how he was going to carry all this stuff, while thinking about it, he heard a sound of a motor, and as the sound got louder he looked up and saw a helicopter in the distance, he grabbed the stuff and dragged it towards a tree close by, he was hoping they weren't using infrared goggles, if they were, he was in trouble.

The helicopter landed close to the camp where the soldiers were sleeping up until that moment as some of them were stirring from their drunken stupor. Don heard shouting from who he was assuming was an officer. Time to get out of there, soon they would discover their missing equipment and figure out someone had been in their camp that wasn't authorized and would come looking for him. Having gotten all the equipment assembled, he grabbed it and left in the direction of Maple Wood, no sleep for a while, at least. He could hear the shouting continuing as he put distance between himself and the camp. He had a smile on his face and his heart was merry. Juggling the equipment on his back to get more comfortable, he managed with the extra weight and bulk. Stars in the sky were magnificent as was the full moon, it was a glorious night, the walk was invigorating and he didn't think he could sleep even if he did stop.

As dawn arrived, he started yawning as his steps slowed; he found a place where he would sleep for a while. Soon he was sound asleep. When he woke up the sun was high overhead with scurrying of small animals. He sat up stretching and yawning, he was wanting to sleep some more but he needed to get to Maple Wood, as he was picking up his load, he heard a vehicle driving somewhere nearby, he pulled the gear closer. It was two of the soldiers in a jeep, it might be them coming to find him, he stayed hunkered down and out of sight, they were looking and he wasn't feeling secure, he stayed still until they drove away and only then did he dare move. With a deep sigh, he was able to get away to a safer place. Moving along under a canopy of trees to find a safe spot he heard the rotors of another helicopter and he knew they were out to find him. This time he planned to make a covering and sit where he was until dark and then move quickly towards Maple Wood.

The situation was more serious than he thought, and as he thought about it, this was a security risk. He wondered what was going to happen to the drunken soldiers; he shuttered to think about them. What he took wasn't the problem; they didn't know if he had gotten any secret information, most likely they would kill him if they caught him. This was not anything he had thought about. His road was not a safe one, right then he wished he hadn't entered that camp, as he thought about it, there was a reason, even a lesson in it having happened. By afternoon he was getting antsy, but he had to hang in there patiently, that wasn't his strength. He did stay and he was thankful that he did. When it was dark enough to move, he came upon a battalion of soldiers, if he had moved any earlier, he would have been caught. He had to go a distance to move around them to get away, he did.

Walking all night with a need to get to Maple Wood he was going as fast as he could. The new day was breaking, he came to Maple Wood. He stopped where he could hide. Taking out some food and water to wait out and know what his next move was, he saw a rabbit and had a strange feeling he needed to follow it. It was a strange thought but he followed it lugging his load, he was having trouble keeping it in sight, he managed to, which left him breathless. After a while he came to a place that seemed odd, the rabbit was gone. Moving around looking very closely at where he was, he was jarred from his search by a voice behind him. "Hi, what are you looking for?"

"I am here to help Chosen Ones. I have been sent."

"We have been expecting you so I am here to meet you, my name is Will," he shook Don's hand.

"I am Don. I have had an adventure getting here." Don lowered his equipment as he told Will about how he had acquired it. "I was sure I was caught for a while, they may be still looking for me. As you can see, this hide out is hard to find," Will told him as they climbed rocks and made their way through some possible snake ridden places, when he saw an opening to a cave that was cleverly hidden he was amazed.

"I see why this is a good hiding place," Don said. "What can I do for you here?"

"We would like to be taught how to better serve the Voice and learn about the Book; we have one."

"I can help you do that and other things. Before I left the shelter I was in, I learned things that I want to teach you."

"Come on inside and meet the other nineteen people. We are a small group."

"I came from a small group, even smaller than this one. They train people and send them out to other shelters. I was one they rescued, I was nearly dead when they found me and now I am in the service for the Voice."

"You are welcome here. Anyone following you will have a hard time finding you here. I will post a guard to watch for anyone prowling around through here." Will took Don inside the cave and was surprised by how nice it was. Chosen Ones sure were clever, and the residents there were studying the Book when he walked in and they looked up to see him. Getting to their feet, they were greeting and welcoming him; he was glad he had come to this place. "May I join you?" he asked them.

"Yes, please do!" was their response.

"What are you studying?"

"What do we need to do?"

"Allow the Voice to lead and guide us to direct you in the way you should go. It is easy to think we know what the best is for our lives, we can only see a very small part of our lives, and the Voice can see the past, present, and the future. We think we know more than we actually can. The Spirit leads us down the road that is best for us as opposed to finding the easy road that we want to take. We are Chosen Ones because we want what He knows is for our own good and to serve him making Him number one over everything. The Spirit is here at the bidding of

the Voice. The Spirit intercedes for us before the Voice for each of us."
Don explained. Maple Wood was full of questions.

All the community wanted to learn and Don was having fun with
his new responsibilities, he took on a leadership role that he hadn't
anticipated, first thing he wanted to do was find out what each person
had to contribute to the survival of all. This was a place where the people
were quieter and went about doing their work without saying much;
they were a group who worked well together because they knew each
other and seemed to know what the other were thinking. Don made
them laugh and consequently they were loosening up to tell him about
themselves. He felt like a part of the big picture here. Soldiers were still
out patrolling, looking for him, the posted guard had spotted them. The
patrols must have found a sign of him being in this area since they were
staying close by. Abandoned buildings around here left them suspicious
so they were staying. People here were staying close to the cave and were
watching very closely. Don didn't believe they were trying to get their
equipment back, something else was going on and he wanted to find
out what it was.

Will found him and they were talking about it. "From what you have
told me, I am thinking the same thing," he said. "I have a bad feeling
about this. We can go to find out what is happening."

"I think so too."

"Come inside so we can get you settled in and we will talk to the
others about it. First thing we need to do is to wait for guidance."

"You are learning well, only the Spirit can make our steps secure."

"After you," and they went inside. Boulders were all around, which
made hiding better. Will knew the way through the obstacle course so
Don could only hope he came through without any bruises; in the dim
light he managed to get through once his eyes adjusted. They came to a
place deeper in the cave where all the other people were assembled and
were working to get their living quarters organized. Don was impressed.
Even if someone came close to the entrance to the cave it was hard to see
with the large boulders disguising the entrance with only small places
where it could be entered, and then a person had to navigate around the

brush that grew there naturally. It was a miracle that it had even been found.

"Let me show you where you get to sleep." Everyone had already chosen their places so Don was surprised when he had a spot that he really liked.

"Why don't we have a meeting?"

"It would be good for us to let you know about a problem we may be facing."

"I would like for everyone to stop what they are doing so Don and I can discuss something with you," Will said raising his voice to be heard, the cave walls absorbed sounds so that loud voices and sounds were muffled. "There are some soldiers patrolling and we think something is going on other than for the reason of Don taking a few things from them, we are going to go out to find what is going on with the troops." They were talking amongst themselves discussing it. All activity stopped and they assembled before the men. "We will be lead and know what we need to do."

"We are going out and the rest of you will need to take care of things in here, do not go outside." Will had told them.

Outside, they headed up to where the soldiers were roaming around. They were a small group and Will and Don were close enough to hear them talking. "Whoever took that knife came in this direction, he seems to have disappeared. We need to find him; we are supposed to stay until his trail is picked up again. If we are found out, we will be shot on the spot." Don and Will looked at each other, quietly they crept back to the cave unnoticed, once inside Don went to his stash and was digging through the stuff he had. Up until this moment, he didn't know what all he had picked up, and when he went into the camp he moved quickly. Will helped him pull out all the knives. There were knives to serve all kinds of purposes and some that were interesting, and not sure what they were looking for, they started examining the handles. Don came across one that seemed different, and Will helped him check it out. If they hadn't known there was a secret to one of them, they would have just admired them. As they were turning it one way and then the other when Don noticed a very tiny notch on the end of it. At first, he thought it was a nick from careless handling and didn't pay much attention. "See if one of the ladies have a hair pin she might let us borrow," Don suggested. Will left and came back a minute later with one while Don kept trying to open it. Finally it opened, but not very easily, and it took manipulating the pin before it did open. The whole bottom came open with a soft pop; this was a very well planned hiding place.

"Look! There is a paper inside," Will said. Don pulled it out and unfolded it, and saw it was a map of the dam that was upstream from them. This was peculiar, or so they thought until they noticed some other papers in the handle of the knife. Pulling them out and spreading them flat, they saw some notes about blowing up the dam and flooding the territory below it. This was a unit who were criminals in uniform. It was looking like a heist, no wonder they were out searching for him, and he stole their master plan. The equipment they were using was stolen. They had to be stopped or Chosen Ones were going to be killed. They were going to have to hurry. "Get back to the cave!" Will was saying. They left and made their way back to the cave. Soldiers were milling around and getting close to the hidden men. Sitting down they started getting the Holy Spirit to tell them what to do. Some of the soldiers were sleeping, some were standing around bored and weren't paying attention as they should have been. In the cave they discussed what was happening with the friends about the soldiers right outside and at the top of the hill above them. As they were talking, there came a voice who told them to wait for the sound of marching feet that sounded as if the army were surrounded, and then attack.

After it started getting dark Will and Don left the cave and went around and circled the thieves as they were setting up camp. The soldiers ate and were bored and restless. They started getting rowdy as some of them were drinking and becoming obnoxious. The Chosen Ones were watching and waiting when they heard what sounded like marching all around them and so did the soldiers, it was the signal. The Holy Spirit had told them to wait for the sound like marching feet and they were to rush out as if an army was coming against them. The Chosen Ones who had been in the cave were in waiting and when they heard the marching feet they rushed out as one. The soldiers stood in fear as they saw the men rushing toward them, the sound was getting louder and with the impending darkness, they dropped everything and ran for their lives. The marching was loud until all the soldiers were long gone, then the only sounds were those made by the men taking over the camp and the sounds of the night. As they were going through the camp, they found military type equipment, food, drinks, and all the personal articles the men had brought with them, including their clothes. They gathered everything together to take back with them. The families left at the cave had come out to watch when the camp was overtaken and when it was time they came out into the camp to collect the loot. The Book was coming to life and great understanding and wisdom was planted in their lives. Will and Don were a team of leaders who were admired and respected as they taught and led.

Don had found his home and he was happy.

CHAPTER TWENTY-NINE

THE LOCUSTS

The drought had become a reality as conditions in areas in the world were suffering from the seriousness of the weather as it was causing hurt and suffering for many. The bunker was stocked and ready for it; the men went out and hunted until finding animals was becoming scarce. They were discussing calling it a day when they heard a faint buzzing that was rapidly growing louder. They looked up at the sky on the horizon and saw a strange dark cloud coming their way. There was no thunder or lightning and it was only blowing in without any wind to signs of rain. Locusts were flying around them and they were swatting at them. These locusts were large and were vicious and they were about four inches long and two inches in diameter. Up close they were quite loud as they were diving at the men as if they were angry. The numbers of them were increasing and the cloud was quickly descending upon them as the locusts were filling the air, the buzzing was a roar by then. "Get to the shelter! These critters are trying to hurt us!" George shouted above the roar. They ran the quarter of a mile back to the bunker. They made it to the bunker without being bitten. A few of the insects had come in with them and they were quickly caught and killed. It was a curious thing about them as they were looking at them, "I have never seen anything like this," Joann said

In the morning as they were waking up they were getting ready for breakfast and Mariann had turned on the radio as the news came on announcing the strange event of the previous day. The unusually large swarm of locusts of the size that they were was baffling, no one could explain where they came from, why they were of the massive size, the aggressiveness of them, or why they mysteriously died. Sam went to the door and slowly opened it and stepped out, "There are dead locusts all over the place out there," he said as he came back inside. The radio announcer was saying there had been massive crop damage as a result of the infestation. The damage appeared to have affected certain places and not everyone had the same experience with the creatures. There were people who had been hospitalized with bites from them and some bites were deep and infections had set in, some died as a result of the severity of their bites as some were out and away from help and they were attacked mercilessly. The insects were highly aggressive and entomologists were collecting specimens for study. The swarm was inexplicable.

After breakfast, all of them went out to see what it was like outside. It was a bizarre sight that was before them. There were dead locusts covering the ground. The difference was in their part of the world the vegetation hadn't been touched and none of them had been bitten. Already birds and other scavengers were busy cleaning up the untidiness of the massive mess. The plague was over and the problem was being taken out of their hands.

In the dark world, the dark spirits were discussing the plague. "He sent locusts! He's killing our people and protecting His own. This cannot be happening!"

The Exalted Dark One replied, "It is, He is destroying everything we've worked for. He will kill off many of the ones we have claimed as our souls. The Voice is punishing them, and the Chosen Ones are living in protection. I saw some of them; they live in an underground bunker. They were caught in the middle of a massive swarm. None of them were bitten." The Exalted Dark One kept a calm demeanor but inside he was panicked. The End would come and it wasn't looking good. The Voice simply would not give up on the sad, pathetic humans. Why did he want them so badly? He tried to reach every one of them.

CHAPTER THIRTY

JEFF

As the drought continued, hardships of daily life were getting worse. Jeff was in the bunker one afternoon, feeling down. Even Lucy, trying as hard as she could, wasn't able to cheer him up. Joann was worried about him.

"What's wrong, Jeff?" He didn't say anything for a minute, he had his head down. "I want to talk to my parents, to see if they're ok."

"Maybe we can find a phone somewhere."

"I can go into town."

"Take someone with you, dear."

"I wonder if George would go?" he asked.

"Go where?" George asked as he came in from outside at that moment.

"Jeff wants to call his parents and he needs to find a phone."

"Sure, I'll go with you. You ok with going in the morning? I need to help Jeremy and Sam in finding food tonight."

"Thank you." Jeff was already feeling better. He went outside to help get food with the other guys. They had a cow and some birds to dress. He'd learned so much about the jobs they did every day. He found the routine relaxing, even though times were tough. He felt stronger than he ever had in his life. He and Jenny spent time together talking, as they got along very well and had gotten close. Whenever possible, they went for walks together. She was a delightful person, down to earth, a good listener, and beautiful. Her smile made Jeff feel like a soft marshmallow.

"Thank you for your help, Jeff," Jeremy told him.

"No problem, man."

"Come on George, let's get cleaned up. Mariann will skin us alive if we don't get cleaned up before we track stuff inside." Jeff was chatting happily during dinner. It was a relief to see the change. George was glad he'd agreed to go with him. The teasing and laughing during the evening ended with Jeremy getting his guitar and playing it as they sang songs that were funny and silly making the evening fun and enjoyable.

The younger women got up and were dancing around the room. It was hard to resist joining in, the rest of them just had to get up and join in with them. It got sillier after a while. Laughing so hard they were crying, they left for their beds still laughing. Eventually, they settled down enough to fall asleep.

Groggy and rubbing his eyes the next morning and stretching his arms, Jeff got up with the smells of breakfast drifting throughout the bunker. His stomach rumbled with hunger. He heard George talking to Mariann. Yawning, he walked into the kitchen.

"Good morning," Mariann chirped.

"Have your breakfast and we'll get going. Our packs are ready to go." George told him. Breakfast was very filling and as always, was good. Eating slowly, savoring every bite and thinking about what he wanted to say to his parents, he finished up. Taking his dishes to the kitchen and kissing Mariann on the cheek, he walked to the door, picked up his pack and he and George were out the door. The first thing they noticed upon leaving the bunker was the dark clouds on the horizon. It looked like rain, and the weather report forecast a thirty percent chance. Rain gear had been included in their packs. Joann was a saint. They hadn't seen any drones in a while, but they stayed alert for them anyway.

"Looks like rain," George observed. "If we hurry, we may not get caught up in it."

Walking faster, they saved on time away from the bunker. A slight breeze began blowing but it was still a warm day. Passing behinds several homes, they moved further back from habitation to avoid detection from possible detection as them being possible trespassers, which they were. Those homes had always appeared to be vacant but they still didn't want to take any unnecessary chances.

"I heard there's a family living about three miles from here who are always traveling. Maybe we can use their phone," George suggested.

"I think we should do that." They took off at a steady jog, and reached the house in half an hour. Scanning the area, they watched to determine if anyone was at home. They couldn't see movement, but that didn't mean there wasn't anyone being inside the house. Everything appeared to be locked up tight. Looking through windows they didn't see anyone, some of the furniture was covered as if the occupants were planning on being gone for a while. George went looking for a spare key and found one under a rock in one of the flower beds.

"Bingo!" George exclaimed. He opened the door and they slowly entered. The phone was in the kitchen and Jeff dialed his parent's number. Please pick up, he thought. Please, please pick up.

"Hello." His mother answered.

"Mom!"

"Jeff, hi, where are you?"

"Don't worry, mom. I'm safe."

"We need to talk."

"Did you turn me in?"

"No, that's why we need to talk. Do you remember our special spot? Meet us there. We have good news for you."

"Ok, mom. Love you."

"Love you too, sweetie. See you soon."

The phone call had been monitored. Jeff had thought he had heard a soft click and a buzzing sound on the line while he was talking to his mom, and he didn't think he had been on the line long enough to have the call traced. He wasn't planning on staying long enough to find out. He didn't realize that soldiers were on their way to the house they were in and they were planning on following his parents, too. He wanted to see his parents, knowing that it would be risky, but he needed to see his parents anyway. He was missing them. He wanted them to know he was ok.

Jeff was suspicious. "George, we need to get out of here right now." Out the door they went, George locked it and put the key back where he had found it. Hastily, they took off. Jogging, George followed Jeff in the direction to where the special place his mother had mentioned. It was a park with a large man-made lake in the center. There were oak trees that overcast the picnic tables. The family went there when Jeff was young. He still loved the place. It was a memory from times long ago, when life wasn't so complicated. The terrain they were running through was rough with lots of large rocks and gravel, the land was rough in itself with the ups and downs they were running on. They stumbled along without getting themselves hurt but they were having to slow down so they wouldn't get hurt, if they slipped they might tumble down the water torn gulley's, maybe breaking bones and getting plenty of scrapes and bruises. They made good time and managed to get into town safely with a minute of two of rest along the way. They could slightly see the highway and saw some vehicles racing back towards the house they had just left. They looked at each other, grateful they had left as quickly as they had. Soldiers converged on the house the men had left. "They didn't stay very long," the commander said. "Spread out and we will see if we can catch them. Jeff is AWOL. He may be one of the Chosen Ones. We have no record of him taking the chip and he wasn't turned in. Find him and take him out."

Since the special place wasn't specifically mentioned, the commander and his unit of soldiers didn't know where to look, but his parents were being watched. As they were getting ready to leave, his father, Henry, saw the soldiers.

"Torry, do you still have those costumes we wore to that fundraiser costume party?"

"They are in the hall closet, why?"

"We need them before we can go out. How fast can you get made up?"

"Give me a few minutes."

Twenty minutes later, they were in their costumes and were quite convincing in their characters. Torry looked like a homeless lady who was mentally deficient as she was mumbling to herself. She had a blue-gray wig on that was shoulder length and wild looking. The shoes she was wearing were in appearance of shoes that had long ago worn out the welcome as modern day attire, the knee length stocking she wore were rolled down at the top and went nicely with the dress she had on. The dress was dark blue with large pink flowers on it and it came to the middle of her calves. The dress had extra padding in it to make her look like she was too decrepit to get around easily with extra weight she appeared to be carrying. As she walked she hobbled from side to side like it was painful for her to walk and with the look of pain on her face, it was believable. Henry was dressed in some ancient pants that had some bold stripes on a background of chocolate brown and the shirt he was wearing was a sky blue one that was faded and had worn thin with a wide collar and lapel. He had orthopedic shoes on of a scuffed dark brown color; the laces in them were frazzled and had been around for a number of years. Torry had padded the back of his shirt to give him a hunched overlook, with him leaning forward significantly, it was working. When they had worn the costumes for the fund raiser the committee raved about how much money the two of them had helped to raise. They were incredibly good with their characters. The makeup was heavy and had transformed their faces into people twenty years older than the two of them actually were, their eyebrows were heavy and it was fun for her to wiggle them at him, she had even blackened their teeth and she was intentionally flashing Henry a funny smile, Henry only rolled his eyes and laughed. Torry shuffled the upper portion of the padding, which made Henry laugh and she was caught up with the humor.

They were ready to go and headed for the back door. Henry made sure the doors were locked and he opened the back door, checking to see if he saw anyone lurking about. He left the lights on in the interior of the house and the outdoor lights were left off. The coast was clear as far as he could see. He took Torry's hand and they walked to the back gate, opened it, peered down the alley, and they stepped out into it. Quickly, he closed the gate. Hobbling down the alley they went from dumpster to the next dumpster peering in as if looking for food or anything of value they could use or sell.

"Mr. Spencer cleaned out his garage again." Torry remarked, Henry laughed.

"That man has too much stuff for his own good."

Henry saw soldiers at the end of the alley. "Keep looking through the dumpsters. There are eyes on us," he said.

"Grab something out of there that Mr. Spencer threw in there. We need to look real," She pulled out some pants that she held up for his approval; they were being boring to the onlookers. The soldiers were convinced they really were homeless people, so they moved on.

"This is a cheap way to get clothes. Let's do it again sometime." Torry was enjoying the moment, in spite of the danger. Moving on they checked each dumpster as they made their way down the alley. Hunched over as if they were old and crippled, they were believable to anyone who would be watching them. They made their way to the park, lugging their dumpster finds.

Torry saw two men enter the park, one with Jeff's significant walk and the other one she didn't recognize, but he was a big guy. Both of them had what appeared to be clothes they had gotten out of the dumpster. The only way she recognized Jeff was by his walk. She and Henry hobbled over to them, still in character. Eyes were everywhere, and they didn't want to risk breaking character. Looking at Jeff she recognized his eyes.

"Jeff, my baby." She said quietly. Her arms were stretched toward Jeff in a manner that appeared feeble and as she did she fell into him and she hugged her son.

"Mom! I'm so glad to see you! Are you ok?" He was staring at her, not believing what he was witnessing, they were strange looking, he understood why they did it and he appreciated the effort. He gave her a big tight hug. He'd been worried about her.

"They're watching us," Henry said. Torry was acting like she was going to fall down, so the others helped her over to a bench.

"Mom, are you all right?"

"Fine, fine. I am just staying in character so the soldiers won't suspect anything. We don't want them coming over here, now do we?"

"Jeff, we thought you were dead. It is so good to see you, son. We need to talk quickly. Our Savior has been talking to us for a while. Since we saw you last, we took the chip and now we want to have it taken out. We were wrong and He has forgiven us. What can we do?"

George answered, "I'm George, a friend of Jeff's. I came with him to ensure his safety. We do have a doctor who can help. You won't be able to come with us since you can be tracked, which is why we'll all need to leave in a minute. He can meet you and take it out. The best option is to meet in two weeks at a place on the outskirts of town and the procedure would be done at our meeting place." George had given them the directions to get them to the house where they were too meet. They said good-bye and casually went their own ways as if they had only run into each other randomly. Leaving to go back home, they hobbled to stay in character all the way back to their house, going back the same way they'd left. No one was in the alley so they dashed through the gate and into the house as soon as they were inside the gate and closed it behind them and the coast was clear of any possible drones. Just as soon as they got back into their regular clothes, the doorbell rang. Henry went to answer it.

"May I help you?" he asked the soldiers standing there. He looked to be about twenty years old. "There has been some criminal activity around here so we were just checking on citizens to make sure everyone is ok."

"Who is it, Henry?"

"This nice soldier is just checking on us."

"You are such a nice young man!" she gushed, attempting to keep her composure as best as she could.

"Can we get you something?" Henry asked.

"No sir. You have a good day," and he was gone.

"Whew! That was close," she said.

Over the next couple of weeks Henry made sure the soldiers knew they were at home so he did things like opening the garage doors and worked on projects so that he was visible with Torry making appearances as well with her gardening and outdoor projects. They worked in the yard, opened and closed the drapes, turning lights on and off. They repeated their vigorous activities over the duration of the two weeks. They could barely contain themselves. They'd be free soon.

After a week, the soldiers gave up their surveillance, figuring they'd disowned their son. Patrols had watched around their house and everything looked normal, the couple even worked outside their home, like most residents of that neighborhood did.

The soldiers had seen some old homeless people in the park, who were approached by two other men. They had helped her sit down. They had sent a plain clothes soldier over to check them out and found they were just some senile old people. She was carrying some old clothes, another eye sore, people like that needed to be eliminated.

They had been married for six years when a woman, Sydney, from Henry's past had found him, after not seeing each other for several years. The two of them had been quite an item when they were in college, and everyone in their social circle believed they would be graduating and marry, with jokes that they'd live in the suburbs with munchkins running around. She was the cute cheer leader and he the star athlete. They were together every chance their busy college schedule allowed.

Graduation for Henry arrived and they made a promise to each other that they would get together as often as possible after she graduated. After she finished college they planned on getting married. For a while, it worked out as they planned, but Henry's job took him away for long periods of time. He worked long hours, and eventually there was a distance that grew between them. The time came when they didn't see each other anymore. When she graduated, she accepted a job offer where she, too, worked long hours. It passed the time while she waited for Henry, but she waited for him and he never contacted her. Henry met Torry at his job, where she was working in the front office, and he married her. They had marital bliss after three years of dating and had a beautiful wedding. The wedding was the perfect event and was the dream and as grand as every bride could wish for, and their life together was happy.

Two years into their marriage, their son Jeff was born. They agreed that Torry would work from home to raise their new son and not use daycare to raise him, and it worked perfectly for them. One afternoon, while Henry was working, the old girlfriend who would have been came into Henry's office. "A little birdie told me you were here. I asked around about you."

"Have you been looking for me?"

"One of your school mates told me where you were, he asked me if I had seen you. Besides, I just moved here and I'm in the market for a job."

"I'll be more than happy to help an old friend."

They went to lunch and that began the start of Henry and Torry's problems. He hired Sydney and they began going out together after work, Henry justified it as a working dinner, it was starting to get heavy after a short time. Torry got word of it, and she confronted him. He first denied it, but once Torry gave him proof that he wasn't at his office when he said he was, he confessed that he and Sydney were together after working hours.

"We just went out for a few lunches, dinners, and a few drinks. Nothing happened. It would have if you hadn't found out. I am so sorry, my dear. Please forgive me for everything." He fired Sydney and never saw her again after that. The trust between them had been broken and Torry's heart was broken. She stayed with him and they made the decision to work it out, they worried about the effects it would have on Jeff, even though he was only a toddler. With counseling, they rebuilt trust for one another. It took years, but after the years of counseling they once again had a healthy marriage they were both grateful for having made the decision that they had stayed together. After Jeff graduated high school, Torry went back to her desk job and she was loving being able to be with Henry throughout the day, he was too.

As Jeff and George were headed back home from the meeting with Jeff's parents they were aware of the coming rain. The breeze had picked up and the air was cooler. The clouds were slow moving. They were about half way back to the bunker when George looked behind them and saw some soldiers who were following them. They had thought that they had been careful but at one point there had been a squadron of soldiers they had to go around, the way they had ducked out of sight must have caught the attention of at least one of them and they decided track them down to find out who they were. The way Jeff and George were running away convinced them something was wrong.

"Jeff, there are soldiers behind us. We need to get away." They broke out into a full run. The soldiers were more weighed down with equipment, so they were slower but they were running to keep up. The clouds were getting closer and the wind had picked up. There were a few hard sprinkles hitting them in their faces as they ran when suddenly up ahead lightning struck a tree and it caught on fire with the wind blowing the sparks all around on the ground and the grass lit up. The wind picked up and flames spread, quickly. With the dry grass and brush, the fire caught everything close. The soldiers kept coming toward them. George and Jeff had to run like they never had before. When George looked back over his shoulder, it was then that they both heard a roar and saw the lightning strike had grown into a wall of fire; he put his hand on Jeff's arm to stop him as they were observing the spectacle behind them. The soldiers were trying to outrun the fire, when they saw they weren't going to make it, they turned around to go back the way they had come only to see lightning had struck on the other side of them, it was another wall of fire and it was closing in on them; they were trapped. The grass and brush was thick and the fire grew by the second, shooting hot sparks everywhere. The smoke was thick and was choking the soldiers, and it was sucking the oxygen out of the air. They were in a panic and were frantically trying to put it out, pulling out water bottles and desperately trying to douse it, when that was failing, they pulled off their shirts and used them. It was of no use, the wall of fire were more than they could handle. The smoke was overwhelming them, they were falling down with no way out and they succumbed to the heat and smoke. There were screams and then only the sounds of the crackling fire were heard, none of them escaped. The wind blew the rain clouds over the fire and extinguished the flames as the rain came down in heavy sheets making visibility impossible for a very long distance.

The terrain was slippery as the ground became soaked, even though they were wearing the rain gear that had been packed, and they were cold and shivering. They picked their way through rocks and small streams. Fortunately, no one was out and about, so they began running to get back to the bunker and to try to generate some body heat. Finally they made it back. The rain pelted them, feeling like needles stinging the backs of their necks. As soon as they returned to the shelter, Joann drew them some hot water for them to get cleaned up and soak their muscles. Mariann took them some soup after they were finished with their baths. Finishing the soup, they told the group how they were saved with the lightning strikes, starting the fire, and killing the soldiers who had been on their trail.

The next day some patrols went out to find the soldiers who had not reported back in the night before and no one had heard from them and they had not shown up for their morning roll call. They knew where they were last heard from and where they were planning to go. Following the direction they were headed, they came to the burned-out patch of charred ground and found the bodies and identified them by rubbing the soot off the dog tags they wore.

"Call this in. They may have been after someone. Head in that direction," he said pointing in the direction George and Jeff had gone the previous day. Within an hour, a regime of soldiers had arrived. The bodies were removed and a search was under way. Spreading out with several yards between them, they came upon the truck of the hunters. It was filled with several inches of water from the day before with the seats soaked and ruined from the windows having been left down. The tires were flat from what looked like gashes made from running over sharp rocks. There were rifles in the gun rack and hunting equipment scattered about the interior of the truck. Birds had been inside, leaving evidence of their presence.

"Looks like an expensive camera, spot lights, two way radios, and a rifle cleaning kit in here."

"What hunter would leave guns in here with the windows down and their stuff like this? Call in the license plate number," The commander ordered. Walking along leaving one soldier to guard the truck they continued the search. It was humid from the rain as the sun had been up for a while. "At least there's been rain, finally." They heard a shout from up ahead, "Commander, come look." He rushed over. He could see what appeared to be camouflage clothing under a pile of rocks that seemed out of place.

"Move those rocks." They found two bodies clad in hunting clothes. "Get the police detectives and the medical examiner out here." Sam was watching the soldiers and went back into the bunker. Sam was wondering where the snakes had gone, he suspected with the stomping of feet they had slithered away.

"Soldiers are outside. They found the hunters' bodies. That means only one thing and that is that they'll be looking for us."

With the bunker becoming quiet, they waited to see what was going to happen right outside the door. The soldiers were milling around and the tank was being examined, they saw signs that something was going on here and they intended to find out. Sam and George were standing in the tunnel out of sight and were intently listening to the commanders talk, from what they could hear, he was intending to have the trash around it removed to find out what was beneath the rubbish.

The soldiers looked up and saw the dump grounds. "This is a toxic waste tank. There are signs all over here. I remember my grandfather telling me about it. Something seems out of place about it." They dropped what they were doing and cautiously approached it. They could see an animal had been killed recently. Someone was living around here, and it was apparent. Sam and George weren't sure what was going to happen but they were hoping for something to change their minds. Both of them were tense as they waited. If the commander were to leave he would station guards to watch, he was a smart man and he intended to go to great lengths to test his theory and if he did, the friends would be found.

There should be more remains of the animal. The hunter's bodies are close by. The animals were killed here recently and the bodies have been here about the same time.

The soldiers were milling around as George and Sam kept a close watch on them. It seemed like they had been standing still and at attention, waiting. There had been some clouds that had been gathering, not the kind to be concerned about, but the kind of clouds to take an afternoon to watch as they formed, those beautiful cumulus clouds. The beautiful clouds suddenly started dropping hail from the sky with only a few at the first and the soldiers were shocked to see this strange phenomenon and they were in a panic to find shelter. Running to escape, not realizing for the moment it was hail, they were thinking someone was throwing something at them. The hail stones were the size of baseballs and they were pelting the soldiers with devastating results. They didn't have any shelter and no head gear to protect them. Their skulls were shattered and they were killed before they had a chance to think about what had happened. The hail only lasted for a minute and it was over.

Going out slowly, watching for any movement they approached the soldiers, they were all dead. "Get their bodies out of here. Many more soldiers will be coming any time." Jeff said.

The men got to work to get the bodies stashed out of sight. Disappearing back in the bunker, they stayed there in complete silence. No one was going in or out while Sam kept watch. More soldiers did come but they found nothing but the hail stones that hadn't had time to melt. It was odd to find the hail stones in the small area where they had come across, leaving and scratching their heads in puzzlement; they were left to find the rest of them somewhere else. No one was going out until they were certain, Sam watched for drones. Their company was gone and the deaths and disappearance remained a mystery. The radio announced the mysterious disappearance of the soldiers and the strange way the other soldiers had died in the fire. The hail stones made the news but no one had any answers. People talked about the disappearances for a long time, some were afraid to venture anywhere near the place, some thought there was a leak and the chemical had dissolved their bodies.

The bodies had been buried and covered over with rocks, leaves, twigs, branches to look as if it were part of the landscape.

Henry and Torry were to meet with Dr. Perry on their side of town. A taxi would drop them off at the predetermined place and from there; they walked the rest of the way. Dr. Perry wanted George and Jacie to go along. In their packs they had the necessary medical equipment along with the usual supplies anyone took when going out.

At a vacated house, Dr. Perry instructed Jacie to inject Jeff's parents with a shot to deaden the pain. A small incision was all that was needed. Using a high-powered magnifying glass, the doctor removed the chips. He used a hammer and crushed the microchips; they were now free from them.

"We have asked the Voice to forgive us and he did. We want to spend the rest of our lives serving Him," Torry said. Jeff hugged his parents.

"What do you want to do now?" Jeff asked them.

"The Voice has told us he has a place he wants us to go," Henry said. "Would you like to go with us?"

"I want us to be together as a family. I will go with you. Do you think we could take my friend Jenny? You will like her. She's great."

"No reason why she couldn't. Don't you think you should ask her if she want to go?" Jeff's face turned red. "Yeah, dad, I should," he smiled sheepishly.

They all went back to the bunker. Henry and Torry had brought suitcases, so they were ready to leave. Jenny did want to go with Jeff when they returned to the bunker and he asked her.

CHAPTER THIRTY-ONE
PRESIDENT GERRIN

Another drought had struck and the conditions were creating food shortages, there hadn't been a drought this severe in several years. Reports from the media stated that many people were suffering the effects of the famine; it was widespread and effecting people in several parts of the world. Chosen Ones knew they were ready and had been prepared long ago for this and all their needs had been supplied as had been promised, they knew these problems would happen and they prepared as they were guided and were trusting they would still be taken care of by their God. But the nonbelievers were struggling without the hope they refused to believe was there for them. Not every place was enduring severe famine conditions but their suppliers were working hard to help all the ones who were suffering, as the president ordered them.

At the World Council, President Gerrin was troubled. "We need to make sure we are will be supplied."

"That has already been taken care of," his assistant told him.

"What are we going to do about feeding all the people around the world? We promised we would take care of them and now…"

"Sir, there is only so much we can do. They can't possibly think we can do everything for them. If we don't take the best care of ourselves, how can we take care of them?" And they did take the best of everything they could get for themselves. No one in the World Council went hungry or without. They threw lavish parties for friends, families, and those who needed to do their work. They went about drinking without any concern for the rest of the world; they indulged in luxury while the world wilted away from them and distributing it among their own. Television cameras covered the elaborate events, which were frequent. After a time, none of them even gave a thought to the world outside of their own limited world. Misery in the world was increasing and the parties were broadcast, causing increasing resentment and discontent. The Council members were living large at the expense of the poor and the poor were not going to tolerate it any more. Promises had been made that if they took the microchips, everything would be better, nothing but lies and deception. It started as angry talk, then rioting, and then the organizers got things under control. Organizers put a stop to the rioting. They brought people together to talk about a solution. As the talks were underway, it was concluded that the President would need to be taken out. The servants who were serving the Council members were angry about what they saw within the confines of the well-stocked mansions. They had families who were suffering along with everyone else. And the wealthy laughed at the outside world as they assumed they were immune from the poverty and they thought they had protection, their lives were comfortable and they had plenty.

A coup was in the making. Servants were giving inside information to the organizers of the coup. They knew the habits of the people they served. These particular ones didn't know how to go about participation in any ousting but they were making money from the organizers. A plan was formulated to go in and loot the mansions where their officials were living whether they were living in the elaborate homes or they planned to serve justice to the pompous leaders.

As word got around about this coup, organizers got together and they explained their plans. They would hit the World Council building and the other mansions as a civilian army, breaking down gates or going over walls from all sides. There were only so many armed guards, overwhelming them would be easy. The servants would show them where to go to get the goods that was in the homes and where the warehouse of stored goods was to be found.

The day was set. Hoping a new leader would change things for them, they chose a man from the organizers to replace the present president, Marcello, and he was a person who knew how to communicate. He was an attorney so he understood the ramifications of what was about to happen. If he were successful with the coup, he would be their newly appointed president. When the day had come, a huge crowd quietly assembled around the vast World Council mansion at the designated time. As one vast army they broke down the gates and some scaled the walls. Within minutes the crowd was rushing towards doors and windows. Guards were appearing and started gunning down the crowd as the fear they were feeling was rising, knowing their time was up. Those who were shot simply fell to the ground, the ammo ran out and the guards were overwhelmed, rioter's bodies were trampled upon as more and more rioters gained access to the mansion. Windows were being broken into, doors were beaten down, and entry was impossible to stop. Guards were knocked down and crushed to death. Those who were not on the front lines when people first broke in were overpowered and beaten. Bodies were left as messes with footprints from the bodies being carried over the floors and the bodies not even recognizable as the ones who had once thought of themselves as royalty.

The President heard the commotion from his upstairs office suite and rushed down the stairs in his wrinkled designer suit. He was hung over from the night before, dizzy, and nauseous. He was well aware of the trouble now facing him. Several of them picked him up and carried him to the top to the balcony where he was picked up and thrown over, and as he was flying through the air and before he hit the floor, he vomited. His body was sprawled out, every part of his now dead body twisted and broken from having been thrown from three stories up. The rioters were in an uproar, as they chanted as if insane from the sight of their "savior" now dead.

Up the stairs, others had his wife and were dragging her over for the same fate. She was screaming and begging for her life. "Please! No!

Not me!" She was wearing an expensive cashmere dress she had worn to a celebrity party that evening where she was adored by her fans. The dress fit her body nicely and its length fell down to below her knees. She was being dragged over to the same spot where the president had been tossed, and as she was being picked up, she was grabbing and hanging onto the rail, still screaming. The mob had her in their grasp with her still screaming and she was falling back onto the floor when she was picked up and hurled over the rail. When her body hit the floor like the president, the cream colored dress she was wearing was no longer the dress that showed off the glamorous life she had been leading. Her body was looking just like the president's body did upon impact. The place was in disarray as furniture and personal belonging were everywhere and the rioters were cheering once again.

They went throughout the mansion, and they eliminated all those ones who were loyal to the President. Their servants were showing them where the subversives were hiding. It didn't take long. They found them hiding and some of them tried to escape out windows and doors, but they were quickly caught and killed. Once they were all killed, the rioters looted the place, taking everything, including fixtures that were a permanent part of the house. The food was quickly confiscated as well as all the valuable artifacts throughout the mansion. The house was left as if it were a vacated, trashed house. Someone started a fire. The mob cleared out as they stood outside to watch it burn. What they hadn't anticipated was how the fire spread from house to house, there were wooden benches, flammable bushes, guest houses, and decorative items that started and kept the fire going and burning. It was so hot that the rioters were having to move back to keep from getting blistered. Sparks were flying like fireworks at their celebrations. Within minutes, the fire was out of control as the wind caused by fire itself threw sparks beyond the property and the whole neighborhood was under fire. A breeze that had suddenly picked up fueled the sparks. Dry grass and some help from arsonists produced fuel that the fire needed. Within a short time, neighborhoods were on fire, occupants were burned up as they were unaware of the danger that surrounded them; many were trapped and surrounded by fire. A few of them got out alive. Time went by and the fires started going out as they were running out of places to go, and ran out of fuel with the help of fire departments arriving on the scene and the wind had died down. Fields that had been plowed and cleared in anticipation of wealthy investors who were planning to develop the area with mansions and upscale shopping centers helped stop the fires.

The Exalted Dark One was finished with President Gerrin. Having him with them was a glorious victory. It was over for this president, and he moved forward with his plans for the new one who would use slick deceptions to further the Evil Ones cause. Walking through the area, the devastation and loss of life was astounding. In the Dark World, the spirits were dancing with glee at the harvesting of new souls they had collected, lost from their tormentor, the Voice. It was a victory! What a day that this was! Everyone out for themselves, murder, mayhem, and lots of selfishness, it was incredible! Now, to get that new president installed, he was going to do great things for them. They had him under their control. The beautiful thing was humans couldn't blame them for everything, much of the havoc was their own desires and not anything they had anything to do with.

The Chosen Ones were listening to the radios and hearing about the devastating occurrences. They were trying to determine if they should be doing anything during these times. They understood they were to sit quietly. There was chaos and they needed to stay where they were and they did. The newly installed President, Marcello, knew the drought was going to end soon so he started promising the world prosperity again. Hope was high and soon the rain came, he became the new savior. Anything he said was believed, it was believed he was the reason the rain came. It was believed he was the reason for the turn of events and the changes in the weather. When he was firmly established, he started taking from them. With the rain came crops, food, and promised prosperity, order was restored. The new president increased his wealth from the minions within society, and he kept his motives quiet. They were in ignorant bliss for giving their money to him, so he didn't think they needed to know what he was going to do and he used them for his own person gain.

CHAPTER THRTY-TWO

KEVIN

Times were what was to be believed to be peaceful and all being well. The summer season ended and the winter hit with a vengeance coming early. The times had brought about changes, technology was advanced and confidence was in what mankind could do, science replaced what the God of the universe did and was doing, logic replace faith, and narcissism was more important than loving one another. Chosen Ones were harming the world just by being in existence. It was reasonable to believe the inflexible attitude of the believers was the cause of all their woes and the reason why the snow storm had left collapsed buildings, bridges were weakened, death tolls climbing as emergency vehicles were not able to get to many places as the road clearing machinery was being used around the clock and not making much of a difference. The seasons would come and go until the end of time as the Book promised, even the severe weather.

At the bunker, the group was forced to stay inside. They were warm and comfortable as they worked inside to maintain their supplies. They held onto the hope that the snow would subside enough to hunt and pick more food, they weren't going to go hungry for a while if the weather eased up sometime soon and the snow did ease up and the temperatures were warming up somewhat and cleared enough for them to go out and hunt and they found wildlife wandering around looking for food of their own. The men wanted to do some hunting.

Getting bundled up; they wanted to get out for some fresh air. The ground had bare spots so that the group could get out and around but it was wet so anyone going out had to be careful where they stepped, so as not to leave footprints. The sun was out and the air was cold but the sun felt good on their skin. The men wanted to do some hunting and they had to be cautious as there was still a bounty on the Chosen Ones so they had to be ever vigilant when stepping out of the bunker. They thought it would be best if they spread out; each of them had their own favorite place they liked to hunt.

Sam headed to the highway to see if anything might be going on. He was breathing deeply, filling his lungs with cold air and was feeling renewed. He was nearing the highway when he stopped. It sounded like he heard some sobbing. Going closer and staying hidden he came to the highway and saw a young boy of about twelve. Sam looked all around but he didn't see anyone. He was dressed in light weight clothes with a jacket that was not meant to be worn out in the kind of weather they were having. It was going to get colder after a while and Sam was disturbed by him being out where he was all alone. Going closer the young boy didn't hear him so when Sam put his hand on the boy's shoulder, he jumped and Sam saw the fear on his face.

"It's ok. I won't hurt you, I am a friend," he told him. "Where are your parents?"

"They dropped me off here. They don't want me."

"Why wouldn't they want you?"

"I was born blind and they got tired of having to take care of me. They said I ruined their life," he was sobbing again.

"Hey, come with me. I have a place for you. Are you hungry?" Sam took him by his arm as he took off his coat and wrapped it around the boy and he led him back to the bunker.

"Yes."

"How long have you been out here?"

"They dropped me off here a little while ago."

"What's your name? I am Sam."

"I'm Kevin."

"Kevin, I can help you."

"Ok. But I'm blind. My parents couldn't take care of me, why do you want to?"

"You are most fortunate; we have some food for you. I have a duty to help and I want to. You're not an inconvenience, you are a person."

They were walking up the road to the bunker with Kevin holding onto Sam's arm and taking uncertain steps on the unfamiliar ground. Sam slowed his steps as he guided Kevin and told him where there might be a spot he would trip over; Kevin started trusting him after a short while. Sam saw Jeremy who was within sight of him when he looked up and saw the two walking towards him.

"Who do you have here?"

"This is Kevin. His parents didn't want him so they dropped him off along the highway."

"How could anyone do this to their child?" Jeremy was angry.

"We need to get him inside." Dr. Perry came over to him to take over his care when they got inside and met Kevin.

"Get some warm water so we can give him a bath to warm him up. I'll examine him when he's warm and fed." Joann and Lucy got busy with the water. Mariann prepared some food for him. Jacie worked on fixing a bed for him. He was still upset and tears were streaming down his face. Cindy sat with him with her arms around him. He leaned into her, which brought tears to her eyes, she was patting him and she laid her face on the top of his head, it had a calming effect on him. The warm water was ready after a little while so they had him take off most of his clothes to get in the water. His lips had been blue when they had found him and as he warmed up he was looking much better from the hot food and warm bath.

After getting him tucked away on a cot with warm blankets, Dr. Perry checked him out. "I don't find anything seriously wrong with him," he said. "We will need to figure out where we need to send him."

"First thing we should do is pray for his sight to be restored," Cindy said.

"Tonight we will make our petition to Him. We haven't done this before but we know He can do anything, we believe, our trust is in Him completely. We can do all things through Him who strengthens us," Jeremy said. They were very excited about making this request. There had been so many miracles they had seen that they wanted to see how the blind could receive their sight.

"How is our new patient, Dr. Perry?"

"Right now, he's asleep. I'm hoping he'll sleep for a while. He's much stressed and rest will do him a lot of good." It was time for them to sit down and quietly play cards and board games to give Kevin his much needed rest. Some of the others started coming in from outside from doing the activities that needed their attention and they were shushed as they came in. As expected, they were surprised Kevin was there.

"As soon as we can we will need contact Pastor Lars to see if he can place Kevin with a family in his congregation," George told them when he heard the story.

"Dinner is ready," Mariann announced. After getting cleaned up they gathered around the table, discussing Kevin, they had come up with a plan to get him placed. Kevin woke up and was calling for help. He was led in to sit at the table with them to eat

"Kevin we're going to move you to another shelter where you will be with a family who will take care of you. We wouldn't mind you being here but we think having a mom and dad will be better for you, ok?" George asked.

"I'm scared."

"Of course, you are. It can be scary. We have help when we need it and He will be with you and make a good home for you. We have a pastor friend you will like."

"Mom and dad hated the Voice. They told me He hated them because of me."

"Kevin, He made you special. He wants to show His greatness through you. He has a plan for you. You just need to trust Him," Joann said.

"I don't know if I can."

"He sent you to us, didn't he?"

"I guess so."

"You would have died out there if He hadn't guided Sam to you."

"We want to talk to Him about giving you back your sight. We are ready, are you?"

"That would be so awesome!"

Cleanup was such a minor detail for Mariann as she happily joined the group in prayer for Kevin. They all gathered around Kevin. As they were spending the evening making their petitions and making their requests known and as they were standing with him, Kevin became excited, "I'm seeing! I can see for the first time in my life!" The friends were excited and watching him in wonder as Kevin was looking around, drinking in the sights. "My mom and dad should have asked for my eyes to be healed."

"What do you think about us leaving to take him to Pastor Lars?" George asked them.

"We have been using the animal skins to make up some outer were that will keep us warm." Jeremy told them. "I learned how to use skins when I was in high school."

"Do you think you can travel, Kevin?" George asked him. "I think so."

"Pastor Lars will work with you to help you get through the fact you were abandoned by your parents." So much had happened to Kevin; they knew that shelter would take him in and love him with all their hearts. Kevin would be ok.

"Kevin, go get a good night's sleep. You'll be bundled up and on your way tomorrow."

Early morning, Jacie got Kevin up to get some breakfast in his stomach. He was taking in everything he saw. The things he could only imagine were a reality.

"How is your breakfast?" Mariann asked.

"This is good. I was usually on my own in the mornings. Mostly, I ate cereal. Thank you Mariann."

"You are welcome, honey."

There was a lot to be learned about Kevin. Despite the disability, he had, he was an intelligent boy and really had a tremendous amount of knowledge by doing lots of listening. He listened to science shows on TV; he touched things and saw things in his mind and saw things through touch that was astounding. Now that he could see he had so much more he could learn. They were all thinking if they had a kid like him they would never have given him up. Jeremy stayed back to get the food supplies. George and Sam were taking Kevin to his new home. The trip didn't seem to take as long with them watching for danger and spending this times watching as Kevin was talking in living color. He saw trees and was astonished by how many he was seeing, he had touched leaves before but to see them was exciting, he was seeing animals trying to find food, the sky, snow, everything, even the holes from the burrowing animals was interesting to him. The colors of the ground made for a fascinating conversation with him. The two men were trying to see things his way and found it as exciting as Kevin did. Not likely would they ever view the world in the old way ever again. Time went by as they were meeting the world through Kevin's eyes and was close to the shelter of Pastor Lars; they were met and greeted by him when they were in range of recognition. "Good to see you again!" he said. "Who is this nice looking young man?"

"Sam found him abandoned by his parents. He needs a home." George and Sam filled him in on Kevin's story. Kevin looked nervous.

"Come on in, buddy," Lars told him and they all followed him inside. "Carrie, would you bring our guests some food and refreshments?" Carrie was the cook and housekeeper for his shelter.

"Hello friends. I will be right out."

"Kevin, we are thrilled to have you here. You'll be safe. We have families who love kids so there won't be a problem. I am so sorry your parents did that to you."

"Thank you."

"His eyesight was restored last night and he is very excited about seeing the world. He was born blind. He is truly a remarkable young man!" George said.

"Why don't you spend the night and leave in the morning?"

"That would be great!" Sam said.

The shelter was bustling to settle Kevin in and situate their guests. Kevin was describing everything he was seeing and it warmed their hearts. It was a great time for them as Kevin was winning everyone over with his enthusiasm.

In the morning, Sam and George were up and ready for the trip home. They watched Kevin, he seemed comfortable with Lars. Lars had a way about him that made him easy to talk to. George knew this was the right place for him. Stepping outside the men noticed the heavy rain clouds.

"Had better get going," Sam said.

"Kevin, we will come back to see you," George said.

They took off as they watched the sky. This was going to be one mean rainstorm. "Please, be careful. If you would rather stay over, please do," Lars shouted to them.

"Our friends will worry about us, so thanks anyway. We will try to get back here soon," George shouted back. "Sam, are you in for a run? We should try to get over that low place up ahead in case of flooding."

"I'm good, let's go." And they took off running. At first the rain came in large chunks of sleet and soon it was a heavy downpour. There was some deafening thunder as they were getting close to the low spot and there was already a fairly swift stream flowing. "We had better get going and fast," George said. Taking off at a full run they started across the stream, as they got to the middle of it there came a flood of water, full of all kinds of trash, brush, tree branches, and everything that was not secured where it was left standing in the path of it.

"Hold on to me, George," he said, "and you need to hang on tight." The flood hit them and they were pulled down stream, helpless with the force that nature had. Both of them were convinced that this was the end for them. They had been pulled under the water and struggling to get to the surface and just as they thought they could no longer hold their breath and the water was freezing cold and then they became aware of a bright light that moved towards them.

Suddenly a strange thing happened and they found themselves in what seemed to be a bubble. They could no longer hold their breath so they let it out and were breathing. They could still see the bright light as they saw the muddy, murky water flowing past them, without any idea where they would end up they could only watch and wait, their clothes were still wet but they were warm. "We must be dead," Sam said.

"I don't think we would be having this conversation if we were," George replied.

"It is very warm in here," Sam said.

"Hey! I didn't see this bubble appear."

"This is so awesome!"

They were in the bubble for a while. The light was still there and they were doing well. After a time, their feet hit some solid ground and standing up the bubble and light disappeared. They walked to the bank of the stream that had turned into a river and they climbed up to a solid spot and sat down, dripping wet, trying to take in what had just happened. It was still raining down sleet, though not as hard, but still coming down and they were on the side of the stream they had to be on to get home. This was a miracle they would not forget.

Getting close to the bunker now they walked up to it and went to the door, opened it and called for someone to bring them some clean, dry clothes. Cindy walked up to them and started laughing, she couldn't help it, they had mud on their faces and she thought they were kind of cute. Since they couldn't see themselves they laughed knowing they must be a mess and a sight to behold. The others inside came to see what they found so funny and they too laughed. "Come on, we need some clothes or we will catch a nasty cold and we will let you catch it with us too."

"All right, all right," Cindy left to get them the clean clothes.

"We must look frightful," Sam said, and he had to laugh at himself.

They were shivering and their lips were blue so the bunker was in a frenzy to get them warmed up. The hot herbal tea was welcome and helped get them warm.

CHAPTER THIRTY-THREE

LABOR CAMP

The Voice was number one. He was always given the credit for all he did for them. Many in his care had suffered from the outside. Recently Henry, Torry, Jeff, and Jenny had come to be with them. Jeff wanted to train to be a pastor. Lars was more than happy for him. He started Jeff out as a study leader. He had proven to be smart and a quick learner. Jeff was talking to the Voice and the Voice was leading and guiding him. Jeff was helping with getting food for the shelter. There was so much he had learned that helped keep these people safe.

In the Dark World, the Exalted One was not happy. They had been sure of winning every soul from the Voice. Not only were they not getting all of them, He was taking them back. How the Dark Spirits hated the Voice! All of their plans were not going as expected. The war had been going their way, but now. Pastor Lars and his group spent time with the Voice asking his help and guidance. He was hearing them and providing answers. These were times of people who had great strength. Never in the history had humans been given such strength as these persecuted people had. They were beaten, imprisoned, tortured, despised, their friends and families taken from them and they still kept seeking the Voice. The Dark World was feeling the pain.

"Pastor Lars, we have word that there are some soldiers who want to see you. The Voice has led them to you. We asked the Voice and he told us He sent them to us," one of the residents said.

"Do I need to go get them? What were you told to do?"

"There are several soldiers who have met together at one of their homes. They asked if you and some of them would meet them there."

"When?"

"They asked if you would meet with them tomorrow."

"I will be happy to." Henry asked if he could come along, Lars had no objections. "Jeff, would you like to come with us? I think this would be some good training for you."

"Yes sir, I want to." Arrangements were being made to keep their shelter safe. Other members took up the duties when they needed to. The Voice provided food in his marvelous way he did things. They were fortunate to have some fruit trees and some nut trees where they were located.

They left early to get to the house where they were to meet with the soldiers. It was a nice quiet morning for walking and the highway was very well travelled so they thought that there was some activities in town to keep people there. By the radio account it was a special weekend of celebrating an anniversary of the founding of the town. Despite the lack of traffic, they steered clear of it and were making good time getting to the house which was located outside of town and in an isolated part of the woods. A lake was located close by down from them where the stream emptied into it and it was in an area that was run by the state. Not many people even wanted to come here. It wasn't land that had much for people to come here for. The security was some of the members who had been in security jobs of various types. One of their security guys was one of the guards at the prison when George escaped. He wasn't one of the camera monitors but he knew the Voice wanted George out. He talked to George on several occasions. Ken was told by the Voice that he was going to take him out that night. Ken also knew the Voice so he knew George was real. Ken did what he could to distract the guards. Pastor Lars told him about where and what George was doing. After he had escaped Ken was thinking about making some changes in his life. It came when it was found that chips were required. He was busy helping Lars build and furnish this shelter.

The shelter had been under construction long before the announcement about the chips. Ken was the man for security and he was proud to do this job for these wonderful people. He watched for the drones and at times shot them out of the sky. People hated being spied on so when they were shot down the government could never pin it on anyone unless they were seen before they were shot. Hunters had fun shooting them for sport and some people went hunting for them as a sport. Young boys who were given guns shot the drones like a time when shooting rabbits and squirrels were used for target practice. Ken was aware of this and smiled at the thought. Getting caught had serious consequences but as with anything, where there was a will there was a way.

Pastor Lars had been to several countries working to bring the peoples to know the Voice. He had seen so much pain and suffering. He knew how the Voice was hated around the world. People had been suffering for their faith for a very long time. This was nothing new. Having the world united as one was new. In spite of the hatred and intolerance, Ken had seen what the Voice had accomplished with his Chosen Ones. The ones who were faithful were so loving and at peace. The purifying of the church was glorious. The work was tough but extremely satisfying. He loved what he did. There was so much to do before the Voice returned to take his people home.

"We should be getting close to the house," Lars said the later that morning after they had been walking for a while.

"Ready!" Henry said. They weren't sure what to expect but they were only doing what they were told to do. Walking with these men, Lars was getting to know them and it was good for him to have someone who he was able to get close to. Guys talking guy stuff. Lars also used this time to give Jeff some more training.

"Jeff, keep the message about the Voice simple. Exact descriptions of tools of worship and the argument of such things aren't necessary. Keep the facts, as you know them from your daily reading true to the Book.

The Voice loves us and his story is too important to let it be diminished by arguing over the artifacts that are here or there. Let love be your guiding light." Jeff was so grateful for Lars down to earth and uplifting style. Lars was his mentor and Henry was getting so much from the teaching that he was learning from Lars. They were so busy chatting they were suddenly aware of the house where they were to meet with Dr. Barringer.

"Stop," Henry said. "If we go around the house we can meet with the doctor before we go in." They circled around and found Dr. Barringer on the other side. They introduced themselves before checking the perimeter of the house. One of the soldiers walked out the door. He was scanning to see if he saw them. He must have been doing it for a while. The group stepped out and they saw him stiffen before he recognized Dr. Barringer.

"Come on in," he said. They drew up together and went to the door. The others were inside waiting. They introduced themselves before explaining why they were there. "We have been making fun of the Chosen Ones until he started talking to us. We have been reading the Book that we found. We know the Voice is real, we have chosen to serve him and we don't want this chip."

"We know. We have been doing things to make the Chosen Ones miserable."

"All right, what can we do for you?"

"There are more of us who want to follow the Voice. We want to get these out and do what the Voice wants us to do. Will you help us?"

"That is what we are here for. Dr. Barringer is here to take care of the chips. We need to find a place for you."

"That has already been taken care of; there is a place close to here that is abandoned. We are hoping you would be our pastor."

"I have some good news for you. Jeff was a soldier who has joined us. I have been training him and will continue to help him. Do you mind if I gave him to you? I need to train him some more so if you would be willing, I will send you to a shelter for your protection for now, ok?"

"This is a good day for us." Henry was so proud of Jeff. Jeff had found his purpose. Dr. Barringer took the chips, injected the chips into some pets that had strayed, sent them away and felt a tinge of mischievousness. The soldiers had food that they shared with everyone who was gathered with them in the house and then they put what belongings they had and started out with the other Chosen Ones. Lars had a special shelter in mind for them to go to for some training until the time when Jeff would be ready. They got back to his shelter and made plans to send a messenger to the shelter he had in mind. The soldiers were happy and were realizing the newness they had just found and were ready to move on and be the servants of the Most High God.

The Rabbit was making his rounds and delivering messages and he stopped by the shelter. Lars sent him to the shelter he had in mind for the soldiers and within a week he heard back from the shelter that they were delighted to have the new members join them and soon they were on their way.

The Voice was happy to see the Chosen Ones were doing his work. They were living according to his mandate. Time was shorter than humans knew. They were strong and they kept their focus. The Dark Spirits were losing them. The world was getting worse with humans finding more and more ways to enhance their dark souls. The Chosen Ones were making the difference. The church, small as it was, was rock solid.

CHAPTER THIRTY-FOUR

THE VALLEY OF THE SHADOW OF DEATH

Jeff and Pastor Lars had been working hard to convert non-believers into the Kingdom of Light. They were being sent out into the streets as the Spirit was guiding them. There were those who having spent their lives hearing the Good News and refusing to listen were having their lives changed. Jeff and Lars went to them and talked with them, validating their understanding of the One and knowing that they were changed, and then they were sent to shelters. Not many people were seeing the truth, but the ones who did had true conversions. The world was set on going its own misguided way. One day, as Lars and Jeff were out on such a mission, they crossed paths with a young person who was asking to be taken in, he had been told where to meet the believers and with skeptics, they went where they were told and they found it was the right thing to do. Jeff had gone off and had promised Lars he would be back soon, and as he was walking away with Lars watching him go, a soldier came up behind Jeff. The young person saw the soldier and knew something was wrong even before he turned around and the look on the young man's face was enough to convince him and told him what had happened. Jeff slowly turned around. "Hello, good afternoon, sir," he said.

"Jeff, we're have been looking for you and here you are. The reward for finding you is worth the trouble we had of finding you. We were told you had crossed over." Jeff didn't answer.

"Get your hands behind your back," he said with his gun pointed at Jeff's head and he complied. The soldier roughly put handcuffs of Jeff, it hurt but he didn't say anything. "Over here," he shouted for others to come over. They came running.

"Well, look who we have here," they mocked. "It's Jeffy."

"I get the reward for catching him. Call the commander over." The commander was there in five minutes.

"Look who I found, commander."

"Good job, soldier." He turned to his man. "So, Jeff, it's so nice to see you again. It's a real unfortunate event that our meeting again has been like this." The commander's face was spread with a snarling grin.

"Where do we need to take him?"

"To jail, he gets his trial like everyone else." Jeff knew the trial consisted of mockery and intimidation; he was loaded into his captor's car and driven down town where he was booked into the jail with all the other soldiers mocking him, hitting, and spitting on him. He was placed in a cell with another inmate who Jeff suspected had been here on several occasions and not for shoplifting. This was going to be rough; he had already made up his mind about what was going to happen and what he would do. This was the road he was going to take. He knew who had died for him and he was ready to repay the blessed one the same favor. As he was sitting on his bunk in the cell he felt strong and he wasn't worried, he started humming a song he had learned. The inmate in his cell was taken aback by this strange behavior. "Are you crazy, man?"

"Seems that way, doesn't it?"

"Do you know what they are going to do to you?"

"Yes, I'm not scared of it."

"You should be. Are you that soldier they have been looking for?"

"I must be."

"We were told and word has spread that any soldier who comes in here will be free game around here. You're in big trouble, man."

"I am not worried."

Jeff was waiting; still humming when a soldier came to get him and he was being dragged out of the cell and still, Jeff didn't utter a sound other than the humming, no defense. He was brought before a judge with several city council members present. As he stood in front of them, Jeff had a look on his face that told them he was unconcerned about it. "Jeff, give up this nonsense. If you don't, you're going to die."

"Sir, I won't give up the one true God."

"You believe in a silly myth," one council member said.

"No, he is very real."

"You are an idiot as are all those who believe in this imaginary apparition, a superstition." Jeff was quiet.

"All you people do is keeping the rest of us from living happy lives, making us feel guilty over ridiculous rules and laws. Those rules are old world and don't apply any more. You are a curse for the rest of us."

The room was filling up with spectators as they were anticipating some excitement. Jeff already knew what was going to happen. Part of his training was learning what to do with subversives. It wasn't going to be a good ending, as far as his physical body was concerned. Members of the Council were throwing accusations at him. "Traitor!"

"Why am I a traitor? Just because of what I believe differently from you? Why do I need to have another god besides the one I have? Why are my beliefs a problem? Do I harm you? Do I interfere with your beliefs? No, you hate my God because deep down, Council, you know He is the God of this earth and beyond it."

"If you serve anyone other than our Supreme Leader, then you are a traitor."

"The God I serve gives peace that the Supreme Leader can't give you in this life and the one after."

"Peace? We're doing just fine with him. Besides that, there is no after life. Once you die you are gone and there is nothing else. You are so deceived."

"Peace is having the knowledge that when you die you are going to a place that is without hate and his place is so full of love, never again having any worries, trials or troubles."

"That place doesn't exist. When you die you are gone and that is the end, aren't you even listening."

"It does exist. You need to change your ways before it is too late."

"Our Supreme Leader is all we need. We don't have to go through anything, only commit our allegiance to him."

"He will die and your hope will be gone. The Holy One is always here and always will be."

"What have those people done to you, Jeff? Their ideals have made you crazy."

"Where are the others? Work with us and go back to serving our Supreme Leader so we can spare your life. We don't want to do this, Jeff. But without your allegiance to the Supreme One, we have no other choice."

"My Supreme Leader is the One I serve who has been with me through all things."

"Where are the others?"

"You would never get them without Him letting you. He protects them. You would die before it happens."

"That is preposterous, tell us where they are."

"No." A councilman stepped forward and punched Jeff in the face. He not only felt and heard his bones breaking and felt the pain, but he was thankful that he was being chosen to be counted worthy to testify for the Chosen One. "Thank you, Father for allowing me the honor of standing tall for you." The Council was furious.

"Shut up! Stop talking to this Voice! He doesn't exist. Fool." The council was in an uproar.

"Take him out and make him pay," The council leader commanded. One of them tripped him, causing him to fall on his face; his hands were still cuffed behind his back so he fell on his face and was knocked unconscious and he laid there. Bones were broken and a bump on his head was swelling. His face was already severely bruised and he was having trouble holding up his head. A soldier came forward dragging him to his feet. He slapped Jeff to make him wake up, he was dazed. They were kicking him and his ribs were cracking and breaking. "Do you still trust in the nonexistent God? Give the Supreme One your allegiance! Do It! Your imagination isn't here. Why isn't He stopping us?" They mocked Jeff.

Weakly, Jeff said, "You had better believe I do believe in Him." His voice was full of conviction, but also no fear. Jeff looked up into the face of an angel through swollen eyes he was barely able to open and only when he saw a bright light. The angels he had heard about. They were waiting for him; at that moment Jeff felt himself entering a new life. It was the most beautiful sense of peace, of no worry, and of comfort surrounding him and assuring him of the things to come.

Soldiers were taking him somewhere he couldn't see, the soldiers made sure he did, wiping his eyes so he could see; he recognized the arena where he had at a times witnessed others being put to death. In the arena, he was propped up against a post where he was tied. When he was securely tied, he heard people entering, finding their seats. They were excited; they had missed out on some of the fun by the looks of him. Finishing him off would give them pleasure. What a traitor, a dirty dog who turned his back to the Supreme Leader, blasphemous.

Standing at the post was the angel giving Jeff comfort without saying a word. Jeff stayed focused on the presence. He felt sadness for the ones who were here and didn't know who the life giving one was. This was to be a moment to give glory to the One would save him forever and ever. "Thank you Great Voice for everything. Forgive them for the wrong they are doing to me. Have mercy on them and forgive them."

The arena was quickly filling with excited spectators and soon they were all settled into their seats. The guards had left, leaving Jeff alone. An announcer was heard asking him to renounce his false God, he whispered, "No." He couldn't be heard so a microphone was brought to him and put close to his face, this time he gathered all the strength he had and said, "No, I give my life to the Giver of Life," which brought laughter and derision. The crowd was booing him but he didn't care. The announcer came over the public-address system announcing his death sentence, "Jeff, you are condemned to die by stoning for your act of blasphemy against the one and only true god, the Supreme Ruler.

Your sentence will now be carried out." A guard walked over to him and loosed him from his constraints. He fell down, too weak to move. The guards had to duck the rocks that were thrown, the crowds were so eager to get this show started. The guards would have been extra entertainment if they hadn't been ducking out of the way.

As the rocks came down, his last words were, "Great Voice, take me home," and with that, he breathed his last. The angel took him home.

"Welcome home, my son. You have been a good and faithful servant." There he saw his loved ones who had gone before him. He saw Kendra smiling at him, with open arms. She was a truly beautiful woman, he had never met her in life, but he knew who she was and she knew him, it was good to be home.

In the arena, the crowds were disappointed that he had died so quickly.

The Exalted Dark One was stewing over Jeff refusing to give in. The Chosen Ones were suffering and they weren't doing things according to his plans. He was becoming angrier and angrier. He knew there were others who were left and he wanted them. He was successful in getting some of the Chosen Ones but most of them were standing firm.

Pastor Lars had come back in time to see Jeff taken into custody and he knew what was to come. He was saddened and he hoped it would be over quickly. He was saddened by the loss of this faithful young man, who had so much potential, his time had come and Lars was happy he got to go home. The business they had come for was finished, the young man they had met was taken to a shelter that was close by and Lars had gotten back to the shelter. They already knew what had happened. The radio was turned on and all they were listening. As was the custom for the poor people who weren't able to participate in the area activities, there was a news station that would broadcast the show. It was not the same as being there but they pleasure they got out of it was the satisfaction of betting on it. Some of the victims would last for a while and depending on what had occurred prior to them being in the area, some died quickly. It was a sports station that would broadcast from all over the world so it was frightening for those who even had a thought about converting to the "unholy" religion calling people to listen to the Voice.

When believers heard about the events they were grateful he had gotten to go home to be with the ones who had gone before them. Memorial services were held honoring him for what he had done and his courage. Other believers were stronger and even more determined to be obedient to whatever they were told to do. The grief was intense and Henry and Torry were heartbroken and the others were giving them the assurance that the angels were singing and dancing.

Chosen Ones were aware of their own going home at any moment. The radio broadcasters were giving full accounts of the Ones who were found and were murdered for their faith. They understood how hard it was for others but those who went home were strong and the Chosen Ones refused to give in to false gods. The dancing in the streets over one of these faithful ones didn't bring about the desired discouragement, only that they had to finish their work to their ever faithful, loving God. There were some who were caught and turned to the god of the world and had given information to the captors that led to the raid and subsequent death of other Chosen Ones.

The Exalted Dark One wanted more than ever to disband the Chosen Ones. Without power in numbers, they'd succumb to him; they were weak without each other. He had some success and it was not enough so, he made plans to get at them, and what a better way than to attack the one who was the weakest of them, the one who'd done so much wrong in his life that it would be easy to turn him from the Way. George, he would be easy.

CHAPTER THIRTY-FIVE

GEORGE

The family of friends listened to the radio to stay informed about what current events were happening. There was dissension everywhere. Greed and hate were driving forces that took a toll on many people and tribes of humanity. There were constant wars between nations and people, and George heard about some of it getting to close to one of the shelters. He and Sam wanted to help them. Plans were for them to try to get to them as soon as possible in an area where bombs were being used. It was like gang warfare with weapons of mass destruction, creating more damage to a broken society. The Voice told them to take Dr. Perry with them. He didn't send the doctor very often, so it seemed odd to them, but they didn't question it. Dr. Perry was kept busy treating people since there weren't very many doctors in hiding anywhere close to them, at least that they knew about.

Mariann made their packs ready. Jacie always had Dr. Perry's bag stocked with his medical supplies. Lucy had been working hard being a gatherer along with her inside work, and things were running smoothly. With the bag ready, the men left after dark to maintain a better cover. In the day time, it was sometimes rough going on the routes they had to take and not leave a visible trail. There were places where they would slip and slide and at times falling down. It was challenging but they arrived at their destination with nothing more than a few cuts or bruises. Time was short so they didn't talk much but spent their energy getting to their destination. It would be another long night. Finding the shelter, they moved slowly as they approached the area. It looked like a war zone that had been reported on the radio where the old down town area was, it was shocking to see the changes since they had been here the last time. There were police spotlights moving and they could hear voices, they were far enough away they were able to get to where the shelter was. Walking to the door, they knocked without getting a response.

"We are here to get you out of here," George said, hoping he was heard. The door opened slowly. The woman who peeked out recognized him and he then opened the door all the way.

"Come in," the man said. "I could only get people out one at a times and it was risky. Only my wife and I are here. Our people are on the lookout for us and are hoping to meet us soon."

"Get her and let us be out of here. Everything looks totally bombed out around here and any day now you might be hit," George said.

The man got his wife and they took off with only a few possessions. Sam led the way with Dr. Perry standing with the couple and they were moving along at a quick pace. There was an alley where the others had gone to get away and the man told them where to go, George was the last one. Things were going well for them as they were getting close to a place where the couple was expected to meet their group. Ducking down an alley, staying close to the walls of the buildings, and using dumpsters and waste for cover in case anyone passing by looked their way. A major street was up ahead that they had to cross to get into another alley way, and they would be highly exposed. Sam went ahead to scout for any danger he could see. Carefully, he managed to cross the street and duck into the alley. The others waited where they were and after a few minutes he came back.

"Ok, we can go." With their senses fully engaged, they made their way across the street. Everyone got into hiding places. Up ahead they saw some movement, the group froze. Within minutes they found out this was the people they were supposed to meet. They quietly hugged each other. Turning to their rescuers, they thanked them, said good-bye and they were gone.

Sam, George, and Dr. Perry started back the way they had come. Sounds of talking were heard as people still roamed the streets. They were getting away from danger when they were leaving an alley, with them crossing the streets one by one. George was the last one. He was almost in the alley when Sam and Dr. Perry heard a shot. Turning around they saw George fall to the ground and not moving. Both turned and ran back to him. He saw a couple of young guys who were shooting at each other. George was hit by a stray bullet. "We need to get out of here. Is George alive?"

"For right now, yes, but I don't know his condition." Sam and Dr. Perry picked him up and took off running as fast as they could. "Set him down so I can check on him." Doing so, the doctor checked on his condition. Performing a quick first aid fix, they got under way to get out of there. "Please don't die, help George and keep him alive, please," the doctor pleaded. They took off and had to find a way back with all the warfare that was going on, it was an unusual amount so they were wondering what was causing all the fighting. With ducking and hiding somehow, they got to the outskirts of town. And with frequent stops they got to the bunker, Dr. Perry was concerned he wouldn't make it with all the jostling and not having the emergency treatment he needed. There wasn't much he could do outside of the stops and taking care of his wound as best as he could. They kept going and in the middle of the night they finally were in sight of the bunker. Entering the bunker, they found Jacie and Cindy waiting. No one had been able to sleep in anticipation of their arrival. "This has been a long night and we have been expecting something to happen but not this," Jacie said. Dr. Perry got straight to work. George wasn't looking very well. The bullet had hit him in the chest at an angle.

Dr. Perry was feeling anxious about George's injury. All the friends were attending Dr. Perry the best they could. Everyone was pitching in and as the sun was making an appearance on the horizon as the morning approached. George was resting and all the friends were hoping against all the odds he would live. "Please, George, don't you dare leave us, you are much needed as our friend and leader. Don't let him leave us like this. Please give him life. Don't take him from us now."

Sam felt he should step up to help. "Ok, I have spent most of my time doing security, now I need to change things a bit. Cindy, you have learned how to do surveillance, so I am assigning this to you. Lucy takes up with helping Jacie and Dr. Perry. Mariann, you're doing your job as we need you, just keep up with your work. Jacie, would you be ok with helping Cindy outside with gathering?"

"I would love to help!"

"I am going to have to keep up with the hunting, so Jeremy and I will hunt and help Mariann with meat preparations. Dr. Perry, how is George doing?"

"Not well. I will be staying close to him."

The group met to get try to coordinate their efforts at keeping the shelter organized and running. George had always been the one who led them and kept up with everything going on within the shelter. It was unnerving for the friends. All of them were strong but they needed guidance. Sam had stepped up to the task. He was capable but had not been in charge since his military service. He still preferred being outdoors even though he had grown used to having to be inside. He was feeling led to be their leader at this time, thanks to his military service. No one felt they could replace George and all of them were struggling, it was chaotic and they were feeling the pressure to step up. George had such a way about him that he could keep all of them on track and right then they had to make a big adjustment and Sam was doing a fine job.

The bunker was a place at this time when all of them were having to work together to solve their problems and find solutions that George had a natural knack for doing, there were some arguments and Sam had to intervene frequently. They were feeling the stress of George being injured, this Sam understood.

George was getting worse and the friends were working to keep up the hope with all that was within them. Sam finally got up and told the group, "Friends, we need to go hunting. We need to keep going, we have work to do. George is in His hands. We need go get busy so we aren't fighting with each other. George is going to make it, so we want him to know that we did everything we could to keep up with our work until he is well." Quietly they got up to go about their work. George's breathing was erratic and Dr. Perry was watching as he started deteriorating. His fever had shot up and the doctor was counting the hours before George was gone. His friends were asking for mercy, they came to the decision that if it was his time, he would be in good hands. As the friends were talking to him, George was hearing them speaking. None of them wanted him to go but they would celebrate their sorrow in honoring their Commander-in-Chief.

He was within the realm of being suspended between life and death where he was aware of a greater place. "Where am I?" he asked a bright light.

"George, you are in the Valley of the Shadow of Death. You are not going to die; your faith has made you strong. I want to test the faith of your friends. They need you so they need to seek me; your time isn't over yet. I still have work for you, you would rather stay here, but I will be with you as you finish what I have for you. For a while, you will be here with me. Your friends need to learn that they should lean on me." The Evil One had stepped in to try to divide them but they persevered and were going strong.

A week went by with the activity going ahead. The friends were finding working together was not as hard as they thought without George's help, Sam had pulled them together and they were getting along very well, they still wanted George back, but until then, they were doing what had to be done. Dr. Perry was tending George when he realized he wasn't hot and feverish. The wound was healing and Dr. Perry looked to his face to see him with his eyes open looking up at him. "Welcome back! You gave us quite a scare."

"What happened? "Dr. Perry filled him in on the shot that hit him. The last thing George remembered as getting everyone across the street and into the alley as he was following behind, he didn't remember the shot that was fired and hit him.

"I was there; I saw bright lights and was being talked to. I had an angel by my side. He told me this was to help all of you. Oww! I hurt, where was I shot?"

"In the chest, you were close to dying."

"That explains why I was told I was in the Valley of the Shadow of Death. I wasn't alone in that place. I had light in that deep darkness. I can't even imagine how horrible it would be going there alone. I think I had lived in that place before I came to know the Voice, it sure felt familiar."

"I am going to go tell the others you are back."

"Thank you, doctor." When Dr. Perry told them George was awake and talking, they bounded to his side with excitement, not wanting to cause him pain, they patted him instead of hugging him. He gave them a sheepish weak smile.

The Exalted Dark One was livid. He had wanted George dead. He was worthless, a criminal his whole life. Another one to give him misery, George was a good leader and was keeping them going, in the wrong direction, this man needed to be eliminated. "Why do you care about him, O Great Voice?" He asked as he mocked him. "He's a criminal, he's nothing to you. How can you want him after all the things he has done? Murder, stealing, lying, drinking, cheating, having no care for you, give him to me! This man is the worst sort."

He was going to the Voice with his accusations against the Chosen Ones, reminding Him of all their deeds of darkness. Discretions were brought to the Voice in trying to claim them for his own. The Voice told him, "They asked for forgiveness so they are forgiven, they are mine."

CHAPER THIRTY-SIX

HENRY AND TORRY'S GRIEF, FORTUNE TELLERS LIES

Henry, Torry, and Jenny were sharing the grief of Jeff's death. It'd been hard dealing with the grieving but with the friends pulling together, they were getting through it as well as they could. Kevin had come to them before Jeff's death; he was a great comfort to them during their time of sorrow. Pastor Lars was also hurting, but as a group and as a family of believers they helped with each other's sorrow. The shelter group was closing ranks as Dark Spirits were working to give these saddened people doubts about the one they served. They all knew the enemy would attack them when they were weakened. Word got back to George, and he called a meeting. "We need to go see Pastor Lars. They aren't doing very well after Jeff was killed." Cindy and Jeremy wanted to go. "George, are you sure you are up to going? You are still recovering and we don't want you to wear yourself out by traveling when you aren't up to it."

"Dr. Perry said I can do anything as long as I get some rest and not to do anything to strenuous. I am doing much better. We need to leave immediately to go be with our friends to give them the comfort they need."

Lucy helped Cindy and Jeremy pack some things they would need for the trip. George was waiting for them when they were ready to leave.

"Let's get the horses so we can get there faster." The horses weren't used very often because being on them made them vulnerable to the enemy. This time they were anxious to get there as quickly as possible. It took a little while to find the horses but they finally did. Jeremy had to make some new harnesses for them and he had made some ropes out of grasses that were growing around the bunker. Mounting the horses, they were on their way. Two hours into their ride, they were met by a man on a horse who didn't say anything for a while. George finally asked him, "Who are you?"

"I am the Spirit of Hope. I will go with you to help you give comfort to your friends. What you do is good, they need you."

"We are appreciative of your company," Jeremy said.

Cindy was singing some catchy songs and the cheerfulness made them feel better. George and Jeremy joined in; Jeremy needed it. He was thinking about having lost Kendra. He wanted to offer some comfort to their friends. The singing was helping to pass the time on the treacherous journey they were taking. They quietly sang most of the way to Lars shelter. The chirping of the birds and the beauty of the landscape was a distraction that was welcome but they stayed aware of the possibility of being spotted. The warm day and taking in the outdoors helped soothe them and make the journey much more enjoyable.

One of the members was outside when they rode up and as he was watching for danger. He ducked into a hiding place as the riders got near. When he saw that they were friends, he came out. The riders got off the horses and let them wander as if they were just out to pasture. They could eat and find water. The shelter member escorted them inside. The friends greeted each other and condolences were expressed. George suggested that they go out to bring in food for them. Cindy went to find and gather for them. They were willing to help them in these sad times. Jeremy stayed with them. "I lost my beautiful wife while we were on a rescue mission to save some Chosen Ones; it was the most painful thing that I have ever had to go through. I thought my life was over. We read the Book and that was when I realized that she was doing well and I would see her again. Kendra would do it all over again if she had to, and Jeff would do the same. He could have given in to serving the Supreme Leader of this world, a false god. Kendra could have done the same, we could choose to serve this world, we have made our choices and all of us would gladly give our lives rather than give up what we know we have. The world sees us as weak, but we are strong, they give in instead of standing up for what they know it right and true. It is much easier to ridicule other people than to face the truth. They have the power to kill as do we; we choose to love them despite them wanting us dead. Our fear is not what they can do to us, but what our Savior can do. Within our community, we come together to love you and you love us, that is how our loved one want us to live. We will miss them, but we have the wonderful hope that we will be reunited with them and someday may be soon. I miss Kendra so much and I think about her every day. I am so thankful that she is truly at home. She is getting the real reward as the Voice has promised. This life is so full of pain and suffering and especially during these hard times. The world has never faced what we are going through. We came to all of you to show you how much we love you and care about you. As members of the Kingdom of Light, we are here to let you know we feel your pain and we stand with you. When something happens to one of us, it happens to all of us." Torry had tears streaming down her face.

"Thank you, Jeremy. You have brought such comfort to us," she said. "It would be easy to feel alone if it were not for the Creator who has sent his Spirit to bring us comfort. We are never alone."

Jeremy turned to Jenny, "How are you, Jenny?"

"I miss him so much, I really loved him. We had gotten really close."

"She is like a daughter to us," Torry said giving her a hug as she cried. Pastor Lars came in from outside. "Thank you for coming Jeremy."

"Pastor, how is Kevin? I haven't seen him since we got here."

"He'll be here shortly. He's outside conducting experiments. I think we have a scientist in our midst. He's remarkable with the science stuff. He adjusted well, and he's learning and we love having him here. Already he's created things to make our lives easier. It's sad his parents didn't want him. Even if they were to come and find him and wanted to take him with them, every person here would fight to keep him. He has learned how nature gives honor to our Creator. His perspective is fresh and innocent."

George and Cindy came in loaded down with all kinds of things for their friends. Cindy explained some uses for some of the finds she had brought in. "Dr. Perry knows about these things so we use this stuff for medicine and Mariann uses some of it for cooking. My job is to go out and find things we can use," she explained. Her face was flushed with excitement. George had found meat for them and he had dressed it out, Jeremy went to help him bring it in before animals got to it. Kevin came in as the meat was at last brought in. "Kevin! Hi guy! How are you?" Jeremy was excited to see him.

"Much better, I still miss mom and dad but everyone here has been so nice to me. I am being taken care of and I really like it here, it has been so much fun. I've been busy helping here. I don't have to make myself food to eat. I am learning to cook, hunt, and I want to be useful." Jeremy laughed.

"Kevin, you look great! We miss you and talk about you often. Too many here trying to mother you," he laughed as Kevin tried to figure out that one. "What kind of experiments are doing?"

"I have been trying to find some uses for some of the plants around here."

"Plants, like what?"

"When you can come back to stay for a while I'll have to tell you more about it." That got a laugh from all of them. It was hard to believe he was only twelve years old, he was one smart kid.

"How did you feel about Jeff," George asked him?

"He was awesome! I wish he were here. We did things together. He didn't deserve what happened to him."

"He got to go to his real home where he is very happy. We miss him but we will see him again."

"I know. That is what Pastor Lars says. It's still very hard, but it'll get easier. Your family here will help you through it. Pastor Lars has been great and has been talking to us about Jeff." Kevin said wrapping his arms around George's waist and George hugged him back.

"It is time to eat, everyone." As they talked about Jeff and how much he meant to all of them, they ate slowly, not wanting the time to go by so fast.

After a good night of sleep, George, Cindy, and Jeremy were ready to go home. "Thank you for coming," Lars said to them. "You have done so much good for us. Now we can move on. One of the benefits of a purified church is everyone can depend on each other. We knew we needed to come, and besides, you would have done the same thing for us."

"We'll see you again soon," George said. "Where did Ken go?"

"He isn't too far away. I will get in touch with him and send him to you."

CHAPTER THIRTY-SEVEN

THE FORTUNE TELLER

Going to the mall was a fun place to stop at a fortune teller's small shop. Young people loved it. They could find out about their dating partners, prepare for the future, or get advice on their current situation.

One afternoon, a young man was having his fortune told to him by a fortuneteller. As he was sitting there, with her looking at the palm of his hand, he stared at her facial features thinking she had at one time been a nice-looking lady. She was about forty years old with her gray streaked brown hair hanging just below her ears. She was a small petite woman with gray tired eyes, with wrinkles around them. He thought maybe she might be sick because of the dark circles around her eyes and the loose fitting dress she was wearing. The dress was red, low waisted, with a wide white collar. She was staring closely at his hand with an intense look on her face, as if trying to figure out what to tell this customer. As he was studying her face, he suddenly saw a transformation that startled him. At first, he was alarmed by the ugly look on the woman's face. Her face momentarily transformed into a grotesque monster. It appeared for only a couple of seconds and then it was gone. When the evil left, she gave him a big smile and foretold the news he was hoping to hear. He had a hard time comprehending the sneering face he had seen. He dismissed it, since she said he would have a long and happy life. The girl he was with went to eat lunch with him after he left the fortuneteller. Both of them were college students and he suggested that they go back to her dorm room for a cozy afternoon. Her roommates had left for home so they would be alone. He wasn't concerned about anything, since he was told he was going to live a long and happy life, with success and lots of money.

The young man was a clean cut, nice looking guy. At the age of twenty-one he was at the top of his game. He was an A student; his parents had threatened to cut off his funding if he wasn't the top of the class from the first year in school. He lived with his parents in the town he was attending school. Classes were fairly easy for him since his father was also an engineer and he worked with him when he wasn't attending classes or being with his longtime girlfriend. His mother was a social planner and volunteered at many events and social functions. What his parents didn't know was about his excessive drinking. He was clever in keeping it a secret from them and had been fortunate not to have gotten into trouble because of it. Both of them were weekend drinkers and attended frequent parties. They were affluent people and expected their children to live up to their expectations in the community. They gave their children the best of everything; it was their way of controlling the kids and it worked for the most part. This son was an engineering major at the college he attended; he was in his third year and was having fun with the nice allowance his parents gave him.

The young girl friend was in her second year of college and she was planning on becoming a nurse. She was a pretty blonde who had been a cheerleader in high school and college. She came from an affluent family and her boyfriend had known each other from high school. He was the quarterback for the winning team he played for. They were always together; both of them were fairly good kids until they started college and the party lifestyle drew them in. They didn't go out as much as most of the other partiers did, but they weren't the same nice kids they were in high school. She managed to maintain a B average in her classes; her mother was an x-ray technician at one of the major hospitals. Her father was on the city council, he was strict with her. In college she had more freedom and at times, she abused it.

It was a Friday afternoon to look forward to. The two of them spent a little while shopping with her parent's credit cards, their arms loaded down with the purchases. With the afternoon slipping away, they tired of the shopping and were planning to go to her apartment. Trudging out of the mall and into the parking lot, they found his car. On the way over, he suggested that they go by a liquor store; there were so many of them it was not hard to find one. Pulling into the parking lot, they parked and went inside. They were in the store for twenty minutes selecting their alcohol of choice. With it purchased, they got into the car and decided to start their celebration early, sitting in the car drinking as the evening was turning into darkness. She decided she was getting hungry and he thought they should go a fast food place for takeout. It was on the next block where they found a hamburger drive through. After a few minutes their food was ready, and they sat in the parking lot eating and drinking some more. He threw the wrappers out of the car window as he leaned over where she was sitting next to him and kissed her. Laughing as if they had no cares in the world, he drove out of the parking lot. She sat close to him touching him in ways that would have been distracting even if he wasn't drunk. A mile down the street, swerving in and out of traffic, he pulled up onto the freeway and made a sharp turn in the opposite direction of traffic. By the time he was up on the freeway, they could hear the distant sirens as police officers had been notified of the driver going the wrong way. Neither one of them were aware of how fast they were going, even as cars had pulled off the road seeing the truck headed straight at them. He was giving her most of his attention, and right before the collision, the truck driver attempted to pull out of their way. It was too late and they didn't even know what hit them.

When the ambulances arrived, they found the two young people were already dead. Sheet metal from the truck had come loose from an improperly secured load and put an end to their lives. The sports convertible top was down as the couple drove. Liquor bottles were scattered about inside and outside the car from all the purchases they had made that afternoon. The car was in an upright position as it righted itself after it had been struck. The car was more of a pile of twisted metal than the once luxury vehicle it had been. The engine had pushed into the back seat with the bodies beneath it.

As for the truck driver, he was dead. At the high rate of speed he was driving, he flipped when he tried to avoid the collision. He had numerous broken bones and his face was so badly smashed that he was unrecognizable. The cab of his truck had been crushed with him under the metal. He skidded down the highway after the rig had come to rest against the center concrete median, and it exploded, sending flames flying, causing debris to hit oncoming vehicles, resulting in other damage, death, and serious injuries.

The truck driver was fifty years old with a wife and two kids waiting for him to get home early for a weekend of a family barbecue with relatives coming from out of town. He was trying to get home as fast as he could. He was a drug user and was under the influence when the collision happened. He was barely aware of the impending disaster until it was too late, and he was driving past the time when he should have taken the break the law required, and he was over his hours.

The prophet of evil said the young man would have a long and happy life. The evil one, who possessed the fortuneteller, was sneering with delight. Lies were his weapons. What did humans expect? The truth? Ha! Fools, these humans were. Complete fools!

CHAPTER THIRTY-EIGHT

A. LUSION

After the death of the young people in the tragic car crash, the woman who made the prediction was busy with her clients coming in. The evil spirits were amused by the number of people who believed in her. At times, she spoke a prediction that was accurate so people were coming to her believing the evil spirits within her. She wasn't the only one who had a booth set up at the mall. The name she called herself was A. Lusion. It was an accurate name, but to her clients, she was a true prophetess. As time passed she had become convinced that she was doing good and making a difference. She was certain she was a real prophetess, but the evil spirits were feeding her narcissism.

One afternoon the Spirit of Truth came to her in human form, "You must stop with these false prophecies or you will die." The Spirit came to her as a middle-aged woman who wasn't an important looking person. A. Lusion just brushed her off. The Spirit was dressed in a long-sleeved purple floral shirt with a deep purple pair of slacks, shoes with thick rubber soles, and her glasses were on a chain that was dangling on her chest. Evil Spirits in A. Lusion were squirming nervously as they recognized the Spirit of Truth, regaining their composure as they told A. Lusion she was jealous of her power. A. Lusion had felt something about this woman who was very kind and spoke kindly, but firmly towards her. The Spirits were speaking lies and A. Lusion chose to listen to them rather than listen to what she felt was the truth, but she did so with an uneasy feeling. Someone had come into her booth so she turned to see who it was and she greeted them. When she turned back to this woman, she was gone. A. Lusion looked around and was confused by how she could have left, and shrugging it off, she turned to her client. "What can I do for you today?"

Sitting in the chair was a distraught young woman in her thirties. She was sad looking, her eyes were wet from crying, and her face was red and mottled. "I just buried my mom, and I am wondering if she is ok now."

Taking her cards, she shuffled them and laid them out in front of her. Taking the client's hands in her own, she gave her a prediction. "Your mom is very happy now, she knows you are here, and she says she loves you and will be seeing you again. Her desire for you is for go on and live your life as you are. Your dad is with her and he is also pleased with you. Keep on serving the Supreme Leader and he will be your guide. They have requested for you to come back here so they can help you with your problems. They are so happy seeing you are so well and they want to see you often." The young woman was laughing through her tears and she promised to come back. The fortuneteller knew her business was secure with this new client. Business was booming for her. Now, the next appointment should be out waiting his turn. Twenty dollars for fifteen minutes was not a bad way to make a living. No matter what, she would never give anyone bad news. People wanted to believe their loved ones were in a better place, and most of them weren't. Maybe someday she would change her ways, someday. She had to make a living.

Her next client was a twenty-year-old college student who asked about his new girlfriend. A. Lusion sighed quietly as she gave him the news, "She loves you with all of her heart. You will marry her and have three beautiful kids. She talks about you all the time as if you are the only man alive. Don't worry about what your friends and parents are telling you, they don't understand her. The two of you will be very happy together. Your parents have heard things about her that has you concerned. She has so much love for you that she needs to share, a lovely girl."

The young man was not comfortable with this but he thought she knew what she was talking about. He had come to her before and liked what advice he got from her. Maybe he could be happy if he loved her in the same way, the more he thought about it, the more he liked the idea. He was a progressive thinker, yeah. He didn't know that he had contracted a deadly disease from her that would soon take his life. She would die in the near future before he did, and before they would suffer excruciating pain as their bodies were torn apart. He left with a joyful expression covering his face.

The next client was waiting for his turn. "Come in," she directed him. He was about sixty years old and was frail. He sat down as if he would break if he sat down with any kind of jolt.

"My doctor wants to do open heart surgery and I am not sure I can survive it, it is a risky operation."

"I can recommend someone who uses natural cures. He has quite a few patients, and he is a doctor of natural science which makes people believe they don't need to see their doctors for treatment and his pockets are lined. Would you like to give it a try and I can call him for you, ok?"

"You think he can help me?"

"I do, your body is made from the earth so natural cures make more sense. Medical doctors know this and they disagree because they make their money from cutting you open."

"I'll do it!"

"Here is his card, call him right away. I will let him know to expect your call." This guy paid her for referrals, and they were good friends. He had gone on the internet and studied plants. In college he had taken some classes about herbs. These scams cost lives, but they justified their practice by claiming these patients weren't following the direction. So far it hadn't been proven that he was the cause of death; most of the people had minor illnesses that would have been healed by that person's own body. He was getting bolder in his claims, thinking he wouldn't get caught. Understanding people's fear made is work much easier, an easy way out was normal and sometimes dangerous thinking.

A. Lusion was on a roll and so were the evil spirits within her. An understanding of vulnerable, desperate people who need good news was profitable for her and others like her. The Voice had all the answers but He told people what they needed to hear, she told them what they wanted to hear. Hope is what A. Lusion liked to think she was offering, her justifying her lies, lying is ok if it serves a good purpose, in the deep recesses of her mind she knew what she was doing was completely wrong, her choice, forget about it, she had to make a living somehow, she swallowed hard. The spirits were delighted as she ignored the sensible reasoning of an all-knowing Voice.

The woman came back to warn A. Lusion about the danger she was in, bringing the news she needed to hear. A. Lusion was nervous and unwilling to give up what she was doing, the power of what she perceived was her gift and the money she wanted and needed. This Spirit gave her another warning and let her know what she would gain by giving up the ways she was embracing for the eternal glory. The evil spirits were trying to make a mockery of the choice she needed to choose and telling her this woman wanted her to be a miserable person. The slick tongue of the evil spirit was winning over this soul, it was her last chance, and she refused to believe there was a place that was as bad as what this woman was telling her about. A. Lusion told her to leave and never to return, she did as she was told.

The day for A. Lusion was great, she had made referrals to her natural science friends, and she made money off her regular and new clients. Walking out and locking up, she walked to the mall exit and she looked out to where her car was parked. In the pit of her stomach she felt something was wrong, shaking it off she walked out to her car. Unlocking it she got in, and started it. Sitting there listening to the engine humming smoothly and after a couple of minutes had gone by while she tried to settled herself, she shifted the car backing out of the parking space and drove out of the mall parking lot. There was still a lot of traffic on the streets so she drove slowly with the lump in her stomach. The street she had to drive down was in a low traffic area, and she felt relief.

At a stop sign close to her house, she stopped. Her mind wasn't on her driving and it was a moonless night. She pulled out into the intersection when a truck speeding down the street, going over the posted speed limit came barreling down the street. A. Lusion never saw it coming, the lights were off and as fast as he was driving she never had a chance, and she was killed instantly. Her car was doubled as it was ripped apart on her side of the vehicle.

The evil spirits who were with her were dancing with maniacal joy as they had kept the Voice from claiming another soul. When A. Lusion did she knew her mistake instantly, the Voice had tried to warn her and she ignored Him, she started pleading for mercy without getting any. She was ushered into the outer darkness where there was fire and gnashing of teeth, including hers. There was fire everywhere and the smell was worse than anything she had ever experienced. This place was desolate. The Evil Dark One greeted her with a dark look on his face and A. Lusion was living in terrifying fear. Looking around she saw other souls wandering around aimlessly and moaning with pain. There was no hope. Fear, pain, suffering, and misery were everywhere. No one looked at anyone else, eyes were empty. She started begging for another chance. "Don't bother, you are here forever. You belong to me," The Dark One told her. Why didn't she listen while she had the chance, drifting aimlessly she thought of all the things she had done during her life. There was no doubt that the Voice was real. The woman who had been sent was the one she sent away was a Spirit of Light, if only she had known, but now she knew who she was.

"The fire here is horrible, I can't take it," she was moaning as were all the souls who were here and there were so many and as far in any direction as she could see. The place was crowded but she never had ever felt so alone.

This place had always been mythical. How could a loving God do this to people? These evil ones were so gruesome looking and they were abusive and ready to destroy. The pain, the pain, if only she could have a few drops of water on her tongue or to go back for just a minute. Relief, please, a little relief. The torment was only to truly die and never see or know anything. She had friends and family she didn't want here, if only she could get a word out to them. The evil ones wouldn't be of any help. Maybe there was a way. Look around, no, only the hot flames and the sulfur smell, the evil spirits, and the Dark One. Why, oh, why did she not see that the Chosen Ones knew what they were doing as many had died and she had been to the arena and watched as they had died with dignity and they refused to turn from the pleasures and riches of the world as she remembered how they looked up and the faces of these people peaceful and serene. A. Lusion was one of those who threw rocks and cheered. How wrong she had been, she had found some of them and had collected the rewards.

Finally, she looked into the faces of the souls here, over there were family and friends and saw many whom she had predicted a bright future for, cringing as she saw the young people who had been killed in the drunk driving accident. Her shame was intense.

Moving around so she could find a way out, she found a sharp drop off she was aware she couldn't cross, and on the other side she could see Chosen One. She suddenly had a glimmer of hope, there had to be a way, "No," one of the evil spirits told her laughing gleefully. This was forever and she started moving about moaning and groaning grinding her teeth in pain with a blank look on her face.

At the scene of the accident, the truck driver was standing outside his truck. His truck sustained damage and he had some minor injuries which he scarcely noticed right now. When his truck had hit and killed the driver of the car, he heard an eerie scream that sent chills through him. The sound of glass and metal colliding was creepy enough but those screams were something he had never heard before and quite likely he would never forget. He walked over to the car and saw the woman's crumpled up body slumped over to the side partially in the passenger seat. He walked away where he threw up. In the distance he heard sirens and soon saw the lights.

The driver wouldn't go back to the car. He was thinking about the screaming he heard and he couldn't get it out of his head, and the realization of what he had done was already haunting him. The police and ambulance were soon on the scene, paramedics were checking to see if she was alive, and finding her dead, started getting her body out of the car and onto a stretcher. Pictures were taken before anything was removed or changed and they covered her up with a sheet. With the body removed, the police started interrogating him. His claim was that she ran a stop sign. Explaining why the car was so badly crushed, he squirmed and had a problem explaining, and he wasn't able to come up with an excuse for why she didn't see him.

Neighbors were questioned and it was found that he had been speeding through the residential neighborhood without his head lights on, and he was drug tested and was found to have drugs in his body. As he was hurrying home to surprise his wife and kids, he wasn't paying attention to what he was doing. He confessed. Eventually he was convicted, went to prison where he was put to death. He met A. Lusion.

CHAPTER THIRTY-NINE
MARCELLO BELIEVES HE IS GOD

President Marcello was the type of man people shouldn't have listened to, but did. His words oozed with lies, but the mentality of the world was distorted and they listened to anyone who told them what they wanted to hear. Mr. Marcello did indeed talk. He was six foot five inches tall, tanned skin that showed his various vacations in luxury resorts. His face was that of a movie star, skin flawless as was his symmetry. His sandy blonde hair was perfectly combed to the side. His bright, sharp green eyes seemed to pierce into the souls of whoever he looked at. His eyes made people feel vulnerable as if he could read their inner thoughts. His perfectly shaped lips, and facial features, surgically fashioned gave off an aura of confidence. He visibly maintained a look of physical perfection. His muscles were bulging with the workouts he spent time in the gym perfecting with the use of steroids. His suits had to be tailored to fit his physique. Men worked to have his looks as surgeons were kept busy trying to keep up with the demand his looks were creating, fitness centers were filled with the desires to have what Marcello was flaunting, women desired him as a hunk of a healthy man of great interest. His face graced magazine covers made the companies huge profits.

He wore tailored suits, designed just for him by high end clothes designers. He hadn't come from money, but his wallet was bulging and he was never lacking. The president could say anything and people would listen. He could go on about most anything and he would be believed with fascination. He had perfected his soft voice and he used his smile to his advantage with an orthodontist making money giving him sparkling teeth. There was nothing he could do wrong; he was sought after as the center of attraction at social functions. His words were like honey, sweet and assuring, and yet, those who listened to the Voice knew the words that came out of his mouth were inspired by the Evil One.

Marcello had come from a small farming area. He grew up tending to his family farm, where they raised food and livestock. His family lived comfortably and not having to do without, but was never wealthy. After years of farming, he decided to become a lawyer. Farming wasn't his forte, he didn't think of himself as being in this type of business giving him such a distasteful image and he figured there were other families who would keep the farm going. He didn't like being dirty. He went to law school, where soon thereafter he began his life as a practicing lawyer. He enjoyed it much better than the life of a farmer.

In his law practice, he quickly moved from an associate to a partner. He had surpassed many of his colleagues who'd been there much longer than he. As an attorney, he learned how being slick in tongue was to his advantage and he used it and perfected it.

The president practiced law for only six years, when politics called to him. He ran for state Governor and won by a landslide. His charm had helped him advance quickly up the ranks of his profession. It was to no one's surprise when he ran for President, and won that too. He had gained popularity during the coup when he had settled the people down and had them organize and take over the mansions of those flaunting their wealth on the televised parties. He believed himself to be of more intelligence than his predecessors.

What no one knew was that he had motives for being president. He had the plans he'd told the people during his presidential campaign, and then there were his personal ones, both were different. President Marcello reassured the people that he would tend to their needs. His soothing voice gave comfort while the world was in absolute anarchy.

The people believed that their troubles were over, but what they didn't know was that an authority much more powerful than the president would soon show His true power, power above all powers. Before his time ended the Evil One would control him.

Behind closed doors, his public stance differed from his private one. He thought nothing of keeping the young girls he had acquired as sex slaves, in which he threatened with death if they left or said anything. They were used for a period of time, and then disappeared without ever being found. His value of human life was that of an earthworm. He didn't care for he was above all others, a god perhaps. The president thought of himself as a solver, a god, a power that could not be stopped. He'd stolen priceless works of art, as much of his belongings had been obtained. He'd stolen people many, many people as well.

He had grown up with parents who were believers and his friends had often ridiculed them, the friends had taken him to meet ones who had a hatred for Chosen Ones and he had chosen to believe in the world system. They had tried to get him back into church but he was set on going his own way. They weren't harsh in their talks with him, but he hated them for trying, and he left home after graduating from high school and never looked back. They sent him letters as they kept up with his career, he eventually ignored them and he was tired of them constantly trying to convert him, so he had them killed and the murders were never solved, both of them were heartbroken when they died. He made sure they knew why he was having them killed, the killer was compensated generously.

He was well aware of the Chosen Ones still alive, but in hiding. He didn't understand his hatred towards them, but all he knew was they had to be killed. There had been some successful deaths of the Chosen Ones and somehow many of them escaped death. This made the president angrier; they needed to die slowly and painfully. They were disgracing the world he wanted to create, a perfect one. Chosen Ones were the scourge on the face of the earth, there had been many killed, tortured, and imprisoned, it was not enough, these people were hiding and escaping, keeping the world filthy, his world would never be perfect until every last one of them were eliminated. He had taken personal pleasure in killing many of them, most of them stayed true to their beliefs, some converted. He was so full of hate and was becoming angrier as he was seeing that he wasn't a god to everyone. The rage was festering and growing, he even took his rage out on people who were supporting him, and misery was spreading as he was becoming possessed by the merciless hatred. Away from the public he let loose his brutality; walking out the door he was charming, slick, smooth, and completely composed.

The hunting games had proven effective, but there had been a few of them that the Marcello had murdered with his own hands. It felt amazing to take the lives of those who listened to that...Voice. But instead of satisfaction from killing them, his hatred consumed him like a wildfire, making him angrier and angrier. He was convinced that the reminder of the Chosen Ones would be found, and once and for all done with and have the world free. There was no room in this world for those who opposed the president.

He made promises to the World Council to take care of them. He distributed the wealth evenly throughout the world so that there were no wealthy people; everyone got a share of everything. Many didn't have to work and those who had the wealth were brought down to the level of the masses. The lazy didn't have to do anything and the ambitious lost everything they worked hard to get. Marcello took what he wanted from off the top so he could live his lifestyle; he did as he wanted. He forced the masses to work so he could live in his own comfort, then all people were allowed to have a home, of one sort or another. Since taking office he had increased his hunt for the Chosen Ones, searching out hiding places using any and all manner and means to find them. Their numbers were swindling, he was out to do as much damage as he could to them.

CHAPTER FORTY

SUN, MOON, AND STAR GODS

Marcello heard of the reports of the deaths of his enemies and was thrilled. He, too, was possessed by evil spirits who were assigned to deceive; their work was going very well. The Dark Spirits were fooling people into a false sense of security. They were leading their victims to believe the stars had their future in good hands and the future was looking good. Eat, drink, and be merry. Nothing else mattered, nothing else was important, and that is what they did. He had his own necromancers available to consult.

The sun, moon, and stars were being worshipped. Massive ceremonies were created and attended to worship the objects in the sky. It was believed that if it couldn't be seen then it didn't exist, even the Dark Spirits were denied that they existed. Dark Spirits were possessing people at the ceremonies. The sun was a powerful force, so it must be powerful enough to help them; it was in the sky, it can be seen, it provides heat, there are hours of the day with bright light, the sun feeds them by giving life to plants which provide food for them and food for the animals they eat. It asks for nothing from a person, never asks for money, never asks to be worshipped, doesn't care if a person loves it or not, never expects a commitment, never is unkind, and never mistreats people. Cancer sometimes, oh well. It takes away the hunger and people sometimes die from not eating, not the sun's fault. Healing powers are possessed by the sum. It is a logical religion, the worshippers say. Believers in the Divine are the ones to blame for the ills of society's problems, the world doesn't want to hear about individual actions bringing about consequences, and eventually it is believed that evolution will solve the problems for a perfect society.

The moon was serene to look upon, and so it was the peaceful symbol. The moon affects the ebb and flow of the oceans waves and currents; it is believed to affect the moods and thoughts of humans. If the changes were not favorable, then it is because the moon god knows best. Lunar eclipses had lives put on hold because of possible impending danger and disaster, especially when starting a new endeavor it could turn out to be evil. The moon could give wisdom and it would serve justice, it is magical and there is a mystery about it that entices the deceived.

Stars were the gods of what was to come and they never lie about the future. When predictions didn't happen as foretold, it was the fault of the seer; they misread the stars. People want to understand themselves and the stars know every person intimately. Worry and fear are easy to read in the stars, a complete guide to get around undesirable futures, the stars are the place to go for all the answers and they give a false sense of hope and peace.

No one wants trial and hardships so they have always sought easy ways out of suffering. People's eyes are blinded, their ears closed, and hearts hardened. In the foolish wisdom of the world the foolish didn't stop to ask about the objects they are worshipping. Those chunks of rock drifting far above the earth are only that, rocks, and are not able to answer back, not able to come when beckoned, without any eyes or tongue to speak. Science has told them they are serving chunks of rocks. Fools never figure that all the false gods are never able to do anything for them other than being what they are.

The Chosen Ones knew the foolishness of these gods. Their futures had been written down many, many years before and every prediction happened as the Book predicted. Their prophet was alive and well. In

Him, and only in Him was there true hope, peace, and certainty. The Creator made the heavens and the earth to remind humans how glorious He is, to worship Him for whom He is. The sun, moon, and stars are for light to keep darkness from being deep, to look at with wonder, to be amazed by Him and Him alone. Mankind, in its desperate need to have the assurance that life after death will give them a comfortable life, will do anything to get it, except to the Giver of Life.

Being a Chosen One requires believing in something not seen; listening to a Voice that speaks quietly, the listener has to listen. His ways take a person to a place of peace that is solid; an assurance of life after death that is living with the Creator of the heavens and earth. Knowing the Voice is listening, has heard and gives an answer, even when it is what is not desired, He says no when it is in the person's best interest. Nothing is by chance; it is for the grand design for the new kingdom that will come when the Savior comes again to take his Chosen Ones with Him.

Chosen Ones have the only prophet who is alive and the only people on earth who can claim a prophet who never dies, the Book never changes with the times, never will. The words are centuries old and have been proven to be true. Each believer has confidence to serve without condemnation, can ask for forgiveness and it is done. Idols cannot offer this assurance; there is no certainly about life after death. The Holy Ones' nature is gentleness, loving-kindness, long-suffering, slow to anger, he is everywhere all the time, he understands every person better than they can understand themselves, he never easily angered. He constantly works to move each person to know Him. With idols people always have to worry about offending them if their lives are going wrong. Seeds of the Holy Spirit need a heart of fertile soil in which to grow. Chosen Ones need to show love for one another and make a difference in the hurting and corrupt world.

CHAPTER FORTY-ONE

A VISIT

As the bunker was bustling with activity there was a knock on the door, there stood Nate with another friend, Ken. "I brought Ken with me and I wanted to see you," Nate said when Cindy greeted them. "Is George here?"

"Yes," she answered, "George, someone is here to see you." George appeared behind her and he stopped in his tracks. Ken laughed.

"George, I am a Chosen One, I am here as a friend." George came closer, not sure what was going on.

"I have been a Chosen One for a long time. When you were in prison, I saw how the Voice had changed you. The Voice told me you were going to leave and I kept the other guards busy when you left. I watched you as you left, and I even fixed the video so as to confuse them. I have worked with editing before, so it was easy to make sure no one saw you. The Voice did everything with the videos, and I just added the confusion. I've worked to get Chosen Ones out of prison; I worked as a senior guard so I know ways to bypass their systems with the Voice showing me what to do." George walked over to him and shook his hand.

"It's good to be on your side as friends."

"It was awesome to have watched you go from an inmate to the man you are today." No one in the bunker knew what to say. "I would like to stay here for a while, if you don't mind." All at once they all found they were talking excitedly and they were talking about the news of what had happened to get George's freedom and they were welcoming them.

"You were taking a terrible risk helping me to escape."

"I was only being obedient to the Voice. The risk I took was like the one you took. All it took was faith in our Voice."

"For once, I'm really living. I wouldn't want to go through what I did again but I am glad I did. It got me to the bottom when I really had nowhere else to go I was picked up and given the hope that I have today." Pastor Lars walked up to them.

"Nate and I are heading back to our shelter. Come back when you can." They said good bye to the others and left.

"George, do you and Sam want to go with us on a trip? The Voice wants to give some people another chance to hear his voice. He will let them die if they refuse. We are going to meet some spirits who will go with us."

"Ken, that's what we are here for."

"I want to go with you, also," Sam said. "I should tell you that his will in no way will be easy. Government officials will be there along with several units of security forces. The Voice told me to go and he wanted some of you to go with me."

"We can be giant slayer with the Voice going and giving us the tools we will need."

"I willingly will lay down my life for Him," George said and Sam was in full agreement. Ken decided not to take anything with them. They would meet with the Spirits and from there depended on the Voice to provide whatever they might need.

"We will be going straight to their place where we are being led to go. There won't be any sleep for a while. The Voice will be letting loose his wrath on them, so we need speed. Time to go," just like that, they were out the door and gone. The shelter started organizing and Cindy and Lucy got busy covering for George and Sam. Mariann bustled about keeping the friends from slacking off when they were needed the most, and Joann helped her. Walking away from the bunker, the men felt something was different. Birds seemed quieter and animals weren't scurrying about as they usually seemed to. It may have been their imaginations as they were realizing that there was very real and extreme danger, and possibly to all their friends. Not a one of them would change their minds, even if they wanted to, they kept going. Up ahead they saw someone just standing while looking at them, waiting for them.

"I am the Spirit of Love. All of you know me. I will go with you to help you with your work." This spirit was someone they did know. He didn't say much, but he didn't have to, and his presence was comforting, "The others will meet you along the way. We will be with you as you go on your journey. No one else can see us except you." It looked like it was going to rain, as they watched the clouds gather in the sky. It looked like a thunderstorm but none of them were concerned. They felt the Spirit of Faith was with them even before they saw him, and they knew the Spirit of Peace was with him. This would possibly be a rough trip, but they were certain they had all the help they needed.

The sweet smell of impending rain was in the air as a cool breeze was blowing in the clouds and the rain was quickly upon them. Just as quickly they were drenched from head to toe as they were soon slogging through mud. They had boots on to protect their feet and were easily sinking down into the mud, making it difficult to walk. Up ahead was a stream they had crossed many times, and as they approached it, they came upon a cow that was stuck in a hole close to the stream. The men were headed over to free the cow when there was a sudden shot that rang out as they were pelted with the large rain drops. Crouching down, they tried to determine where it was coming from. As lightning lit up the sky they saw a hunter with a rifle who had shot at the cow, but he was trying to aim again to shoot when the lightning flashed again. At the same time they saw him, he saw them and he turned toward them with his rifle. What they saw on his face was frightening, the look was that of someone who was angry and out to cause harm. He couldn't see the Spirits with them. Sam and George couldn't see the Spirits, but they knew they were there. George, Ken, and Sam stood still where they were. As the lightning lit up the sky again the hunter raised his rifle and shot. It was very dark and they didn't know what he had hit, but it wasn't one of them. The thunder rumbled and a few seconds later, the lightning made a loud cracking sound as it lit up the sky again. It was then they saw the hunter bent over with his hands covering his face. One of the spirits had put his finger in the end of the gun and they could see it, making it blow up in his face. He was lying on the ground writhing in pain, "My face! My eyes! I can't see!" The man shouted. He wasn't going to be a problem for them. The Spirit came to them and told them to keep moving. The Voice didn't want them to help him. They walked and looked in the hunter's direction as they passed by him, and the lightning showed his face which was gone. He was screaming with pain. He was cursing at them. It ate at their hearts knowing that he didn't hate them, but the Voice. It was not a time to be happy as any lost soul was a tragedy. As they walked by his thrashing body, George looked down upon him and whispered, "May the Voice bless you with his peace." The man hurdled curses at them. They kept moving without flinching.

This was not going to be a boring trip, as the Voice had warned. Up ahead the stream was flowing quickly as rain pelted down. They could see a fast-moving current had already picked up. The Spirit of Faith led them to a spot they were not able to see, but he saw everything, so they were following knowing they were safe with the Spirit who knew the way. The Spirit of Peace gave them comfort as they placed their feet, one foot in front of the other, in the right spots. It was dark and difficult to see and without seeing where they were going, he told them to stop.

"There is a boat right there; the Spirit of Self-Control will go into the boat with you to help you keep from panicking. These waters are rough and you will need to sit still. The boat will be rocking violently and it will be frightening for you. You only need to believe and listen to me." They walked over to the boat and were trying to get into it as it rocked and made it a problem for climbing in but they managed to get in. The boat was torn from the bank and tossed in the middle of the torrent of water. It was a rocky ride, but as Faith told them they sat still as the boat felt like it was about to capsize at any moment. As it was going down the stream, tree branches were bumping the sides of the boat, scraping rocks along the way.

The Spirits were speaking gently to them; panic was rising up in them as they fought to stay focused on the Spirits' voices. It was tough, at that time the Spirits were not visible and the water was loud as it thundered around them. Peace was persistent in his trying to help the two men remain calm. Being thrown around in the stream, they started to see that they really weren't going down. With the element of danger all around them, they settled down and listened as Peace spoke. The Spirits' voices were getting through. The stream finally started flowing slowly, and the sky wasn't as dark and threatening as the storm passed over them. They could see stars and the moon peeking through the scattered clouds. Faith pulled the boat up to some large rocks and beckoned them to leave the boat; the spirit of Kindness met them as he helped them out of the boat. The Spirit of Goodness had a fire going and something delicious was being cooked over the fire; that was when they became aware of how hungry they were.

"Here, sit down and eat, it is all ready for you," he said. They did and it was as good as it smelled, they were even surprised by the wine they were served. When they were full and they had rested, the Spirits urged them to get up and be on their way.

"We will follow this stream for a while," Faith told them. Feeling refreshed, they were off at a good pace. There were many rocks along the stream, some of them slippery but the Spirits kept their feet firmly planted. They were moving with less speed but still moving steadily along. None of them were aware of time. At times, it seemed like they had been moving for many hours and then it seemed like only a few minutes. It wasn't until the skies started getting darker that they had any idea how long they had been gone. The sun had only a short time before they could see the stars twinkling and a crescent moon was rising up. The mud was thick and sticky, and navigating it was taking time. At times one of them would lose their boots and have to stop to pull it loose with a sucking sound, as the boot would be stuck in several inches of mud. The stars were out in all their brightness, showing just how big the sky was. A beautiful moon was giving them pause to admire it, and before the sky had lightened up to much they had put in some miles.

The air was crisp with the fresh-washed smell; water was dripping and had a soothing sound to it as they walked. Night animals had come out to look for food, making scolding sounds at times as the men had gotten to close for their comfort, hissing their unhappiness.

The night went by in a blur; the horizon was lightening up as the stars were disappearing, leaving the moon lonely before it finally found its way past the night. When they stopped for breakfast, they found Kindness and Goodness there beside the fire they had made. Ken, George, and Sam plunked down on some soft grass wondering where the food had come from as the Spirits took care of them and their needs. They were served with beautiful smiles, feeling gratitude to have this rest time and a chance to eat and get refreshed. Not sure about what they were eating, they ate until they were full. Off in the distance they could hear some exploding and sounds like land being cleared with heavy machinery. It sounded like some large rocks may have been blasted to make way for some land development.

"Time to head off towards that forest over there," Faith informed them. The forest looked ominous and foreboding. Heading in that direction where they were being lead, they found themselves walking along on uneven ground where flash floods had cut streams and trenches, some being deep and sharp. Though the landscape was treacherous going, it must be quite stunning if looking at this from above. Traversing this terrain was difficult even when dry, but with all the water it was dangerous as the water was rushing through there. The sun was well up over the horizon and the day was warming as they were making their way along. It was going to be a beautiful day. Ken, George, and Sam had become great friends. Ken was so delighted to get to know George as a human being rather than as a prison inmate. He was learning about how he had come to the troublesome path in his life. This long trip seemed to be as much for them as for whomever they were to help. They were a canvas that had started out blank and the master painted a marvelous portrait with seemingly random strokes of his brush. The work was ongoing until the final moment when the picture was complete in eternity, showing the finished portrait.

They came upon the place where they could see the effects of the explosion. It was a town that was being torn down, and they stood where they were, staring. People were being loaded into open trucks with guards pointing rifles at them. As they watched, they saw an older couple trying to get into the back of the truck with the prodding of the guard as he became impatient with them. When they made several attempts to get in and failing, the guard shot them as the ones in the truck were screaming and in a panic. Some children were trying to run away and they were also being shot and killed. The men were horrified as they watched helplessly. The truck filled up and the driver left with the people standing up in the back, working to keep from losing their balance and falling. The guards were laughing with apparent delight at what they saw as accomplishments, hoping they would be recognized as having found them and get a chunk of the reward money. Obviously, they were Chosen Ones. Another truck pulled up to take the place of the previous one, and it too became filled with some of the Chosen Ones being shot and killed as had the former truck had left. Walking away was hard as they were feeling helpless and saddened by what they had just witnessed. They went on their way to do the task assigned to them.

They could see that the forest was close and this place seemed overgrown and wrought with danger. Besides the danger of the forest, it appeared the rain was catching up with them. By this time they were getting hungry and it was time to stop for lunch. They hadn't seen the Spirits in a while and were hoping they were going in the right direction. In their backpacks they had some jerky meat and some hard bread, which they ate with their water, and the dried fruit finished off their lunch. The rain was fast approaching, so they were off, not sure where they were going but feeling like the direction they were going was the right way. Upon entering the forest, they had to contend with many seen and unseen obstacles. The forest floor was littered with the usual assortment of leaves, twigs, roots, bugs, and snakes. As it started to rain the moving crawling things were going for protection from the weather. With the dark clouds, it made seeing in the shade a bit more of a challenge. Mostly all they heard were the rain drops hitting the leaves on the trees and the splattering on the ground. With all the dripping water, they were getting a bit of a chill as they were soaked. The birds were chirping, but otherwise it was quiet. All of them wondered why the Spirits weren't visible to them. Their presence was felt.

"We're a long way from the bunker," Ken said.

"I have no idea where we're going," George was wondering aloud. "It looks like we will know when we get there," Sam was saying.

The rain clouds passed after a light rain and the sun was shining even though the sun was barely making it through the trees in the small patches, it was pleasant for the men. The ground was spongy with rotting and fresh leaves. Squirrels were racing from tree to tree and were scurrying away as they were getting to close, the birds were chirping and singing their happy songs, bugs were crawling about and occasionally other animals were spotted. The day was beautiful, even getting humid as the afternoon passed. About dinnertime they came to an open grass land where deer were out in the open eating the lush green grass. "Do we go straight across or do we go around?" Ken asked.

"Go straight across since we need to hurry," Sam said.

"Here we go," George said.

Out in the middle of the meadow they were marveling at how incredible it was. Some snakes were slithering away as rabbits and other small animals were startled. The sun was warming up the land. Lifting up their eyes, they noticed a man approaching who looked to be in his thirties. He looked athletic; as they got closer to him they could see he was a nice-looking guy wearing a very big smile. The blue jeans and red and black plaid shirt rolled up to his elbows showing off his muscular arms only added to his charm.

"Hello," he said. "Are you the Chosen Ones I am supposed to meet?"

"We are Chosen Ones but we didn't know anything about meeting anyone."

"I was sent to you to guide you."

"Where are you taking us? And who sent you?"

"Don't worry about it I will take care of you." They continued to walk and George felt as if they were going in the wrong direction in a subtly different way.

"What is your name?" Sam asked him.

"Just call me Harrison." George whispered to Sam, "This doesn't seem right, the Spirits were more direct with us." Sam was watching the direction they were headed, they seemed to be going at a forty five-degree angle away from the route they had been going.

"Who do you work for?" George asked him again.

"I am here to lead you."

"Where?"

"To the place I have been sent to take you." By this time, they were on the other side of the clearing. The men were having feelings that something was wrong. Entering a thicket of heavy underbrush, they were veering off in different directions, planning to meet a short distance where they could see some large boulders. The plan was to find a way through the rough territory and meet at the designated place. Harrison turned to face Ken and stared at him.

Ken grew up in a close family with two brothers and one sister. His parents were a happy couple who made sure the kids were raised right and had good solid values and work ethic. One brother was a pastor, one had gone overseas to help believers stay safe; he was a Special Forces soldier with plenty of training in survival skills. His sister was a doctor and she did missionary work around the world. His parents were getting on in years and Ken had put them in hiding where they were continuing to help others. Ken had turned to law enforcement, and he also had special training and he was useful in helping with keeping Chosen Ones undetected so the drones wouldn't spot them. He knew how to remotely disable them and had been teaching shelters how to do it.

He was a six foot one man with a toned slim body; he stood straight and he seemed confident. His dark brown hair, soft gray eyes, straight white teeth, and deep dimples made him seem boyish when he smiled. At the age of thirty-nine, he was quite the good-looking man who had married his high school sweetheart. He lived with his two kids in the shelter with Lars, and they were planning to move to the shelter where his parents were living as soon as he finished up the work he and his family had to do. He was devoted to the work he was doing and there were times the thought about why he did what he did. There were doubts and fears he didn't tell his family.

"You weren't sent to help us, you have other plans, and you want to hurt us." He looked around trying to find George and Sam without seeing them. He was unaware of them having gone in a different direction, Ken was in trouble, Harrison had raised his hand and then Ken noticed the spear that had appeared out of nowhere. "You are going to die!"

"Why?"

"You are doing the work that is making the Supreme Leader very angry, and I am here to stop you. You won't bow down and serve him, he wants to take your soul with him to eternity. If you die you will live with him and he will give you everything you could ever want or need. Wouldn't you like to live with him? He wants you and going to help those people you are to meet are going to go to be with him and you can save yourself trips by letting me take you to them, you would be much more useful that way." Ken felt anger burning within him, it was ugly and he was shocked to feel the way he did, he had always thought of himself as a calm kind of guy. He felt the pain of it as it rose up within him, he turned to walk away when he heard the hissing, and then Harrison raised his hand and Ken saw the sharp claws and the transformation as he turned into the Evil Snake that he was. The eyes were yellowed and the pupils were tiny pinpricks, the teeth were severely yellow and razor sharp, his body was black with long arms reaching out in a menacing manner, causing Ken to inhale sharply. The demon was reeking of sulfur and making Ken nauseous. The sharp pointed ears were twitching in anticipation of retrieving a soul. Ken was close enough to reach out and touch this creature and it was slowly moving in for the kill and as the raised hand came down with the claws coming close to his face the sneering demon was in his game, Ken was about to die, he was willing to and wasn't afraid, which added some irritation to the demon's demeanor. With his hands raised up in a defensive position, waiting for the inevitable to happen, the demon's face suddenly had the sneer replaced by a look of surprise and then sheer terror as it looked over Ken's shoulder, Ken turned to look to see what had caused the fear, he didn't see anyone or anything, he turned back to the demon and it was backing away, in a hurry. He knew what it saw even though he couldn't, he smiled.

George was also looking around trying to find the other two. He heard some sounds around him and felt a chill. This was not a part of the forest. He felt what was like wings hitting him on his head and it was hurting him as the creature relentlessly attacked him, fear bubbled up within him. The creatures were gathering as he was seeing more dark shapes flying around, getting closer and closer. And as they got closer he could see their faces, the teeth were sharp and dangerous looking, the faces were menacing and their intentions were clear. Some of them were hovering around him and some were landing on the ground getting closer. He turned and saw these creatures had surrounded him with their mouths open and ready to attack him. The ones on the ground were the size of small animals but the one coming toward him was large and coming to him as if he were the one in control. "What do you want from me?" He asked it.

"George, you have committed murder, you have been a thief, you have been full of hatred, and you have despised your precious God. You are mine forever, this is your last day, there is your place reserved for you in the furnace of doom. You are useless in this world and I am here to take you with me. Denounce that Holy One of yours because He doesn't care about you like you think he does this is my world where you have wandered in and now, come along." He was moving slowly closer and George could smell the nastiness of him, there was a cold chill that set the hairs on his arms and the back of his neck standing up, it was looking hopeless for him and the dark creatures were moving ever nearer. "I have gotten permission to take you with me, so give up." George closed his eyes as he heard shrill screams, he opened his eyes as he heard the sound of rushing as if the wind had blowing and he saw a brilliant white robed spirit with a sword in his hand walking between himself and the cringing creatures as they were walking backwards in fear, the spirit didn't say a word as he kept walking and pointing the sword at the evil creature, George remembered that he wasn't given the spirit of fear, he had the love and had been given a sound mind. He was free indeed! The light stayed with him until everything had quieted down. George sat down knowing how helpless he had felt, the light brushed against him as it left. George stood up and started looking for his friends.

And Sam had stumbled along trying to find a place to meet Ken and George when he was picked up by something he couldn't see, there was no warning, he was carried into a shadowed place where he found himself falling and as he landed he looked around and all he saw was darkness. He looked up and he saw light from above, he stood up stretching his arms to find out how wide his prison was. The hole was very narrow and he was about to get sick, it was the claustrophobia pounding into his head as memories came at him with a vengeance. An awareness of something in this hole made the fear scream within him, he was having flash backs of being in a war zone and the enemy had attacked. Grenades were tossed, landing close to their positions, they had been spotted, comrades were killed and he needed to find a place to hide, he had found a hole and crawled into it. He had heard a gun going off and the grenades were hitting their targets as screams of death was resonating all around him. Even in the hole he could smell the blood, he needed to get out and get some help. Where was his rifle? He struggled to get out of the hole, by the time he was out and the shooting had stopped, his comrades had been hit and medical help was around when the warriors had been hit. Medics were tending the wounded a short ways away and Sam was trying to help, the soldier had a serious head injury, he realized as he wiped sweat from his eyes, the medics were wanting him to sit down so they could attend to him but he refused until his comrades had been attended. His injury was a minor head wound but the hit was enough to knock him out. The evil spirits were tormenting him trying to get him in a state of mind to take control and start blaming his God. Then he heard a quiet voice, "Sam, trust me."

He was sweating but he stopped and quietly said, "I do trust you, help me." He touched the sides of the hole and found some roots he used to pull himself out of the hole and as he climbed out, sat down catching his breath, getting his heart beat back to normal, he was hearing the spirits scream on the battle field and he got up to walk away and the further he walked, the less of the screams he could hear including his own as he was feeling his fear and then a calmness come over him. "Sam! We have been looking for you, Harrison is an evil spirit and he led us here."

"I had something horrible happen to me." They sat down to rest and talk about what had just happened to each one of them. They were shook up but otherwise doing well; as they were talking about it the Spirit of Light came to them.

"This is a place where demons are worshipped and they live here, you have been given freedom from some things you have been afraid to face."

"Well done!" Faith told them. "Rest here and eat. We will be arriving at your destination soon." With his road you will come to Terrell where you will start your work. You will find shelter there. Be careful, these people will be wary of you. Go to the abandoned church that you will see as you enter into the town and we will send the people to you." Over the hill they saw the small town down below, and it was a busy day there. It was nestled up against the wooded area that was behind it, the shops lining the main street were the creation of the people who lived there as if they were in a world of their own. Homes were sprinkled on all side of it as if guarding it from unseen threats. The Spirits had gone on ahead of them to prepare the towns people, as the three men entered the town the people stopped to stare at the three crumpled looking men. Ken saw the church building so they headed for it, the people were following them. Going into the church building, the men were looking around, looking for a way to use it, it looked abandoned and had been unused for years, as time had taken a toll on it. They set their packs down as people started coming in.

"We were sent here to give you a chance to have your lives changed; you are going to die if you don't come to repentance." Ken told them gently. "Why don't you all have a seat somewhere?" George, Ken, and Sam went around making places for them to sit. These people were very suspicious and curious at the same time. Finally, they were all seated.

They were told what their future was without Him, no hope, and in eternity with unimaginable, horrific suffering. Suffering in this life was nothing in comparison to the afterlife. George and Sam got up to tell their stories of how they had their lives changed and were living in freedom; the congregation was listening with their full attention. An invitation was given to those who wanted this new life. The response was overwhelming.

For the next three days, these men stayed where they were to do as the Spirits guided them. By the time they were to leave, the town had changed. Many of them had participated in the demon worship, as the town was known for its spiritual activity, it was dealing in tourism for occults and as of that day, it was a day the demons were promising retaliation for the treason.

On the morning of the departure, one of them offered to take them back on a plane. "That would be great!" George exclaimed. Saying good bye, they headed for the airport. Mayor Stone drove them to the airport, talking excitedly and asking questions. George, Sam, and Ken gave him warnings about the demon activity that would come to them and try to destroy what they now had, he needed to keep the friends on constant alert and they would come to them and try to destroy them, he needed to keep the friends on constant alert and not get slack about their faith, and the attacks were going to come, not if they would come. Mayor Stone had a somber demeanor as he considered this and promised to do everything in his power to be watchful. He told them about what they had been doing and how the town had prospered through the use of the occult. This had been a tradition for so long and with times as they were, it was time to clean up and put the house in order. George explained to him that now he would have to start planning for going into hiding as they were going to be hunted down and placed where their fate was to be determined by the world authorities.

They shook hands with the mayor and the pilot had to sneak them on his plane as they didn't have the chips and would have been arrested had they been caught. The mechanics were so busy with their work they had to do that getting on the plane was fairly easy. They headed for the airport close to their bunker.

Flying over the woods where the demons were residing was chilling, they didn't see anything but it seemed dark and dangerous; they were taking deep breaths and sighing with relief for having a shorter trip home. Flying over the airport, they could see platoons of troops who were milling about and doing drills to keep their skills honed, some of them were using the firing range, some were in formation, and they were carrying their weapons so the friends had to be careful. Max landed at the end of the runway and was preparing to take his plane to the hangar, it was a small airport that had been taken over by the military but was still used by the local pilots. Max knew many of the soldiers. Private planes flew in but when they did it usually caught the attention of the soldiers so Max had to come up with a cover to get the men off the plane safely. He taxied down to the end where he was to turn to park his plane in the hangar. "When I get to the end of the runway, you need to jump out and run as fast as you can, I will pause briefly to give you time after that those soldiers will want to know what I was doing, they are suspicious about pilots who are in aircraft not their own." They were ready and waiting, Max got the plane to the end where there was a field of grass without any buildings. When he stopped, they jumped out, fell to the ground and rolled into the grass, disappearing, and were gone. Sam had given him general directions to the bunker.

The friends had their packs loaded with food and water, not likely would they be hungry but it was just in case something happened. They had a way to go to get back to the bunker as they had to walk so they headed out, staying out of sight of the highway, Sam looked over to the road and saw a truck that had a cover over it, "Wait here for me," he told the other two. He left his pack with them and started towards the truck with George and Ken wondering what he was doing, they were apprehensive and curious until they watched him as he went slowly to the back of it after having watched to see where the driver was, not seeing a presence for a few minutes, Sam went to the back of it, cautiously lifting the tarp, peering inside, he was studying it. Satisfied that it was safe, he dropped the tarp gently and took off in their direction, when he got to where they were waiting, he had a grin on his face that made the other consider him as having lost his senses.

"I found our ride back," he informed them.

"Sam, I didn't think it was all that warm out here, but maybe, just maybe, you are a bit overheated,

"George replied.

"No, really. The truck is pointed in the direction we are going, so let's take advantage of the wheels." Sigh, "Ok, here we go." With that, they started out for the truck, walking soundlessly, and creeping into the back of the truck. They had just settled in for an indefinite wait when they felt a movement of the truck as someone was moving about up front as the person was getting in. The men looked at one another in surprise and were thinking about what they had gotten themselves into. Instead of the fate they thought was about to be given them, the driver had stopped to take a nap and had gotten out to walk around for a minute to walk himself up. Sam kept a vigil as he peeked out the back of the truck to watch for oncoming traffic as they were traveling along and the turnoff to the bunker. The truck was empty, fortunately for them, as the driver was driving recklessly and freight might have caused them to get hurt. The trip was short as Sam announced, "Get ready to jump and run, we are almost to the road." There were no vehicles behind them so they were crouched and ready to go. "Jump!" The driver had been driving recklessly but not very fast, they jumped and rolled, landing on their packs, they moved off in a direction the driver would not be able to see them in his rear view mirror. The grass was grown up after the rains and provided the protection they needed. Some cars drove by, Sam got up to check the direction for other traffic, there wasn't any sign so he motioned for them to cross the highway. They had a quarter of a mile to walk to the turnoff but they made it and went through the weeds to find their way home.

"I am so ready to get back," George said. "I think I could sleep for a week."

Later they were back at the bunker and they had a captive audience as everyone got to hear about their adventures.

CHAPTER FORTY-TWO
CHURCHES AS A SYMBOL

Churches had been a symbol of life that was good, meeting together for support and learn how to live a life that keeps civilizations at peace with each other. The Book was taught and living by the rules and having a way to live without hate made people civilized. The rules were for only one ruler who taught followers how to live and treat one another to keep harmony in every society. There would be respect for each other, loving one another, and have only one King who ruled with perfect justice, giving room for healthy happy living. Families would thrive, children obedient, and needs would be provided. The umbrella of protection was for real life and real living. The rules were simple and fair. Each person would have plenty for their own needs. The human race was to be a reflection of Himself and He alone was to be worshipped and honored without other gods in His place for He is a jealous God. It was good. The Church He set up was to teach its followers how to live in this perfect harmony. The church allowed itself to be corrupted, they made allowances to make room and excuses that the Evil One convinced the Church that it was the loving Godly thing to do. It was hard to tell the difference between the Church and the rest of society, it didn't separate itself to stand up for what the one true God had intended for it. The Great Church chose to compromise, neither hot nor cold.

The Exalted Dark One was elated. "Humans just don't get it. We don't want them to go through all the ridiculous trials that make humans suffer. All of these weaklings just need assurance that they are on the right path and that's what we can do for them. I will lead them and distract them away from listening to another one. We can let them think they have it all. Keep them believing that anything that feels good to them is right. Have them ignore the inner voice that tells them what is right is wrong and what is wrong is right. Drown out the Voice. Make them believe those who have a voice for Him is so old news and they aren't with the times. We want them to think that because they are a "good" person they won't come to be with us. If they think about having faith in Him they might change their ways and we don't want that to happen."

CHAPTER FORTY-THREE

HENRY AND TORRY FIND
THEIR HOME IN TERRELL

The people of Terrell were happy about their new friends coming to give them the Good News but now the Spirits were leading them a direction they weren't sure about, only that they needed to get some help. The demons were afraid, their territory had been violated and they were angry. The airplane pilot, Max, decided to go to the shelter to see if he could get a pastor to come to teach them and have a doctor to remove the microchips. The Spirits of Light were working to protect them from the evil forces at work and were at war fighting the people everywhere, especially those who were the weakest, there were ones who were being attacked and suffering physical illnesses from turning away from the demons. The mayor had been warned and he was concerned, this town was choosing to fight with what they had learned.

One of the people had been meditating on the words he had learned from the friends who had brought word to them about living life as a believer. He had been sitting quietly when he was confronted with one of the suicidal demons, he could see it. "You will not and cannot be accepted as one of them," it told him. "You were in so deep and it is too late for you, the things you have done are unforgivable. It's not like you were only lying, you were converting people to believe in us so there is no way for you to be accepted. They didn't tell you that, it is true." To make its point, it took a claw and raked it across the man's face, leaving a gash that was bleeding. The man reached up when he felt the pain and touched the cut, pulling his hand down, he saw blood on his hand. The fear in his eyes made the demon laugh with a laugh meant to harshly condemn him, his head dropped to his chest with the shame he self. It was true that he had done those things, he had done many things that were wrong, he knew he was undeserving of compassion, it was true. The demon was laughing and urging him to end it all. Out in the woods he had thought he was alone with the demon, unaware of the presence of another person, he was startled when someone touched his shoulder, causing him to jump. He looked up to see the mayor standing at his side; he stood up and faced him. The mayor saw the gash on his face and was alarmed. "Connor, what happened?"

"I was attacked by a demon who wanted me to kill myself and I was considering it." Connor related to the mayor what had transpired, he looked around and the demon had left without Connor being aware it had left.

"Connor, that isn't true, as long as you have life, you can have forgiveness. You have been forgiven. Let's go back. We are all guilty of breaking every law and we have all been forgiven, even if you didn't actually commit the act but considered it, we are going for some help. I was talking to George, Sam, and Ken and they told me many things about it."

A meeting was arranged with Mayor Stone discussing having Max leave to see about bringing back a pastor. None of them had the Book so they wanted to learn more about the Voice. The Spirit of Faith was working to strengthen the Chosen Ones as the Spirit was guiding them on their journey of prophesy. Through the Spirits, the people were finding the refreshing cleansing of new life, with many of them becoming aware of what could have become of them if they hadn't seen the light. It felt like they were awakening from a dark dream and found light amidst a frightening nightmare; it felt as though they had had their eyes closed and suddenly they were seeing the world in a different perspective. Carrying heaviness around wasn't noticed if it had been carried around for a very long time and when the weight was lifted it was eye opening and refreshing, being able to dance when it was too difficult before.

The mayor talked about how this tiny town had changed, finding a new beginning opened their eyes to the wisdom, they lacked before. The oppressive spirits that had one held them in tight bondage had been losing their grip on those minds and souls but, the Dark Spirits wouldn't give up so easily. This town was so isolated by the horrors that were present and the darkness had been like a wall to those wishing to settle for a normal life. Those residents were to be delivered over to the dark forces. It had been a town desperate for hope they didn't even know they needed until they found it. The Voice had watched over that town, and guided the Chosen Ones there, to give hope and faith to thirsty people and with the Living Water they were thirsty for more, much more.

"I want to leave as soon as possible since Connor was close to dying and we need help as soon as we can get it," Max was saying.

"I had some of my family who lived over there and they knew Jeremy, I have been there with one of my cousins who was a friend of Jeremy's, it has been a long time since I have been there but I think I may be able to find the farm where the bunker is again."

"We don't know anything about what's going on there other than what these new friends told us." Jeremy pointed out the proximity of the place. "I'm good at finding things on the ground that I see from the air. I have been flying for a long time, you know."

"Connor is doing much better and he is right in the middle of making preparations with the full cooperation of the rest of us," Mayor Stone told him.

"Get a doctor to come back with you, if you can, so we can get these chips taken out before the outside world finds out about us, we need to get things done, and quickly, everyone had been working hard on getting ready, time is against us so leave when you can and we will continue with our efforts." The mayor was efficient in his job, not only as a mayor, but as a leader and as a friend.

"I'll need to fly them here and back. I think it may be a good idea to get my chip taken out when I get back here. For the final trip, I'll talk to the doctor about removing the chip when I land the plane, then hike here on foot."

"Before you leave to take the doctor home, we'll make sure you have anything you may need."

"I need to go check my plane to make sure it's ready."

"Anything we can do to help?"

"Everything should be ready to go since I check it often. You stay here and watch the town."

"Our friends told us to talk and to stay open for guidance, we need to be listening. It is time for us to have a town meeting to get our concerns out in the open and come up with possible solutions."

"Good idea, since I'll be flying to an airport where the military are stationed. When I flew our friends we saw them, but I was able to get them safely away by flying along the back-run way out of sight of the soldiers. Fortunately, I had to stop for another plane, and when I did they jumped out and ran into the brush. I'll have the chip taken out right before I start back here."

Later in the afternoon the townspeople got together to go before the Voice to plead for the safety of Max. The spirit of Faith was there encouraging them. These Spirits were with them as the Dark Spirits were fighting to reclaim the souls they had considered to be theirs. The Spirit of Doubt was deployed to stop Faith. Doubt was good at what he did, and he found one of the weak people and started to try to turn their attitude negative. The friends had warned them about the spirits' work and what they would do. Faith fought back and the Spirit of Doubt fought for them. Fear was coming at them and the mayor brought these people together to strengthen them.

The entire town met together to pray. The mayor started off the prayer as others joined in. The Spirit of Love was busy and the Spirits of Light were strong and the Dark Spirits were afraid and desperate. The walls needed to fall down. Terrell came together to hear the story about Connor and were astounded by what had happened to him, they saw the cut on his face and they were afraid, if this could happen to him, then it could happen to any one of them. No one had any experience being on this side of the demons and they were worried. The time had come to get some help and answers.

The mayor stood up and announced, "We will never be able to take anything for granted from here on out. From now on we are going to have twenty-four hour a day prayer time. For those of you who are able, come sign up for times that work for you. We are in danger. If any of you start feeling the pull that is leading you astray, come to us and we will strengthen each other. Please don't be ashamed, we need each other and we must stick together. The evil one will work hard so he can divide and separate us from each other. If you feel that happening, find someone and you will be prayed for. Do not let the enemy conquer. We are trying to get a pastor who will teach us more of what we need to know. This town needs to strengthen one another. Focus on what we have been taught so far, the Evil One must be rebuked, we can do that."

The ones who felt the sting of the snares of the evil spirits stayed with the mayor and those who were led stayed with him and he gave them the comfort with everything he knew and to encourage them so they knew they weren't alone in their struggles. The things they were learning was priceless, they had made a decision to stand firm and together they were finding they were having success. The friends from the bunker had done their work effectively; they had listened to the teaching that had gotten them riled up enough to fight. George was a leader who kept them on track and going in the right direction. The friends from the bunker had been working outside and beyond the world they had made for themselves; they wanted to go far beyond their small world to make a difference far and wide. Max planned to fly to the airport to try to get them the help they needed the next morning. Everyone in Terrell were hyped up and ready to get started with getting their hiding place ready for a teacher, it was sobering to know how vulnerable they were without having more good solid teaching. People passed through their town but it was not a popular tourist town because of worshippers of demons with sacrifices, many found them distasteful and chose worship of various other sorts. Terrell was considered only a stop to get from one place to another. Most of the people living here were suspicious of strangers who showed up here, since it wasn't attractive to outsiders. It was a seemingly unfriendly place and closed to anyone not having connections to it.

After a good night's sleep and having made his pre-flight checks, Max was ready to go, Mayor Stone drove him to the airport and dropped him off, he went into the terminal where he had a cup of coffee with some of the other pilots and members of the armed forces, they were laughing as one of the other pilots was telling some jokes, Max had a donut in his hand as he told the guys he would be back later and to keep his spot on the runway open, they laughed and waved him off, some of them followed him out of the room so they were making their way to their own planes. His was in the hangar so he went through the rigors of the pre-flight checks that had to be done, he got in the plane, started it up and listened to the engines and they sounded normal so he was ready to go on this trip. After he finished up he got into the plane. Strapped in his seat, doing his final instrument check, he took it out and heard the chatter in his headset while waiting his turn, shortly he was cleared and took off to be ready for the final clearance and he taxied down the runway when given the word. His flight plan had been filed, so he took off and was in the air. The flight would be a short one, but dangerous. But Max was confident and had no reason to believe anything would go wrong, he had done this many times, he knew he was protected and wasn't worried.

The flight was smooth as was every other flight he had been on, he was about halfway back to the airport where he was to land when suddenly he smelled smoke and as he looked out the window, and saw that both of the engines had caught on fire. He saw the black smoke and yellow flames, he needed to find a landing spot, but where? It looked like he would have to crash land and his work would be for nothing. There was no power, this was it. Preparing to crash he was braced, except the plane wasn't going down. It was floating soundlessly above the tree tops and soon he saw the airport, still the plane was floating as though being suspended in midair, he couldn't see how it was possible. Max was baffled, his hands weren't even on the controls and still he was headed in the right direction, the airport. The instrument panel wasn't were working the way it should, he drifted the rest of the way to the airport and the plane stayed up and when he saw the runway right in front of him, he didn't touch the controls. Landing was a bit rough and he was jarred from his shock. No power but he drifted to a stop, without his hands on the controls. Realization hit him, he had been taken down with his with his invisible pilot and he had become the co-pilot and his pilot had spared him. He sat motionless in the pilot's seat without moving as he heard voice on his headset asking him what had happened, he had no way of telling them the unbelievable story. When he went into the hangar the mechanics were talking about the incredible landing they had just witnessed.

"How did you do it silently?" they asked him? "The engine caught on fire and I lost the other one when it caught on fire. I had no power to land; I had no power from several miles away." They couldn't believe it. When they checked the plane, they saw no signs of a fire and a further check, they found no reason for engine trouble. Max understood. Divine protection was on his side. It was an amazing experience he wasn't likely to ever forget.

He chatted with the mechanics for a little while before he took off to go to the bunker, he was trying not to act as if he were in a hurry.

"I'll be back in a few days. Take care of my bird for me."

"Yes sir." The mechanics answered. As he walked to his plane, he could still hear them talking about the landing. He went to retrieve his pack. As he was walking away from his plane he saw military aircraft landing and some that were parked. It might be tricky getting out of here with the passengers he planned to take back with him. He saw some soldiers walking around and waving at them he walked back through the terminal so he would leave through the front door as if he had a ride to take him somewhere. "Ok," he thought to himself, "how do I do this?" As he was flying over the landscape he saw the general direction of Jeremy's farm while he was still in the air, he knew the general direction he needed to go, and hopefully find the bunker. He hadn't come this far without help. No drug on earth could make him feel as high as he felt right then. He shuffled his pack and started his trek to the bunker with a sense of purpose. No one at the bunker was expecting him, so he wasn't sure how to approach. He finally decided to walk up and hope it went well.

Walking along he was hungry, so he pulled out some food he had brought with him, the sandwich was tasty as was some of the fruit, it would be a while before he would sit down to eat and the water was refreshing. There were some farmers out plowing and he waved at them when they looked up. He had high hopes and wasn't worried about anything at that moment. He felt like life had handed him a new chapter that would be filled will lots of challenges but also events that would amaze him and give him a new outlook on the once oppressed life he had just walked out on.

He was a small man of five feet six inches tall, his hair was light brown and thinning, he had lots of energy and those who knew him teased him about having a jumping bean in their midst, his constant movements kept him from putting on weight as should have happened at the ripe old age of forty three. He had a knack for fixing things and managed to repair or improvise repairs. Having him around was like a breath of fresh air.

Max also knew how to fly helicopters and at times he would fly paramedics out on rescue operations when the ambulances couldn't get to places in rough and in back woods places he would fly in or it would take horses to accomplish the feats. He loved flying, his parents had paid for flying lessons for him when he was in high school, he was a good pilot and like do to do air shows where he did trick flying for their entertainment, no one liked being in the aircraft with him.

He was married with a son who was eighteen years old. His wife, Betsy rolled her eyes at stories she heard about him, but she was proud of him for the awards he had gotten. They lived in Terrell with him and his son, Seth, where they were at the moment working with the rest of the town getting ready for their hiding place. Seth was a good hunter and was an asset to the town. He had been taking flying lessons and was showing promise as an excellent pilot. Betsy made and repaired the clothes for her neighbors and friends.

He was thinking about what he had to do as he came to the road to the bunker, he hoped was the road. Sam was out as usual watching when he saw Max before Max saw him. As he got closer Sam recognized him. "Max, what's up my man? Is everything ok? We certainly weren't expecting you."

Welcome!"

"All is well. We are all excited about the changes we have made but I'm on a mission here."

"Come in and meet everyone. You can tell us what brings you here and we will see what we can do for you."

"Thank you, Sam." They went inside and Sam made introductions all around.

"Max, you must be hungry," Mariann was holding his arm as she took his pack and was directing him to join in to eat with them.

"I am. I was told you're the best cook in the world."

"I don't know about that, but no one complains." She laughed. Lucy whispered to Cindy. "He's so cute!" Cindy agreed. "Easy, Luce, he's married." They laughed. Max was not only good looking, but he was charming and funny. George and Sam noticed the change in him. His eyes had once been stark were now twinkling. Now, they wished Ken had been here to see him.

George asked him, "How are our friends back in Terrell?"

"They are all going great. We are so grateful to you for coming to us with the Good News. We were hoping to have a doctor come with us to remove the microchips. Also, to have someone come to teach us, recently we had some issues that had us scared. The enemy you told us about had come in our midst and we did like you told us to, we have been doing the things that you told us to do and it has worked, if you hadn't told us; our town never would have survived the attack. We thought if we can have someone to teach us we can be better equipped to stand firm, our town would appreciate it more than you could ever know. I came here to ask for help. Do you think you can help us?"

"How did you get here?" George asked him.

"I flew my plane. I still have the microchip so I'm able to do anything I want to. Our plan is to fly a pastor in who would be willing to stay with us and a doctor I can fly back here when we get the chips removed and when I get him back here I will get mine taken out and hike back."

"That's dangerous; we aren't worried about that, we will help you."

"We had a meeting before I left. It was a risk we thought was worth taking. We felt led to come here."

"At another shelter there's a couple I think may be able to help you."

"I knew this was the right place to turn to."

"Early in the morning we can go and ask them. They're nice people and they love be able to help."

"Their son was murdered by soldiers he was a part of and they want to do whatever they can."

They spent the evening talking and Max told them what had happened since they had been visited. He told them about the plans for hiding. Dr. Perry agreed to go back with him and hopefully, Henry and Torry would accompany them. Cindy and Lucy brought in some tea and snacks before bedtime. Jenny had been helping Jacie and Mariann. Joann had been resting, as she hadn't been feeling very well lately. Taking it easy and talking to Mariann as both of them were getting their proper rest.

Joann and Mariann were happily spending time talking about days gone by, they were having fun talking about all the things in their pasts that they had done that were the same or similar. They were content to living as they were for the reasons that they were living the way that was leading to the eternal life where they would finally rest. There were things they missed, such as working openly and not being hindered. Lucy was doing more cooking as she had been paying attention to Mariann's cooking lessons and she was getting to be a very good one.

Sam came in from outside the next morning as breakfast was being served. "The horses are outside and ready to go," he announced. He had gotten up before the sun came up to go find them and have them ready for the others.

"Sit down Sam and eat," Mariann told him. The plan was that Sam would go with Max and Dr. Perry to bring the horses back. From the other shelter they were going to pick up Henry and Torry and go to the airport. Sam would return to the bunker with the horses. The three men went out to get on the horses. They were taking two extras for Henry and Torry in the hopes they would be willing to go with Max. They left with Max as he regaled them with his war stories.

Max talked about his life as a Navy pilot. He had dropped bombs in the wars he had fought in. His commander reprimanded him frequently but had to admire his ability and effectiveness. This man had the same passion for what he was doing as he did back in his younger days. Dr. Perry was hoping he wouldn't get to experience the same kind of thrill Max seemed to thrive on. Max was certainly a colorful man, his dry sense of humor had them laughing in spite of the possibility of being heard so they were trying to keep quiet, which proved to be harder with Max's exploits. They had to wonder how much he was exaggerating, but it didn't matter, and he was making their trip enjoyable nonetheless. It didn't seem like it took long to get to the shelter where their guard was posted and he saw them coming, he went inside to inform Lars, who came out to see who had trespassed. When he saw who his visitors were he instructed the guard to welcome them in.

"Hello, what brings you to the shelter?"

"Good to see you, Pastor. This is a business deal we were sent here for. This is Max. Max, this is Pastor Lars. Max is from a small town that some of our friends were sent to give them the Good News. The entire town has become Chosen Ones. I will be removing the microchips for them. The reason we are here is to ask you if you could spare Henry and Torry. Recently they were under some serious spiritual attacks, so they need some help to learn more about the Book and learn His ways. Do you think you could spare them?" Max had such a hopeful look on his face that Pastor Lars had to laugh.

"Come in and we'll ask them." All of them stepped inside. Henry and Torry were cleaning and straightening up the mess that came with having a group living in one place. When they saw their visitors, they gave them friendly smiles. "Hello, Dr. Perry. Who is this new friend?" Henry asked.

"Meet Max, Max meet Henry and Torry. You two are the reason Max is here."

"Us?"

"It's a real pleasure to meet you. I'm from a small town that recently converted and is desperately looking for someone to come to teach us about the Book, we know so little and need to learn."

"Honey, sit yourself right down here," Torry said patting a chair next to hers, he obediently sat down.

"Henry and I have just been talking about doing more. This sounds like what we've been looking to do. What do you think Henry?"

"This sounds exactly like what we would like to do. Torry, let's do this. Pastor has been teaching us. It'd be an honor to go; we will bring the book with us so we can share." Max was elated and he got up and went over to them and gave them a hug.

"How soon can you be ready? We'll fly back."

"Would you be ok with spending this night here and leave in the morning so we can have this last evening with our friends here?"

"Absolutely," Max said.

The next morning, they quickly made preparations to be on their way. Sam had the horses ready.

"Henry, when was the last time you and Torry rode a horse?"

"A while, for sure."

"You may be sore at the end of the day," Sam said.

"Is everyone ready to go?" Max asked Dr. Perry, Henry, Torry, and Sam. They were ready to go. Sam helped Torry up on her horse; she thought it was funny and it was just like her to find the humor. It didn't take her long to start groaning, "Oh, it's been a while, all right," to which started them laughing so hard they were afraid they'd fall off their horses. No one could help but love Torry. She had a way to find humor even in the most unpleasant of situations. Henry thought these people didn't know what they were in for, but it was too late to turn back. He smiled at the thought of helping new Chosen Ones. There were so many people they had been working with and training.

Riding along absorbing the warm sun and being out on the beautiful day, they were cheerful and having a friendly conversation when they heard a plane flying low and then plummeting to the ground crashing. There had been a plane that they heard but had not seen and it had been close. They heard the loud crash and then the explosion as smoke filled the sky and fire was spreading as sparks were flying up and scattering causing other fires to start. The woods they were riding through at the time were thick and shady and all of them were safely under the protection of the trees. Soon this part of the woods would be crawling with law enforcement so they got their horses moving in a hurry. As the riders were running their horses, they spotted the emergency vehicles up ahead. Fearing they would be caught, they turned the horses to go deeper into the trees and try to get around anyone who might see them and as they were moving away, they came upon the plane crash. It was a small plane with only room for two passengers, the wings had been sheared off and it didn't seem likely there were any survivors. They needed to find a way around so they could get to the airport.

Max had an idea, "Sam, do you think we can back track and back into the woods to get around? When I was in the air flying in I saw some country that is rough but I think it may be the best way to get around, it will slow us down and we need to be very careful."

"We are going to have to take another route and it looks like you have a pretty good idea how we should travel, so let's go that way," Sam answered. With that they turned the horses that way and went the way Max had suggested with Max leading them. They were seeing two helicopters flying about and hovering close to them. The cover of trees was essential to them to make it through and most likely they would be encountering drones. Space available at the moment was shrinking. "Get your horses running or we are going to get trapped here," Sam urged them and going like the wind they ran the horses, after they were out of the danger of getting caught they stopped to see if anything was happening behind them, except for the breathing of the horses and the animal sounds around them, it was quiet.

"Whew!" Sam said, "I thought we had been seen there for a minute back there."

"I was concerned about it also," Henry said.

"From here, I estimate we will be at least an hour later getting to the airport." Walking the horses as they tried to be as quiet as possible, trying to listen for any problem they might come across and as they were moving along, each was thinking about the plane crash, it wasn't good, no matter whom it was. When they had gotten around where the crash site was, they started moving faster as they guessed the crash site was keeping people busy and not concerned about intruders.

Torry was getting sore but she didn't complain, she was happy they had managed to get out of another narrow escape, she was excited and having a nice time riding through the beautiful place where they were seeing wild flowers and little animals, she smiled. She was watching birds soar overhead as her horse was following the others. Henry was watching her with an amused look on his face and he knew she was sore since he definitely was. Max and Sam were cautiously watching.

Time went by and before they knew it they could see the airport. Walking the horses and with watchful eyes, all of them were looking around. Henry and Torry were riding behind them and they were all watching

"This is where it may be problematic. I'll have to try to put my plane between you and the hangar so you will have to hide in this tall grass and wait for me to get over here. My plane is white with red and blue stars on the front of it; I'll slow down before I get to you. I'll tell the air traffic controller that I was hearing a noise coming from the plane and had to stop to check, to prevent raising suspicion. You get in at that moment and we'll take off quickly." They sat there for a few minutes thinking about the plan and came to the conclusion that it made the most sense.

Max took off on foot towards the hangar as Sam stayed with Henry and Torry until they were safely aboard the plane. The horses had been tied up out of sight of the airport where they could graze until he

was ready to leave. Max told them where to wait for him at the barren
end of the runway with a large pile of trash that had been discarded
and forgotten. They found the spot where they would wait and be
comfortable, but still maintain a clear view, it would take a little while
for him to come get them. The drone of the activity of the airport made
Dr. Perry and Henry sleepy and they were snoozing as Torry and Sam
watched and Sam spotted the plane first.

"Time to get going wake up." Sam shook them to wake them up
from their nap. The plane was getting close and as he got close and where
they wouldn't be easily seen getting into the plane he stopped and opened
the door as they jumped to their feet with their bags ready to jump into
the plane, and they ran to it. Henry and Dr. Perry helped Torry in and
quickly jumped in right behind her. Unless someone from the hangar
was using binoculars and suspected something going on, they weren't
spotted. Max slammed the door shut and quickly entered the cockpit,
strapped himself in, revved the engines, and taxied down the runway and
was airborne, Sam turned to watch the plane as it disappeared.

In seven days, Sam would be back to meet Max and get him back
to the bunker. As he was about to go into the hangar and before taking
off Dr. Perry would take out the chip. When he got to the airport back
home he would put the plane away as if he would be coming back soon
to fly it again, only he would never fly it again. Sam turned to watch the
plane as it disappeared. The short trip back was ended and Henry and
Torry got out meeting with Mayor Stone, who had driven his car to meet
them at the appointed time. Riding in a car again was surreal for them.
It had been a while since they had done so, and it was an odd feeling.
Waves of memories from their old lives came back, lives they had gladly
given up for the new life, without regrets. They met Max in front of the
airport and after all of them had gotten in, Mayor Stone left as fast as
he was able to. Five minutes later they arrived in the town and Henry
and Torry were surprised how abandoned the place was, especially for
such a well-kept, maintained looking town. They were informed of the
type of town it had been.

"We've already moved everything to our hiding place. We plan to burn the town soon. It looks like everyone has been busy finishing it up. There used to be an underground mine here, at one time someone had fixed it up and used it as living quarters."

"We'll help you in any way that we can," Henry told him.

"You've already helped by being here to teach us. We're extremely grateful."

The town was quaint and charming. Torry thought how much she would have loved to shop here, if it hadn't been the location of the occult. Mayor Stone drove through town to a spot only he knew about, the mine was on a back road that was barely there; it had been sitting idly for quite a long time. As usual, Torry thought of this as a great adventure, Henry was thinking how bad this trip was going to be, but he was coming around with a lot of nudging from his dear Torry. He was apprehensive about this "adventure" but he was in for a surprise.

Much to this couples amazement, the mine was not what they had imagined. Torry was excited and Henry thought, 'this is livable!' Max knew they would be surprised; he was laughing at their reaction. People saw them and came rushing over, "Greetings! You have no idea how relieved we are to have you here! Come with me. Let me show you to your rooms." Henry said, "Rooms?"

"Yes. We decided to make your living area special since you have been so gracious and kind to come here."

"You were sure we would come, weren't you?" Henry quipped.

"We had high hopes and we decided we would trust that you would want to help us."

"You've learned a lot."

"We try to believe we will be taken care of since we have seen things happen."

"We are most certainly impressed and it is good to be here."

Entering their quarters was an eye-opening experience. The people had spent most of their time working on these rooms. The couple felt gratitude for these lovely people. "Let's go meet with them. The mayor is bringing our things in." It felt like a five-star treatment. In the living area, many people had assembled and were waiting for them, the assembled were quiet, waiting to find out about these newcomers.

"Thank you for asking us here, we are deeply honored to be here; to teach you all the teaching we would like to pass on to you. We will pass on the knowledge that we know, and hope that it gives you the peace that you so desperately need in these times. We will teach you about hope, peace, love, and everything that you should desire. We want you to be whole and armed to fight the good fight. "Henry spoke first. When he said that, the people were anxious to start learning. Many questions were asked all at once; so many that Henry was laughing and telling them he would address them. The Mayor came in.

"Ok, ok, let's give our teachers a chance to eat and get some rest. The seminar will begin soon. If you would like to get started a little later in the day, we can, I feel we have done the right thing in coming here. Is this ok with you?" he asked as he turned to Torry. "More than ok!" Torry exclaimed. "Teaching and passing on the Good News is what we do, but more so what we love to do!"

Mayor Stone had everyone sit down to eat and get rested, no complaints there, as it turned out, these people were very kind and accommodating, they understood the new residents were there to stay. The mayor was not only in charge of this group of people, he was very caring about each and every one of them, a very good reason he had been elected mayor for many years. It was very obvious he was an admired person; a bonus was he had been encouraging to each person in accepting the new way of life. Yes, it would be fair to say that Henry and Torry were in the right place.

They had been sent to the exact place where they needed to be. Torry was having a great time getting to know these friends and loving having an entire town of people becoming Chosen Ones. And to have veteran Chosen Ones go to them, Terrell was never going to be the same after Torry had been given the opportunity to spread the cheer she had within her that was inspired, it gave the receiver insight and clarity, with a sense of purpose about themselves. The Giver of Life had gotten hold of them and they couldn't get enough of it. Dinner was over and there was some small talk with laughing, then Henry asked everyone to help with clean up himself and the mayor included. After the eating area was. Cleaned, he asked for all the people to sit down for a time of teaching. Torry gave a testimony of her life and how she had come about the change in her life. Henry gave his story including the shameful things he had done in his past. They chose to be open about their sins as they wanted to be real, and it put them at ease, giving an opening for openness. All present were listening with fascination. Many were crying and feeling the shame of time spent in the ways that displeased the One who loved them the most.

Henry and Torry really didn't know what these new converts would think about them, but they found that these friends were at ease knowing they weren't alone and being looked at as the imperfect people they were, sinners, people that they were, sinners, people who had made mistakes but turned their lives over to be renewed. The Dark Spirits had so much to fear, they were brooding, they were unhappy, they had not succeeded. When Jeremy, Ken, and George were sent to them, the world, as they knew it has become a more beautiful place, for the Dark Spirits, it was terrifying, they would fight back.

CHAPTER FORTY-FOUR

TERRELL HAS CHIPS REMOVED

As of the morning dawned bright, there also came lines of the believers coming to have their chips removed. Dr. Perry told them about Dr. Barringer putting the chips in animals and turning the animals loose, and they loved the idea. One of them had been trapping, so he went out and found a fox caught in one of the traps, which he brought in. They decided to feed the chips to the fox in the case they were being tracked, the authorities would possibly find them excreted in the animal's waste, hopefully the animal wouldn't be harmed. This little joke had them laughing at the thought of the chips being tracked and those doing the tracking feeling foolish. They were having a fun time and Dr. Perry was smiling at the thought of going back to the bunker and telling the friends. What would Jacie think of him now? She was always trying to get him to laugh.

The week was passing and the chips had been removed, the fox had quite a feast before he was turned loose with his load of hardware that the poor thing was carrying around. Max and Dr. Perry were getting ready to return so the kind doctor could get back home. The townspeople wanted to send gifts back with them. "Dr. Perry, we want to show our appreciation to you for everything you have done for us. You freed us from the enemy so we don't have to be concerned about being tracked and we could never repay you enough for that."

"It has been my pleasure to serve you and it has been my honor, really. Thank you for allowing me to serve you."

"Off we go," Max informed him and off they went and as they were headed out he turned and waved with a smile for these hospitable people, he was feeling useful and that he was really doing work that was gratifying knowing he was doing more than just prescribing medication and the week had invigorated him. Mayor Stone was driving them to the airport. "Where are the other vehicles from the town?"

"We sold them and used the money for necessities for the mine," Mayor Stone told him.

"What will you do with this car? You can't sell it."

"I plan to take it to a place where I will wreck it and set it on fire. All identifying information has been removed from it. I have arranged for transformation to get back home."

"Transportation?"

"Yeah, a donkey." Dr. Perry was amused.

"Here we go," Max said. The airport was only a few minutes away by driving in a vehicle.

"Get out of here, quickly. Max will get the plane ready for our final trip. There's a place on the other side of the air field that has a pile of rubbish close to some wild bushes and thick brush where you can hide safely, the place where you hid before. Be careful and watch for snakes. And as I make a turn for takeoff, I will need you to come out and quickly get in the plane as fast as you can. I can fake a glitch in take off but you need to hurry so we don't raise any suspicions. I will have the door open for you, be ready."

The Mayor drove them to the airport, stopping the car before they came into view of the terminal, and being on the alert for any traffic that might drive by, Mayor Stone told them it was safe to get out. "It has been so nice to meet you, Mayor."

"My pleasure, Dr. Perry," he said as they shook hands and Dr. Perry headed for the meeting place. Mayor Stone then drove Max to the terminal and as Dr. Perry was out of sight he saw the car stop in front of the terminal and Max got out and went inside to check in to file his flight plan. He chatted with the people he knew and then walked out to his plane. As he was checking his plane he talked to the mechanics, they had looked for possible engine problems after finding out about the engine trouble he encountered a week before and they found it to be in perfect working condition. He was about ready to go.

'I need to hurry,' Dr. Perry thought to himself. Keeping himself hidden and staying low, he walked to the trash pile and hid on one side of the large pile and maintained a well-hidden view of the hangar without being spotted himself. The pre-flight checks would take a while so he spent his time observing the trash he was sitting on. He found rubber tires, plastic containers, cans, bottles, partially used liquids of questionable origins, various bits and pieces of junk, and a lot of unsavory, decay in various stages and other smelly things lying about. He was so preoccupied trying to identify the debris that he was startled when he heard the plane approaching. Just as soon as Max was where his plane blocked the control towers view of the hangar and other possible prying eyes, Dr. Perry quickly jumped up and ran up to the plane. He dove into the door of the plane Max had open and ready and he ran and jumped in knocking his breath out as he landed with a thud from the mad scramble as he dived in head first and Max slammed it closing it behind him. Max jumped into his seat and took off like the tail of his plane was on fire. "That was impressive, Doctor." He laughed. For an older man, he still had athleticism.

"I may regret that for a long time. I hope I didn't break anything. I know I have some bruises."

They both laughed. Max looked at Dr. Perry, and jokingly, "Physician, heal thy self." Dr. Perry winced. His ribs hurt from landing on his chest as he tried to get into the plane and he was out of breath.

"Doctor, buckle up."

He buckled himself in and sat back, slowing down his heart rate with deep breathes. But with hardly any time to relax, Max landed the plane before Dr. Perry knew it.

Max landed smoothly on the tarmac, and he climbed out first in order to help Dr. Perry get out. He ran out as fast as he could with his bag and went for cover before anyone spotted them. He hid behind heavy brush while Max took care of the plane.

It was a moment of sadness for Max. That flight was the very last time he would ever fly again. Knowing it was a better one than any other time in his life. He had some friendly bantering with the mechanics and the mechanics noticed something different about him he was lighter, friendlier. He had known some of them for a long time, going back to when he first became a pilot. They noticed Max was new and improved. He didn't talk or act like he used to. He wanted to get away as quickly as possible so after saying good bye, he waved to them as he turned to leave. It was with his backpack slung over his shoulders. Getting out of sight of any possible eyes that could be watching and Dr. Perry stepped out to meet him at the designated place where he had been waiting for him as they had agreed upon.

"We'll wait until we get back to the bunker before I remove your chip. You can spend the night and we will get you on your way in the morning. Is that ok with you?"

"Good idea." Down by the road where they were walking they found Sam waiting for them. He quietly stepped out in front of them. He had moved so quickly and quietly that they jumped and laughed.

"Are you trying to give us heart attacks, Sam?" Max asked him as he kept laughing, Sam was laughing with him as well. He was having fun at their expense. He walked with them to the bunker. Along the way they had startled some animals that were hiding in the brush and some birds took flight as they approached so they chose to move around so that they were less visible and not draw attention to themselves with the wild life being startled. Satisfied that they had a path that was more secure they finally arrived at the bunker. They were greeted by their friends and updated with all that had happened since they had been gone, they told of how they had made it through the flight and of teaching the town. The troops at the airport had seen Max around enough to think he was only conducting business and thought very little about his comings and goings.

"Max, are you ready to get the chip removed?" Dr. Perry asked him.

"I am." And it was removed.

"Dr. Perry, are you going to put this chip in an animal?" George asked him. George had heard the story about the antics with the fox. "I may have a bird you can use. That would confuse anyone searching with it flying around."

"That'd be interesting for the trackers." George had a grin on his face and he went out to get the bird. The fox plan was a good one and so was the bird.

"Time to get your things ready for your walk back home," George was saying. He warned Max about the training camp and the forest. Another route was planned for him that they hoped would be easier and safer, it would take a little longer to get there but it was also more scenic.

"I'm ready to get back to see how things are going with Henry and Torry being there. Everyone seems to love them. I expect Torry is already having them laughing, last night was good, but we have so much to learn. I can tell all the Chosen Ones are ready to help anywhere and anyway they can, I hope that we will be able to give back."

"Each shelter has special skills that they are known for, when yours get some training, your will have a special skill set. The important thing is that you have made the changes that are needed for when your time comes when you die; you will be in good company. If ever you need us, we will be here for you," George told him.

"Send our love to Henry and Torry," Joann told him.

"I sure will. And thank you for everything you have done for us. Good bye for now."

"Bye," the friends waved at him. Max began an even longer and more dangerous journey back to his home. He made if home safely after walking through the night and resting during the warmer part of the day. Terrell was happy to have him back safely.

CHAPTER FORTY-FIVE
THE GIRL WITH THE KNIFE

The men had gone out hunting again, to find meat, vegetables, and herbs. They found everything they needed in the afternoon; they had enough food for ninety days. "All right, let's go back. Mariann's going to be happy with this find," Sam said.

"She sure will." Jeremy replied. "This is going to be some good eating once Mariann gets it prepared. All of us need to pitch in to help her. I think everyone has learned how to prepare the meats. She has taken it upon herself to make sure we know how to do it and she has been great in teaching the other shelters how, great teacher she is."

"I'm hungry, already." George piped in.

"Keep your eyes open. I will take care of her." They heard the Voice and had no idea what was meant by it. A wild, strange looking girl, who was dangerously underweight and about twenty years old stood in front of them. In her state of mind, none of them were sure how she had managed to get to them knowing she was around. Her black hair was tangled with leaves and dirt as if she hadn't washed it in quite some time; her dark brown eyes were red and wild as if she were high on some type of narcotic and by the look on her face, they were certain she was going to hurt them. She wore tattered jeans and a dirty white t-shirt, her purple shoes were muddy and the laces in them were untied, threatening to trip her any time. In her left hand, she held a long knife about twelve inches long that was covered in blood. The blood on the blade was dried on it from having been used in the not so distant past.

"You're all dead. You people make me sick, the way you believe, how you act. Where's your Voice, now?" She mocked them with her shrilly voice and her hostile words. It didn't have the intended effect on them.

At that moment, she swung her knife up, in an attempt to try to kill them. As she moves she was suddenly brought to a halt, her dark brown eyes rolled back into her head, her face was ashen white as she fell to the ground. Sam checked her pulse, "She's dead." She had drool and mucus dripping from her mouth.

"We are always being looked after," George said.

The girl had been a part of a family living in a shelter where some of the group's friends were living, she had been caught because of her carelessness and her heart was not with them. She had wandered away from the shelter where she had friends. These friends used drugs and lived in ways that took her far from the Grace and the Chosen Ones. The friends she had ran from when they found out what she had done to the person when she went to kill her families' friends. When she took off she took a stash of the drugs with her. Her determination to take out her anger on the ones she thought of as her enemies took her to the bunker where her family had fled to when they made their escape as they were rescued in town. The family was some of the ones the bunker friends had rescued. The bunker was the closest place and she had planned to kill all the friends at the bunker before she went to her family's shelter to kill them, her family had already been moved to another shelter. Her hatred, compounded by the drugs, made her violent as well as unpredictable. The knife she held in her hand was stolen and she had killed a person she had come upon as she makes her way to the bunker. The person was out hunting and just happened to be in the wrong place at the wrong time and he had known she had the drugs and was trying to take them away from her, he knew her.

They made it back to the bunker, with their load of food, and told the rest of the friends about what had just happened. The girl was known to them and they weren't sure what to do with her body so they put it down the road away from them so the authorities wouldn't come in their direction to find any witnesses as they did their investigation.

Outside the bunker there were about twenty people looking for them. They couldn't see any trace of activity, no footprints, no trodden grass and dirt, nothing. The police knew the hiding place was in the general area, but finding it was impossible. There were bones of animals found, obvious sign of them having been killed and skinned. But here were no traces of anyone having there. The bunker friends were wondering if the girl had turned them in before she had died because of the speed with which they had shown up after her death. Inside the bunker, they turned the radio on to find out what the latest news was that was being reported. "Reports have shown that the Enemies of the State are currently being investigated. Police are as of now unaware of their whereabouts, but the commander said in a statement that he has a large group of hunters currently looking for them. He also said it shouldn't be too much longer until they are found. They do know of the location of their hide out, and explosives were used to get the Enemies out of their hiding places. That proved to be unsuccessful, but the commander is continuing his search. Hopes are high that they will be found. More will be reported when we have further information. That is all. Thanks for listening. This has been your early morning news, have a great day and we will be back tomorrow at the same time."

Outside, the hunt continued. The hunters passed by the entrance of the bunker countless times, yet they had no clue it was there. The Voice sent two of his Spirits to guard the door. The commander had convened with his troops. "They've been here, I know it. We're going to find their hiding place, they can't hide forever. Find them, kill at will. No mercy on them, they're enemies. Am I understood?"

"Yes, sir!"

"Outstanding! Now go!"

"Does anyone not understand what I want? I want their souls. I'm tired of your failure. How can you not find them?" The Exalted Dark One was on another rampage. He'd grown so tired of not killing off the Chosen Ones. The Voice was preventing him from finding them. Every time he set up situations to have them killed they were stopped. He protected those disgusting, pathetic, little creatures.

"Sir, we've been working hard, but we have become aware of a small group of the Chosen Ones that have somehow managed to escape our soldiers. We don't know how, but they have. The commander is trying to find them, even hiring citizens."

The President looked up at him, with a glare. His eyes were burning with a fire and he snarled like a beast, "How did they escape our soldiers. We don't know how, but they have."

Marcello was glaring at him as if he could do harm by his non-contact actions. "Go out and get them and do not fail."

"Uh, y-y-yes sir. I am so s-s-sorry, sir."

"Get out there and find them, or you'll find yourself with the lot of them."

CHAPTER FORTY-SIX

MARCELLO'S VANITY

Others were reporting in to Marcello with results that put a smile on his face.

"Sir, many Chosen Ones have been eliminated. Our cooperatives have turned in the heads of them. The plan is going well."

"Good, good. It seems that our...uh...problem is being taken care of."

"Yes sir. The monetary incentive has proven to be quite effective. There are still some of them out there, but it shouldn't be too difficult to take care of them, as well."

"This is going to be fantastic! We found more of those undesirable people." President Marcello had received word that some of the Chosen Ones had been found and there was going to be a massive public display that evening. He wanted the people to see them being burned, and also to remove any doubts on who was in charge here. With people seeing them being burned, and also to remove any doubts on who was in charge here. With people seeing this, he would retain all control, the one thing he wanted more than anything else. His motives wouldn't be questioned; no one would be brave enough to. "We'll see who can do what, Chosen Ones. Your Voice is nothing compared to me."

Later that evening, Marcello stood in front of his enormous gold trimmed mirror, and admired his ravishing looks. "It's time to go." He'd noticed that he talked to himself when he was by himself. We all have our own absorption, and he was convinced everyone was out to get him. He even put more guards around him, he was thinking they were out to get him. As he was admiring himself he noticed some wrinkles around his eyes that he hadn't noticed before, 'I need to schedule some surgery,' he thought. He went to get ready for the entertainment for the evening as he took great pleasure in murdering the Chosen Ones who were being caught. It was time to get going. It didn't take long and his driver was ready and waiting for him.

There was a crowd of about one hundred thousand people standing in the town, waiting for the Chosen Ones to die, "To all the people here, thank you for attending. You are much appreciated, being here in support of our cleansing. We cannot, or will not, have uncooperative persons roaming amongst us. This shows that if you are not on our side, you are and enemy of the state, and this…this we cannot allow! Now, without further ado, we shall commence the punishment." He got up in front of the crowds as he knew they were inpatient to get the show started.

He made a ceremony out of the event; there were bands, food, and plenty of entertainment before the big event at the end of the day. Lights were set up to maximize the effects of the fiery furnace and the discomfort of those who were put in it. Children were present and they had their own games and entertainment and were allowed to watch the big show. It had the making of a carnival which drew huge crowds from all over from the surrounding towns for when they had enough enemies to put in the cage. The more they caught, the bigger the crowds so they would keep the prisoners in prison until they had quite a few of them, if they survived prison.

It was considered a special privilege to be the one to start the furnace, one needed connections with someone or it was a lottery. The fire starter was given a special status. So, when he was given the signal to start the fire, it was done with a ceremony all its own. There were seven Chosen Ones standing in a large closed in cage type setup. It had been a while since they had caught any more so they had to make do with only the seven of them. The glass on the cage was of a tempered glass that could sustain extremely high temperatures. There were tubes on the underside of the cage for heating it. The fire starter went to the backside of the cage, and turned on the gauges to start the fire. The Chosen Ones locked inside the cage immediately felt the temperature rising. The oxygen was used up inside and it was enough to cause them to fall over dead. They sang, and gave praise to the Voice. "If you command us, we shall die now for you. If you do not spare our lives so that we may live for you, we will do as you command us. Our lives are not our own, but yours only to give or take."

"It shall soon be the time that I shall give you the reward of your servitude to Me. Fear not, for I am with you. Remain loyal to my Work, to me. The path through me leads to eternity in Heaven."

The President himself turned the gauges on to start the fire. He turned the temperature up to two hundred fifty degrees. The men stood in the cage were still standing in the cage and they weren't being burned by the heat. The crowd cheered for their death, yet they did not act like people in intense heat Marcello turned the heat up to four hundred degrees. Still, the men were standing up. Marcello turned the heat all the way up, as high as the machine went. At five hundred degrees, the men hadn't even started perspiring. The crowd's attitude shifted from encouraging to angry. The men were supposed to have turned to ashes, yet they stood there, still very alive. As the crowd was getting into an angry state of mind, a storm hit that threatened to blow them away with booming thunder and lightning strikes that raised the hair on the crowd, there was no cover over the stadium where they had been attending this event. Lightning struck a light pole causing bolts of electricity to surge through the seats of the spectators, there were a huge number of deaths that night as many of them were not able to get out in the panic, not only the lightning strikes killing the crowds, there were those who died when they were trampled in the scramble. The storm seemed to stay over the stadium casting down vengeance on the murderous crowd, fear was creating havoc. By the time it was over, the eight men in the cage were standing and watching. The eighth man in the furnace turned to them and said, "You are free to go now. Go in peace." He touched the lock on the door and they walked out where they were met by an appointed one who took them to a shelter to serve out their days until the end of time.

In his increasing anger, Marcello walked away. The crowd was seeing not seven men in the cage but eight, the crowd wanted them dead. Marcello's hands were far too important to be riddled with the blood of the men, at least not publicly. He climbed into his chauffeured car, and drove away, back to his mansion where he would sip expensive cognac in his comfortable leather chair where he drank until he was sitting the next morning trying to remember why he was sitting in the chair. His head felt like he was going to die any minute and his mood was dour.

On the news, the next day it was reported that the prisoners had been killed in the stampede as the lock on the furnace had been broken and the prisoners had walked out and many in the crowd had been tramples to death. The cameras and equipment had been destroyed by the storm, of which it couldn't be explained about the storm and the events that had occurred the night before. No one was alive to account for the prisoners, there was fear of these people and the rumors and superstitions were abounding, they needed to be killed.

Not having the power to roam freely and to do as he wished angered the Exalted Dark One, but he was still more than pleased with his spirits' work throughout humanity. He was still upset over the Voice and the fact that even with the state of the world, as it was, there were still people choosing the Voice and even willingly dying for Him. The Exalted Dark One still had more souls than the Voice. The numbers were satisfying. He despised having to ask permission to do his deeds. The closer to the end of times came, the angrier the Evil One became and he was desperately and feverishly trying to do as much destruction as he could.

CHAPTER FORTY-SEVEN

MAPLE WOOD

The Chosen Ones had the spiritual armor on and it was the armor that the Voice promised them. It wasn't one that could be seen with the naked eye, but rather one on a spiritual level. This armor, the Helmet of Salvation, the Shield of Faith, the Belt of Truth, the Shoes of Peace, the Sword of the Word, and the Breastplate of Righteousness kept and protected them. With this, the Chosen Ones survived and thrived. There were trials they went through but they had to stay close by reading the Book.

There came a knock on the door and Cindy answered it, to her surprise there were six men standing there, "Come in," she told him, for reasons she didn't know, she felt no fear as normally she would have with strangers invading the place of safety. "What can I do for you?"

"We are here to take you with us to go on a journey to another place for some work you need to do."

"We have met before when we went to Terrell" George said as he walked in as Cindy had answered the door.

"We are Salvation, Faith, Truth, Peace, Gospel, and Righteousness. We are to take you with us and the Spirit will lead the way. I am the Spirit who will be your guide. The others are here to help you as you go where you are being taken. Faith will hold you up as Righteousness will keep you on the path, as Gospel will help spread the Good News with Truth," he explained to Cindy. "Time is running out so Salvation is here to go with lost souls. We must go. Don't worry about anything here. Your food will be multiplied and you won't run out of your essentials."

Truth took the lead as the others followed with Faith helping them to trust the Spirits to stay close to the friends. Outside they were surprised to see horses just outside their door. Faith stayed in the front of the group and they followed him after getting on the horses. The horses were gentle and the riding was at a gentle easy but constant pace.

They were expecting this to be a fairly short trip, but it turned out to be a long one. It took four days to get to their destination. Along the way, they passed through several towns, and soldiers were out patrolling the streets. Law enforcement was seen but it was the soldiers who were the most numerous. With Faith at the lead they knew they were in good hands. Faith stopped in a small town of North Ridge. The Spirit told them they were to give the town's residents the Good News.

The town had two hundred people living there and it was a town where farming was the main source of income. They produced wheat, corn, and in the fall several kinds of vegetables. There was a small grocery store that was the gas station. The hardware store sold implements for the area. Most of the people didn't travel far from their homes as there were too many responsibilities and taking time away put burdens on them. In recent days, there had been a stirring of the Spirits and they were ready to make changes.

"These people have wanted to hear the News and have asked the Voice to help them," the Spirit said.

"They won't be able to see us; we are here to help you. We will stay with you, by your side. The enemies who would cause them problems have been moved out and won't be coming back. These people are the true ones so you can be bold and testify to them about the Good News." It appeared the whole town of North Ridge was out to meet them.

"They will see Righteousness in you. Share the Gospel with them planting the seeds so that Salvation will step in as you speak and they listen. The Voice is depending on you or these ones will be consumed with the dark spirits. I will speak through you with Gospel. Don't worry about what to say. You are a vessel for the Spirit." The group divided up and everyone took groups of people to talk to them about the Voice. As the day began to slide away, these new converts were becoming believers. Salvation had come to this tiny town of lost souls, and they now knew the Voice, and wanted to know more.

George was curious. "What will happen to them when we leave?"

"We will be here with them. The Voice is sending other Chosen Ones to come here. They need to be taught about the dark spirits who want to destroy them. Your work here will be finished. We are with you even when one of you goes home. They have been making preparations for many years for this time and haven't realized it yet." The Dark Spirits were in this place and were already at work to destroy the mustard seed of hope that they had, they were going to be up against the Kingdom of Light.

Truth spoke up, "The world doesn't understand that Truth is what it is. It can't be changed no matter how many lies are used to try to discredit it. Pure truth is such a beautiful gift; the problem is that it hurts along the way. In the end truth will not and cannot be stopped. There have been prophets who had been sent here for these people."

After ten days of spending time in North Ridge, the townspeople were on the path of salvation and they were assured that they would have a teacher among them to teach them so they were planning their survival as the Evil One would come in to rob, kill, and destroy them. Having shared with the gracious people and knowing they were going to have a better life, they got on their horses for the trip home. It seemed strange that the horses were never stopped and searched as was the custom of soldiers who looked at them with looks on their faces that spoke of confusion. They were seeing something unusual and were afraid to come against them, George was wondering if the Spirits were allowing themselves to be seen in some form. The friends hoped it would lead them to know who the real God of the world was. On the way back to the bunker they took the time to rest and appreciate the beauty of the land and being out to travel. During the two weeks they had been gone they had been working and were ready to get back. There would be so much to do.

When they got back to the bunker and opened the door, they stopped and stared. When they thought their supplies would be multiplied, they were not expecting what they found. They were expecting to have a supply of food, certainly not supplies of new clothes, shoes, and other personal items. This was a miracle! Not a one of them knew what to say for a while. The bunker had been fully stocked, not only with food but with many other essentials they needed and plenty of other things they hadn't thought about needing or wanting. It was all very exciting for them to know that all things were supplied without even having to ask for it.

CHAPTER FORTY-EIGHT

BOMBS OUTSIDE THE BUNKER

BOOM! BOOM! BOOM! BOOM! The walls of the bunker shook with the sounds of explosions. Every one inside the bunker was jarred awake by the sounds and the shaking.

"What is that?" Lucy shouted. "What is it?"

"I don't know!" Cindy shouted back. They could barely hear each other over the loud sounds, the sounds were so close.

"Everyone stay where you are!" George shouted at them. He was going to find out what that was. He went outside the bunker, after dodging flying objects that were falling down from the pile of trash surrounding the bunker but he got outside and walked up through the tunnel. Once he got close to the outside, he saw that bombs were being dropped all around them. Then, he heard the loud speaker,

"Come out, come out where ever you are." The man's voice coming from the bull horn resonated in the still air. He couldn't tell from where the voice was coming from, but he knew there were people nearby who seemed to be trying to bomb them out. As far as he could see there had been a barrage of bombs that had been dropped. The platoon was randomly searching out places without having any actual knowledge of people being hidden as had been reported on the radio. Any structure standing was fair game for searches and with the dead men who had died on the property; it seemed a reasonable place to search as the men had most likely told someone they were going back to search with suspicions of despised Chosen Ones may be living around this area somewhere.

"What is it, George?" Jeremy asked from behind him.

"Bombs, they're trying to fish us out. We need to go inside now."

They sealed the bunker door after cluttering the walk way into the tunnel to the door as they ran inside. George wanted to check on the rest of them, to make sure there were no injuries, there were. When they got back to the common area, objects had dropped from places where they had been stored up high and the rattling had knocked them loose and they fell. There weren't any serious injuries that a bandage couldn't fix; there were several cuts and bruises. Dr. Perry and Jacie were working to check to make sure they were all doing well.

After the wounds had been bandaged George took inventory of what was going on, he suspected there must have been a drone that had picked up their whereabouts. It obviously hadn't spotted the entrance or they would have broken down the door and taken every person into custody. The booming could still be heard, but the bunker had stopped shaking. What they didn't know was that a massive man hunt had begun again, and there were hordes of people looking for the bunker, and a way into it to destroy them, once and for all. The bombs were to get them out in the open.

All that they could do was to sit tight and they did, all of them were accounted for and inside in the safety of their hiding place. Time passed as they were wondering what was going on outside. George and Sam went to the door and cautiously peered out; it was deathly quiet so they opened the door enough so they could step out into the shadows, creeping along the corridor up to the surface, ever watchful. As they got to the top, they could see the troops were packing their equipment in a hurry and were doing it so quietly and they were disturbed by something. George and Sam got brave and went to the top and saw the sky had turned an ugly black. "Get back inside, quick!" George ordered, and they ran in.

"What happened to you?" was the question they were asked.

"A tornado is about to hit and the soldiers are trying to get out before it does." Even underground the friends could hear the rush of the air, and then it was silent. The door had been securely locked. George and Sam went out the door again, standing in awe of what the scene was before them, the tornado had struck ever piece of equipment and turned them into rolled up balls of twisted metal and the soldiers bodies were scattered all around, dead. Some of the men appeared to have been blown away as there weren't as many bodies as there had been before the wind hit. The trees were still standing and the birds had come out again with their singing, the bodies were mangled as they were most likely hit by the debris that flew around, nothing outside and on top of the bunker had been blown away, it was surreal to see only the enemy had been targeted.

The news reported the twister in the news that evening as it had swept through the area doing damage and loss of life. The path had swept through choosing its path of destruction; it had been a narrow path but destroyed everything it touched. There was a search made along the path as the damage was assessed and bodies collected for burial. Many bodies were never recovered. The bunker was kept secured until after the authorities had come and collected the bodies of the soldiers and carted away the mangled equipment. They were inside the bunker for several days.

CHAPTER FORTY-NINE
THE WORLD BELIEVES MARCELLO IS GOD

Many people chose to believe the Supreme One was their Savior. They had everything they needed to survive the collapsed world economy. Handouts were given to those who renounced the Voice and the tokens seemed to please the people. For a while, those who cooperated were happy. There was no financial problems, no worry of having the militia break down their doors, just bliss.

The Voice saw what was happening, he saw that people had renounced him and that their souls were darker than night. The flame of humanity was burning low and in danger of going out. Human nature at its core is evil, pure, unadulterated evil. And so, to bring back the sons and daughters He had wonderfully made, diseases plagued the nations.

There were no cures, not even the best medical care given to non-believers could save them. None of the diseases had ever been discovered and infected more people that could be medically seen. Populations all around the world were being infected. The Supreme One watched with a lifted heart. "You see? My work had been made easier. I sit back and do nothing. And the miscreants that bow to me die and I don't have to put in the effort." His body was so absorbed with dark spirits that even his laughter was a hiss. The only part of him that was human was the

310

flesh that covered him. He was overcome by the darkness; he was the essence of darkness.

He murdered the people he didn't like or the ones he believed to be a threat to him. The wars were to kill the ones he was choosing. He knew there were still the Chosen Ones around and he was warring against them and at every turn they were kept in the safety of His wings. As much as he hated them he was not completely successful in his endeavors. Time was getting short and he was becoming more hostile and angry. They are going to die because it was essential to his plan.

CHAPTER FIFTY

THE PARTING OF THE RED SEA

In the bunker where the two pastors and two other Chosen Ones who had been rescued from the labor camp had been recuperating from their injuries and were healing very well; they were gaining weight and their health was rapidly improving with Mariann's good cooking and Jacie was closely monitoring them. They were needed in other shelters to help in teaching, training, and leadership roles. There were clever hiding places and many of them were fairly nice and they were being well taken care of as their needs were being met as they did the work that had been given for them to do until their time was up or the end of time. While they were recovering, the friends were getting rescued people to new shelters and had some who needed to be moved to their new destinations. Lars had already gone to be with his family and was teaching his flock in his shelter and was doing very effective work inside and outside of it. He was busy training and sending help out to where it was greatly needed and very much appreciated. Omar had healed and had been sent to Lars to get ready to go out and he was called to do.

On the day they were to leave to take Everly out to his appointed shelter they were feeling like they would have a memorable trip and they shouldn't be afraid. Leaving was a sad occasion for the friends. The farewell breakfast was a time to get messages to other shelters and then this newcomer was sent off. Everly, who was to be placed with friends had a long trip ahead of them and they were to be escorted to meet the Chosen Ones who were to take him the rest of the way. A messenger had been sent out to the shelter where he was to go and they waited until he returned to find out where they were planning a rendezvous to get him placed. The messenger told them to meet at a dried up and wide river and they would camp there for the night and return the next day.

Saying good bye, George and Jeremy started off with Everly. The weather was agreeable and all of them were well rested. The next escorts would have fresh supplies for them so all of them used what the bunker friends took along. This was to be an overnight trip. People who had to survive by hiding had to do lots of physical work so their bodies were in a great condition and they had built up incredible endurance, they had to carry heavy packs and carry food they packed that had been brought back to their shelters as the hunters kept them supplied by the grace of the one true God, it kept them healthy and hardy. The hiking was pleasant and they were constantly on the lookout for danger.

The route they were traveling had become familiar with time. In an emergency, they could find quick hiding places from the natural terrain or from planned uses of logs or rocks they placed in natural looking formations. It was safer to go from one of these places to the next. Their clothes they wore were colors to blend it to where they were; they even had clothes that were seasonal in coloration. Jewelry was not worn so as to keep from having light hit them and give the enemy pause and give them away.

"Are the two of you going to stay in the place where you are going or will you move somewhere else?" George asked the men.

"I am, but it is only a temporary place; I will be moved around to train people to be teachers. There are people coming to the Voice so we need to prepare for them. Every person counts. Any one of us would travel great distances for just one person." All of them understood what he was talking about so they nodded in agreement.

With danger as a possible companion they watched with rapt attention as they had opportunities to see the color variations of in the landscape. It was breathtaking that before now they had never actually taken the time to notice the beauty around them, the differences in colors were astounding. Danger may be intense but having to slow down to really notice creation was satisfying not only for their ultimate survival but for their good health. It made having to walk long distances less of a burden and more of a happy way of life. Time passed in a way that was not wasted as it would be sitting around without a purpose. They saw ways to worship their Creator as they saw his creation.

With them getting used to going distances they were finding it didn't seem to take as long as it had a one time, in the beginning of having to hide. George remarked about the river bed they were nearing, it was dry. As they started crossing George suddenly looked and as did the others and they noticed the drone flying overhead. George pulled out the rifle he had brought with him and shot the drone to disable it. Sparks flew as the drone lost power and it spiraled the short distance to the ground where it crashed and the dust around it swirled about it before settling on it. They knew they had been seen, it wouldn't be long before someone came after them. All of a sudden Jeremy cried out, "Soldiers behind us!" The thought occurred to them that they had been spotted quite some time ago judging by the speed with which the soldiers had found them. They froze and then they were urged forward, they started running and they made it to the other side with the soldiers in pursuit close behind them. They knew they couldn't get away so they stopped. Just as the soldiers got out in the middle of the dry river bed everyone looked up to see a tsunami size wave headed straight for the troops, they tried to run but they were not able to get away. The wave came down upon them and the water was so violent and the soldiers were carrying so much equipment they didn't have a chance to make it out alive and they disappeared in seconds. The river flowed normally with the swift speed a river runs with water flowing and water still coming, after the wave passed and it was carrying mud and anything that dared to be in the way. No bodies were seen but they were sure there were some in there somewhere. It looked like parts of bridges, houses, and cars had been hit, anything in low lying areas and at the river edge that flowed past and went down stream.

The group was left standing at the edge of the river marveling at the power they had just witnessed and after a few minutes they got their voices. "The Voice sure does know how to get things done!" the others laughed.

"We should be meeting your new escorts soon," George said. "I think this river is where we are to meet them."

Jeremy was following along making sure these men were safe and was walking with George when he saw a group of people up ahead. "I think we have found them," he said.

They met the escorts and introductions were being made all around. "What was that gunshot we thought we heard and then we heard a loud roaring?"

"George shot and disabled a drone that had been tracking us. Soldiers had been tracking us and we were in trouble," and they had a discussion about what had just happened. "We get to see these remarkable things as well," one of them said.

They had set up a camp as the newcomers set up their small tents they had with them. There was a nice fire going, food was prepared and set out, stories were swapped; it was not usual for Chosen Ones to get together with groups of new friends so they had a fine evening together and as the sun set, the fire dying down they fell asleep one by one and slept fitfully through the night. The moon was shining big and bright, the air was comfortably cool, the night passed with all of them in their bed rolls, sleeping soundly.

The sky barely had any light showing when the first person started waking up. It had been a long time since anyone had slept in what now would be called luxury, a nice mattress, they had to get used to sleeping where they were, some had found ways to make sleeping more bearable by finding materials to soften hard places; creativity was essential. The fire was stoked and one of them had brought coffee and it smelled delicious as small cups were set up and the camp was waking up to have a cup of this brew. A simple and filling breakfast was served as the camp became fully awake. It was going to be a beautiful day. Birds were stirring and flying about as the sun was showing its face on the eastern horizon. The brilliant orange layered with yellow and the deep blue. Unseen critters were moving about foraging for their daily food. An owl close by was giving its early morning hoot. The morning was glorious!

"Friends, it has been a real pleasure meeting you. I hope we will see each other again on this side of eternity, if not, then," George said.

Cleaning up the camp and hiding any signs they had been there, they parted company and headed in their respective ways. It didn't take George and Jeremy long to get to the river, it seemed so docile now. It was hard to believe how ferocious it had been only yesterday. If they hadn't seen it, they wouldn't have believed it. There was a lot of mud and the water was a red clay color. A cow carcass went floating by with a log seeming to be chasing it. Trees and branches were everywhere. Not the best times to get into the murky waters to cross so they needed to find somewhere to get across. Jeremy walked to the bank and was looking up and down for a clue to their passage. "I think I see a place that may be passable a little way downstream." George walked up to his side and saw the place.

"You are right, head that way," George said. About a quarter of a mile downstream they saw that it was the best place to cross. There the water was only inches deep and large rocks provided the steps needed to keep their feet dry, since the rocks were rough, it would be easy going. Jeremy and George brought walked across and working to keep their balance.

Walking at a comfortable pace, listening to the early morning sounds and breathing the fresh air soon had them singing to pass the time and gave them a cadence set to the rhythm of the tune. Jeremy was walking in front when he put his finger to his lips to shush them; he waved then to a spot where they could hide. "I think I heard something." They listened, in a minute they saw a uniform of the military come into view; they were far enough away that they weren't seen but to close for comfort.

"They must be trying to find that unit that was washed away yesterday. I don't imagine they had time to contact their commander before that wave hit them, they must know where they were before the drone was disabled. Probably, they think we had something to do with their disappearance. We might want to find a better place to hide," George said as he and Jeremy were looking around. Jeremy saw a grouping of some large boulders further on the left. The sun was up in the sky and it gave them the advantage of having it on their backs. It was in the soldier's eyes. Watching them, they were certain they were searching for the unit.

"We are going to have to get out of here and fast," George said.

"Move back the way we just came from and then we can go around them." They did an about face and headed back toward the river. The ground was dry so they weren't worried about leaving tracks. They were hoping their friends were far enough away so as not to be found. It was decided to move and keep moving through the whole day and into the night. As many soldiers, they had been coming across must mean there was something secretive going on, George was wondering about it.

The troops were slowly waking in their direction, so they needed to get out as fast as they could. Staying low and keeping with trees, rocks, brush, everything between them and the troops; they were getting distance between them, drones were a huge concern and they would not be able to do any shooting. They made their way back to the muddy river, they didn't have much time for planning away across and they didn't want to leave tracks so they started downstream and looked for a good place to get over, with speed they were making time and progress when Jeremy found a place, logs had piled up and jammed in a narrow place where the rapids would run swiftly when the river was full and running "If we walk carefully, we can get over, if we slip, it may not go very well, so here we go." Jeremy went first and George came up right behind him, holding to the tree branches they made it. On both sides of the river there were rocks and trees, and that is where they headed, sitting down under the trees on the boulders for a short rest. George was looking around for signs of anyone who might be in the vicinity when he saw a drone on the horizon.

"Look, a drone. The other one disappeared so they are out looking for us, they know we are here. I hope the others are safe."

"We had better get going," Jeremy said standing up as the other two joined him. The trees provided good protection for them and the troops were in good condition, they didn't know about the prey they were chasing.

"Before it gets too late I think we should make a camp instead of traveling the entire night, if we travel when we are overly tired, we won't be able to move as fast, we need some rest and they will make camp before dark which will be to our advantage, they are depending on the drones to find us so they are confident we won't get away," George suggested. They walked until well after dark, there was a town up ahead they could see by the traffic they heard on a nearby highway, time to find a place to stay for the rest of the night. They came to a landfill and by chance they found some abandoned cars that had been dumped and amongst the cars there was a camping trailer with broken out windows with a door barely hanging on, it was a rusty, worn out place and was sitting by itself. "Must be home for the night," Jeremy said. Going inside they would have to make the other small guests leave, the smell was musty and old having been left for an undetermined amount of time, home for the night. Getting some food out, they ate before lying down as they needed to get up before the sun. They slept fitfully as they were aware they may have company and when they heard sounds they awoke to listen and to determine the origin of where it was coming from so that if there was danger to them they could get away.

When the sun came up they were well on their way having gone around the town, walking for several hours, avoiding places that would be populated, they hadn't come within a drone's range, that they were aware of anyway and they were keeping watch. It was a long way to the bunker, it was making them nervous, but they had no choice. As they needed to change directions to head to a shelter that was not too far away they went that way. "We need to go to the shelter our friends were going to," George told them. "That last town we passed is close to that shelter, so let's go there, I am sure I can find it."

After walking for about five miles, they came to an apple orchard, "The shelter is not far from here, a messenger who came through here told me about it." Passing it they walked along eating the apples they picked up before leaving. A couple of miles away they saw two men walking with one of them having trouble moving, Everly, had turned and saw them coming towards them, he froze, at looking at them he thought he might know them, within minutes he was close to them and was puzzled at seeing it was George and Jeremy. "Why are you back so soon? I am happy to see you just the same."

"We were on our way back when we came upon soldiers we believe are out looking for us. We are in danger of being found, let's get under cover, this is to open," George told him. George and Jeremy got on either side of Micah to help him along, Everly was relieved to have help as he was getting worn out.

"If we can make it a little further, we will be at the shelter and safe, with your help I can get us there faster. I need to go slow for Micah's sake. Have you seen the sky? It looks bad. Some bad weather is on the way."

Twenty minutes later they were in the shelter, safe. Soldiers had come up behind them and were closing in when the clouds suddenly came up and there was no time to find cover, as the clouds were passing over with the wind blowing, it was eerily still and they were unnerved, then they were hit as with a strong wind blew them around and they were blown up against one of the apple trees where the wind accompanied by lightning struck the tree causing branches to break loose and coming down like spears and killing them as it pierced their bodies and they bled to death.

Others would be coming this way so the made haste to get to the shelter and they were having to half drag Micah to get there faster. Inside the shelter, Micah was being gently cared for, he was exhausted and he fell asleep as soon as his head hit the pillow. George and Jeremy stayed for a few days to be sure they could get back home and the soldiers had given up finding them, the news had mentioned the death of the soldiers in the strange way they had died. It was assumed that the Chosen Ones had died the same way. A company of soldiers had known they were on the loose so they were chasing after them. When the drone had been shot down it had picked up the whereabouts of the men and the battalion was chasing after them.

George and Jeremy make their way back going through some rough territory that kept them well hidden. The friends left to go back to the bunker, they didn't encounter trouble and when they walked into the bunker, they were greeted by all of the friends who had no idea of what had happened to them. "We thought we wouldn't see you again," Sam said, obviously, he had been watching. All of them were relieved.

CHAPTER FIFTY-ONE

OMAR AND DACK

There was no worry or fear of what was to come. There was no certainty of that very time, for they didn't know when it would be. What the Chosens did know was that being servants of the Voice would give them a reward that no human could possibly comprehend.

Omar, one of the rescued ones from the labor camp, was staying with Pastor Lars. He was a faithful follower of the Voice and had a strong conviction for Him. Lars had used him for training new converts as they were sent to shelters that took them over great distances to ensure as many shelters were strengthened by learning and obeying what was written in the Book. He was an easy going and gentle man who had a solid character.

At the age of thirty-eight he had worked as a construction worker, filling in as a supervisor from time to time. He had worked in large cities but was from a small town, and when he wasn't on a job site working, he liked to go hunting and fishing, sometimes alone or sometimes with a friend. He had been married but his wife was killed soon after the microchip deadline had passed when she was caught and killed for the reward, losing his wife had been hard, but losing his unborn daughter had been even harder on him. He often thought of what it would have been like, to hold his baby girl for the first time. He would never know what that experience would be. It would have been their first child, and he'd never get to be a father.

He was five feet nine inches tall with a broad chest and shoulders from the work he did. His sandy blonde hair, soft blue eyes and lop-sided smile gave him the look of someone who was never bothered about anything and he did take things as they came with the exception of losing his family. Having studied the Book he understood what and why it happened, but still, it didn't stop him from feeling the pain from the loss. Omar buried his pain from everyone, including himself. His parents had been overseas when the chips were being injected, but they weren't able to get back home in time for the deadline. He didn't know what had happened to them, but still he trusted the Voice.

"Omar, would you travel to a shelter? It's a week's hike from here. A messenger wants to get a family back here for training and they will go back after training and will leave to go to a shelter that is quite a distance from the one they are in."

"I'd be more than happy to help." Omar had a funny feeling about this trip but he was still willing to do whatever needed to be done. After reviewing his route, he was ready to go. Lars wanted to send someone else to go with him but he declined. He felt danger was coming his way and didn't want anyone else to be put in harm's way. He would be going by himself and that meant having to watch for everything alone.

Drones weren't seen too much out in places without a population, unless unlawful activity was suspected. He watched for them anyway. Training camps were out in the woods at times, mostly around their bases.

Fishing would be a relaxing to spend his evenings, quietly sitting by a stream or lake; contemplating being in the presence of the Voice knowing his life was being lived in obedience. Omar had estimated the trip was about forty miles to his destination, and he was hoping to get there in three days or less. This time of year, he wouldn't have any trouble finding water. The ground was wet, the air was humid, and the sky clear and birds were flying about with cheerful songs.

Mid-day of his second day out he was making good time and he thought he would arrive sometime late the next evening when he heard a sound that made the hair on the back of his neck stand on end. He whirled around when he heard clicking behind him. Standing there in front of him were soldiers pointing their rifles at him. He was thinking that he had thought it was an animal creeping around instead someone trying to sneak up on him.

One stepped forward. "Drop your pack and put your hands up. You're under arrest." Omar complied. The commander grabbed his hands and put handcuffs on him with his hands behind his back, and threw him roughly up against a tree with his face taking the blow and he was frisked for whatever he thought was a weapon.

"What am I being arrested for?"

"We have information about you that you are one of the Chosen Ones. If you renounce the Voice and accept the Supreme One, you'll be released, no questions asked. You'll sign a statement renouncing the Voice."

"Even if you offered me everything in the world, all the power, and all the glory in it, I will not give up Voice, who alone offers eternal life."

"I should shoot you right now for your blasphemy, but I won't. We have ways to change minds. You'll regret it otherwise if you choose to persist."

"I'll regret changing my mind." The commander was enraged but he held his temper. He roughed up Omar and Omar was thanking the Voice for the chance to stand for Him.

"I have only one master." The other soldiers were following close behind as if he was carrying a bomb that was set to go off with a push of a button. The Book had said Chosen Ones would be hated and Chosen Ones were to be joyous to be counted as worthy.

"I thank you Voice that I have this opportunity to honor you this day," he was quietly saying. A soldier standing near him overheard. He'd witnessed people going through torture and saw what happened to them. This was the first time he had ever heard someone being thankful for it. He became curious how the Chosen Ones could act without fear of what they knew would happen to them. In that instant, he wanted to be his guard, to know more.

A half-mile from where he was arrested, they came upon a van that had been hidden from sight. Several soldiers were standing around it waiting as the prisoner approached. The soldiers stood at attention. The opened back doors and Omar was thrown inside, where he struggled to sit up. The young soldier, Dack, made sure to get in with him. He intended to find out more about this prisoner. Two other soldiers climb into the van with them. Dack knew he couldn't ask questions, otherwise he'd get reported and end up like the prisoner. The van driver got in with a soldier riding as his passenger. It might have been a bumpy ride if it had not been for the driver wanting to keep the others from being jostled. They drove to the military base two miles away. The driver pulled up to the gate and was waved through. The van parked in front of a building set apart from the others. The soldier riding in the front of the van got out with his rifle at the ready position and he walked to the back of the van, unlocked the doors, and the soldiers inside pulled Omar roughly by his arms. When they got to the place they intended to interrogate him they parked the van and the soldiers in the front came around to the back to get him out. When the doors were opened the soldiers in the back with him push him forward and the soldiers standing just outside of it grabbed him roughly by him arms and pushed him to the ground as his face was pushed down. He was getting some scrapes and bruises in the process. When they were satisfied that he was secure, he was pulled up by his hands as the cuffs dug into his wrists inflicting pain as they did so. Omar never made a sound as he was jerked to his feet, and Dack was amazed. That had hurt him, yet he did not complain or resist.

Omar winced as they pulled him to the front door of the building where the doors opened and Omar was pushed through it. He was rushed back through another set of doors where they took off the cuffs and he was pushed into a cell, the door slammed shut. Rubbing his bruised wrists and cringing as he sat down on the cot, the pain caught up with him but thankfully there were no broken bones. Looking around the cell, he didn't see any other prisoners. The cell was in fairly good shape and it was clear that hadn't seen many inmates going through here. He could hear talking and laughter at the intake desk as he settled down on the cot and it was sounding like he was being mocked. He didn't mind it; Chosen Ones had been living with it for years. Within the hour, an officer came back to book him with charges.

"Turn around with your hands behind you." Cuffs were put on and he was escorted to a small room that looked like a miniature size courtroom.

"Choose to renounce the Voice and commit your allegiance to the Supreme One, and we'll let you go," he was told.

"No," was his answer.

"Then it is your choice, you will be sentenced to the box until you've changed your mind."

"I choose the box."

"Very well, the forms are here when you're ready." He was led to a room where he was given prison attire. After changing, with a guard watching him and a gun pointed at his head, the cuffs were put back on him and he was led through double doors to the outside, where he saw a concrete structure that looked like a port to an underground bunker. There was a narrow slit, a window and an air duct. Walking to the backside of it, he saw a small-hinged door with a padlock on it. The officer took out a key to unlock it, and forced Omar had to crawl inside.

"Hold it; I'll take your cuffs off." They were taken off and Omar crawled in. It was hot. The lock was put in place with a click. The guards were laughing and talking as they went back into the main building, and then Omar heard nothing. It was hot, dark, and silent.

In the darkness, he felt around. The floor was dirt. In a corner, he found a bottle and opened it. He smelled the contents. It was water. His eyes were adjusting, and he saw there was only the one small window that allowed air in to prevent suffocation. "Great Voice, I thank you for being with me. You say all things work together for good for those who are called according to your purpose. I would rather live like this than to have everything the world has to offer. Thank you and may you be honored and blessed through me."

He laid down for a nap and when he woke up he could hear Dack was calling to him through the window slit. "Omar, here is your dinner."

"Thank you."

"I'm Dack but my friends call me Duck."

"Nice to meet you, Dack."

"This isn't much but it'll fill you up."

Omar was determined to keep a good attitude towards his tormentors. He prayed and sang praise to the Voice. There was no room to stand up in the box. At best, he could sit back on his feet. Since there wasn't much else he could do to pass time, he did sit ups and pushups. Mentally, he kept busy doing exercises: math, history, and most importantly, he spoke to the Voice. He didn't allow himself to give up and give in to despair that was always lurking in his mind, that which pushed for his destruction.

In the labor camp, all four of the Chosen Ones had disciplined themselves to be strong, but here he was all alone, which made it harder without support.

"I can do this. I can with the Voice who is here, who cares for his people," he said out loud. Dack volunteered to take Omar food. He wanted to talk to him, to find out what drove him. When he would approach the Box, he heard joyful praises to the man's God. It wasn't a man breaking down; he was praising the Voice as if He was in there with him.

Days went by and Omar stayed strong. One day Dack got up the nerve to talk to him about the Voice. "Omar, it's burning hot in there. How can you stand it? It's hundred and two degrees outside the box."

"I have the Voice with me. If I die, I go home to be with Him and if I live, I live for Him. The heat in here is nothing compared to the eternal fires I would live in if I give in to a false god. I have Spirits here who are going through his with me. I am without worry or fear. Dack, you need to be worried. Without the Voice, you are forever lost."

"I don't believe you. I don't see anyone in there with you. Maybe you're going crazy. You'd have to, being in that heat."

"You breathe air that you can't see. You can feel it, when the wind blows you can feel. A tornado gives full vent to its power; you can see what it can do without seeing it. The Voice will one day vent his full power. I know what the Voice has done for me."

"Tell me more. I'll be back." With that, he left. It was true that the heat was taking its toll on his body, and he was becoming weaker. He would sleep when he could. Once a day an officer would come to see if he was ready to sign the papers and it was obvious to him that his condition was deteriorating rapidly. Dack came as often as he could. He saw special qualities in Omar, he was hearing the Voice, and he had to do something before Omar died.

"The Voice has been talking to me, Omar. I think I need to get you out of here."

"Do you now believe in Him?"

"Yes, I do believe in Him. I have been thinking about this a lot and I am ready to have what you have."

"What are you going to do?"

"I'll unlock the door and tell you how to get out to the back fence where I have cut the wire. I'll be there waiting for you. Do you think you can make it?"

"I will give it my best try."

"At dinner time, I'll sneak you some extra food that'll replenish your energy." Omar ate what he had and tried to get loosened up and stayed by the window to get oxygen. Dinner time came with another guard bringing his food; he was disappointed but thought something had come up. When he finished eating a thought that had just popped into his head told him to go to the door and try to open it, he went to the door and pushed on it, it wasn't locked, and he knew that at some time Dack had been here. At night, the yard around the box was well lit, but soon after total darkness had fallen and the night lights were on there was an electrical failure casting everything into natural darkness. This night the moon was not in the night sky so it was dark. He carefully opened the door and slipped out, and a last minute thought occurred to him, he locked the door. They were in for a shock to find it locked, but no Omar.

Making his way across the darkened yard, he found the location with a bit of searching. When he finally found it he slipped through the cut wire as he snagged his prison garb making a ripping sound as he kept going. His leg had a bleeding gash, but he felt no pain. As he got through the fence and had jumped to his feet and just before he started into a run, he was caught by his arm by someone unseen.

"It's me, Dack." Relief was on Omar's face.

"I thought it was over for sure," Omar said and Dack laughed.

"I was wondering if you would check the box door. I had to sneak back out with the pretense of leaving the papers for you to sign. When the sun went down I cut some lines, and created the electrical outage, it wasn't easy. I had just got off duty, so time wasn't on my side. I'm taking all my vacation days, so as far as anyone knows, I'm going island hopping." They both laughed. Omar loved the way he thought things out, he was thorough and analytical.

"It might be a good idea if we get out of here. See that road over there? A patrol will be coming around soon. I'll fix the fence so it will be a while before they figure out how you got away."

"Thank you, Dack. So, you've been hearing the Voice?"

"For a while, yes. I had friends, who were Chosen Ones, and they disappeared one day and I didn't get a chance to find out any more from them. When you got here, I understood a lot more in the few minutes I was around you than I have ever understood by the way you have handled yourself under these conditions. I asked Him to show me what to do and I've been really listening and He has been talking to me. I understand now. You've shown me more recently than I have had in my whole life, and I'm ready to go with you and learn. I have to thank you for having been a fantastic mentor for me."

"I'm happy that your eyes have been opened. We should move on." Dack led him to a spot that was out of sight of the road where Omar saw a pile of something.

"What's that?"

"I stashed some things a few days ago for you. There are some clothes, food, and water in there for you wrapped in sealed plastic bags to keep them clean and the pests from getting to them. Since I'm still in my uniform, we can take my truck to wherever you need to go." Omar was very happy to hear it, but he was weak and traveling by foot would've been too strenuous for him.

"Stay here along this road, out of sight, while I go get my truck. I'll be quick. I told my commander that I saw something and was concerned and would check it out. I told him if I found anything that I would report back to him, if not, I would see him when I got back from my vacation." He left, with Omar getting into the hiding place.

He got out some food and water, his hands were shaking, and by the time he was finished, his body felt energized and full. He saw a large truck driving slowly, slowing down as it neared his hiding place, it came to a stop right in front of him as Dack got out and went to the passenger side to help Omar in.

"Get in and get down just in case we come across the patrols." Omar picked up his things and made a dash for the truck.

"Where to?" Omar gave him directions. Twenty minutes later, they arrived at their destination.

"It's important for you to find a place to hide the truck. We don't want to draw attention to our shelters, and eventually you'll have to sell it. Most of us sold ours or if the car wasn't worth much, we'd disable them as if they'd broken down and we abandoned them."

"Oh, that explains why we have found so many. We could never figure out why vehicles were sitting abandoned on roads and the registered owners never came back for them. We even tried to find the former owners of cars that were sold. The ones we had captured were the ones who had gotten careless, rarely did any of them convert and they didn't give away any information. I didn't participate in what they did to them. I am sorry that I didn't see what I have been missing before now."

"There was a reason. "Dack had been driving slowly along when Omar saw a good place for hiding the truck, and pointed to a place where the trees were thick and the land sloped downwards. Towards what may have been a lake, Dack weaved through the trees until he found a good spot to leave his truck. They got out and found some branches to put around and on top of the truck so that it would difficult to see from the road was hidden from an aerial view.

"We'll walk the rest of the way," Omar told him. They pulled their things out of the truck and hiked down the road.

"The Voice will let them know we've arrived." Sure enough, someone did come out of a hidden door, straight to them. "Hi, I'm Baxter. The Voice told us you were coming. Welcome."

"I'm Omar and this is Dack." Baxter shook hands with them. "Dack is a brand-new convert. He was one of the guards where he just helped me escape from incarceration. I was sent to bring some friends back with me to train them before sending them out to places needing teachers. Dack will help."

CHAPTER FIFTY-TWO

TAMMY

Tammy was an obese bully with black hair that hung down to just below her shoulders, her skin was pale and she had brown eyes. Her weight had blossomed to two hundred pounds. Considered to be a loud mouth know-it-all she had an opinion about everything. Whenever she was around where two people were talking she couldn't help herself, she just had to jump in to answer the question even before knowing what they had been talking about. Being rude, obnoxious, disrespectful, and a troublemaker, her big accomplishment was her drinking, which had her calling in sick and she called in frequently. She was not liked at all and sadly, she didn't even know it. When she wasn't at her regular job she was a stripper. Her regular job was working at a convenient store during the day. She could put on acts, which helped her keep her jobs; she could fool her superiors into believing whatever she told them. Her co-workers didn't like her. At twenty-five years old she had no prospects for marriage, she thought she was to smart and was waiting for the right one to come along, her expectations for the right one was for an educated man who thought she was the most beautiful person imaginable.

Living with her parents and not paying rent or any bills she didn't go to school do anything to try to improve her life, she was immature and irresponsible. One night she went to the club where she worked nights stripping and it was her turn to dance when in walked one of the Chosen Ones to get one of the girls out who was being held as a sex slave. The Chosen One, Rex, looked up to see Tammy and was very embarrassed as he quickly looked away. He knew what kind of place this was, he did not want to come in here but a Chosen One, twenty-one-year-old Beth, was being held against her will. Rex was directed by the Voice where she was and who she was, he immediately recognized her and he went directly to her where she was about to be dragged out of the room and into a back room where she would endure abuse without getting the money that was paid for her services. Rex went to her and grabbed her by her hand, at first, she resisted until she looked at him and saw who he was. As quickly as she could she scrambled to her feet as he led her outside where George and Sam had been waiting and he handed her over to them. The crude man didn't have time to react and Beth was out the door before he could react. He glared at Rex but otherwise he didn't go after her, instead, he went looking for another victim. The club was packed so they were scarcely noticed.

Beth was in front of Rex when he got her out, Tammy's act was over and she had noticed Rex where she left the stage and wrapped a flimsy robe around herself. Being quite a handsome man and being taller than those who were in the club, it was hard not to see him and Tammy came running after him, trying hard to keep from drawing any more attention to himself than he had to, he tried being polite to her, she was pulling him toward the side door by the stage where there was a bouncer standing guard. He had a big grin on his face as he caught on to what she was doing and she was determined to do as she pleased with him. He was going to get out of sight of security and then make his escape and he was hoping there was an exit door somewhere nearby. He tried to put on an act to fool the guard, and it worked.

With the saucy smile on her face she was still dragging him and her intention was to get him into her dressing room. Being a married man, Rex refused to give up and was trying to get loose her grip that she held on to him without the guard noticing. As he walked by the guard, he gave him a smile as if he were a lucky man. His heart was racing as he acted like a willing participant in the game going on. Tammy was thrilled to have caught this most fortunate catch.

George and Sam were outside hiding and waiting for Rex, "He should have been right behind her," George said, turning toward Sam. Along the wall staying in the shadows. It was easy to move through the parked cars in the direction of the door, walking casually he went through the door staying with a group of burly men out for a good time, while the attendant was collecting the cover charge fee from the hostess, Sam slipped through undetected. While moving through the cheering crowd he put a smile on his face, waving as if he had seen a friend, he kept his eyes away from the bright stage lights which made it easier to look for Rex. Not a trace of him in the room, looking for a way to the back he saw doors on both sides of the stage. Rex had gotten Beth out so he went to the stage door nearest the front door, there was a bouncer guarding it so he needed to come up with a diversion, looking around for something he might be able to use, he saw some bar rags waitresses had left lying around so he nonchalantly sauntered over to pick them up.

One of the waitresses came up to him to find out what she could get for him. "I am waiting for someone," he told her. She had an irritated look on her face but left to attend to other customers. He continued to make his way across the room where he found a sweater draped across the back of a chair with the owner of it presumably off to the restroom. He sat down close by as he examined it. He found a loose thread and he started pulling. It unraveled easily enough. Pulling out more and when he finally had what he thought was plenty, he cut it. The owner returned and sat down on the chair and kept watching the show. Sam wound the thread around four of his fingers as he stood up and put it in his pocket. He walked over to collect the bar rags, and using the rags as if he was compulsive about cleaning, he swiped the rags across the tables, making his way to an empty table. As he walked he picked up glasses, some of them still had liquid in them, and he set them down on the table he had selected at the back of the room. It wasn't likely anyone would be paying him too much attention with the show on the stage, so he wasn't worried about getting caught. He was aware of cameras in the corners of the room so he had to make sure what he was doing couldn't be in view of them.

Wrapping one of the rags around the center pole under the small table, he tied it securely as he moved to the table close by. He made sure another rag was tied in the same way with the thread stretched out taunt between them so that in the dim light what he had done wouldn't be seen by unsuspecting bar patrons. Getting up he walked over to the wall close to the bouncer to wait without looking toward the stage. The dancer had the audience's rapt attention. Having gotten used to him standing there and he soon forgot about him, Sam worked his way closer to the shadows by the door with only the lit exit sign as light. The bouncer was watching the show which made it easier for him to get through the door when he needed to make a dash for it. The bouncer moved closer to the stage for a better view. Sam saw a young couple walk to the table he had set up, the young man walked around the table to pull out her chair for her. In his nervousness to please her, he stumbled over the thread and caused the table to tip, and the glasses slid off and crashed onto the floor. Shards of glass flew in all directions, and heads turned toward them. He was embarrassed as some of the patrons laughed, the bouncer had started toward them until he saw that nothing was wrong except the young man's blunder. The bouncer moved and turned away and Sam made a dash through the door. He found an unlocked door and slipped inside to see what was going to happen. Nothing did so he opened the door slowly and looked out; nothing. Now, to find where Rex had gone, going along the long, narrow, dimly lit hall he listened at each door, the door near the end of the hall he heard a loud woman's voice and a man's voice he couldn't hear what he was saying. Sam checked the knob to see if it was locked, it was, bracing himself to knock it down he backed up and ran into the door with his shoulder, splintering the wood of the cheap door. The bouncer didn't come racing back with all the noise of the music out front kept his break in easy.

Rex was standing up with Tammy sitting on a plush seat with the hopeful look on her face as she had plans. Both of their eyes wide with surprise as the door splintered and the room was invaded. "Police!"

Pointing to Rex, he motioned for him to leave, which he was anxious to do. Tammy started to cry. "Shut up!" Sam told her. Both men backed out the door. Out in the hall they made a dash through the door to the alley where George was waiting for them. "Took you long enough," he told Sam.

"I needed to have a distraction to rescue poor Rex. By the way Rex, why didn't you just walk out?"

"She threatened to scream rape. I was waiting for her to turn her back. At the moment before you broke in she was starting to take off her clothes, she was trying to make me think I was interested in her. I was so disgusted with her lurid behavior."

"We need to move faster so we can get away from here," George said.

"Beth, how are you doing?"

"I have been kept safe so far but that was about to change, you got there just in time. I was so scared; they have been hitting me to try to scare me into submission. I had a friend who was killed by these people and they aren't interested in our well-being. I am so happy you showed up."

Jenny had been the one who had first become aware of Beth's plight. She had known Tammy, she was always reporting the girls to Ghost, causing harm and even death to them, Tammy took pleasure in what she did, it gave her a perverted sense of power in being rewarded by Ghost and finding favor with him. She was pleased to eliminate what she thought was her competition. Before he was arrested and put in prison, most people were afraid to tell Ghost no. It was how Tammy was kept in comfort. Jenny heard the Voice tell her about Beth. Young Chosen Ones who were attractive had become target for sex traffickers, defiling them. George had Sam come along for his uncanny ways of getting in and out of precarious situations. With Sam and George on each side of her, they hurried her along the street as drunks were staggering along, crashing into things. "George, let's act drunk, and Beth, act like you are with him and we are going to your apartment. It will make a good cover and no one will bother us. Laugh like you are having a good time." Both of them did and if he hadn't known any better, Sam would have believed it. Sam found some empty liquor bottles and picked on up for himself and George. They were staggering, talking loud, being as obnoxious as they could. The patrols pointed at them in ridicule, but left them alone. When they got a safe distance away, they took off at a quick pace.

"Sam, that was brilliant, I can't believe it worked."

"When in Rome," he remarked. "Besides, you two were very convincing, I almost believed it."

In her dressing room, Tammy was mad. When it was over, she figured out the man who broke down the door was not a police officer. That good-looking guy had gotten away and she was sure he would have paid her well for her services. The bouncer appeared in the doorway and was staring at her body, without taking his eyes off her, he asked, "What happened?"

"One of the customers tried to rape me."

"The one who came back here with you?" He didn't believe anything she told him, he knew something else was up with her with all the customers who came back to her dressing room for him to believe her story.

"No, the one who broke down the door."

"Where did they go?"

"Out the back door to the alley."

"I will go see if they are still lurking around back there." He left to see about it. In the alley, he only found some homeless people digging through the dumpsters. Going back inside, he found Tammy sulking. She had no feelings for anyone, only that she had been jilted. "Why don't you go home?" he asked her.

"I think I will. Will you take me?"

"No, I have to work for a while." He found her sick and repulsive, she was only a part of the job. Her attitude and personality were malicious and he avoided her as much as possible. "I can have your car pulled around to the front if you would like." She would have demanded that he do it anyway, so he just offered. She was immensely slothful. She handed him her keys from her purse and he took them to go out to have someone go get her car for her. In parking, it the attendant who brought it to the door and left the door unlocked since she was coming right out. Entering the front door of the club, he was met by the hostess, "Did Tammy come out yet?"

"No, I haven't seen her in a while."

"Thanks," he said as he walked back to the bouncer and told him the car was ready. The bouncer went to her dressing room where she was getting her things together to leave. "Your car is out front and here are your keys." She snatched them out of his hand and left in a huff. The hostess rolled her eyes as she walked by, both of them watched her get into her car through the door the bouncer was holding open.

Leaving the parking lot, she hit the accelerator making the tires squeal, leaving skid marks on the pavement. Her mother lived in an area where they were isolated and had no neighbors close enough to be nosy or noisy. Tammy pulled onto the driveway leading to the house when she was startled by a man raising himself up from the back seat, reaching around her neck with a knife at her throat. "Pull over," he demanded. She wet her pants as she pulled over into the grassy side of the driveway. "Turn it off!" She did. "Open your door and get out." She complied. "Get in here," he said and she climbed in. She was terrified and knew something terrible was about to happen. She was thinking that she knew him from somewhere but she couldn't quite place how. "You accused my brother of raping you and he was sent to prison. You are a liar; he didn't do it." After he stared at her with hatred in his eyes, he watched the fear in her eyes before she lost consciousness after injecting her with a poisonous substance. Getting out of the car he took a can of cigarette lighter fluid and emptied it on her and the interior of the car. Before leaving, he lit a match and tossed it on her body. Instantly the flames spread, as he was running away from the scene, the car exploded. Tammy got paid back for what she had dished out to others.

At the bunker, Beth was trying to settle her mind and was receiving comfort from the friends. Dr. Perry checked her to make sure she didn't have any serious injuries and Jacie and Jenny were sitting with her. She was recounting how Tammy had found her and had turned her in.

Mariann made her some soup to settle her stomach. "Where are your parents?" Jacie asked her.

"They were sent to prison, I got away and found a shelter mom and dad was headed to. They took me in and I was helping them. I was delivering a message when Tammy found me. I could have gotten away except there was that bouncer who grabbed me and took me to the club where they were about to make me work in that horrible place. Tammy was so mean to me and the other girls. The bouncer hated her but he knew what she would do if he didn't do what she wanted him to."

Sam had been sitting by the radio with his chair tipped back on the two back legs when the chair fell forward with a crash as the front legs hit the floor. They all turned to look in his direction, and he reached over to turn it up. What they heard had them looking at each other. "Tammy's car has been discovered on the road to her parents' house where they had heard the explosion and saw the fire. The car exploded burning her body beyond recognition; she was in the back seat at the time with the ignition switch turned off. Her body was identified by the jewelry she had been wearing. It is believed she had been murdered," Sam announced.

Sitting there George was thinking aloud, "As I was waiting for you to come out with Rex, I saw what I thought looked strange. There was a car in the parking lot and I saw someone get into the back seat and he ducked down out of sight. I was more interested in watching for Sam so I didn't give it much thought at the time."

"It is sad to say but the only ones who will miss her are her parents," Jenny said.

CHAPTER FIFTY-THREE
CARSTON'S STORY

Carston had been rescued from the labor camp, just in time, because he wasn't sure that he'd still be alive much longer in that place.

The many labor camps had built reputations of slavery and abuse, immeasurable against any other times in history. The guards had used whips as punishment, but mostly without a reason to do so. The whips were the guards' symbol of power above those whom they'd captured. Because of the almost constant whipping, the inmates were covered in open wounds that developed quickly into infections that were left untreated, and had killed many of them. Compliance with the Supreme One ensured the medical treatment only for those who trusted in him. Those who remained faithful to the Voice often times died from their bodies going septic, if malnutrition or dehydration didn't get them to them first.

There were different levels of inmates in each labor camp. Level one was the inmates who were labeled as the least risk, and were given jobs such as cleaning, painting, working outside the camp with armed guards and they were the ones believed to have lower intelligence and incapable of planning an escape, many times they did escape. Level two were the medium level risks and they were forced to work in the gardens, livestock pens and did the work of repairing equipment under the watchful eyes of the guards. Level three were the inmates considered to be the most risks, the ones who would cooperative the least and possessing the most intelligence. They were forced to work in the shops, running farm machines or having to lift heavy equipment and punishment and having to do other labor intensive jobs and other harsh labor work assignments.

Carston was level three and his body looked like it'd been attacked by a wild animal. He'd been whipped countless times, as a way for the guards to reeducate him. He refused every time to turn his back on the Voice. No pain was worth selling his soul to the Darkness. He'd worked long summer and winter days outside, with little food and water. His work assignment had been to clean the roads having to use his back and he was feeling the strain of it. The work was less picking up trash, as it was more digging. He had to tear up the asphalt and repair the holes in it. While it had been hard on him, his arms were powerful with muscles.

Many of the slaves were forced to dig, plant, gardens in the spring and summer months and harvest at the end of the summer and fall. There were those who had to make machine parts for the military year round and since Carston was an intelligent man, he was used for the higher-level jobs. Those who were weak were given the jobs of laundry, or kitchen duties. It was the guard's duties to keep the workers alive for the work, eventually when they were failing to meet the expectations, they were put to death. So many of them had untreated wounds and were at the point of starvation, so either starvation or serious infection.

After his rescue, Dr. Perry treated his wounds, healed his body of the near-fatal infection and malnutrition. The bones in his body stuck so far out he looked as though he was on the verge of death and was severely malnourished and dehydrated. He would not have survived much longer if he had not been rescued when he was. When he was taken out of the horrible camp he was hurting so bad he thought he wasn't going to make it. Getting up on the horse sent a shock of pain through him and he thought he would pass out. Dr. Perry tried to keep him and the others from being jolted to much as they tried to hurry as fast as they could. Remembering all the pain he was thinking that he wouldn't have been alive to see tomorrow's sunset being half starved and enduring that kind of pain. Dr. Perry had managed to deliver all four of them to the bunker without losing any one of them and he was sure the others were feeling just as bad if not more so, he had some gashes on his body. There were only four Chosen Ones in the camp, the other inmates were there for brutal crimes which made it easy for them to add to the abuse the four men endured.

At the bunker, they were lavished with more care then they could even believe was possible, good food, good care, loving-kindness, gentle hands, and a warm environment. It seemed like heaven on earth. George had sent word to his family that he had been rescued and was doing well.

His stay at the shelter helped him heal, both mentally and emotionally. Once his body had overcome the injuries and he was healing of the inflictions he'd suffered, he joined the rest of the shelter in celebrating life. He had conquered and was healing beautifully as the Chosen Ones worked to make him whole again. Carston was still haunted by the memories of the labor camp but those very memories were no longer personal demons, he chose to forgive. Many of the fears that had once haunted him were no longer having power over him.

As his stay passed, he knew he needed to get back to his family, and to other shelters that needed his pastoral guidance. He had a wife and two children. His son Quincy was ten, his daughter Abby was eight. It soon became time for him to begin his journey back home. It'd been so long since he'd seen his family.

"I've been gone for too long away from my family, and my wife will be relieved to have me back home"

He was getting around without pain, gradually, Dr. Perry started having him do chores to test his strength and he was pleased by his progress, his color was looking good as his strength was quickly returning back to normal, everyday he improved. Dr. Perry had given him a clean bill of health and he had his duties as a pastor to return to. Carston felt like he should be going to a shelter that was isolated so he could help them through their hardships.

His wife, Janice, was a strong woman. They had discussed possibilities of different things happening so she was prepared as much

as it was possible without it actually happening, things a person expected
to happen, hoped it wouldn't, and shocked when it did. She had to take
care of their two children. When word got back to them that Carston
was finally coming home they were so excited they were jumping up and
down but it would take a little while for him to get back to them because
he needed to stay where he was so he could get his body healed and
his strength to return. The messenger told them he was being properly
spoiled. Janice couldn't stop the tears.

George felt Carston needed a traveling companion, and he knew
of just the one to go with him. There was a man, nicknamed Rabbit,
who could go with Carston on the long road ahead. Rabbit had been
nicknamed as such because of the ferocious way he worked. He was
a thirty-year-old who had gone to college and worked as an electrical
engineer he designed and tested the products he helped to create. Once,
he's been overweight, the life he'd once had before the Chosen Ones
were forced in hiding. On his down time, he played video games for
hours upon hours. His weight shot up as his ability to move about
comfortably decreased. One day, he realized what he had done to his
physical health, and was tired of being obese, and so he began working
out. The time he'd once spent playing games was devoted to losing his
weight. As he lost pounds from his body, he was able to do more things
that he'd forgotten was possible, after most of his weight was lost. When
he had joined the Chosen Ones and his life changed he spent those once
wasted hours working around the bunker, doing the hard labor and he
became muscular as a result. He was fast on his feet, thus, earning his
nickname of Rabbit.

That evening, the bunker had a sendoff party for Carston and Rabbit.
Making trips had become harder, even harder than before. Traveling to
shelters took a long time, since they were scattered everywhere. Some of
them took a week to get to, others took months as they were quite a few
miles away but most of them used relay teams to move believers from one
shelter to the ones that were great distances away. Carton's home shelter
would take a couple of days, given there were no complications along
the way. He planned on stopping at the two shelters that were along the

route, to stock up on supplies and rest. The time of the year was in the early part of fall, they had light jackets on and blankets for night, some shelters were fortunate to have coffee, the ones who did had people there who had owned stores and they shared with others. Carston and Rabbit had some coffee to get their day started.

The next morning, Carston and Rabbit woke up early to get a head start on the day. It would be a long enough hike as it was. There were a few of the fellow Chosen Ones that were up at that hour, the ones who prepared the bunker for breakfast and the day that was ahead of the group. Mariann ran to them, hugged them and gave them some extra treats for their trip. "Oh Carston! I wish you didn't have to go! You will be missed, you know that?"

"Yes ma'am. I'll miss you all too. After everything you've done for me, I could never give enough back to you."

"The only thing we want for you to do for us is to make it home safely and spread the word."

"I will." With that, they left the safe confines of the bunker, and were off.

Two hours into the walk, the sun was up and the beauty of the earth was showing the most brilliant of the fall colors that man itself could not create. It was autumn and the wind was comfortably cool and the trees were stunning red, orange, and yellow. The Voice had given them the gift of His creation with the world as it was where they were. No violence, nor destruction. It was simply beautiful.

They'd walked for two days when the air around them changed, something felt wrong, then they stumbled upon the campsite that had been torn to pieces.

"Carston, there's bodies. Looks like three men, two women."

Carston looked fifty yards ahead from where they stood, and there were bodies lying on the ground. Swiftly, they jogged to the campsite and checked·for pulses as they intensely watched for intruders.

"Rabbit. They're dead. They were killed maybe about ten minutes ago."

They checked the bodies to find any identifying items rolling them onto their backs. There wasn't any, but they found a Book in the pocket of one of the dead men.

"I think I recognize one of them," Rabbit gasped.

The bodies were lying on their stomachs, with bullet holes in the back of their heads. It looked as though they'd been surprised by head hunters and shot point blank. They were planning on getting a rich reward for these despicable people.

"Quick! Hide!" Rabbit had heard some voices and twigs cracking. They both scrambled to hide in some bushes.

"Smith, this was incredible. We've got to find more of these people, nothing like killing while they're busy with their little prayer-incantation stuff," there was laughing.

"Wait, someone's been here. They were on their stomachs, they've been moved. There's someone here, find them!"

The group of soldiers, numbering at least twenty, immediately spread out. Carston and Rabbit remained in their hiding spot, trying to breathe as quietly as possible. They watched as the soldiers patrolled within a matter of a few inches from where they hid, aching from the awkward position they were sitting in. One soldier walked by them, even looked down straight at them without seeing them. Carston was hoping that they would not be found. Surely the soldier had to have seen them. They were covered with leaves or tree branches. They were only hidden behind a giant bush. But the soldier never saw them and kept walking past. The soldiers gave up and left, frustrated and angry they wouldn't be making another kill, Carston and Rabbit waiting until they were long gone before getting up to leave.

They had been so preoccupied with finding the bodies that they didn't notice the fuel cans that were close to the death camp. When the soldiers came back they had intended to burn the bodies and when it had been discovered someone had been there, the soldiers carrying the gas cans had set them down in a hurry, knocking them over, spilling the contents on the ground that was covered with dried leaves, grass, and tree branches. One of them had lit a cigarette when he was told to spread out for the search he threw his lit cigarette on the ground in the liquid fuel, he wasn't watching what he was doing when he took off in pursuit on the intruders. One of them had a motorcycle parked by the fuel can. The ensuing fire spread to the motorcycle, melting the soft parts before heating the full gas tank after the fuel line melted, blowing the motorcycle, and causing fire to spread even further. The soldiers ran back while Rabbit and Carston took off while they were distracted. The owner was the one who threw down the cigarette. He had brought it out so that he could leave early.

They had to move fast and Rabbit was concerned about Carston, "I will be ok. We had better get out of here as fast as we can." They took off. The sky was darkening with a thunderstorm moving in. They came to place where they found a shallow cave where they could put a tarp on the front of it for some protection. It wasn't long before the storm hit and the rain came down in sheets, the wind had picked up and fortunately they had secured the tarp. Eating some of the dried meat and fruit they had packed, they stayed where they were watching the rain as it approached them until they were sleepy. The air was cool with the fresh smell of rain and the comfort of the warm sleeping bags they had gotten a good of sound sleep. The storm passed as the morning light appeared, the sunrise was stunning with the sun starting to show behind the remaining clouds. The world was wet and cool.

As the morning light was showing itself, the men were waking up to a new day with the freshness of it. Stretching, it was time to get started, with a yawn they got up. Mud was going to be a problem if they were being pursued. The spot where they had camped was dry so they gathered some wet vegetation to spread over the spot they had spent the night, at least at first glance it would not be noticed. Next, moving without leaving foot prints was going to be a challenge. They walked through the wet grass which was abundant and walking on rocks they kept from leaving footprints.

The middle of the day they saw up ahead the shelter they were looking for and Rabbit went to the door and knocked. It was a hard place to find, it was hidden so well, Rabbit had been there on numerous occasions so he knew where to find it. The door was opened by a young man about eighteen years old, with a head full of fiery red hair and freckles sprinkled on his face. He introduced himself as Liam.

"Welcome to our shelter. How may we help you?"

"Thank you, my name is Carston and this is Rabbit. I'm Pastor Carston. We're going to my home shelter and we were hoping that maybe, if your shelter would be so kind as to allow us to stay to get rested. We've got another day until we get there."

"Of course, please come in."

They were welcomed by the small shelter. It was small, a military-like structure with only five people there. They were hospitable, giving them a hot meal and comfortable beds to spend the night.

After eating, they explained to the shelter what they'd found at the campsite. Liam chimed in. "Two of them were my parents. The other three were our people from here, too. They were going out to a town not even a week from here to talk about the Word. We were prepared for death of our residents. They were, too. I just didn't think it'd be them, so soon." Tears were coming to Liam's eyes. His pale face had splotches of red as his emotions were surfacing and his sorrow was apparent. Carston felt empathy for the young man.

"I know it's hard, but I'm glad we found them and were able to let you know."

"Thanks. They were great people, very passionate about the Voice and doing His work. At least they don't have to worry anymore, about anything."

"We're going out to spread the Word. Would all of you care to join us? We could use more people. You can join my shelter and hand in hand; we'll do some great work." All agreed. They wanted to go out and finish the work that was started by the fallen Chosen Ones.

"The others were people we had taken in several other people here have been killed by soldiers so now there are only me and two other couples living here. I know that we are being hunted. The soldiers get really close to us and it wasn't far away that the others were caught and killed."

"We are headed to a shelter that is somewhere around here. We would like for you to go with us," Carston said.

"I know the place and there is a shortcut that will save you a lot of time and miles. I will take you. Mom and dad would want me to go to a safe place. I know where they are and they are waiting for me, I am sad now but I will see them again. We had talked about this and I know what to expect. I am happy for them." Liam said.

"You had great parents." The two couples walked in and Liam introduced them to the new arrivals. The talked about the plans for leaving and they were in agreement and ready to go. Carston spent the rest of the evening with Liam to help him through his rough time, Liam was quietly sobbing as he talked, and Carston hugged him.

Before the sun came up everyone in this shelter had freshly stocked packs and full stomachs. One of the couples had a small cart they had used for hunting so they then used it to carry their personal belongings in it.

"Follow me. There's a shorter way to get to the shelter. The terrain is going to get rough, so watch your step. This way will save us time."

Knowing that Liam knew the area much better than the rest of them did, they followed him. Liam had grown up in the area, so he knew it like the back of his hand. The way he was taking them was through rough terrain, it was difficult to navigate at times but Rabbit saw how they were going to get there sooner. He'd spent his entire childhood out there with his parents who had been hard workers, spending more time at work than at home with each other and Liam. After times had turned for the worse, his parents lost their jobs and were faced with cooperating with the World Council or be left for dead.

They met a man, shortly before losing their home to foreclosure since they were wary of the microchip, that at first seemed to be homeless, his parents soon came to know the Voice. They asked Liam to give the Voice a chance and thereafter the family became Chosen Ones.

Carston was getting acquainted with the new travelers. What they were not aware of was that the shelter they just left had been found and invaded, the soldiers had assumed that the people they had killed were the only occupants and they celebrated their victory. One of them had some explosives with him so they thought it would be fun to blow the place to pieces after looting it and what shouting as debris littered the sky and rained down to the ground after the explosion. The traveling party was thrown to the ground from the shockwaves of the explosions as it was massive and they were not far from it, they were only out of sight. They were thrown to the ground and up, scraping their elbows and knees and bumped their heads on the rocks on the ground. They all got to their feet and stood, staring at what they knew was the shelter they'd just come from. Liam broke the silence with, "They found it. We need to keep going." They fixed their packs on their backs and kept hiking. If they stayed there too long, they'd be discovered and who knew what would happen.

The men who used the explosives didn't have enough experience with them to know they didn't need to use so much. The men must have been injured, Carston was wondering how they were but he wasn't about to go back to find out. The shelter was discovered after they'd left. The soldiers assumed that headhunters had already been there and killed off anyone who lived there, but they took the remaining food to keep for themselves. The soldiers watched their work, as it burned to the ground. They laughed and partied. Howling and screaming could be heard in the still air as they celebrated what they'd done. They had proper ear protection; at least they were smart enough to do that. They didn't know about the traveling party so they were safe. Carston suggested that they not stop until they had put some distance between themselves and that shelter, no one objected.

Liam guided them through terrain difficult to navigate. The land wove up and down, with boulders and loose dirt that would have been impossible to walk at night. Walking through trees and the underbrush and getting their shoes loaded with mud and grass. The day was warming up and the sun was making the humidity high; they were perspiring heavily with the exertion from walking and the extra weight they were carrying. They were making it faster than they thought, especially with

Liam as their guide. Before they knew it, they were just a mile from the shelter.

During the long hike, Liam had managed to avoid all dangerous terrain. Without his guidance, they would've walked to cliffs and through thorny brushes, unseen because trees and brush hid it. The group was surprised when late in the day they saw where the shelter was located up ahead. The route they took gave them some scratches but Liam really knew the way and it was worth the few scratches, it was a scenic walk. The guard who was posted had been out and seen them so he was waiting to see who was approaching and when he saw Rabbit he ran back to tell the others so that when the approached the residents weren't alarmed.

They saw some of the shelter's residents working outside. They assumed they were seen, but the workers seemed to be preoccupied by their work. A guard had already spotted them a way back and it had been reported to the leader of the shelter. The closer they got they saw a person dart in the door and go right back out as quickly. The guard greeted Rabbit as the rest of them paused to greet them. Carston's stomach fluttered with the thought that his family was there, and at last after being gone for as long as he had, he'd see them again. Before he knew it, Carston's wife and kids dashed to him, the family rushed to each other and were happily embracing, "I am so happy to see you too," Carston told them. His heart melted as the family were crying with the joy of being together to again and he kneeling down and kissing their heads as he wrapped his arms around them. They'd grown so big but they were still the beautiful children he remembered from the last time he'd seen them.

His wife put her arms around him and whispered in his ear, "I've missed you." He placed his hands on her cheeks and smiled, as tears ran down his face. He had missed his family, and the time away made his heart ache. "I'm back, now." The group was escorted inside the shelter, where Carston made the introductions for the others. "I would like to introduce my friends here. Most of their group was killed, and if it would be ok I'd like for them stay here. They could use some support and love from this shelter. And this young man here," he pulled Liam next to him, "is a very special person. We found his parents killed and we were unfortunate to have had to break the news to him. He was our guide here, and I think you'll all find him to be exceptional." The shelter gathered around them and welcomed them with warm hugs.

"I will tell you of what happened to me, but for now, let us eat and the time will come for that." They gathered for their dinner. It was a fine hot meal that was even better after a long trip. After, they gathered for stories and to learn about what had happened since they were together the last time.

Rabbit had been quietly listening quietly to the conversation when he made an announcement "I would like to stay here to help out. I feel like Liam and I are like brothers, we have a lot in common." Liam was nodding his head in agreement. This pleased the others living there. No one wanted him to go. Liam gave him Rabbit a hug and told him, "You are my brother."

Carston recounted his days at the labor camp, and showed off his scars. "Those are days I cannot forget. They are days that I was tested. I am here, healthy, and ready work. I bear these scars as the Son bears his, He who died for us. My body was broken, but my spirit was not."

There were looks of horror on the faces listening to him, they were so happy to have him home.

CHAPTER FIFTY-FOUR

JENNY GOES TO BE AN ASSISTANT TO DR. BARRINGER

Dr. Perry had worked with Jenny to train her in medical studies. She had proven to be a natural as a nurse and he felt that by giving her proper training, she'd do great things. Jacie had given her nursing classes and Dr. Perry gave her the doctor perspective, with face-to-face, supervised hands on work, and his medical books that he'd kept.

Dr. Perry knew that nurses were needed, and when Jenny was done with her training, she'd be able to go to many places to help to tend to the healing those who were injured or sick. He thought of speaking with George about sending her off to Dr. Barringer, where he had more cases and was desperately in need of a nurse.

The test Dr. Perry was helping Jenny with to test her knowledge of what she had learned, she had come a long way. Jacie had put her through a thorough training and the doctor had books he was teaching her from, she wouldn't be a doctor but he was making sure she was a good helper for Dr. Barringer since he didn't have a nurse. Both he and Jacie were confident she would be a fine helper.

"Jenny, are you ready to be Dr. Barringer's new nurse?" he asked her as she was finishing the cleanup she was working on.

"Yes, you and Jacie have taught me so much, I really love what I am doing. I never thought of myself as a nurse."

"Jenny, we need to see about getting you to Dr. Barringer soon, he really needs some help, we will talk to George. Dr. Barringer will continue with your training."

"I will go whenever I can get there, anytime." They went to find George where he was chatting with Mariann and he was helping with some cooking.

He found George and asked to speak to him in private. They found a quiet corner. "George, as you know Jenny has been working with me, learning about the medical practice. I believe she's ready to start, and Dr. Barringer is in desperate need of a nurse and we have trained Jenny, we believe she is ready and we want to see if you can get her to him. He is over close to Terrell where he is available to help Chosen Ones from a more centrally located shelter. I wanted to talk to you about sending her there with him where her skills can be put to better use."

"If you think that's where she needs to be, I want her where she's needed."

"Excellent, I'll let her know."

"Jenny, my darling, could you come here, please?"

"Of course." She had her head buried in one of the books Dr. Perry had given her. A break was needed, so she closed it and sat down with Dr. Perry. She had been studying and was trying to continue learning so she was hoping to be able to go help Dr. Barringer.

"Jenny, you're ready. I spoke to George and it's time for you to go with Dr. Barringer. He needs nurses. With him, you'll have the opportunities to put practice into action. You'll be leaving soon to go to his shelter. What do you think about that? Will you be ready to go tomorrow, will that be good for you?"

"Really, George will take me? I am so excited about being able to go. OOH! I'm so happy!" She jumped up and hugged him. "Thank you!!"

He laughed and shook his head in amusement. "Get your things packed and we will help you get things ready that I want to send to him.

I do know that Dr. Barringer has been asking about you, Jen. He has some things he wants to teach you, you are in demand."

"Come on Jenny, I will help you get ready," Jacie said putting her arm around her shoulder.

George sat down with Sam to discuss the trip they'd be making in the morning. They both agreed that they'd be the ones who would take Jenny to Dr. Barringer's shelter. Plans were finalized and Jenny was ready within a short time. "Remember that forest, outside of Terrell, the one where the evil spirits were found?"

"I do."

"I'd like to avoid that place. I think we might be able to go around it. We should go through the forest, but more to the North. It'll take longer, but it should be safer. What'ya think?"

"Sounds like a better option. I can mark down our trail on the map. But there also was the military base in that general area." They would be going through the forest where they had come across the evil spirits on the way to Terrell, just in a different direction when they passed through the woods.

"You're right. Tell you what; I'll go pack up our gear if you can figure it out. I'll be back to help after I'm done."

"Good. I'll be here."

The next morning, they were off on the hike. Jenny was pleasant, her excitement overflowing. Jenny admired the doctor and she thought of him as a grandfather to her. Sam and George were laughing, enjoying her happiness. They left with bags of things she wanted to give Dr. Barringer and Dr. Perry had gathered for him. Sam and George groaned as they were to be the baggage carriers who were to carry them, Jenny rolled her eyes as she teased them about being weaklings. They didn't mind very much. The journey was going smoothly; under their feet they saw trodden grass, what looked like military grade vehicles had driven through. Cautiously, they continued but they all had bad feelings that the vehicles were still around.

Walking along George and Sam noticed that the grass seemed to be packed down where vehicles had been driving through where they were and in a large patch of ground where there seemed to be a training camp that had been set up with a cleared area with a possible camp fire and it looked to have been recently. Sam was watching to see if he could find out where they had gone. It didn't make sense for them to have camped out where it was so open when a little further away there were trees unless they needed to have everything and everyone closer than camping under the trees would allow, a special operation that hadn't made the news, yet. With Chosen Ones, what they liked to call, under control, he wondered what war operations they may have been conducting no matter they had to be on the alert. "We had better get hidden before they decide to come back," Sam was telling them with urgency in his voice.

Sam was leading the way towards the trees and a spot that would make a good hiding place when they heard some shots being fired, they missed hitting them but it was close.

"GET DOWN!" Sam yelled suddenly "GET DOWN NOW!" They fell down into the grass that was high enough to hide them if they stayed low. "We need to get into the trees so let's go," Sam instructed, Sam was in front with Jenny behind him and George watching from behind. In the rush, Sam got ahead and Jenny lost sight of him, when he noticed he was thinking George would get them to safety. Shots rang out right behind them so George told Jenny to hurry and catch up to Sam but to stay low, she started running thinking that she knew where to go, so she hurried, George was trying to find out where the shots came from so they could get away. When he turned to go with Jenny, she was out of sight so he thought she may have caught with Sam, he ran until he got to where Sam was.

"Wait, Sam. Where's Jenny? "Sam looked around them, and saw she wasn't with them.

"Where is she?" Sam asked.

"I don't know." They panicked, hearts racing, and fearing the worst. They were there to protect her, and they lost her. George felt guilty, but there was no time for that. They needed to find her before something bad happened.

Not being able to see she had gone off in a wrong direction and had tripped on a half-buried tree branch while they were running and fallen, rolling down the fairly steep downgrade. She landed directly in front of soldiers, armed soldiers. All three of them had been spotted and they were on their way to get them. Jenny screamed to warn George and Sam, they heard and knew about where she was. They were creeping through the grass after having stashed their bags where they couldn't easily have been found. They were listening and heard the low voices when they heard Jenny, she was in trouble. Moved as quietly as they could, they came to where she was and she was sitting on the ground with several soldiers standing over her.

The soldiers were staring at her, shocked and happy that a Chosen One had landed directly at their feet, literally. One soldier had a scanner out, attempting to find a chip in Jenny's arm. Another was asking her if she had one. She remained still and silent, not answering any of their questions.

They could hear the soldiers ask several different questions about her identity, if she was one of them, and they kept pressing her. She sat up, obviously hurt, and said nothing. Her face was blank, no hint of concern, which annoyed them. The soldier were getting agitated that she refused to answer them, and they became angrier. One was looking at Jenny in a way that made Sam and George uncomfortable. If she wasn't rescued from the grips of the militants, and being a woman, she'd wished she was dead after they were done with her.

Sam and George overheard a soldier say, "She's not alone. They never travel alone. Let's go find the others before Commander gets here. He'll be thrilled to see her and her little friends captured. And hey, aren't you up for promotion? You would get a nice promotion and a raise for this pretty little girl's head." They laughed. Sam and George needed a plan. They weren't getting Jenny or them.

As they were waiting, some more troops walked up, "Those guys got away, we are going after them, I am sure we can catch up with them before they get to far away."

They retreated where they'd have enough time to come up with a plan. They leaned against a tree, sipped some water. Jenny seemed unconcerned and they hoped that she knew they would never abandon her. There was no time to lose.

Jenny did know, she didn't know what was going to happen but she did know that the Chosen Ones never neglected the others. Enduring Ghost had helped her and knowing how Cindy and Lucy had suffered gave her courage.

More troops were showing up and were mocking her as a Chosen One, Jenny only smiled, she was not going to give in to them and this situation was confusing for the soldiers. She was making hard choices and decided to not let it bother her. A couple of them were going to poke her with sticks when their commander showed up and ordered them to get her so they could move her to a secure place and locked up so she couldn't escape. She was snatched off the ground and they were moving in the opposite direction from where George and Sam were hiding. They were moving fast so they had to get going to keep up. Raising their heads, they checked to see what was happening and they could only see the troops up ahead.

Sam and George were feeling guilty for not being able to keep Jenny safe. Sam was taking it especially hard, in combat he had seen comrades' die and he had felt helpless to do anything about helping them. George was feeling guilty because she was a young girl who innocently headed out to help others and George had taken a human life that hadn't done anything to him; he was only doing his job. Each man was suffering from fear that neither one had known they were enduring

Sam had been a POW for a short time, his hands and feet had been tied the whole time he was held in captivity where he spent most of the time in a box that wasn't much bigger than a grave. He hated the indoors because he was afraid of being trapped with the friends he had, they were patient with him and he thought he had gotten over this fear.

George felt so protective of Jenny, she had been through so much he just couldn't stand the thought of what he greatly feared was about to happen to her.

When they looked up to see where the troops were, they had gone a distance, the day was turning late and George was sure they would stop soon for the night. Trudging alone they started closing in on them. They soon stopped. Jenny seemed to be holding up well.

"George, what do we do?"

"Let's go. We'll get an answer, I know it."

They went back to their hiding spot, where they could hear the soldiers talking, only to find patrols had already been sent out. They were still close enough that they could see Jenny being dragged by her hair off into the distance.

"We trail them, but stay far enough behind that they don't know we're there. We can't let them get out of sight or else we'll lose them and never get to her." George nodded in agreement. They walked behind the soldiers, cringing with the sight of Jenny being dragged along behind the troops to an unknown destination, she kept her feet moving and they were moving her fast. Up ahead she spotted their camp, she was led to what looked like a cage on a trailer, jail that was portable, where she was pushed into, she kept quiet as she watched what was going on in case she could find a way to escape, she was trying to give them a reason to get careless. There was lots of activity as they were preparing their dinner and getting tents set up for the night, she was listening to what was being said. Now she knew why the soldiers were all over in places that were in the middle of nowhere, this was some interesting information. Patrols were out looking for George and Sam, it seemed they had concluded that they had gotten away, Jenny knew better, there had been rescues, including here, they may have gotten away but they were not far away, they would be here soon. She had her eyes and ears open.

How could this have happened? If only they'd paid closer attention, she'd never have gotten left behind.

It was getting late, and a couple hours later it would be dark. They continued following the soldiers when they saw the camp site, along with Jenny being thrown into a cage that would normally be used for animals, she seemed to be still holding up well.

They stayed back to ensure their cover. "George, we need to watch to see how they set up their camp, keep your eyes open for other troops who may be around, they will have guards posted. We need to sneak up on them and get them out of the way. Closely watch to see where they keep Jenny, what we do will have to done fast or else they will catch on to us." Waiting for a while to watch as the camp got settled, they saw where Jenny was, she was calm.

"How are we going to get her out?" George asked.

"Wait for a while and they may open the door, and when they do, watch where they put the key. No one would believe someone would dare to walk into their camp to try a rescue, we have done this kind of thing before," Sam reminded him. Jenny was on the outside of the camp and so far, they only saw one guard and he seemed to be quite young.

Jenny looked around her. She observed the activity of the soldiers and saw that they were setting up tents and other modular structures. The militants weren't known for camping out like this. It was interesting that they were doing it now.

She soon found out why. Two soldiers were talking about ending the entire population of Chosen Ones, once and for all. They were camping out to take back as many as possible, all at once. They'd grown tired of them running around among everyone else. Chosen Ones were not only hated, but now considered to be diseased. Jenny chuckled quietly to herself. 'Uh huh.' She thought.

Going silently around the camp Sam and George were checking out possible ways to get in and out with Jenny. Sam had an idea and he motioned for George to follow him back away from the camp where they could talk without danger of being overheard. "They are using only one guard and he is being careless in doing his job, what I propose that we do is to wait until the camp quiets down for the night and then we sneak up on the guard. I can knock him out without him alerting the others, by the time we take him out and get him tied up the rest of them should be asleep. I noticed that Jenny has been watching what is going on and I am hoping that she has seen where the key is to get her out." They moved back into a position where they could watch. Jenny was still alert and observing everything going on. Sam and George could see her. She was fine, for now. But time wasn't something they would risk. They continued watching the guards and noticed that there were fewer of them walking about. It seemed they were going to bed early, presumably to get an early start.

Two soldiers still sitting up were saying that the others that they knew Jenny were with had likely gotten away. They wrote off Sam and George, and they were relieved. At least they thought they'd abandoned Jenny. They would never suspect they were coming for her. Jenny sat down on the floor of the portable jail, knowing that Sam and George were out there, probably close, waiting to come get her out there, she would wait.

The two had noticed that there was only one guard assigned to Jenny, and he was failing miserably at his job. He was paying more attention to throwing his knife at a nearby tree than watching Jenny; they looked at each other and smiled. This would be easy.

Going silently around the camp Sam and George were checking out possible ways to get in and out with Jenny. Sam had an idea.

They scooted further back away from the guards to talk without being heard. "Ok, so here's what we're going to do. We'll have to wait until it's nighttime. The darkness will provide cover. It looks like most of them are asleep, so the only one we're dealing with here is that guard, and I doubt he'll be trouble. We'll sneak up on him and I can knock him out without him alerting the others and get the keys, by the time we take him out and get him tied up the rest of them should be asleep. I noticed that Jenny has been watching what is going on. The guard has the key."

They moved back into a position where they could watch. It was getting late and the soldiers were yawning, conversations were dying down as they were starting to go into their tents. They seemed to have forgotten about Jenny and she was still watching them closely. For the most part they had been ignoring her, they must had a low opinion about her intelligence, there were comments about her not being smart enough to keep from getting caught which she made no reply which was interpreted as them being right. Jenny's guard had approached the jail with a plate of food. He unlocked the door and set the plate down, just inside the door and on a small shelf that had been built in on the wall. He closed the door and went back to his seat by the tree, where he continued throwing his knife.

"Wouldn't you think he'd be a better soldier?"

They laughed. He was a terrible soldier. After a couple of hours Sam and George noticed he was the only one that was in the nearby vicinity, so they crept on, crouching and keeping as low as they could. The guard's back was turned to them, but they could see the slow heaving of his chest, the rhythmic flow of breathing in and out as he has found a comfortable position. Sam carefully crept in front of the guard and verified he was in fact out for the night. Reaching over and tipping back slightly they were looking for something to tie him up with and they just happened to see a rope that was laying close to the guard and it was just long enough to tie the guard up.

George grabbed it, tied him to the tree securely. With his mouth gagged and the rope looped across his mouth to prevent him from alerting other soldiers. The guards weren't the most sanitary people, and that was fortunate for them. There was trash lying everywhere. George found a wad of duct tape, in which he gagged the guard with, being careful not to ram it too far into his mouth. With his mouth gagged and the rope looped across his mouth, it prevented him from alerting other soldiers. The guards weren't the most sanitary people, and that was fortunate for them. They searched his pockets for the key without success, so they were going to have to find out from Jenny where they hid it. With a hand gesture, Sam motioned George to follow him. While everyone else in the camp was sleeping soundly, Jenny was awake and alert. She saw two shadowy figures coming towards her.

By the time Sam and George reached the small jail, Jenny was standing outside of it, waiting for them to their surprise. Without a word, they each took her by the arm and they calmly walked out of the campsite.

Once out of sight and out of earshot they turned to her in amazement. "Ok, girl, spill it. How'd you do it?"

She looked at Sam with a smile on her face.

"Well, did you see the guard bring me food?"

"Yes."

"The whole time I was sitting there, they were talking about me. They said I was too stupid to escape or to be rescued, and that anyone else that I was traveling with couldn't possibly be smarter than me. When the guard came to bring me food, he closed the door but left the key in the door. He was distracted by the talking of the other soldiers. I picked up my food and ate it and when I was through I pretended to stretch and yawn as if I was about to go to sleep. So, when no one was looking, I reach through the door and grabbed the key, and closed the door all the way to avoid drawing attention. That guy never gave it another thought. Once I saw you two coming, I opened the door. Whoever made that jail also put a key hole on the inside of the door." She giggled from the amusement of the irony. "They made it too easy. When I got out and was waiting for you I threw the keys on the ground as if he had dropped the keys after I relocked the door." The men laughed.

"We watched you since before you got there and you were very calm; weren't you afraid?" George asked.

"No, I knew I would be rescued. This wasn't the first time you have rescued me and I knew you would not leave me here. I found out why we keep seeing camps of them in strange places, they are looking for our hiding places."

"Jenny, you were great! I don't think you need us. If ever we get in trouble, we want you to be there. We already use a lot of caution so it is no surprise that they are out looking for us. You are on our side and I am happy you aren't our enemy." She laughed.

They continued on their way, but drones were flying throughout the sky. It wouldn't be an easy trip. Distance had to be put between them and the camp. First, they had to get their packs and not being sure if the patrols were close by, they stayed on guard. They found a place where the soldiers had thrown down their cigarettes and left trash on the ground where they had gone through on their way to hunting for them, this was the way the three of them would have gone if they hadn't had to go rescue Jenny. "I wonder if they went as far as the forest we need to walk through?" George asked Sam.

"That is hard to say, if they don't see any signs of us they may give up, at least until they find Jenny gone."

"They should have found out by now. They will be doing everything they can to find us. Instead of going through fields, we will need to go a long was around to stay under trees at all times," Sam said. "I know where we can go that is useless for anything other than animals roaming, the soil is to poor for growing anything and there are so many large rocks no one wants to do anything with it."

"There are some homes along the way, we can sneak in and get things we need, if we take only small amounts from a home we may be able to get away with it. Hope the way is clear and we are safe."

They were getting close to an open field and up in the sky they saw a drone, they moved back from the edge of the field to be under the trees more. The drone flew away and they moved along under trees keeping a sharp look out in front and behind them. One of them had stopped off in the distance as if something was found, then out stepped some soldiers who waved at the drone and it kept moving. The three of them kept moving. The soldiers were going in a direction they thought to meet up with the rest of their comrades. "Move along faster, if they don't find us they will send in more troops, right now they believe the ones here can find us. We just thought they had given up on finding us, not so."

"We should continue moving. There will be more drones monitoring this area. They know the soldiers are camping there and I don't want to risk detection. We'll get distance between us and those troops, and then we can find somewhere to take a short nap." George was tired, and could see it on Sam's and Jenny's faces. It had been a long day and they needed a power nap until they could get fully rested.

They finally found a place, and set up an easy site to sleep. As they were about to lie their heads down for a couple of hours, they saw drones flying up ahead. The only way they could see them was by the flashing lights that were installed on them, making them look like small UFO's. They quickly grabbed their things and hid under cover by the trees. They watched as a drone stopped suddenly, as though it had detected something, but it resumed its flight. After waiting to see if a drone or soldiers were nearby, without seeing or hearing anything, they kept under the trees for their nap.

George let them rest up, for just a short while, and then woke them up to keep moving. They could see by the sky that it was nearing dawn. "Time to go, we're getting close."

Sam found the trail that he knew about, and they set themselves along it. As he had said, they could easily see anyone before being seen first. It was safer and quicker. To the left of the trail was the tree line, leading back into the forest. They talked to each other quietly, when eerie blood-curdling screams could be heard. They hurried along as the sun was making its way down the horizon. People living in the houses they found were off to work; they watched for a while and finally picked some houses they would visit. George was blowing his breath out through pursed lips as they chose a house; going through the neighborhood with only a few houses tucked around a small park, they didn't see anyone else, not even a dog barked. The house that was selected had a narrow trail behind which they walked down. There was a gate that wasn't locked so they went through it; the windows didn't have any window coverings so they looked in a saw no one or any movement. Walking across the neatly groomed yard they checked the door, it was unlocked, they went in and there was no one home. The kitchen was at the back of the house where they found all kinds of food, it was then that they chose to stock up their packs and they thought these people weren't going to miss what they took. Jenny filled the water bottles as Sam and George filled their packs.

As they were headed for the back door, they heard a car pull up into the driveway. "Go, go, go!" Sam said. They took off, making sure they closed the back door and the gate on their way out. They were running as fast as they could, "Whew! That was close, too close," Sam said as they were breathing hard. They got away and needed to move fast. Trekking deeper into the woods, they slowed down. Hopefully, the occupant wouldn't notice missing food or see where they had been in the house. Before they heard the car drive up, they had tried to make sure nothing was noticeably out of place.

There were more drones they managed to avoid, and by nightfall they were hoping to get into the forest. They were having trouble moving as exhaustion was starting to get to them. "Find a place where we can get some sleep or we will not keep our focus on danger," George was saying as he was looking around. They did find an outcropping of rocks that had a place under it where they could crawl and be out of sight. Perfect, they climbed under them and soon were asleep. George and Jenny were suddenly awakened by Sam shaking them, "Move up under the rock, quick!" he whispered. Instantly they were awake as they scrambled up under the rock further. Sam put his finger to his lips letting them know they needed to be quiet. They heard the voices, and they stayed still and quiet. The voices were fading as they moved away. Sam indicated they were to stay still, after a while he moved to go out to find out what as going on. "They left."

"Who were they?'

"Some patrols, there is a road up above us, I don't know if they were looking for us or just happened to stop here. We have been asleep for several hours so I think we should be on our way."

Climbing out of the hole they saw that the sun had travelled a way across the sky. "I know where we are now," Sam said. "We can get to the forest after dark. I know a trail we can use, if anyone else is on it, we will be able to know." In Sam's mind, he was going over what had just happened, and it had just occurred to him that he been in a situation that he was afraid of. He had taken care of people he cared about, saving their lives and he was not feeling fear.

The group stayed where they were until dark. They had food and water so they just rested. When it was dark enough, they walked into the forest. They were close to where they were going to take Jenny and she was doing well, "Are you ok if we just keep going so we can stay at that shelter?" George asked them. Sam and Jenny nodded their heads. They kept going. A way into the trees they heard some eerie creams.

"Evil spirits, they're trying to get into our minds. Believe that you are covered and are protected." George warned them.

But the spirit had its sights set on Jenny. Jenny was being pushed away from the others. They were walking close to one another, when Jenny's body was pushed back, onto the ground, by something unseen. And then, the evil spirit showed itself to her.

It was something straight out of nightmares. Black scales for skin, long four inch claws protruding from its fingers and toes, eyes darker than smoke and coal, its face.... the face was a tangible form of all of the hatred, the face was pure hatred.

It snarled and hissed at Jenny. The voice was enough to make her skin crawl. For a second, she was horribly afraid. It spoke to her. "You are a pathetic, worthless, little girl. You've never done anything in your whole, a sad life that would make you worthy. You've been a stain on society, never had a reason to live. Look at you, you're nothing." It had Jenny pinned to the ground, with its clawed hands squeezed her throat.

Jenny heard nothing more after that. "Help me, it is attacking me and wants me to give up everything that matters to me. LEAVE ME SPIRIT!"

"The Voice is nothing more than a noise."

"Great Voice!" The spirit hissed, and still tried to confuse her, but to no avail, it was gone. She heard no more of the taunting. George and Sam found her on her back. They saw the spirit on her, looking like it was choking her there were red marks on her neck and bruises on her throat. They helped her to her feet; she was shaken but otherwise nothing was wrong with her other than having gone through a bad experience.

"Jenny, we'll be there soon. This is a sad moment for us. You know you'll be missed, right?" Sam and George felt bittersweet about Jenny leaving, but knew it was what she was called to do.

In another couple of hours, they came to the shelter where Dr. Barringer was awaiting them.

"I know. I'll miss you all too, I'll go back when I can. Please tell everyone I'll be thinking about them. "Will do. All right, then we're here."

The shelter was in sight, finally they had made it. There were some of the Chosen Ones outside working, but the guard they had at the front door had seen them before anyone else. He went in and alerted the others that they had visitors.

Dr. Barringer ran out to greet them. "Jenny! How nice to see you! Gentlemen, thank you for getting her here to us. You must all come in and rest. That was quite a trip you made." They laughed; it had been. And they were planning on filling him in on everything that had happened.

"Dr. Barringer, would it be ok if we stayed for a couple of days? We need some rest."

"You're welcome to stay as long as you need."

"Thank you, doctor." George replied.

CHAPTER FIFTY-FIVE

BETRAYAL

The bunker friends were listening to the radio one day when the announcer was talking about dogs being used to track down Chosen Ones. It was hard to find scents as they had been diminished over time. Officials were buckling down to find those they knew were still around. With all the moving around from place to place and so many people who went hunting, camping, and hiking in the wilderness areas, it was a challenge for them. There was some success but it was limited.

Another story came over the radio about a man named Micah who had been outside when a drone flew over and he had gone into the shelter, unaware of the drone. He had gone to the apple orchard to pick some of the apples; he was only going to get them and return. The shelter was raided within a couple of hours and all of the residents were arrested and taken into custody. The public trial consisted of ridicule and the officials trying to coerce them into renouncing their God. None of them would.

Two of the people who were arrested were the parents of the young girl, Melissa, who had tried to kill Sam and George with the knife. George had sent a messenger to let them know what happened to her, and her parents were heartbroken. The details were horrifying and it was hard for them to understand why she had turned out the way she did. They had loved her, but she was so set on going her own rebellious way, there wasn't anything they could do. When they were arrested, the officers told them she had come to them and reported where they were hiding. They sent the drone to verify their location and had spotted one of the tenants outside as he had come back in.

Melissa had opened an account at a bank where she was given a large sum of reward money for turning them in. The officer laughed as he said he would get the money instead, along with a promotion. If they renounced their God, they could get the money. Both refused. The officer was thrilled; he was going to collect her money since he had found her dead alongside the highway. An autopsy had shown the cause of death was a drug overdose. The mystery was why she had been found where she was found. No one really cared as far as he could tell. Sam had suggested that they put her body where it would be found. They had planned to bury her but they knew they couldn't do it without drawing attention to themselves. It was suggested that they allow the authorities to make assumptions about her that would lead them away from them, and it worked.

When Melissa had reported her shelter to them, the officials thought she was about to give them information about another shelter but she had started slurring her words so they couldn't ascertain where the other one was located. They had hoped she would come back in to talk to them so as to get drones in the area. They were planning to scout within several miles of the one they had found in hopes of finding more than one hiding place. Melissa had been a great help and he was almost sorry she had died. He was going to find more of them, many more of them

The Chosen Ones were subjected to many types of torture. Melissa's parents were put on public display as tokens of the rewards to be earned by finding these people, and that they had been turned in by their own daughter. They had made the choice to stand up for who they believed in and took it with all the dignity they had. After their public display, they were separated from each other. He went to a labor camp where he died within a few months and she was put into prison and later died of starvation. Micah was beat to death by another inmate within a short time after he was sent to a labor camp. The reunion in the afterlife was a grand meeting with other believers, some very new and recent, greeting them. The Voice smiled with his welcome home greeting. One by one the other friends from their shelter made their way home also.

The friends at the bunker were listening to the radio and heard all the fanfare of the killings. It was announced that drones would be patrolling the skies in search of more of them. There were more betrayals as the lure and freedom was tempting others. A few of those who were in hiding felt the strain of having to hide and the fear of getting caught, only a few of the Chosen Ones in the shelter moved out quickly as messengers relayed messages and came to their rescue. Times were becoming more perilous as time went by.

The friends in the bunker were going to go out to do some hunting when Sam was trying to open the door to the outside. It was stuck tight and he could not get it to open. He found this quite odd since they had never had a problem with it before. George walked over to help him but it was of no use, no matter what they tried to do, it would not budge. Jeremy had been watching them, "That door was designed to open easily and the special locks on it were to protect us when we were inside. We had better sit tight for a while. I suspect we aren't being allowed to go out for a while." To this they agreed even though they thought that it was peculiar. There was no urgent need to have to be out, so they worked inside until the door could be opened. Cindy was feeling as if there was something going on outside. Sam was fighting panic as he felt trapped. With the help of the friends, he felt the calmness he needed.

Three days after having been trapped inside, Sam got the door open and he made his way to the outside, where he was stunned by what he saw. There was trash everywhere as he saw evidence of a camp. No one was around and it was quiet with only the sounds of wild life. The ground showed signs of activity as if someone had been staying around for the last several days. This was the reason the door had been stuck. He glanced around and saw where camp fires had been used, with holes dug into the ground to restrain the fires. The place was a huge mess. Whoever had been there had moved on to other places. It looked as if they had been digging in the trash piled on the bunker and they seemed to have lost interest after a while.

"George, Jeremy, come look," Sam called out as he went back inside. They walked over to him with concern on their faces. "Now I know why we weren't able to get the door open. Come look." Going to the door, they opened it without a hint of it sticking. George and Jeremy were behind him as were the others in the bunker. When they got to the top side, they stopped and stared at the mess before them. It looked like they had been staying there with a purpose and had no concern for what it looked like when they left. Walking out with great care, they were observing anything that would indicate a presence not their own, and there was nothing to be seen, not even in the sky. Sam led them out and they were silently looking through the trash to get any indication of who it was who had invaded their area. Sam suspected troops were out trying to find any of the Chosen Ones after what they had been hearing on the radio.

Mariann, Cindy, Lucy, and Jacie were helping them salvage any useful items they could find. The men thought it would be best to leave the trash as it was, in case any of the soldiers came back. They may think it was odd and become suspicious. George had them go back inside. Hee told them that they were going to have to stay inside more and only go out when it was absolutely necessary; it was just too dangerous. For hunting they would only use bows and arrows, and most of the activities outdoors would be at night. Things were going to get worse.

Listening to the radio, they were hearing about how serious the world was about these Chosen Ones. Before the chips had been forced on the human population, there had been Chosen Ones who had worked hard to spread the Good News. Many had been killed or imprisoned for their witness, and as a result, there were some of the lost who were finding the saving grace after the Voice continued to reach out to them. The shelters were sending out rescuers to help these refugees. There were good times in the midst of the bad times. The seeds of the faithful were planted in the hearts of the ones who were to come, to know the only one who could give them new life. The Spirits of Light were carrying out the work assigned to them by the Voice, as he softened the hard hearts. He gave them fertile soil to nourish the seed of Eternal Life. With the sprouts and growth of the Wisdom, there grew hope for new believers who were living life anew in a wildly evil world lacking in divine wisdom.

Printed in the United States
By Bookmasters